EDGE OF EXTINCTION

Edge of Extinction

Kim Borg

E. L. Marker
Salt Lake City

E. L. Marker, an imprint of WiDo Publishing
Salt Lake City, Utah
widopublishing.com

Cover design by Steven Novak
Book design by Marny K. Parkin

ISBN 978-1-947966-37-6

To 16-year-old Kim. We did it.

"As new species in the course of time are formed through natural selection, others will become rarer and rarer, and finally extinct. The forms which stand in closest competition with those undergoing modification and improvement will naturally suffer most."

—Charles Darwin, 1859

"Our only chance of long-term survival is not to remain inward-looking on planet Earth, but to spread out into space. We have made remarkable progress in the last hundred years. But if we want to continue beyond the next hundred years, our future is in space."

—Stephen Hawking, 2008

Prologue

Jungle, Unknown—
22:30, 9 March, 2086

Alone, he ran.

Wet ferns slapped against his face and arms as he pushed forward blindly. The moonlight could barely penetrate the thick canopy above, blanketing the jungle in shadows. Soft rain droplets mixed with the sweat dripping down his face. Despite the rain and the darkness, he ran. Terrified, he advanced through the trees, moving quickly but cautiously, trying not to lose his footing against the slick gnarled roots. His ears throbbed with the sound of his own heartbeat.

Don't slow down.

Don't fall.

Need to hide, need to get away.

The thumping of heavy footsteps followed close behind. The trees rustled in the distance from some unknown force, some unknown creature, as it chased him through the black, storm-lashed night.

Ahead the forest thinned slightly as a clearing opened up, a path in the jungle. The man felt a small sensation of dread swell in his chest. He slowed a fraction as he burst from the thick undergrowth onto the enormous dirt path.

A shadow flashed across the path before him. It was small, about the size of a human, but it moved with incredible speed. For a moment he wondered if his eyes were playing tricks on him. The shadow reappeared, closer this time and moving slower. As it came toward him it was growing in extent. It was not human sized at all. It was enormous; a monstrous figure obscured by the darkness. And it was coming toward him.

The man panicked. He tried to stop running mid-step, but in doing so he lost his footing. He slipped in the mud and hit the ground hard, rolling several times before sliding to a stop on the wet earth. A rising pain began to fill his abdomen; the impact must have been more severe than he realized. He was in the middle of the path, totally exposed. With his face buried in mud, he opened a single eye in time to see an enormous three-toed claw sinking into the sludge beside him. He squeezed his eyes shut again, ignoring the pain coursing through his gut.

Hold still.

Maybe it didn't see.

He held his breath. He could hear the creature standing above him, breathing deep hollow breaths. It was sniffing, searching. He could feel the warmth of its breath against his back.

Don't move.

Don't breathe.

From behind, the man heard the nearby trees shake and snap as something else huge crashed onto the path. The creature that had been pursuing him had finally caught up.

The second creature entered the clearing and paused. For a moment, the jungle was quiet as the two beasts sized each other up. Suddenly the creature with the huge three-toed foot hovering over the man broke the silence with an ungodly roar; a deep resonating bellow which vibrated the ground beneath the man's face. In return the second animal snarled aggressively; it was a guttural, gravelly hiss. Suddenly, three-toes lunged forward, stepping clear over the man who still lay silently in the mud.

Without missing a beat, the man sprang to his feet. To his right was a large tree with thick buttress roots which wound together creating a hollow, just big enough for a small person to fit inside. He ran to the tree, clutching at his stomach, and jammed his body into the crevice. His ears were ringing from the trumpeting roars and growls as the two titans brawled behind him. He could still feel his heart thumping in his ears. He tried to turn his body to see the creatures outside but he couldn't move. Glancing down, he saw his field-medic kit. The carabiner which connected the kit to his belt had jammed between the intersecting roots.

He was stuck, facing the huge tree, staring into darkness.

From behind, he could hear the battle raging; the wet smacking of flesh against flesh, the crunching of bones, the snapping of nearby branches. The sounds of these monsters were from another world. The three-toed creature moaned and growled from deep in its throat, projecting a profound and deafening sound, reminiscent of a lion's roar. The second beast hissed and snarled, more like a crocodile or snake. Each sound sent shivers down the man's spine.

Another blood-curdling wail rang out, vibrating the man's eardrums. Judging by the sound, it was the second creature, the one that had pursued him through the night. Warm thick liquid splashed across his back. He reached a loose hand to his shoulder and felt the sticky substance: blood. The hissing and snarling slowly subsided, giving way to deep and raspy breathing; followed by a loud thump as a huge body crashed onto the earth. Lightning cracked and thunder rolled as the victor bellowed a deep and triumphant howl over its adversary.

The man held his breath again, praying the winner would not come looking for him. After a few moments he could hear the sound of large footsteps moving away, into the jungle, into the distance.

The man remained frozen for several minutes, too terrified to move. He could still feel the warm and sticky blood on his shoulders. After a few moments, his heartbeat began to slow, his breathing returned to normal. A shiver rippled across his body as he started to feel cold. The jungle was silent again, save for the sound of the pounding rain and the occasional distant thunder crack.

He'd made it.

The man tried to wriggle free from the hollow but he was still attached to the medical kit, which was firmly wedged between the tree-roots. Carefully, he maneuvered a free hand down to his waist and unclipped the carabiner, and the kit, from his belt. As soon as he was free he backed away from the roots clumsily.

He looked up and down the path for any signs of movement. As he did so, he stepped backward, slipping slightly as he came into contact with the huge pool of blood seeping toward him. The man turned sharply and found himself standing only meters from the fallen creature. It was a hideous beast, like something out of a child's nightmare. Its hulking mass moved slightly. A shiver skipped across the man's spine. For a moment he made eye contact with the beast, his stomach tensed; but its eyes were empty and dull; it was dead.

The man clutched his stomach as the pain continued to intensify. He pressed lightly on his right side, just below the ribcage, and groaned in agony. He doubled over, trying to breathe through it. As he opened his eyes again, the man saw something strange. Lying on the ground at his feet was a beautiful yellow feather the size of his forearm. It was completely out of place in the depths of the jungle. He crouched down and picked it up. It was unlike anything he had ever—*WHACK.*

Darkness.

University of Oxford, Oxford—
21:00, 10 March, 2086

A middle-aged man sat alone in the basement of the Earth Sciences department at Oxford University. It had always amused him the school was still referred to as "Earth Sciences," despite the fact his lab was full of core samples from around the solar system. The Geologist stared through a microscope at a sample he'd received earlier that morning. The container was covered in a bright red sticker which read "TOP SECRET." He marveled at the shape and color of the mineral magnified under the fluorescent light. It looked so familiar, so ordinary, and yet he knew this mineral had been extracted from the surface of some unknown planet.

A soft chime, accompanied by a flashing red light, sounded on his desktop. It was the communication equipment. He stared at the light for a moment and frowned. The signal was coming from off-world. He engaged the message.

The holographic projector on his desk remained dark, which meant whoever was sending the message did not want their face displayed. A raspy voice came over the speakers.

"*Terra, this is ET,*" said the voice. "*Alexandrite confirmed. At least a hundred carats. But that's not the best part. There's more to this place than we thought. Think silver value.*" The voice paused, clearly excited. "*We're gonna be rich.*"

"Who's that?" came a cockney voice from behind.

The Geologist paused the message and turned abruptly. He'd forgotten the janitor came in afterhours to clean the lab, after everyone had left for the day.

"Apparently that was ET," said the Geologist snidely. "Guess he figured out how to phone home."

The janitor didn't react.

The Geologist frowned. "Not familiar with Spielberg? He was only the Shakespeare of twentieth century film." He eyed the thick black hair hanging loosely over the janitor's eyes and the thin layer of stubble which covered the bottom half of his face. His clothes were old and worn; he was not a man of means. "I guess I shouldn't be surprised."

"What's Alexandrite?" asked the janitor curiously.

The Geologist eyed the tall thin man suspiciously. "Alexandrite is the rarest gemstone on Earth, which means it's incredibly valuable."

The janitor frowned. "Then why did he say 'think silver value?' Wouldn't silver be less valuable?"

The Geologist shrugged, turning back to his desktop. "No idea. Silver isn't even a gemstone. Guess ET doesn't understand much about geology."

The Geologist continued to play the message. "*We're gonna be rich . . . But we're gonna need backup. Shit is starting to hit the fan here. I'll do what I can from our end, but it looks like we might need to enact the failsafe protocol. You know what to do.*"

With his back turned, the Geologist couldn't see the thin smile creep across the janitor's face.

EVOLUTION

Museum of Natural History, New York City—
18:00, 25 July, 2086

Dr. Amber Lytton wrapped a scarf around her neck, flicking her long auburn hair behind her shoulders. Her friend and colleague, Dr. Joel Carter, handed her a pair of black gloves as they walked briskly toward the West 81st Street exit of the Museum of Natural History, bickering about the presentation they'd just delivered.

"I told you this wasn't the right audience for that," snapped Amber, not looking back at Joel who was trailing several steps behind. The annoyance in her voice was palpable.

Joel opened his mouth to speak.

Amber cut him off. "You've got to stop doing this. We have six more cities to visit and if we want anyone to actually fund our research then we need to stop pissing everyone off by telling them humans are a fucking virus!"

Joel grunted, "I'm just telling it how it is. Humanity needs to wake up and stop living in a bubble. The world is already dead because we screwed up the planet. The Anthropocene has wiped out more species than the goddamn meteor that killed the dinosaurs. But most of the ten billion people who live here are just ignoring the problem hoping someone else will fix it."

Amber rolled her eyes. "I know, I know. Everyone is stupid and you're the smartest person alive. If other people saw things your way we'd be better off as a species." They'd been having the same conversation for most of their lives.

Joel and Amber had been friends since birth. Their mothers met during pre-natal classes, immediately striking up a friendship. Joel's father had left his mother shortly after he was born. Amber's parents, on the other hand, had been madly in love, but her father travelled frequently for work. And, although her mother had no trouble balancing home life and a career, she appreciated the companionship offered by Joel's mother.

Amber's tone softened. "You know I'm with you on this, right? You're like a brother to me. Not many people can say that these days."

With their mothers so close Joel and Amber became each other's surrogate siblings. Their relationship was rare in that respect. Since the introduction of global population policies in 2031, it had become increasingly difficult to have a child legally. Strict licensing laws prohibited couples from having a child if they didn't pass a series of tests to determine their "fitness" as parents. And even licensed couples were restricted to a single child in an effort to curb overpopulation.

The laws didn't stop everyone from having children. But those who broke the rules weren't let off lightly. They were stripped of their rights as a global citizen; voting, education, healthcare, and welfare were no longer freely provided for illegal *breeders* and their families.

So, Amber, Joel, and their mothers became their own little family, living happily in the densely packed suburbs of Melbourne, Australia.

Amber finally slowed her pace so she could look Joel in the eye. "I believe in population control and environmental protection just as much as you. But you can't tell an auditorium full of potential funders the planet would be better off if dinosaurs hadn't died out and humans had never existed. They don't want to hear it. Especially from a paleozoologist. Who are you to tell people they shouldn't exist?"

Joel bristled. "Well, maybe you should toughen up and start being more vocal. I'm sure they'll like the message more from a behavioral ecologist."

Amber paused as they approached the large windowed exit doors. "Don't take your frustrations out on me. I wasn't having a go at your specialty. My point is, our expertise is in evolution, not extinction. *Cerebraptor* was a huge discovery for us. Not everyone can say they found the raptor with the largest brain-to-mass ratio of *any* species in the fossil record. But the funding from that grant is running out. And if we want to continue doing research at Dinosaur Cove then we need at least some humans to be on our side; hopefully ones with deep pockets."

Joel didn't respond. He tugged at his sports coat uncomfortably. Despite Amber's advice, Joel never dressed up for these occasions. He wore jeans with a navy blue sports coat over a plain white T-shirt. With his ear-length sandy blond hair, he looked like a surfer itching to get back to the waves, not like an academic who had just delivered an important presentation. But that's how he liked it. He despised the song-and-dance that came with securing research funding.

Amber pushed open the large glass door. "C'mon, our next stop is the Irwin Institute in Buenos Aires. Maybe you could just dial it down a little for Mr. Irwin? He's the best chance we've got to secure a private grant."

Amber shivered as they exited the building into the wet metropolis. Outside was unseasonably cold. Rain drifted across the wind gently, but the pair stayed dry under a large glass veranda as they waited for their car to arrive. Amber wished she had worn something warmer. Unlike Joel, Amber dressed to impress on these occasions. Her black and grey dress contoured perfectly to her petite and athletic physique. Although her father's family had been in Australia for generations, her mother's Irish origins still dominated her appearance; porcelain white skin, deep blue eyes and dark auburn hair which snaked down the length of her back.

"Chilly, aye?" said a deep voice from behind.

Amber and Joel turned back toward the doors. A young security guard was swinging gingerly on his heels, eyeing the pair and smiling.

"You two look familiar? Been on the HV or something?" His voice was thickened by a deep southern drawl. The dark brown skin of his face contrasted starkly with the white of his teeth as he grinned.

"Not recently," said Joel, turning away indifferently.

The young man snapped his fingers and stepped away from the door. "I know you! You're the scientists that were on the news a few months ago! Didn't you discover some new sort of smart dinosaur or something?"

Amber smiled. "You have a good memory. That was almost a year ago and it was only on a small local newscast. What's your name?"

"Black, Diamond Black," he said, offering his hand. Diamond was tall and lean, giving him a slightly formidable appearance. And yet, there was a friendliness to his demeanor that Amber found endearing.

She shook his hand. "Amber Lytton, and this is my associate, Joel Carter. That interview was so long ago and we were only on for a few minutes. I'm surprised anyone would remember our faces, let alone why we were there."

Diamond smiled, pleased with himself. "Yeah, the old memory has always been sharp; particularly when it's a subject that interests me. So, where you off to?" He followed Joel's gaze down the driveway.

"Buenos Aires. And we're in a bit of a hurry, too," snapped Joel.

Diamond chuckled, a deep and hollow laugh. "Sorry, sir, am I holding you up?"

Amber laughed. "Don't mind him, Mr. Black. He's just a bit sour no one liked his speech. I guess not everyone likes dinosaurs as much as we do."

Diamond smiled. "I used to love dinosaurs when I was a kid. My uncle's really into all that stuff. He's been on HV, too. Was even knighted a few years back by the King of England; 'Sir Hugh Irwin' is what they call him now. But I still call him Uncle Hugh."

Joel spun around, intrigued. "Did you say Hugh Irwin? Hugh Irwin of the Irwin Institute in Argentina?" Joel's demeanor was suddenly warm and friendly.

"That's my uncle. I'm actually going to visit him soon. He's got some special job that needs extra muscle."

Joel stepped closer and shook Diamond's hand. "Diamond, was it?"

The soft rays of car headlights flashed across the carport and a shiny white self-driving Tesla rolled to a stop. The car door slid open automatically, sensing the proximity remote in Joel's pocket. Inside were two forward- and two backward-facing seats, creating a small seating pod.

Joel continued to shake Diamond's hand, smiling warmly. "Well, what a small world. It was a pleasure meeting you."

Amber rolled her eyes before stepping into the car and sitting on one of the forward-facing seats toward the rear of the vehicle. A small keypad lit up on the center console and she began punching in coordinates for the airport.

"Maybe we'll see you in Argentina sometime soon?" Joel grinned childishly before climbing into the car, taking the seat opposite Amber.

Diamond saluted the pair as they got into the car. "I hope so," he winked, as the car door slid back into position and the car pulled away from the curb, disappearing into the rain.

JFK International Airport, New York City— 20:00, 25 July, 2086

Seated at a small bar near the departure gates of JFK, Joel and Amber sipped their drinks casually as they waited for their flight to Buenos Aires. Joel swallowed the last of his drink and glanced at Amber, who was busy reading from a small portable info-tablet. He saw how intently she stared at the device, absorbing every word. For a moment, his mind drifted to fifteen years earlier, during their undergraduate days at Monash University. He saw her sitting in her bed, studying with her info-tablet, wearing nothing but a bed sheet. He was looking up at her with one eye half open, through the strands of his long blond hair, pretending to sleep so he could watch her in secret.

Amber looked across the bar and saw Joel's soft grey eyes staring at her. "What? Do I have something on my face?" She rubbed at the corners of her mouth.

Joel stifled a laugh. "Nah, nah. You just remind me of Uni-Amber whenever you play with your info-tablet."

"Are you talking about my early morning 'study sessions' back when we were dating? When you would pretend to sleep so you could stare at me like a pervert." She smiled coyly.

Joel cocked his head. "You knew about that? I thought I was so sly!"

"Why do you think I was studying in the nude? In winter?"

Joel ordered another drink from the bartender; their flight wasn't for another hour and there was very little to do during their wait. As he sipped the cold beer, he thought again about their University days and their brief romantic liaison.

It was the end of their third year. Joel had arrived at Amber's mother's house to find her on the floor of her bedroom. Her face was red, her eyes were streaked with black mascara, and she held a tissue bunched in her hand.

"What's wrong? What happened? Are you okay?"

Amber was breathing heavily, trying to talk through the tears. "I can't do this. I'm not good enough to do this. You wouldn't understand . . ." she trailed off and began sobbing softly.

Joel stood awkwardly in the doorway, confused. "Take a deep breath and calm down. What can't you do? What happened?"

Amber took several deep breaths, trying to calm her mind. "It's my course. I'm just not good enough. I tried so hard all year but I just couldn't . . ." She cut herself off again.

Joel was finally starting to understand. He walked into the room and crouched down in front of her, placing a sympathetic hand on her knee. "You failed a class?"

Amber shook her head. "No, I mean, I might as well have. I got a Credit in Marine Ecosystems. A *Credit.*"

Joel hesitated for a moment before he burst out laughing.

"I told you, you wouldn't understand!" blurted Amber through angry tears. "You don't ever go to class and you get High Distinctions for everything! You don't know how it feels to try and fail! I'm worthless. I might as well just give up now," she mumbled, burying her face in tissues again.

Joel continued to chuckle. He pulled Amber into his arms and hugged her tight. "I'm sorry for laughing, I know I shouldn't. But you're being ridiculous. You're not worthless; you know you're not worthless. It's not your fault if you weren't blessed with my God-like intelligence and epicness," he smiled, running his fingers through his messy beach hair with exaggerated motions.

She smiled, despite herself.

He shook his head. "And you didn't fail, you got a Credit. That's still better than sixty percent of your class! You need to start believing in yourself." He tilted her head so he could look into her eyes. "Hell, I believe in you. And I don't believe in much these days." He smiled his trademark charismatic smile. The type of smile that took over his entire face.

Amber looked up through red, bloodshot eyes. "I'm such a mess."

Joel shook his head. "I don't think you're a mess. I think you're amazing. It's kind of cute you're so upset over a Credit. I love that you want to be the best you can be at all times and that you're so passionate and intelligent and hard working. It's actually kind of a turn on," he half-laughed.

Joel continued to stare deep into Amber's eyes. He felt a sudden surge of electricity pulsing through his chest, something he'd never felt before. The look in her eyes said she felt it, too. Joel took a chance. He leaned in, closed his eyes, and kissed Amber on the lips.

In that moment, the nature of their relationship changed forever.

Joel's mind slowly returned to the present as he took the last sip of his beer, now tepid and warm. "Remind me again why we never worked out as a couple?"

"You still thinking about our Uni days?" She shrugged. "We were young. And, if I remember correctly, you got fed up with all my 'adventures,' as you called them."

During their Postgraduate years Amber developed an affinity for fieldwork. She volunteered for any and every expedition she could find where she could observe extinct-in-the-wild animals in wildlife parks, comparing their behavior with their wild ancestors. She began travelling to remote parts of Africa and South America, even Antarctica, gradually spending less and less time at home.

Joel preferred to stay close to Melbourne, investigating the remains of extinct Australian flora and fauna in the relative safety of the University laboratory.

He scratched the purposeful ten-day growth on his chin. "Oh yeah, your little adventures. I remember now. You'd leave for months at a time, sometimes to places that didn't even have Wi-Fi. Those days sucked."

Amber nodded. "I know. You made me feel so guilty. You wanted a stay-at-home girlfriend who was into fashion and beauty products and all that girly stuff. But that was never me."

Joel half-smiled. It was true. Back then he wanted the type of girl his friends were with; someone who worked in marketing or social media, someone who took an hour to get ready so they could look like a Photoshopped version of themselves. But more than that, he wanted a girl who thought he was the center of her world. Someone who wouldn't disappear for months on end as if it were no big deal.

He sighed. "Like you said, we were young and dumb."

The airport speakers sprang to life, "*Ladies and gentlemen, boarding has commenced for flight BQ156 to Buenos Aires. Please make your way to Gate 7.*"

Joel swiped the small black point-of-sale machine imbedded in the bar with his GeniousWatch. The machine flashed with the price of their bill and the word "ACCEPTED." He tilted the empty beer bottle upside-down to extract the last remaining drops and the pair left the bar, making their way to the gate.

Arcadia

Irwin Institute, Buenos Aires—
11:30, 26 July, 2086

Charles Kendal found himself seated in a cramped room. In the center of the small space was a large semi-circular table surrounded by a group of very irritated people. The walls were clearly white once, but they had stained yellow over time. The whole building had a faint musty smell, like a damp towel left on the bathroom floor. Charles sat away from the others, near the rear corner of the room. An e-cigarette hung loosely in his mouth as he leaned back on the hard wooden chair. Vapor floated aimlessly about his head like a tiny cloud.

Charles stared through the window and watched as rain streamed down the pane. Typically he didn't like to leave the UK, but he was grateful for the chance to travel somewhere tropical and sunny. He sighed audibly as he watched the rain fall in a steady torrent outside.

Looking around the room, he recognized the various faces seated at the table. While he hadn't met anyone in person, he had memorized all the names on the attendee list. On the far side of the room sat a short stocky man in his forties, wearing a pale cream Armani suit, which was obviously too small. His thick dark hair, stubbly chin and rounded red cheeks betrayed his Italian heritage; Leonardo Montello.

Beside Montello, Charles recognized the Australians, Amber Lytton and Joel Carter. Near the center of the semi-circular table sat two young Russians. They couldn't be much older than thirty, perhaps even younger.

"Welcome!" A deep booming voice appeared at the back of the room, resonating in the small space. Charles turned his attention to the ample frame and dark chocolate skin of Hugh Irwin as he strode casually around the table to the front of the room, chewing a cigar stub. He eyed the various faces sitting around the table, grinning.

Irwin took his position by a very old-looking podium and cleared his throat dramatically. "Ahem. First, I'd like to thank everyone for taking a moment out of your schedules to hear what I have to say. I understand you are all very busy, but I assure you, this will be worth your time."

"Mr. Irwin? I'm a bit confused. I thought we were here to pitch for the IRC grant?" interrupted Amber.

Charles eyed Amber appreciatively. He'd heard she was quite tenacious, but judging by her small frame she wouldn't be of any concern. Charles turned his attention to Joel. He was rugged and fit, not a typical academic at all. He looked more like a laborer with lightly tanned skin and a solid frame. Charles sized him up; it wouldn't be easy, but he could take him if he had to.

Irwin chuckled. "My apologies, Dr. Lytton, but we may have been a little misleading in our invitation. Please allow me to explain. You're all here today because you are the best at what you do. And we have a proposal that requires an interdisciplinary team of scientists to do something no one on this planet has attempted before." The lights dimmed slowly as a holographic image of the Earth from space rose in the center of the table.

"Ever since extra-terrestrial life was discovered in 2044 the world has been united in our efforts to explore the skies. While the life we've found so far hasn't quite been the sentient beings we were hoping for, the discovery of those plant-like organisms has given humanity hope we are not alone. And, more importantly, there are other places capable of sustaining life."

As he spoke, the holographic Earth rotated slowly.

"The push for space exploration and commercial travel has grown rapidly over the last fifty years. With the development of the Ultra Shuttle we were finally able to approach the speed of light." The hologram changed again; "flying" through space was a 3D Ultra Shuttle. It was a silver cigar-shaped tube, with three large tapered wings which fanned out from the sides and roof of the craft like the feathered tail of an arrow. Also like an arrow, the nose narrowed sharply into a pointed tip. Small portholes lined the cigar-tube and a huge glass window wrapped around the entire front of the craft.

"The tourism industries on the moon and Mars are booming. And scenic tours of Venus and Jupiter are becoming more and more popular." The 3D image flipped around so it showed the view from inside one of the portholes, looking outward. The outside flashed from blackness to an external view of the moon, Mars, Venus and then Jupiter.

"As our ability to travel further into space improves, so does our knowledge of neighboring worlds. We've known for a while now Earth is the only planet capable of supporting complex life in our solar system. Intense heat, unimaginable cold, poisonous gases, and unstable surface activity make human residency outside of Earth impossible. It costs the tourism industry billions to maintain habitats on the moon and Mars; importing oxygen, food, water and materials; regulating habitat temperature, air pressure, UV protectants, you name it.

"While people celebrate the latest advances in technology and stellar exploration, the problems on Earth continue to grow." The view from inside the Ultra Shuttle switched back to the Earth from space. It showed super storms gliding over the Pacific, floodwaters consuming low-lying coastal villages, and animal bones protruding from dried-up riverbeds.

"The warnings of climate change and environmental destruction were ignored for too long, and with each passing year the Anthropocene impact worsens. Even with the introduction of population control laws, there are now ten billion people on the planet. It was only a matter of time before fossil fuels, forests, and thousands of animal species vanished. Turbulent and unpredictable weather and never-before-seen natural disasters continue to wreak havoc across the globe. Some scientists are even suggesting the human race is now beyond the tipping point of extinction. It's no secret, science and industry alike dream of finding a hospitable planet somewhere in our galaxy. Somewhere to start afresh." Irwin could see his audience was starting to lose interest. They'd heard it all before; pipe dreams of the rich and hopeful.

Irwin smiled.

"What people don't know is that the most extensive expedition has been conducted in secret for decades by the International Space Alliance."

Everyone shifted in their seats.

The projector faded to black and was replaced with a new image. A footprint hovered in the space above the table.

"Dr. Lytton, can you tell me what this is?" asked Irwin.

Amber frowned and leaned closer to the table as the image rotated. The impression was large and imbedded in clay. She inched closer to get a better view, waiting for the image to rotate further. "It's a footprint. At a guess, I'd say a member of the Crocodylidae family; saltwater or Nile crocodile? I can't quite place it. How old is the print?"

A grin crept across Irwin's lips, unable to contain his excitement. "When this image was captured, it was estimated the print was between twelve and twenty-four hours old."

Confused murmurs spread through the group.

Amber shook her head, as if her hearing had failed her. "I'm sorry, did you say twelve *hours*? That's not possible. Whatever made this print was huge; at least two hundred kilograms. Everyone knows the last mega-fauna died out years ago. Is this from the San Diego zoo?"

"You're right, the last wild mega-fauna was declared extinct in 2068. That's any animal weighing one hundred kilograms or more for those unfamiliar with the term, excluding humans of course." He chuckled jovially and patted his stomach. "But this is not from a zoo or wildlife park."

Confused looks were exchanged across the table.

Irwin smiled. "You know our world is dying; what you don't know is the ISA has spent decades searching for another planetary body capable of supporting human life. I know what you're thinking, it's impossible, right?" He paused for dramatic effect.

The image in the center of the table began to shift into another planetary shape. While it looked strikingly similar to Earth, the continents were misshapen and the land was covered in lush forests and deep blue oceans.

"We found it."

The group fell silent.

"We found exactly what we were looking for; an unspoiled planet with liquid water, a breathable atmosphere, and an average global temperature of about fourteen degrees Celsius. It was named *Arcadia* after the paradise from Greek mythology. From remote observations, there is evidence of complex life already on the surface. But in order to make a proper assessment of the planet's viability we need to send a team there for further research." Irwin's voice quaked slightly.

He turned off the projector and waited for the lights to return. "I want to send you to the surface of Arcadia; a team of scientists to collect data and determine if the planet is fit for relocation. Due to financial constraints and conflicting political interests there will be no second chances on this."

Irwin began to pass around small sheets of translucent paper which rotated through the images from the projections they had just reviewed, along with a dossier detailing the mission.

A deep Russian voice interrupted. "Not to sound too skeptical, but how's this even possible?"

Charles turned toward the source of the voice, the young and broad-shouldered Russian, Mikhail Ozero. Even while relaxed his biceps bulged within his shirt. His hair was black and short, shaved close to his head. His face was hard but his eyes betrayed his youth. Charles figured he would struggle to take on the big Russian physically, but he should be able to outwit him.

"The fastest ships on Earth can travel up to near the speed of light, or NeSOL, which is around 240,000 kilometers per second," continued the woman seated beside Mikhail: Veronica Nizhny. She was also tall and lean. Her long black hair was pulled back into a neat and precise shoulder-length braid. Her features were also hard, yet with subtle femininity that Charles found appealing.

"But, even traveling at NeSOL, it would still take five years to reach the nearest star, and over 100,000 years to reach the nearest galaxy to the Milky Way. So, how is this possible?"

Irwin's smile widened, he had been waiting for this question. "Drs. Nizhny and Ozero raise a good question, and the answer is nothing short of spectacular." Irwin punched at the controls of the projector. A large shuttle appeared above the table, rotating slowly.

"Ladies and gentlemen, meet *Hermes*; the messenger god."

Unlike the Ultra Shuttle, which was long and sleek in design, *Hermes* was big and stocky. It was mostly white in color, with an enormous window which wrapped around the entire front half of the craft. From the outside, the windows were tinted black, like the hollow reflectiveness of a shark's eyes. It was the size of a small house, with two large wings jutting out from below the huge black windows, a smaller pair of wings at the rear, and a single fin on top of the tail. The nose tapered to a rounded shape and mounted on the end of each wing was a thin blue cylindrical engine.

Irwin beamed. "*Hermes* was built using the latest developments for space exploration. A fusion of military and industry expertise, it was created specifically for this mission using a revolutionary type of engine. As

Dr. Nizhny pointed out, most modern crafts are equipped with a *Light Drive* which is capable of traveling up to NeSOL; however, this mission needed something faster. To overcome this obstacle, our team of scientists created a device capable of doing what no other could; the *Phoenix* engine."

The hologram zoomed into the stern, through the huge bulkhead doors. The engine room was entirely white and glowed with an ominous energy. A huge and bizarre-shaped contraption sat in the center of the room. It was as tall as two men and attached to the ship at the top and bottom through an interlocking metallic structure. Like the rest of the room, the engine was clean and white, except for a capsule which sat in the center of an opaque chamber, emitting a soft reddish-orange glow. The light around the edges of the chamber seemed to dance and jump, like tongues of fire pulsating on the surface of the sun.

"I know the concept of teleportation is not new to anyone here. However, the teleportation we know is reliant on pre-existing booths set at various places around the world. Kind of like the first telephones, where you could only make a call to another telephone at a fixed location. What makes the *Phoenix* unique is its ability to transport an object between locations *without* pre-existing hardware; a bit like a cellular or mobile phone, where a call can be placed to anyone anywhere in the world.

"It's because of the *Phoenix* we were able to find Arcadia, hidden in the furthest regions of the universe. Before the *Phoenix* we'd been searching our neighboring systems using drones fitted with *Light Drives.* It took years just to reach the first star and decades to explore a tiny fraction of our neighboring systems. Once we had the *Phoenix* our ability to search distant worlds increased exponentially. And once Arcadia was discovered, the *Phoenix* was redesigned to transport the most technologically advanced craft ever built; the *Hermes* spacecraft was born."

Irwin paused and noticed Charles Kendal slouching in his chair, half-asleep, with an e-cigarette still hanging from his mouth. "Dr. Kendal," said Irwin with tension in his voice. "Am I boring you? Is this information about another Earth-like planet old news?"

Charles shifted in his chair and took the e-cigarette from his mouth. "Sorry, I was just waiting for you to stop bullshitting and get to the point."

Irwin's face flashed red. "Excuse me?"

Charles took a drag from his e-cigarette. "For one, your *Phoenix* drive sounds incredibly flawed. You liken it to a phone, which is ridiculous, because even mobile telephones relied on pre-existing hardware for sending and receiving information. What you're describing is science fiction."

Irwin huffed. "Fiction? I've just told you, we used this device to find Arcadia. That is fact."

Charles ignored Irwin's comment. "Plus, you've been working on this for decades, developed new technologies, broken the laws of space-time, discovered a magical Earth-like planet, and now all of a sudden you have financial and political constraints? Something doesn't add up."

Irwin shifted nervously on his feet. He looked away from the group; this was the question he had hoped to avoid answering today.

"There is something else." Irwin sighed heavily and stepped away from the podium, sitting casually on the corner of the table. "There has been some disagreement among the project team about the feasibility of Arcadia for colonization. Another research mission was deployed just over six months ago. Shortly after they arrived we lost contact with the shuttle. And we haven't heard from them since."

While the others gasped under their breath, Charles leaned back in his seat again, nonchalant.

"Do you have any idea what happened?" asked Amber after a moment of silence.

"No. That's why we need to move fast. This expedition is also a rescue operation."

Charles laughed. "Move fast? You lost contact six months ago and only now you decided to send a rescue team?"

Irwin balled his fist unconsciously. "We started moving as soon as we could. We didn't have a spare *Phoenix* engine lying around. We had to build a new one, and a new ship. And we had to find the right people for the next mission."

Irwin glanced around the room, noting the air of hesitation. "I understand this is a lot to take in. I know some of you may be doubtful, but I assure you the reason you are here is because we need you. You have been handpicked for your skills, your field, and your abilities." He gestured toward the Russian couple. "Take Drs. Nizhny and Ozero. In addition to being some of the top cosmonauts of their time, they are also established scientists in the fields of astrophysics and astrochemistry."

Veronica and Mikhail exchanged glances and smiled.

"Leonardo Montello has more knowledge of medical biology than any other living person." He nodded to Amber and Joel. "Then there's Dr. Lytton and Dr. Carter; the world's top behavioral and paleozoological team." Irwin pointed to Charles. "Even you, Dr. Kendal, despite your disposition, are one of the foremost exo-geologists in the world."

Suddenly a short man hurried into the small room and whispered in Irwin's ear.

He smirked and nodded his head. "Yes, yes, bring them in. It seems the cavalry has arrived." Irwin gestured toward the door as two men dressed in American military fatigues entered the room. Charles stiffened in his seat. *There weren't any military names on the invite list?*

The first man was average height, in his late fifties, with greying hair and cold eyes. A long scar lined his clean-shaven jawline. The second man stood over six feet tall with deep chocolate-colored skin. While his movements were stiff and serious there was a softness in his face.

Irwin gestured to the man with the scar, "I'd like to introduce you to Lieutenant Jeremy Grey and Sergeant Diamond Black."

Amber and Joel exchanged a curious look. *Irwin's nephew,* mouthed Amber.

The pair made their way to the front of the room, standing either side of Irwin, almost disinterested in the rest of the group.

"Lieutenant Grey and Sergeant Black will be leading the rescue portion of this expedition, so as far as you're concerned, they are in charge."

Charles sat up in his chair. "What? We're being led by a couple of mindless, gun-toting mercenaries? I'm surprised this one is even old enough to carry a firearm." He gestured to Diamond.

Before Diamond could react, a deep throaty voice interrupted the exchange.

"Excuse me?" Lieutenant Grey leaned forward. His voice was rough and cold. His eyes narrowed, measuring Charles's nerve. "If you have a problem with authority I'm more than happy to leave your ass behind."

Charles didn't flinch. He raised an eyebrow, eyeing Grey carefully. The man was all military, from his hairstyle to his tone of voice. He wasn't like the others in the room, he wasn't an academic or a scientist. He was hard and severe.

"Aye, aye, captain."

Grey held eye contact. "That's Lieutenant to you, *civilian,*" he hissed.

Charles's face hardened, but he held his tongue. He'd come too far to lose his cool now.

"Don't make me repeat myself," said Grey.

"Gentlemen, please," urged Irwin. "We need to work together on this. There are no second chances. Failing is not an option." His voice echoed throughout the room.

ISA Training Facility, Buenos Aires— 16:00, 26 July, 2086

As the group waited to be called into the examination room Charles filled a paper cup with water, trying to keep away from the others. The group had been asked to complete an examination to make sure they were physically and mentally fit for the mission. Charles was nervous. He had been preparing for months, rehearsing the right responses.

He stared at his faint reflection in the large glass water tank. The face staring back at him was so old. His thick jet-black hair was now speckled grey and his hairline was clearly receding, the skin beneath his eyes and neck had begun to sag, and when he relaxed his facial muscles he could see faint wrinkles around his brow and eyes. Charles sighed heavily as he scratched at the greying stubble which had started to form on his chin.

Suddenly Charles saw another face in the glass; the younger and more attractive face of Dr. Lytton approaching from behind. And she was mad.

Amber took a cup and filled it quickly. "Why are you still here? You obviously don't believe in the mission and you have no respect for Irwin or the ISA. So, why are you here?"

Charles shrugged apathetically. "I've never been to space before. Imagine, being an expert on extra-terrestrial geology and never actually leaving the planet." Charles eyed Amber's physique appreciatively. She was short, but what she lacked in height she made up for in confidence. "I think the better question is what are *you* doing here?"

"Are you serious? This isn't the nineteenth century, Dr. Kendal. You don't think a woman is capable of being a scientist?"

Charles raised an eyebrow. "Actually, Dr. Lytton, I was referring to both of you." He gestured to Joel who was half-asleep on one of the waiting room chairs. "I find it hard to believe an intelligent woman like you isn't asking more questions. Like why they needed a behavioral ecologist and a paleozoologist? Why not an exobiologist, someone who has studied extra-terrestrial lifeforms?"

Amber opened her mouth to speak but couldn't find the words to respond.

"Exactly." Charles smiled, satisfied with the last word.

He made his way to the rear window of the waiting room, trying to find a new refuge from the others so he could stay focused. Outside, the rain had cleared and a murky grey sky was visible through the thick glass. Charles took a seat facing the windows. Once again he caught a glimpse of his weathered reflection.

At least I'm still young where it counts.

"Charles Kendal?" A thick Russian accent came from behind, followed by the sweet scent of a woman's perfume.

Charles turned around slowly. "Excuse me?"

Veronica walked around the row of seats and stood before Charles. She was tall, staring down at him. "You are Charles Kendal, yes?" she repeated. Her accent sent electricity through his veins. There was something sexy about a thick Eastern European accent. Her features were sharp, from her perfectly applied makeup to her perfectly shaped eyebrows.

"Indeed. I see you've heard of me?" He leered at her like a schoolboy.

Veronica smiled warmly, revealing a set of perfect white teeth. "I have heard of you, yes. They say you are one of the best exo-geologists on the planet?"

Charles smiled, he loved compliments from beautiful women. "I can't deny that. What else have you heard?"

Veronica's expression stiffened. "I have also heard you killed a man."

Charles's smile vanished. He placed the empty water cup on the ground and pulled the e-cigarette from his pocket. "You shouldn't believe everything you hear."

Veronica frowned. "So, it was all made up?"

"What would you know?" snapped Charles. "You weren't there. No one was there." His voice weakened and his posture dropped. His eyes began to soften and bore the unmistakable sign of pain. Charles's hand, still clasping the e-cigarette, began to tremble slightly.

Veronica relaxed slightly, feeling a little guilty. "You're right. I wasn't there."

Charles sighed, "No one was." He paused and glanced back to Veronica; her eyes were now sympathetic and understanding. He concealed a smile and continued, "We were in one of the University research labs. It was late. No one around except us. I don't even know how it started. All I remember was smelling smoke and suddenly the room turned into a fireball. Have you ever been trapped in a burning building, Dr. Nizhny?"

Veronica shook her head.

"It's suffocating. The heat is so intense it sucks all the oxygen from the air. You can't breathe, you can't see, smoke fills your lungs as you gasp for burning mouthfuls of air. And even though they tell you not to, you panic. And you run. You run so fast you don't even think about anyone else. You only think about getting the hell out of there." His voice softened and trailed off into silence.

Veronica placed a comforting hand on Charles's shoulder, sensing the emotion in his words.

"It was only when they found his body I remembered the janitor was still inside." Charles pulled away from her, closing his eyes.

"He didn't make it?" Veronica could not hide the doubt in her voice.

"Yes!" snapped Charles. "He must have passed out from the smoke or something! Why is that so hard to believe? I'm lucky to be alive but people treat me like it's a goddamn conspiracy!"

Veronica searched his face again; his eyes were watering, but his outburst was off-putting; there was something she couldn't quite put her finger on.

"I'm sorry, yes, of course. You're the victim here." Her words were stiff.

"Excuse me? Who are *you* to judge *me*? Who are you to walk over here and stir up shit from my past then judge me about something you know nothing about? You're just a glorified weather girl; a stuck-up, pretentious, weather girl."

Veronica's eyes narrowed. "I might be a 'glorified weather girl,' but I'm also the one who'll be flying you to Arcadia. Your life will be in my hands."

Charles looked up again. The pain in his eyes was gone, replaced by something sinister. "Let's just hope nothing terrible happens to those delicate little hands of yours. Accidents happen every day."

"Dr. Kendal?" a nurse poked his head out of the examination room. "They're ready for you now."

Charles switched off his e-cigarette. "It's been a pleasure talking with you, Dr. Nizhny. I hope we can be friends."

○ ○ ○ ● ○ ○ ○

"Good morning, Dr. Kendal," said the young practitioner, running her hands across the desktop and flicking through various electronic files. "Take a seat, please." She gestured to the empty chair opposite her desk. Charles sat and crossed his legs. The entire desktop was made from glass. It was a huge touch screen computer which could be manipulated by the practitioner seated in the control chair.

The doctor ran her fingers over several colored squares on the desktop. "First, I'm going to run you through a series of standard questions, okay? Good. Full name?"

"Dr. Charles William Kendal."

"Okay, Dr. Kendal, when and where were you born?"

Charles paused for a moment. "Oxford, England. August 24, 2042."

"In the last twelve months have you taken any narcotics including illicit stimulants, depressants, or hallucinogens?"

"No."

The doctor slid a hand over her desktop, opening another file. "Do you have any allergies; food, medications, hay fever?"

"No."

"Have you ever had a sexually transmitted disease?"

Charles scrunched his nose. "No."

"In the last twelve months, have you had any form of surgery; this could be a major operation such as an organ transplant, or something minor like plastic surgery?"

Charles's demeanor became stoic, staring at the back wall with an empty gaze. "Did you know a hundred years ago plastic surgery was considered an invasive operation? The body was literally sliced, the skin peeled, bone chiseled; all in the name of beauty and self-improvement." Charles touched his jaw absentmindedly.

The doctor frowned slightly. "As a medical physician, I am somewhat familiar with the history of plastic surgery."

"It's incredible to imagine what life was like before genetic selection. Children were born with physical and mental disabilities, parents had no say in their child's gender or height. Imagine a world full of ugly people and retards? It really makes you appreciate the world we live in." Charles glanced out the window at the busy city streets; the sky was tinged a hazy yellowish-brown as the sun climbed across the afternoon sky.

The doctor frowned and followed Charles's gaze out the window. "I'm afraid I—"

"But as we know, perfection comes at a cost," Charles interrupted.

The doctor began to lose her patience. "Dr. Kendal, could you please just answer the question?"

"Surgery, you say? I had my wisdom teeth taken out a few months ago. They were so badly impacted they had to virtually reconstruct my jaw."

The doctor nodded and made a note. "Well, that's all for the written test. If you'll just follow me we'll take you through your physical examination."

Charles opened the door to his right revealing a room full of monitors and white-clad personnel, just in time to see Montello receive a large hypodermic needle injection into his backside. Montello wailed in shock and bit down on his knuckles. Charles shuddered and proceeded through the door.

Missing

ISA Training Facility, Buenos Aires—
05:00, 5 September, 2086

Amber opened her eyes and checked the luminous red light of her GeniousWatch. It was five a.m. She closed her eyes again, the training facility didn't open until seven a.m.

For six weeks, Amber and the rest of the *Hermes* team had been at the ISA Training Base in Buenos Aires. After signing a strict non-disclosure statement, they had been living in isolation at the facility, undergoing a strict physical endurance regime, psychological counselling to prepare them for deep space, and learning how to operate the *Hermes* and its equipment.

Hermes was truly the picture of modern technological advancement. In addition to the incredible *Phoenix* engine, it was equipped with the latest military and space technology. It had magnetically induced artificial gravity, an internal satellite for enhanced communication, as well as the two lifeboats. The lifeboats were also fully equipped. They had four compact two-person multi-terrain vehicles, or MTVs, an armory of direct-energy bullet-free weapons colloquially called lasers, and a handful of chameleonic tents for camouflage.

As their training neared completion Amber had become increasingly restless. Her sleep patterns were disrupted by the sheer excitement of impending deployment. Today they were finally going to launch, finally going to leave Earth and make their way to Arcadia. Amber opened her eye again, certain at least an hour had passed: five fifteen a.m.

Amber huffed and peeled the covers back. Determined to make the most of her time, she quietly changed into her training clothes, careful not to wake the others sleeping peacefully in the barracks. She opened the external door and silently slipped into the crisp pre-dawn light.

Amber pulled her ponytail tighter and leaned forward to stretch the back of her legs. The air had a briskness to it which was refreshing after spending the night in such a humid room. Despite their protests, energy preservation laws made it illegal to use air conditioning and other heavy-duty appliances overnight.

The training base was eerily quiet at this time of the morning. Amber moved quickly across the grounds toward the security gate.

Ronald, the security guard, waved as she approached. "Morning, Dr. Lytton. Up early again?"

Amber smiled and leaned over the bench of the small security office. "Good morning, Ronald. I can't sleep. Any chance of sneaking out for a quick jog?"

"Dr. Lytton, you know it's against the rules for any recruit to leave the base this close to launch." He watched as she began to stretch her legs by bending forward and touching the ground with amazing flexibility. "You've already twisted my arm a bunch of times the last few weeks. With the launch so close we have to be careful."

Amber sighed heavily, exaggerating her disappointment. "Please, Ronald, just this one last time. This is a dangerous mission, I might not even make it back to Earth. It could be my last run on this planet."

"Dr. Lytton, you know why we have these rules. If anyone finds out about—"

Amber interrupted, "I'll be really fast, I promise. Just one lap around the base, please, please, please."

Ronald grunted. "Fine, okay, okay, quick. If you're not back in thirty minutes I'm declaring you AWOL."

"You're the best, Ron!" She leaned across the bench and kissed him on the cheek before ducking under the boom gate and sprinting around the corner, out of sight.

Amber was beginning to feel claustrophobic at the base. She hadn't spoken to anyone outside the facility in weeks; no visitors, no internet, and no comms. Their only connection to the outside world was the central communications room where a team of ISA staff monitored news and media outlets.

While Amber wasn't particularly fussed about being disconnected from society, her greatest frustration was being removed from the natural world.

Normally, she would spend hours visiting national parks and zoos, observing the behaviors of captive animals and absorbing the atmosphere. Despite her outgoing appearance, Amber disliked social situations, and society in general. It was something she and Joel had in common. Amber felt out of place in the city. She had always felt a strong connection to the natural world.

The ISA base was situated outside of Buenos Aires city center, on land that once belonged to the Otamendi Nature Reserve, before it was cleared for agriculture and industrial developments. While the facility took up most of the land, a small stretch of parkland remained outside the exterior walls to maintain some distance between the public and the base. As Amber's strong legs pushed her forward along the walking track outside the compound, surrounded by small shrubs and greenery, she felt free.

Amber slowed her pace as she rounded the far end of the base. Ahead she spotted a small shadow crouched in the middle of the path. As she approached she could see it had a long tail, flicking back and forth like a snake, and pointed ears which turned and twitched.

Her heart jumped. Could this be one of the few remaining wild cats in Argentina? Amber moved very carefully, trying not to disturb the cat as it ate a small rodent in the middle of the path. It was difficult to make out its coloring in the pre-dawn light, but as Amber moved closer she could see its back had black splotches. Her heart leapt again. It was a species of small leopard! Maybe a pampas cat?

Amber stopped approaching and crouched quietly a few meters away. She pressed a small button on her GeniousWatch, illuminating the space above her wrist with an image of a 20th century camera. She lined up the holographic image with the cat and pressed the camera icon. As she did so, the watch made a clicking sound to indicate the holograph was successfully captured.

At the sound of the click, the cat turned its attention toward Amber, hissing viciously and arching its back. Her heart sank. It wasn't a wild cat at all. It was a feral cat with black and tan markings. The very reason why wild cats in this area were declared extinct-in-the-wild. The cat hissed again, picked up its half-eaten meal and ran into the darkness.

Amber switched off her watch, disappointed.

"No, I haven't told anyone else," came a voice from the other side of the base wall.

Amber froze.

"And it can stay that way, for the right price," continued the voice.

Another voice entered the conversation. "Are you blackmailing me?" The second voice was more hushed and raspy.

Amber approached the large stone wall that surrounded the base. The voices were muffled, making it difficult to tell who was speaking.

"Is that really the right question to ask right now? I'd have thought the more appropriate question was 'how much is this secret worth to you?'"

"You small-minded git," grunted the softer voice.

"Hey, whoa, let's be reasonable!" The louder voice became agitated.

Amber heard grunting and shuffling. Loud wet slaps echoed over the wall, the sound of a fist slamming into flesh. Amber held her breath, she was clearly overhearing a fight between two people but didn't know what to do. She heard the louder man start to beg the other to stop; he moaned in agony as the softer man continued to lay blow after blow.

Amber couldn't stand it anymore; she stepped back and took a deep breath, ready to shout out to make her presence known; maybe she could startle them into submission?

She heard a sickening crunch and the scuffling sounds stopped altogether.

After a moment she heard the soft raspy voice again. "Goddammit, look what you made me do."

Amber felt her stomach sink. She turned around and began sprinting back to the gate.

Fuck! Fuck! Fuck!

Her mind was screaming.

It was just a fight. Just a fight between two men. Men fight all the time. Someone was probably just knocked unconscious.

But what if it was more serious than that? What if someone was badly hurt? What if someone was just killed? What impact would that have on the mission?

Amber felt guilty. She didn't want anything to affect the mission she had trained so hard for. Did she really need to tell anyone? It was just by chance she was there. In fact, she wasn't supposed to be outside the wall at all. And if she hadn't been outside the wall, she would never have heard anything, and the launch would go on as scheduled.

But she did hear something.

○ ○ ○ • ○ ○ ○

Veronica drank her coffee slowly, taking tiny sips to avoid scalding her mouth. She sat at one of the small tables in the dining room of the ISA training facility and blew gently on her coffee to cool it. She was the only one inside the large dining hall, beside the chef who was busy preparing breakfast in the kitchen next door.

Laying on the table in front of her was a slate of crystalline glass framed with a soft black rubber around its edges. It was one of the ISA's info-tablets. Veronica swiped her hand just above the surface of the glass and the holographic display within the screen changed. Beneath the surface of the screen sat the 3D face of a stranger; at least he had been a stranger six weeks ago. Veronica had spent hours staring at these images and memorizing the dossiers. She wanted to know everything she could about the missing crew before they departed.

The face on the screen was of a middle-aged Asian man wearing a white lab coat. Veronica closed her eyes and began to recite the details in her head.

Dr. Yoshirou Kato, better known as Yoshi. Japanese ancestry. Completed his medical degree at Kyoto University. Served in the Ground Self-Defense Force as a medic for fifteen years. Forty-three years old.

Veronica opened her eyes and smiled, knowing she had the correct profile.

From behind, a pair of strong arms slipped around her waist, squeezing tight. Mikhail leaned his chin on her shoulder and pulled her closer to him, she could feel his breath tickling the side of her cheek.

"When we get back I'm going to buy you the biggest, most impressive engagement ring anyone has ever seen." His accent was thick and his voice deep, producing a soothing tone, reminding Veronica of home.

Veronica smiled and squeezed Mikhail's arms. "How many times do I have to tell you, I don't care about that sort of thing? All I want is you and one day a family."

Mikhail slipped into the seat beside Veronica, holding her hand lovingly. "I know you don't care about the bells and whistles. But in order to have a family we need to be legally married for at least two years. So, if we have to marry, why not enjoy ourselves?"

Veronica smiled. "For someone so big and macho you are a hopeless romantic, you know?"

Amber burst through the doors into the dining hall, flustered.

"Amber? Are you okay?" asked Veronica, noticing her erratic movements.

Amber approached the table and took a seat beside Veronica; she took several deep breaths and wiped the sweat from her brow. "I'm fine, I just got back from a run. Guess I took it a bit hard on the return." Her eyes darted around the room, searching for something.

Veronica poured Amber a glass of water. "You sure you're okay?"

Amber drank the glass in one breath. "It's okay. Just adrenaline."

The dining hall began to fill with ISA employees as the breakfast bar opened. Eventually Joel and Charles joined Amber, Veronica, and Mikhail, eagerly discussing the impending launch. Everyone was visibly excited. They had all trained hard to get to this day. Everyone was willing to risk their lives because they believed in Irwin's project.

Diamond and Grey soon entered the dining hall, too. But they sat away from the others, on a table with Irwin and some of the more senior staff, as they had every morning.

"What do you think they talk about?" Mikhail said to Veronica.

But Veronica wasn't paying attention to Mikhail. She was pretending to eat breakfast as she watched Amber in the corner of her eye. Amber was still looking around the room, trying to see the face of every person who walked in and out of the dining hall. The longer they were there, the more frustrated she seemed to become.

"What?" said Veronica, realizing Mikhail was staring at her expectantly.

Mikhail nodded toward Grey and Diamond. "What do you think they talk about every morning?"

"Probably just security stuff. Things we don't need to worry about." Veronica gulped her last mouthful of coffee and looked at her GeniousWatch. "Come on, everyone. Last training session starts in a few minutes."

"Yes, mum," laughed Joel.

Amber shook her head. "We can't start yet. Montello isn't here."

Veronica shrugged. "He contacted me earlier saying he wasn't feeling well so he's going to give the session a miss and try to sleep it off before we launch."

Amber bit her lip.

○ ○ ○ • ○ ○ ○

Irwin stood before the stunned group in the small meeting room. He wasn't behind the podium this time. He stood with his palms flat on the semi-circular table. Everyone's face had dropped at the news; Montello was missing.

"We have every available person on the base looking for him. Turns out he's been communicating with his wife, in direct violation of our NDA policy. From the conversations we've uncovered it appears he was having doubts about the mission, talking about quitting and going home. At this stage we're declaring him AWOL."

Veronica frowned. "But what about the message he sent me this morning?"

Irwin nodded. "We believe he sent it just before he left, to give himself a head start. Shortly after that message was sent, his GeniousWatch was deactivated, making it impossible to track his whereabouts."

Amber stared blankly at the table surface, deep in thought.

"I know this is hard to hear. And the timing couldn't be worse. But we're going to press on today. We're still launching at 20:00 as planned. As I said at the beginning, there are no second chances."

The crew slowly exited the room. Amber stayed seated at the table for a moment, still mulling over the news. Veronica was the last to leave when she saw Amber still at the table.

"You coming?" she asked. Veronica saw the vacant stare in Amber's eyes and the paleness of her face. "Are you sure you're feeling okay?"

Amber looked up, slightly shaken. "I, I think I know where Montello is," she stammered.

Veronica's eyes widened. "You what? Why didn't you say something to Irwin? Where is he?" Veronica slipped into the seat beside Amber.

Amber shook her head, as if changing her mind. "I don't know for sure." She turned to Veronica with tears in her eyes. "Vee, I heard something this morning. I was outside the wall, and I heard two men arguing. They started fighting and then, then I don't know."

Veronica placed a hand on top of Amber's. "Shh, it's okay. Was it Montello's voice? What happened after the fight?"

Amber shrugged. "I don't know, I couldn't place the voices. But I know it ended suddenly. I think someone might have been killed."

"Jesus," breathed Veronica. She took a moment to process the information. "Okay. So, it might not have been Montello at all, we can't really say for certain who or what it was. All you know is you heard a fight and then it went quiet."

"Or it could have been Montello being murdered by someone on the base!"

Veronica maintained her cool. "Calm down. What time did all this happen?"

Amber shook her head, "I don't know, five thirty, five forty maybe?"

Veronica pressed several buttons on her GeniousWatch, bringing up the message from Montello. "Then it mustn't have been him. He sent me this message around six."

Amber saw the timestamp, 06:02. She exhaled heavily at the sight of the message, as though a weight had been lifted from her shoulders.

"See," said Veronica, smiling. "Nothing to worry about."

LAUNCH

ISA Training Facility, Buenos Aires—
20:00, 5 September, 2086

In the late hours of the warm September evening, Joel and Amber approached the hulking mass that was *Hermes*. From the glass-walled sky-bridge on which they stood Joel could see the entire port side of the large ship. Nestled inside two precisely cut holes on each side of *Hermes* were two miniature Ultra Shuttles, commonly called "lifeboats." Unlike a regular shuttle which was designed for interplanetary flights, the lifeboats ferried passengers between larger ships or space stations and the surface of a planet. At the other end of the overpass, the airlock door of the second level opened wide before them.

Joel felt Amber squeeze his arm in excitement as they stepped through the airlock at the end of the bridge. The compartment was cylindrical in shape, forming a perfect circle at each end of the lock. It smelled of fresh plastic and adhesives; like a new car straight out of the factory.

Amber approached the inner airlock door excitedly and pressed the release button.

Nothing happened.

Joel smiled a wide and toothy grin. For someone who was always so organized and well prepared, he delighted in seeing Amber make mistakes.

Amber caught sight of Joel by the still-open outer door; his face said it all. She laughed at herself. "Shut up. Can you get that instead of smirking like a crazy person?"

Joel shook his head as he pressed the panel beside the outer door. The door closed silently, sealing the compartment. "Try it now."

Amber pushed the release button again, this time the inner door slid open. Almost immediately they could hear the voices of Mikhail and Veronica inside. As they entered Joel could see they were at the edge of the science lab. Screens and clean white equipment lined the walls. Instruments were strapped firmly into place. The whole scene reminded Joel of a hospital research facility. The upper level of *Hermes* contained the cockpit at the front, science lab in the middle, and equipment storage in the rear. It was connected by a vertical ladder to the lower level which housed a kitchen and meals area, sleeping quarters, and bathroom facilities. Behind the bathroom and equipment storage were two pairs of large bulkhead doors which led to the stern of the ship, the engine room.

Hovering over their heads was the glass window which wrapped around the entire front section of the ship. The window was made from a high-temperature quartz glass. The extreme tinting which caused the glass to look black from the outside was far less impactful inside. Instead, the tint simply reduced the brightness of external lights.

Veronica called from the cockpit, "There they are. Come on, you two, we would like to be off the ground in fifteen minutes."

Amber and Joel made their way through the science facility into the front of the ship. As they passed through the section doors they could see the large control panel was lit up with hundreds of flashing light pads and buttons. The wraparound window provided a panoramic view of their surroundings.

Mikhail sat at one of the two pilot seats beside the control panel. Behind him were two rows of passenger seats where Charles, Diamond, and Grey were being strapped in by Veronica.

Joel and Amber took their seats. As Veronica began to clip Joel into his safety harness he felt his heart start to race. It wasn't something he liked to admit, but Joel was afraid of flying. While he had learned to manage his fears over the years, the prospect of being launched into space filled him with nervous adrenaline.

Outside, the sky-bridge began to retract, allowing a robust tug-cart to tow *Hermes* into position on the runway. Joel watched through the thick window as the craft moved slowly toward the flight strip. He closed his eyes and concentrated on his own breathing to slow his heart rate.

As Veronica took her seat and strapped herself in, the ship's speakers clicked to life. Irwin's deep voice resonated throughout the massive vessel, "*This is it. This is your moment.*" A portion of the front window projected a huge image of Irwin's face. "*As you know, once the* Phoenix *is engaged our ability to communicate will be limited. But we'll be here to ensure you get off the ground safely. And we'll be here when you return."*

Amber glanced toward Joel. His hands were gripping the armrest so tight his knuckles were white. She smiled reassuringly.

"*On behalf of the human race, I'd like to thank you for your bravery and determination. I know you'll do us all proud. Good luck.*" The cockpit fell silent and the window reverted to an opaque grey-green color, partly obscuring the view outside.

The tug-cart pulled *Hermes* slowly away from the control center onto an old airplane runway. *Hermes* came to a jolting stop as the tug-cart detached itself and raced back to the control center.

Mikhail and Veronica began their pre-flight checks.

Joel felt his stomach tense, everything was becoming too real. He felt his skin turn cold and his hands become clammy. He closed his eyes again and started counting his breaths. A soft comforting hand touched his arm; it was Amber, sensing his unease. He smiled awkwardly and took a deep breath. While he'd never explicitly told her about his fear, he suspected she had always known. For some reason, it was mildly reassuring to think she knew what was going on in his head.

"All systems are operational," said Mikhail.

"Ready to engage," said Veronica.

"*Clear for ignition,*" the voice of an ISA control operator echoed over the speakers.

A soft whirring sound grew quickly in volume as the engines were initiated, quickly increasing in intensity until a thunderous sound reverberated around the ship. In the corner of his eye, Joel could see one of the blue engines begin to distort the air around it as the intense heat built up.

Mikhail started counting down, ". . . three, two, one, ignition." He held his hands over the glowing face of the control console as Veronica pushed the throttle. The winged engines engaged and the shuttle lurched forward. Everyone was thrown back in their seats.

The enormous ship gained speed quickly. Within seconds the front was off the ground, followed by the rear. Veronica pulled down hard on the steering levers, sending the craft into the air at a near-vertical ascent.

Joel felt his stomach lurch.

"Engaging boosters," called Mikhail.

There was an enormous blast from the rear of the ship as the final engines were deployed and everyone was thrust further into their seats as g-forces assaulted their bodies. Joel started to feel faint, as though the blood were being sucked from his body. Suddenly the ship began to shake uncontrollably. Joel's vision started to narrow into a point. He squeezed his eyes shut, concentrating on his breathing again.

The shaking grew more violent. All internal lights in the cabin dropped out, plunging the team into near-darkness. *Hermes* continued its ascent. The cabin temperature increased dramatically. The turbulence grew worse as they climbed further into the sky.

Joel opened one eye. Through blurred vision he could see Mikhail and Veronica calmly working the control panel. While their actions were precise, Joel could sense their alarm. Nausea began to swell in his stomach; his head was pounding, his stomach twisted, he wanted to cry out but was paralyzed by the forces.

Then, just when it felt as though the ship was going to tear apart, the shaking, the heat, and the noise vanished in an instant as the shuttle burst out of Earth's atmosphere.

Silence.

Joel felt the pressure on his chest weaken; the ringing in his ears was gone, and the shaking had stopped completely. Cautiously, he opened his eyes. After a moment the opaque windows faded clear once more.

Veronica and Mikhail exchanged glances and smiled, letting out a silent sigh of relief. "ISA, we are clear," said Mikhail.

The team visibly relaxed.

Joel glanced toward the section of window which covered the roof of the cockpit. Through the glass he could see the pale grey-blue of the Earth's polluted atmosphere. He recalled the image of Earth Irwin had shown the team during their initial briefing, "The Blue Marble" image taken by the crew of the Apollo seventeen spacecraft. It was one of the most famous images in history; swirling white clouds dancing over an azure ocean, the massive white face of Antarctica sitting at the South Pole while the entire continent of Africa took up most of the remaining image.

Joel stared at the sickly sight outside his window; even in the middle of the night, the American continents were illuminated by light pollution. Just beyond the Atlantic Ocean, the sun had started to peek over the horizon, casting light over the west coast of Africa. It was almost indistinguishable from "The Blue Marble" image, yet with virtually no trace of green left on the continent and an unhealthy yellow tinge to the clouds. Antarctica had shrunk by almost a third, and coastlines were distorted by changes in the sea level. Joel looked away from the window, feeling a pang of sadness at the dismal state in which they were leaving their home.

"Don't get too comfortable," said Veronica, half-smiling. "That was the easy part."

She flicked a switch on her console and a small holographic keypad appeared before her; the *Phoenix* controls. Her fingers danced through the hologram, entering the coordinates via the keypad. Once the coordinates were set, Veronica moved her finger over the "enter" key and paused. "Preparing to engage the *Phoenix*."

"All systems operational," replied Mikhail.

"Here we go," she breathed.

As soon as Veronica's finger hit the button, the universe seemed to move in slow motion; stars became long streams of light blurring together, surrounding the *Hermes* in a ball of blinding whiteness. It was impossible to tell if the ship was moving forward or backward, or if it was moving at all. Nothing seemed real, space and time stood still. Inside the craft the same blinding white light enveloped everything. The physical space of the ship seemed fluid, liquid, transparent.

As quickly as it began, the white light began to fade, the physicality of the ship returned. The streams of stars were replaced with tiny dots once more; space and time returned to normal.

Joel stared out the window; it looked unchanged. Infinite blackness, interrupted only by a small blue planet, but this was not the same small planet. Even from a distance it was clearly distinguishable from Earth; the large bodies of land were covered in vibrant greens and blues, before turning stark white as ice took over at the poles. It was beautiful. Like being sent back in time.

"Dr. Ozero, status report? How long until we reach the planet's surface?" asked Lieutenant Grey as he unclipped his harness and stood unsteadily in the artificial gravity.

Mikhail scanned his hands over the illuminated holograph of the console. "We're pretty close," he replied. "Should be an hour or so to reach orbit. The lifeboats are pretty agile, so it'll be a short flight from *Hermes* to the surface after that."

Grey patted Mikhail on the back. "Good work. Now, did you two decide who's staying behind?"

"Staying behind?" asked Amber, stumbling away from her seat. "You're not coming to the surface?"

Veronica shook her head. "We've been discussing it for a few weeks now. After losing the first team we figured it was safer to keep someone on board *Hermes* for insurance."

Amber's face dropped. "That's a bit grim."

Veronica smiled. "It's the logical decision. We have a lot of equipment which is easier to operate from *Hermes* so it also makes sense to have someone on board for cataloguing and reporting back to the ISA." Veronica turned back to Grey. "In answer to your question, we decided to take turns. It seemed the fairest option. Plus, with multiple return trips we can ferry additional equipment or data between *Hermes* and Arcadia."

Grey nodded in agreement. "Very well, then."

Joel unclipped his belt and made his way toward the rear of the ship to check some of the personal cargo he'd brought aboard. Inside one of the larger and heavier boxes was a series of antique paper books from the beginning of the century. He carried his cargo box to the science facility and began unloading the books onto nearby shelves.

"Bit impractical, aren't they?" said Mikhail.

Joel paused. "What? Books?"

Mikhail leaned over Joel's box so he could see inside. "*Paper* books. They're a waste of space. Don't you think?"

Joel shrugged and continued to unpack. "Not entirely. There's something special about information preserved on a page. It doesn't rely on any electricity or power. It can't be tainted by revisions or corrections. The words written on these pages are immune to changes in ideology or opinion. They reflect what was 'true' at the time they were written."

Mikhail pulled out a book from Joel's collection. The front page had a map of the Earth without political borders, a simple rendering of each landmass. "What's this one about? It looks like a geology textbook?"

Joel smiled nostalgically. "This, my friend, was one of the first books to explain dinosaur evolution through the use of plate tectonics. The fact we can find creatures with amazing similarities and yet biologically different proves these creatures were once part of the same gene pool but something pulled them apart over the millennia." Joel turned the book over; the back cover was an unrecognizable landmass. As though someone had taken the continents and pushed them together to form a single body of land stretched across the face of Earth like elastic.

"Pangea?" said Mikhail, trying hard to recall his high school science lessons.

"That's right. The last supercontinent to have existed on Earth."

"Last? You mean there were more?"

"Absolutely!" said Joel, unable to hide his enthusiasm. Where Joel lacked at public speaking he excelled at tutoring. "There've been a few over the last four billion years. Pangea is just the most recent one. We often see the Earth as a stagnant body of rock just 'existing' in space but in reality there's lots of activity happening under our feet, quite violent in fact. Not to mention the bombardment of activity from space, too. In fact, some scientists believe tectonic activity can actually be triggered by meteorites smashing into Earth, if they have enough mass and velocity behind them."

Mikhail smiled politely and nodded, clearly losing interest. "Well, you learn something new every day," he said, promptly turning away.

Joel, mildly disappointed at losing his audience, placed the book on the shelf with the others. "Kids these days," he mumbled to himself.

○ ○ ○ ● ○ ○ ○

In the lower section of the ship, the living quarters, Amber sat on one of the bunks, staring through a small porthole and watching the diminutive blue planet slowly grow in size. It was a beautiful sight, with white clouds swirling through the atmosphere. The land was a collage of greens, yellows, and reds and the enormous oceans were a deep rich blue. The image before her seemed so familiar and yet so strange. It certainly put the view of Earth to shame.

"Wake up!"

Amber gasped at the sudden appearance of Charles behind her. "Oh, hi Charles."

Charles smirked mischievously. "You sound disappointed to see me? Were you hoping I was your boyfriend?"

Amber laughed. "You mean Joel? No, no. We're not together, not romantically. I mean, we dated briefly, but that was a long time ago."

Charles took a seat on the bunk beside Amber, eyeing her hand curiously. On her right middle finger was a silver ring. In its center was a heart, topped by a crown and held by a pair of hands which blended with the ring band. "Funny, because your ring tells another story."

Amber glanced at her hand; she hadn't thought about the ring in years, despite the fact she never took it off, to the point it had worn a slight indentation at the base of her finger. The band was a traditional Irish ring, representing love, loyalty, and friendship; the Claddagh. The wearer could symbolize their relationship status depending on the hand and orientation wherein the circlet was worn. Amber's ring was currently on her right hand, with the heart pointed toward her wrist and the crown pointed to her fingertips.

Amber laughed. "I forgot I even have this on anymore. I got it for my eighteenth birthday and have worn it every day since."

Charles cocked his head. "I thought you were meant to be Irish? Every Irish girl I've met knows that if you wear the ring pointed toward your wrist it means you're taken."

"You're right," said Amber, removing the ring from her hand. "Best uphold my ancestors' values and keep it facing the right way." She held the ring for a moment.

While it was true she had received it as a gift for her eighteenth birthday, she failed to mention it was Joel who gave it to her. She also left out the part where, years later, Joel had changed the orientation of the ring to symbolize the start of their romantic relationship. She had left it like that ever since.

Amber placed the ring back on her right hand so the heart pointed to her fingers and the crown to her wrist.

Charles winked playfully. "So, that means you're single, right?"

Amber scrunched her nose, "Not if you were the last man on Earth."

Charles's demeanor stiffened. "Ah, but we aren't on Earth, are we?" He moved toward the window and pressed his face against the small porthole. "Looks like a pretty boring place if you ask me."

"Shouldn't you be more excited?"

Charles lay down on his bunk so he was still facing the window. "Why's that? Do I look like someone who enjoys boring things?"

Amber frowned. "You're an exo-geologist. This is a giant rock in space. Just sort of figured you'd get a kick out of being the first to see it."

"But we aren't the first, are we? The whole reason we're here is to find the other team. They were the first to see it. We, on the other hand, might be the last. I guess that's something," he laughed dryly.

Charles pulled an e-cigarette from his pocket.

Amber's face dropped. "You brought an e-cigarette on board? You can't vape here!"

Charles frowned. "Who's going to stop me? The old one or the dumb one?" He laughed to himself.

"Why do you have to be such a jerk?"

Charles stopped laughing and replaced the e-cigarette in his pocket. "Maybe it's because my mummy didn't love me enough? Or because my daddy beat me? Or, maybe I'm just a jerk and I don't care what you think. You should try it, it's very liberating."

Amber frowned. "Is that why you left that man to die? Because you're a jerk?"

"Oh Christ, not this shit again." He turned his attention to Amber, leaning into her personal space so their faces were only centimeters apart. Amber could see the small wrinkles in the corners of his eyes, the soft grey and black hairs of his hairline. She could smell the toothpaste on his breath. "Best not to speculate on things you know nothing about," he hissed.

Amber opened her mouth to respond but snapped it shut again as something behind Charles caught her eye. "My God," she breathed, pushing him out of the way to get a better view through the porthole.

Charles turned.

"It's another ship."

Hermes, Orbit—
08:00, 6 September, 2086

"*Hermes, this is boarding party, we're about to dock with the unidentified ship, stand by.*" Grey's gravelly voice rang out over *Hermes'* speakers, tinny and distant. *Hermes'* windowed façade had been hijacked again, this time by the internal comms system. The front section of the cockpit displayed Grey's enormous face inside his spacesuit helmet. His grey military haircut was lit up by the helmet's internal lights.

"*Copy that, boarding party,*" came Veronica's reply. "*Switching visor-cam to external.*"

Aboard *Hermes,* Veronica punched several keys on the main control panel and suddenly the window image changed so it was facing outward, displaying the interior of the lifeboat. As Grey moved his head left and right, the camera attached to his visor moved too, so the crew aboard the *Hermes* could see everything Grey could see.

Grey turned his head and the image inside *Hermes* showed Mikhail, sitting by the controls of the lifeboat, gently guiding it toward the derelict. Beside him, Diamond was strapped into the co-pilot's seat, staring out the window in awe. From Grey's vantage point, the crew could see the ship in detail through the window of the lifeboat. It was almost identical to *Hermes* in terms of its size and shape. But this ship was a dark and desolate mass with a missing lifeboat.

Veronica's voice echoed in Grey's ear again, "*Advise that pressure suits and helmets must be worn at all times. We don't know what state this ship is in, and judging by the look of it, life support systems are probably dead.*"

Mikhail carefully steered into the lifeboat-shaped hole where the missing boat should have been. The craft fit into the gaping cavity like a puzzle piece. Mikhail had lined everything up perfectly, but was unable to dock as there was no return signal from the ship.

"*Affirmative,*" replied Mikhail. "*Dock and airlock appear to be disabled. Looks like we're going for a walk.*" Mikhail brought the lifeboat within meters of the ship, close enough to "walk," but with enough space for the team to manually open the doors.

Grey, Mikhail, and Diamond wore golden spacesuits which hugged the body like a wetsuit. They used an internal compression system to protect the wearer from depressurization and regulate body temperature.

Grey clicked his helmet into place. It was a rounded dome which connected to the neck of the suit via an airtight clasp. From inside, the visor was entirely transparent so the wearer's vision was never obscured. Externally, it was also gold plated, making it impossible to identify anyone.

"*Okay, Dr. Ozero,*" said Grey into his helmet mic. His voice echoed throughout *Hermes* and inside the helmets of Diamond and Mikhail. "*Let's go.*"

The three men hovered weightlessly inside the airlock of the lifeboat. Unlike *Hermes*, the lifeboats weren't equipped with anti-gravity technology. Torso-sized oxygen tanks sat awkwardly on their backs like rectangular golden turtle shells.

"*Engage lifeboat airlock,*" said Grey.

Mikhail opened the safety casing surrounding the large green "open" button. He pressed the button, and they momentarily felt their suits try to expand before the pressure regulators kicked in and brought the material flush against their skin. Once the small airlock had depressurized, the external doors released and the team pushed away from the lifeboat, floating toward the doors of the dead ship.

Mikhail looked over the ship's external airlock doors, examining them carefully with the flashlight on his helmet. After a moment he found what he was looking for and pulled a small panel away from the ship. "*Just as I suspected,*" he said, twisting the manual release lever inside the panel.

The doors to the ship didn't move.

"*Hey, what gives? Why aren't the doors opening?*" asked Diamond.

Grey pulled his body forward so he was flush with the airlock. "*The ship's dead. So, there's no power to open them.*" Grey wedged his fingers between two doors and pulled. After several heaving strains the doors came apart.

The three men pushed themselves through the gaping doors into the darkness of the ship's interior. Three distinct beams of light danced inside the ship from each man's helmet lamp. Objects floated weightlessly around the interior; glass beakers, medical instruments, and notebooks, suspended in space.

"*Science lab,*" said Grey, scanning the floating debris.

Diamond pushed through the lab to the back of the craft. In the rear was a handful of weapons and several crates of unknown contents. "*Storage in the rear,*" he reported.

Mikhail pulled his weightless body down the ladder to the lower level. "*Looks like living facilities down here.*" Mikhail paused, "*Uh, lieutenant! I think I found one of the crew.*" His voice shuddered slightly.

Grey pulled himself down the ladder to the lower floor. Suspended in space, in the middle of the living area was the frozen and lifeless body of a woman. She was grey-blonde and she wore a gold-plated ISA jumpsuit. Her body was mutilated and swollen well beyond its normal shape; with ragged, pale skin and bloodshot eyes, she barely looked human.

Grey pulled himself closer to the woman; he examined her eyes and face, and touched her bloated skin lightly with his gloves.

"*Exposure,*" said Mikhail. "*In space, the pressure is so low the boiling point of fluids is lower than body temperature, which causes little gas bubbles to form. The body swells up and, combined with a lack of oxygen, you die in only a few minutes.*"

"*Nasty way to go,*" mused Grey.

"*It is. But, I don't think that's what killed her,*" said Mikhail, hovering over the woman's chest.

Grey turned his attention to the woman's torso; his eyes followed the beam of light cast by Mikhail's torch. Directly over the woman's heart was a hole the size of a softball.

"*Looks like she took a laser blast straight to the heart,*" said Mikhail.

Grey looked around the walls of the room, moving his helmet torch slowly until he spotted what he was looking for; a hole in the ship's wall. It was roughly the same size as the one in the woman's chest, clean and round, but this hole was at an acute angle, not fired directly.

"*Hull breach?*" asked Mikhail as he followed the light of Grey's torch.

"*Looks like it,*" said Grey, not taking his eyes off the hole.

"*So, who fired the shot?*"

"*Lieutenant Grey,*" Diamond's voice came over their helmet speakers. "*There's a guy up here. He looks messed up. Like a human balloon, it's pretty gross.*"

"*Might be our shooter,*" Grey directed his comment to Mikhail. "*Sergeant, anything else to report? Describe the body.*"

Diamond looked over the suspended body hovering beside the airlock of the remaining lifeboat. "*Can't make out the face, but pretty sure it's a middle-aged male, skinny, got an ISA jumpsuit on with a pilot's badge. He's just outside the airlock to the second boat. Looks like he was trying to make a break for it but didn't get out in time. Hey? There's something else? Either this guy is a junkie or someone stabbed him with a needle. It's still in his arm.*"

Mikhail turned to Grey. "*Poisoned?*"

Grey shrugged. "*Maybe.*"

Diamond continued, "*Oh, I also found the black box and grabbed a couple of info-tablets from the lab. There's some samples that look like they were collected from the planet's surface but they're frozen now.*"

"*Good work, Sergeant. Anything else?*"

"*Nah, can't get any content from the box or the tablets without power, but I did find out the name of the ship.*"

"*The name of the ship?*" queried Grey.

"*Yup. The name of the ship is printed on the top of the tablets;* 'Atlas.' *Now why would they name the ship after a book about the Earth?*"

"*Atlas is another figure from Greek mythology,*" said Mikhail. "*He's the God of astronomy and navigation. And he's the father of Hermes.*"

"*Whoever's naming everything on this mission really likes Greek stuff!*" laughed Diamond.

○ ○ ○ ● ○ ○ ○

The remaining crew members sat impatiently around the laboratory table of *Hermes* waiting for the airlock to re-pressurize. The doors slid open seamlessly and three gold-clad figures walked through with the gear they'd collected from the other ship.

Charles was unusually withdrawn. While the others hung around the airlock, he stood by the cockpit doorway, watching quietly.

"So, what happened over there? What did you find?" asked Amber.

Grey hung his helmet on a hook beside the airlock as he explained what they'd learnt about the *Atlas,* "... and there were two bodies on board, one had been shot, and both showed signs of exposure."

"Two bodies?" asked Charles from behind. It was the first thing he'd said since Amber had spotted the ship. "What happened to the rest of the crew?"

Grey glanced to Charles by the cockpit door and shook his head. "One of the lifeboats was missing. Best guess is the rest of the team are still on the surface."

Charles felt his muscles tense involuntarily. "Any idea who the bodies were?"

Grey dropped the dead info-tablets on the table. "Hard to say with certainty. Their bodies were pretty mangled. But hopefully the black box will have some answers."

The team migrated to the cockpit, gathering around the control console. Again, Charles remained off to the side, hovering just inside the doors.

Veronica carried the black box to the console. In reality, it wasn't a box at all. It was shaped like a basketball that had been cut in half; flat at the bottom and rounded at the top. At its peak was a small projector lens. The box was designed to capture all instrumental flight activity, radio communications, as well as any direct logs made by ship personnel. It received data via wireless antennae and stored the information on an internal processor.

Veronica sat the box on top of an internal power supply pad attached to the control console and the device sprang to life. The small projector lens lit up and the words "STARTUP" were displayed in large white holographic letters above the box. After a moment the word was replaced with a shortlist of options:

NEW ENTRY

REVIEW LAST ENTRY

REVIEW ALL ENTRIES

DELETE LAST ENTRY

DELETE ALL ENTRIES

Veronica swiped her hand across "review last entry" and the image of a woman's face appeared on *Hermes'* front window. Bunks could be seen in the background; she was using the video logging system in the living quarters. The woman was older, early sixties, with grey-blonde hair.

"That's Dr. Erika Schmitt," said Veronica, recognizing the woman's face from the profiles she had studied so diligently. "Exozoologist and member of the SETI mission that first discovered Arcadia."

Mikhail and Grey exchanged a knowing glance.

Erika's face was red, her eyes watery, and she was bleeding from a small gash on her temple. "*I don't know what to do,*" she said in a distinct German accent. "*This feels like a bad dream. I don't know who to trust anymore. I tried to send a message to Earth, but I don't know if it'll get there. I think he's cut the comms. I don't know how, but he did. I've subdued him for now with a little anesthetic cocktail.*" She held a small bottle in her left hand and a syringe in the other. "*I don't know how long it'll last. God, I just hope the others are okay. We should never have come here.*" From behind, a man's voice could be heard, interrupting her monologue. She jumped from her chair. "*Shit! Shit!*" she cursed, rushing out of frame. The image cut to black.

For a moment, no one spoke.

"Play the previous entry," said Grey, breaking the silence.

On the box, Veronica selected "review all entries" but only one file was listed; the one they'd just watched.

Grey frowned. "The previous entries have been erased? What about flight data?"

Veronica pressed a small button on the base of the black box and the image on the windows became a series of numeric data which streamed like falling snow. The data was incomprehensible to most of the team. Veronica and Mikhail scanned the information, noting important dates and coordinates. The last entry, however, was clear:

HULL BREACH.

DEPRESSURISATION INITIATED.

BULKHEAD DOORS ENGAGED.

BULKHEAD DOORS MANUAL OVERRIDE.

WARNING: PRESSURE DECREASING.

WARNING: PRESSURE CRITICAL.

SYSTEM FAILING.

SYSTEM FAILURE.

SYSTEM SHUT DOWN.

"What does that mean?" asked Amber.

Grey stared at the last line of the log, narrowing his gaze. "Something's not right."

DESCENT

Lifeboat, Descent—
16:00, 6 September, 2086

Veronica sat alone at the control panel of the lifeboat. She glanced at the empty co-pilot seat, where Mikhail would have been sitting, and sighed. The boat was much smaller than *Hermes*. It was like transferring from a cargo plane to a light aircraft. Behind the two pilots' chairs were four pairs of seats, occupied by the rest of the team. Like *Hermes,* the front window of the boat wrapped around the entire front half of the vessel, creating a one-hundred-and-eighty-degree view of the world outside. Behind the seats was a small L-shaped walkway. Toward the port side of the ship, the walkway led to the small airlock hatch. Toward the stern, it led to an internal doorway which separated the passenger compartment from the storage compartment.

"Okay, everyone, listen up!" said Veronica. "Make sure your safety harnesses are secure, we're about to enter the planet's atmosphere. Things are going to get a little bumpy." As she spoke, she began to ease the steering lever forward to commence their descent.

Joel felt his stomach tense again as the ship lurched forward. He was fine aboard *Hermes* once they'd left Earth's atmosphere. But now, the mere thought of plummeting back toward the ground turned his insides cold. Joel focused his attention on the front window, watching as the blackness of space shifted to a brilliant deep purple, then a rich dark blue. Streams of white clouds washed over the window as the craft moved further into the stratosphere. Suddenly the boat was surrounded by a vivid iridescent blue. The clouds below were big and fluffy against the blue backdrop.

Amber leaned over Joel to see through the left-hand side of the wraparound window. "It's incredible! It looks just like Earth!"

Veronica heard Amber's remark. "It doesn't just *look* like Earth. The atmosphere composition is just like Earth, too. But it's not quite identical.

There's a higher concentration of oxygen due to the volume of plant life and a lower concentration of carbon dioxide and methane."

"So, we'll be able to breathe fine down there?" asked Diamond from the rear.

"Not only is the air safe to breathe, but we'll be landing near the equator where it's a balmy thirty degrees Celsius, with around seventy percent humidity."

"Phew! Sounds sticky. Can't we go somewhere a bit cooler?" asked Diamond.

Veronica sighed. "We need to find the second *Atlas* lifeboat. We don't have the exact location but the data from the flight recorder gave us a rough area of where to start searching. It's on the continent marked L-two, near the equator."

"What about aliens?" interrupted Charles. He was staring intently through the window watching the ground grow in size and shape as they descended.

"Well, like Irwin said, we know there's complex life on this planet already. That's why we're taking extra precautions. We've got camouflage tents, plenty of firepower, and four brand new multi-terrain bikes. We also have a perimeter safety fence, and, of course, two highly skilled Marines."

Charles leaned closer to the window. "Why doesn't that make me feel any safer?" he said to no one in particular.

The craft moved below the cloud line. In the distance a mountain range cut across the land; it was covered in thick greenery, stretching as far as the eye could see. The mountain ended suddenly a few kilometers away from the coast in an almost sheer cliff face. Toppling gracefully over the cliff were two large waterfalls, creating a series of long rivers which snaked across the landscape, making their way through the lower forest, to the coast.

Veronica eased the boat down, bringing it closer to the canopy so they were practically touching the treetops. The trees grew so thick they obscured any view of the ground.

Joel tried hard to concentrate on his breathing. He hated being afraid of flying, hated feeling weak and vulnerable.

Suddenly the trees disappeared and a large flat clearing opened up. It was a wide field, covered in grass and small shrubs. Veronica reduced their speed and gently brought the craft down, suspending it for a moment over the empty field like a hovercraft. As she lingered, blades of grass shivered from the blazing engines. The boat finally touched the soft grass, barely making a sound.

Veronica switched off the engines, cracked her knuckles and smirked. "Piece of cake."

Joel slowly released the breath he'd been holding. He unhooked his safety harness and turned to see Amber already standing by the airlock. She was visibly excited, almost bouncing on the spot, as she waited for the cabin to finish pressurizing. Joel stood unsteadily and made his way between the seats to join her by the airlock. The light turned green and Amber released the external doors. Together, they stepped outside slowly, absorbing the sights, sounds, and smells of Arcadia.

The clearing was open and flat, covered in a lush layer of grass varying from only a few centimeters to areas which grew up to knee height. Small patches of flowers dotted the edge of the clearing and in the center a huge tree stump sat like a sentinel in the empty space. At the edge of the clearing, trees towered over their heads like skyscrapers. Thin shafts of light filtered through the canopy as the trees swayed in the breeze. A chorus of chirps and croaks filled the air, giving the whole scene a distinctive living atmosphere.

In the corner of his eye, Joel saw the beaming smile plastered across Amber's face. He'd never seen her so happy.

Charles sniffed the air and covered his mouth. "This place smells like shit."

Amber ignored Charles's comment. "It's incredible. It's a rainforest, an actual living rainforest! I never knew trees could grow so tall! Can you believe forests like these used to grow on Earth?" Amber began fondling some of the fern trees at the edge of the field. "My grandmother told me stories about the last rainforests. And I've seen virtual-reality forests before. They capture the images pretty well. But this is something else; the textures, the smells." She inhaled deeply. "Phew! That *is* ripe."

Charles stood beside the lifeboat. Unlike the others who were beginning to explore the area, he was facing the center of the clearing. "Doesn't that bother anyone else?"

"Calm down, it's probably just animal crap," said Joel.

Charles shook his head. "I'm not talking about the smell, champ. Where's the rest of the tree?" He pointed to the tree stump.

The stump sat alone in the empty field, surrounded by knee-high grass which swayed gently in the wind.

Joel shrugged. "Well, clearly it fell down. Probably from a storm or something."

Charles raised an eyebrow. "And then what? Ran away on its little tree legs?"

Joel paused, turning his attention to the tree stump. Charles was right, the rest of the tree was nowhere to be seen; no rotten log, no fallen branches. In fact, the stump was flat, almost like it had been—

"Hey! Get back here!" called Grey, interrupting Joel's train of thought.

He threw a large insulated case onto the ground just outside the airlock. "You can go sightseeing later. We've got work to do." Grey disappeared inside the boat for a moment before reappearing with another case from the storage room. "We need to get those tents propped, set up a perimeter fence, and get the communication equipment up and running. Dr. Nizhny, how much time do we have before nightfall?"

Veronica checked her info-tablet. "Taking into account the position of the sun and the average rate of the planet's rotation, I'd say we have about two, maybe two and a half hours of light."

Grey nodded. "Okay, all hands on deck. If there is anything running around that jungle I'd like to know we're secure before nightfall."

○ ○ ○ ● ○ ○ ○

As Mikhail sat alone in the cockpit, a small pinch of loneliness dawned on him. His mind flashed to a large bottle of vodka he had stored in the kitchen. He thought about the smooth clear liquid sliding down his throat, making his insides feel warm. Suddenly Mikhail found his mind slipping back to almost ten years ago. He was alone, again, but surrounded by bodies; bodies lying half buried in snow. He could see their blue skin lying under the fresh white powder as he huddled, freezing, in the wreckage of the small commercial plane. It was almost two days before they found him.

When he was eventually rescued, the investigators determined a freak cold front had struck the craft without warning, freezing the fuel lines. There was nothing he could have done to save his five passengers. It was a miracle he survived. Mikhail was only eighteen at the time, but the guilt of that day had never quite gone away. It didn't sit well with him he had survived and everyone else had lost their lives. It just didn't seem fair.

That's when Mikhail started drinking. He drank to forget. He drank to fall asleep and to numb the pain. It was only when he met Veronica three years ago that he finally overcame his demons. She made the pain go away, better than any drink ever could.

He had never told Veronica about the accident.

Mikhail slapped himself in the face, hard. He couldn't let those thoughts sneak back in. Not again. He quickly moved away from the cockpit, forcing his mind back to the present and making his way to the observation table at the back of the science laboratory, determined to keep busy.

The observation table was black and imbedded with small glowing red nodules spaced a few inches apart. Hovering ghostlike above the nodules was a three-dimensional model from the planet's surface made entirely from projected light. Lush green vegetation and beautiful bright colors lit up the space. It was incredible.

Before they left, Veronica and Mikhail had deployed dozens of round baseball-sized monitoring units to act as surveillance for the ground team. The surface of each unit was flawless, just a smooth black orb, capable of three-dimensional panoramic views, acting like a perfectly rounded fly's eye with hundreds of microscopic lenses. Veronica had mapped out an area within a ten-kilometer radius of Base Camp and strategically set up the orbs in various locations so Mikhail could keep an eye on everything from *Hermes*, and so they had visual records for their database. The orbs also transmitted data from a series of microscopic sensors which measured temperature, air composition, pressure, and heat signatures.

Mikhail looked over the data carefully to make sure everything was still operating correctly. The readings hadn't changed since his last check, before the lifeboat departed. Ambient temperature: thirty degrees Celsius. Humidity: seventy-three percent. Air composition: sixty-nine percent nitrogen, thirty percent oxygen, one percent argon. Air pressure: one standard atmosphere.

Mikhail frowned at the final reading. Several of the orbs closest to Base Camp were recording thermal signatures. This was expected now the team had arrived. But another orb, labelled P1-08, situated ten kilometers southwest of Base Camp, had also picked up a thermal signature. Mikhail's heart jumped; this could be his first sighting of alien life. He turned back to the projector and located the image from P1-08. It was right on the edge of the surveillance area. He stared at the image, waiting patiently for signs of life. Nothing. Just a thick tangle of trees and bushes. Mikhail sighed. He looked over the readouts again and saw the thermal signature was gone. He made a note that P1-08 had a glitch and moved on.

Next, Mikhail turned his attention to the array of monitors imbedded in the walls of the science laboratory to review the output from the planetary radar. The radar couldn't be more different from the small baseball-sized monitor orbs. It was a huge disc, stowed on the underside of *Hermes*, designed to act as a communication satellite for the ground team. Once the team finished setting up the ground receiver they would be able to communicate with each other as well as *Hermes* using their throat mics. The satellite was also designed to capture images of Arcadia from space, providing a 3D rendering of the entire planet.

Mikhail stared at the rotating image on the screen in awe. When Irwin described Arcadia as Earth's twin, no one really believed him. But the similarities were stark. Arcadia rotated on a tilted axis, with northern and southern magnetic poles. Most of the planet's surface was covered in liquid water, with large continent-sized bodies of land, interspersed with smaller islands. From space, one could easily mistake Arcadia for the Earth itself, if it wasn't for the misshapen landmasses, the lack of manmade satellites in orbit, the pollution-free atmosphere, and the rich tapestry of greens and blues from the land and water.

Mikhail turned back to the beautiful images on the projector table. He watched the scene unfolding around Base Camp as the team set up their equipment. He saw Veronica, the love of his life, his partner and safety net.

As the loneliness began to creep in again, Mikhail's mind flashed once more to the bottle of vodka stored in the kitchen.

Base Camp

Base Camp, Arcadia—
18:00, 6 September, 2086

Joel and Amber worked in silence as they set up the communications equipment. Amber's messy red hair fell in loose strands over her shoulder, sticking to her skin which was damp from the humidity. She brushed the hair from her face and swore profusely. Joel smiled to himself. Seeing Amber in the field was a far cry from the glamorous and professional exterior she put on when they were on the seminar circuit. Amber knew how to work a crowd, she knew how to play the part of the polished academic. But that wasn't really her. Deep down she was still the adventurer she had been when they were kids. She wasn't afraid to get her hands dirty; in fact she enjoyed it.

"Hey, Dr. Carter! Come help me with this!" called Diamond.

Amber nodded. "Go on, I've got this."

Joel turned his attention to the campsite. Veronica and Diamond had finished erecting the tents and were now unpacking the remaining equipment. The tents were small domed spheres, perfectly camouflaged against the flat terrain, thanks to the latest in military technology. They were made from an experimental fabric which reflected light from the surrounding area, rendering the object virtually invisible. The fabric behaved similarly to a one-way mirror; from the outside it was perfectly concealed, but from the inside, occupants could see through the dark mesh. Similar technology was also used on the outer surface of the lifeboat to further conceal their presence.

Toward the edge of the clearing, Grey and Charles were erecting the motion-operated security system; two-foot-tall tripods, arranged at one-hundred-meter intervals around the perimeter of the camp.

Diamond was standing over the remaining equipment, which was sitting beside the now-camouflaged boat. He was trying to extract a strange-looking weapon from the pile, but it was blocked by heavier gear. Joel walked over to the boat and together they freed the weapon.

"What the hell is that?" asked Joel.

Diamond slung the strap around his shoulder and smiled. "This is an M1050 laser-guided shoulder-fired explosives launcher. Standard issue in the Marines nowadays. Imagine if a rocket launcher and a grenade launcher had a baby."

Diamond adjusted the strap, holding the device up so Joel could see it clearly. It was roughly the size of two large hand-lasers back to back, with one hand grip at the front and another at the rear. In the center was a rotating compartment which looked like the bullet chamber from an old-school revolver, feeding the long thin gun barrel at the tip.

"They use a compact bullet-sized capsule with compressed C4 explosives that discharge on impact. Can blow a hole in the side of a building with ammunition the size of a peanut." Diamond placed the back of the launcher against his shoulder, holding each of the hand grips, and stared at Joel through a small scope sitting just above the rear hand grip. "She's a beauty, don't you think?"

Joel cast a sideways glance at Diamond. "How often do you use it?"

Diamond lowered the weapon and chuckled. "Never. Guess she's more like emotional support."

"She?" said Veronica, raising an eyebrow.

"Aw, it isn't like that, Dr. Nizhny. I consider it a sign of respect that one of the most formidable hand-held weapons known to humanity is female."

By the comms equipment, which was now up and running, Amber waited patiently for Veronica to reach the far side of camp so they could test if the system was operational. She gazed lovingly at the forest just beyond the campsite. None of the virtual simulations she'd seen on Earth could replace the real thing. The atmosphere was thick with humidity. Amazing and wondrous smells lingered somewhere in the underbrush. The sun cast beautiful oranges and pinks as it began to set over the nearby mountains.

Amber had been fascinated with nature since she was a young girl. Her grandmother had been an environmental conservationist in the 2020s and 2030s, when the effects of the Anthropocene were approaching their tipping point. She told Amber stories of being strapped to enormous trees in the Daintree Rainforest, trying to ward off bulldozers. Sometimes their protests would last for days. They rescued hundreds of animals from affected areas, helping to establish the very nature reserves Amber visited as an adult.

It was her grandmother's stories that inspired Amber to study environmental sciences. Unfortunately, by the time she reached university, environmental conservation was an obsolete discipline. Replaced by new fields like paleozoology, which explored the environmental and biological history of life on Earth.

Without realizing it, Amber had started to wander into the forest, drawn by its natural beauty.

"*Hey!*" called a loud voice in Amber's ear. She was startled at the sudden sound. It took a moment for her to realize it was Grey using his throat mic from the opposite side of the clearing. "*Stay behind the perimeter line! I don't want to lose anyone on the first day!*"

Amber stopped in her tracks. Sitting only a meter away, at the very edge of the clearing, was a half-concealed two-foot-high tripod, poised and ready to fire at anything that moved beyond the invisible fence. On top of the tripod sat a small silver sphere with a thick concave lens running half its length, like a giant watchful eye. Above the sensor was a small but powerful laser the size of a grape, designed to fire if the motion sensor was triggered.

Amber waved sheepishly to Grey before turning around slowly, embarrassed she had not been more careful.

At the other end of the clearing Grey was shaking his head. "Damn academics. No sense of safety. It's no wonder Irwin insisted on sending military personnel this time around."

Charles watched Amber retreat to the safety of the camp with her tail between her legs. "Why is that exactly? Why did they decide to send extra security this time?" he said, casting a sideways glance to Grey.

Grey continued testing the reflexes of the security tripod, waving his hand in front of the rounded "eye" and ensuring the small laser followed his every move. "I guess when your entire team and their ship go missing you assume the worst. And you do whatever you can to avoid making the same mistakes."

Charles frowned. Grey was a hard man to read. His voice lacked emotion, his face hardly changed; never showing surprise or intrigue.

Satisfied with the tripod's reflexes, Grey switched on a small button at the base of the stem. A soft hum began to emanate from the device as the laser charged. After a few seconds the humming faded and Grey began to move to the next site.

"How do you know they're on? There's no light or anything?" asked Charles.

"That's because light attracts curiosity. We want to blend in, not stand out."

Charles didn't appreciate Grey's tone, but he bit his tongue. "So, how do you know they're on?"

Grey pointed to the base of the sphere, where it met the top of the tripod. A small red bar protruded from the center of the three black legs, pointing to the ground. It was embossed with the word "ARMED".

Charles frowned. "That's it? Kind of hard to see from a distance, isn't it?"

"That's the point. We don't want anything outside the perimeter to see these at all."

Charles stared at the small red tab. "That's going to make exploration a bit of a bitch, isn't it?"

Grey extracted a small remote from his pocket. "Not really. Once the circuit is complete we can control all the sensors using this."

The small parcel in Grey's hand was flat and white with only two buttons; "ARM" and "DISARM".

"And what if we need to leave the camp and you've run off with the remote?"

Grey returned the remote to his pocket, keeping his eyes fixed on Charles. "Then you can disarm the system from the lifeboat. I'm surprised you're so interested in the security system? In fact, I'm surprised you volunteered for this job at all? I was under the impression you weren't a fan of authority."

Charles shrugged. "Don't get me wrong. I despise authority, especially the military. But I'm a big fan of self-preservation."

Hermes, Orbit— 20:00, 6 September, 2086

Mikhail had been keeping himself busy by unloading the remaining crates from the storage compartment and organizing additional supplies into convenient portable parcels. When he and Veronica eventually switched shifts in a day or so there would already be a cargo crate full of dehydrated food, water purifiers, additional electronic equipment, and batteries ready to take to the surface.

Once the parcels were ready, Mikhail returned to check on the radar recordings. The image of the planet without cloud cover sat on the monitor. The shape of the landmasses stood out as though they were puzzle pieces floating on the water. Mikhail stared at the shapes of the landmasses. There was something strange about them. He touched the screen, sending the image to the projection table, replacing the images of the monitor orbs. He stared at the globe as it rotated freely.

Mikhail touched the largest landmass, which formed a large inverted L shape, stretching almost the entire length of the planet's western hemisphere. He plucked the continent from the map so it moved freely across the surface of the sphere and dragged it toward its eastern neighbor. The nearby mass was shorter than the one beneath his finger, but it was thick, forming an inverted J shape. The inverted J fit neatly into the inverted L.

Mikhail smiled.

He began rearranging the rest of the continents, moving each into position. They clicked together like a giant jigsaw until he'd created a supercontinent. There were minor gaps between the pieces but the overall result was uncanny.

Mikhail smiled at his creation. "Continental drift in action."

He leaned away from the screen and stared at the image. Something about it itched at the back of his mind, something oddly familiar. Beside the monitor he noticed Charles's e-reader and began flicking through his exo-geography books, looking for the image. He searched the digital bookshelf for hours but there were no known landmasses which matched the one he'd created. In desperation he moved to the bookshelf with Joel's heavy, and completely unnecessary, paper books. Mikhail began pulling books out, flicking through the pages, and dropping them to the floor. Before he knew it he'd emptied almost the entire shelf. Still nothing.

Mikhail stared at the pile of physical books on the ground and growled to himself, "Stupid paper books."

He began putting them back on the shelf, grumbling about their weight and size. About halfway through, Mikhail came across a familiar cover: a map of the Earth without political borders. He tried to recall what Joel had said about the book, something about plate tectonics? He turned the book over and his heart froze. It was his supercontinent. He glanced back at the projector and held up Joel's book beside the image; there was no mistaking it.

"Pangea," he whispered.

Base Camp, Arcadia—
04:00, 7 September, 2086

Diamond was awoken by the sound of rustling outside his tent. He checked the time, it was four a.m.

Why would anyone be up now?

Maybe someone going to the latrines?

The rustling moved away from camp, not near the latrines at all. Diamond sat up; curiosity was getting the better of him. He moved quietly, trying not to wake the Lieutenant who was sleeping soundly on the other side of the tent, and shuffled closer to the mesh fabric. It was hard to make out clear shapes through the darkness, but he could see something moving outside. It was tall and it was heading toward the ship.

Diamond felt his heart jump into his throat; had the security sensors failed? Was there an alien creature in the camp?

He held his breath and reached for his trusty explosives launcher sitting by the tent flap. Diamond burst from the tent, aiming his launcher in the direction of the mysterious figure. His heart was pounding.

"What the—?" exclaimed Charles.

Diamond quickly lowered his launcher and grabbed his chest. "Charles? You scared the shit out of me!"

"You?" said Charles. "I'm not the one aiming a rocket launcher in your face!"

"What're you doing up this late?"

Charles was standing a few steps away from the lifeboat. He growled, "You mean you can't hear it from here? Goddamn Australian snores like a freight train. I haven't had a wink of sleep all night. Was going to try and get comfy in the boat."

Joel and Charles were sharing the two-person tent beside Diamond and Grey.

Diamond listened intently. "You mean Joel? Can't hear anything from here."

"He's stopped now. But just listen, he'll start up again." Charles's voice was tense and frustrated.

Diamond shook his head and laughed. "Night, Charles." He retreated into his tent, climbed back into his bunk, and began to drift into a light dozing sleep.

After a few minutes, Diamond could hear rustling outside again. He growled under his breath, wondering what Charles was up to this time. He kept his eyes shut, trying to ignore the noise. The shuffling continued to move around the camp.

Diamond rolled over so he was facing the mesh of the tent again. From this angle he could just see the outline of Charles's shadow beyond the lifeboat. The figure started tapping on the boat, making a soft but annoying clanging sound. Diamond gritted his teeth in frustration. He sat up abruptly, ready to go outside and give Charles a piece of his mind.

It was then he noticed the shadow was different this time; it was taller and hunched over, with a tail stretching out behind it.

Diamond's blood ran cold; there were three shadows.

He felt his heart begin to race again. Quickly he crawled across the floor of the tent and picked up his launcher, carefully easing the flap open and pushing the barrel through. He stuck his head out, slowly aiming his launcher in the direction of the shadows.

They were gone.

Diamond rubbed his tired eyes. His heart was still pounding. He glanced around and saw the shadow of a nearby tree dancing across the camouflage mesh of the boat. He exhaled and laughed to himself for getting worked up over the silhouette of a tree.

CONTACT

Jungle, Arcadia—
06:30, 7 September, 2086

The *Hermes* team set off early the following morning. According to the data they'd retrieved from the *Atlas* flight recorder, the crew had initially taken both lifeboats to the surface. Almost two months later, one of the lifeboats returned to the ship and stayed there. Without the Earth's global positioning system, it was impossible to determine the exact coordinates of the remaining lifeboat, but the flight data gave them a rough idea of where to start searching.

Veronica had mapped the area into a large grid so they could coordinate their search efforts. Today they would try to cover the south-southwest quadrant. They travelled light, but made sure they had enough equipment to catalogue data and collect samples along the way.

While their primary objective was to recover the *Atlas* team, they were also there to determine the planet's capacity to support human life. At first glance, the planet certainly appeared perfect. Beyond their camp, the rainforest was thick and vibrant, filled with beautiful plants, enormous trees, and buzzing with activity. The atmosphere was warm and tropical, with a cool breeze wafting in from the ocean to the east.

Plants fought for sunlight through every level of the forest; from the enormous trees which stretched hundreds of meters over their heads, to the sneaky vines which crept up the trunks of the trees, and the broad flat-leaved ground-dwelling plants. Beneath their feet, the leaf litter was thick and rotten, providing the perfect environment for fungus and mold to thrive.

"Holy shit!" called Diamond from the rear of the group.

Everyone stopped.

"Look at the size of this!" Diamond had frozen mid-step and was pointing into the thick shrubbery beside him.

Joel and Amber scampered across to see his discovery. It was an enormous beetle-like creature, the size of Diamond's head. It was wrapped in a hard exoskeleton, assembled in segments which were colored in beautiful bright yellows, oranges, and reds. Its head was small compared to its body; like a grape attached to a melon.

Amber was almost bouncing with excitement. "It's a giant beetle!" she declared as it waddled around on six spindly black legs.

The beetle seemed oblivious to their presence. It continued to walk along the ground, shuffling through the leaf litter, using a small pair of serrated mandibles to search for food. Suddenly the armored exoskeleton on the beetle's back opened and a pair of enormous translucent wings extended from inside. Its wings began to buzz, flapping so fast they were virtually invisible. The giant beetle lifted off the ground and it started to float away into the thick jungle.

Suddenly the enormous beetle exploded in a puff of red and pink, splattering the surrounding area in entrails.

"What the fuck?" cried Amber.

From behind she saw Grey, with his arm outstretched, holding the Marine-issued explosives launcher against his shoulder.

Amber was livid. "Why did you shoot it? We came here to observe and report, not interfere!"

Grey's demeanor remained indifferent. He lowered the launcher. "Can't be too careful. Who knows what alien bugs are capable of?" Before waiting for a response, Grey turned away and continued trekking through the forest.

"It's just a bug. Asshole," growled Amber under her breath.

In truth, the beetle troubled Amber. The statistical chance of coming across another planet so similar to Earth was extremely remote, but it was plausible. When they first arrived, she was impressed at the physical similarities between the two planets. At the time she assumed these were just the required building blocks for sustaining complex lifeforms. But the chances of finding a planet so similar to home across so many minute details were incalculable.

Joel saw Amber staring into the middle distance. "You're worried about something."

"It's just, I don't know how to describe it. You know that saying 'if something seems too good to be true—'"

"Then it probably is?" said Joel, finishing her thought.

Amber looked over her shoulder at the remains of the giant beetle. "That beetle unnerves me a bit."

Joel shrugged. "Like Veronica said yesterday, Arcadia has a higher concentration of oxygen compared to Earth and the more oxygen in the atmosphere, the bigger insects will grow."

Amber sighed. She knew just as well as Joel the correlation between insect size and oxygen levels. She also knew the same correlation ceased to exist on Earth once birds entered the evolutionary ring. The only insects that could outmaneuver the agile avian predators were much smaller. Given Amber could not recall hearing or seeing anything reminiscent of a bird flying around the trees, she had to wonder just how big the insects on this planet could grow.

As the team delved deeper, a ravine began to rise around them. Large rocks and boulders slowly emerged on either side until the team was enveloped by steep slopes. Light struggled to filter through the taller trees overhead, providing a comfortable shaded path on which to walk. An enormous rotting tree-trunk, which had fallen down some time ago, lay strewn between the rock walls, bridging the chasm overhead. Everything was covered in greenery, from the determined plants which grew on the rock face, to the long thick vines which dangled overhead.

The further they moved into the ravine the narrower the path became, until it was the width of a single car lane.

"It's so damn hot. Why did we have to land where it was so damn hot?" complained Charles.

The others ignored him.

"Is this seriously the only way to find the *Atlas* crew? Wouldn't we be better off splitting up to cover more ground?"

"Everyone stays together," said Grey tersely.

Grey didn't normally deal with civilians. He found them frustrating to work with, always complaining and questioning his authority. And academics were the worst kind of civilians. They seemed to have a pole up their ass like they were superior to anyone in uniform.

"But *why* do we have to stay together?" pressed Charles.

And they questioned *everything*.

Grey ignored him and continued to march through the thick jungle.

Veronica walked beside Grey as they led the group into the ravine. While she knew Grey was in command of the mission on the ground, as the shuttle pilot she couldn't help feeling a sense of responsibility. Her expertise in astrophysics was useless in the jungles of an alien planet, but she had always been a natural leader. The wellbeing of her crew was her first priority, like a mother bear protecting her cubs.

She knew Grey didn't see her as a leader. She was literally half his age and had never served in the military. In his eyes, she wasn't fit to be in command of anything.

"Are you sure this is the best way? What if it's a dead end? We should stay in the open," said Veronica as they meandered along the thin path.

Veronica could practically hear Grey's eyes roll.

"I'm sure," he said flatly.

Veronica dropped back several steps pretending to examine a small patch of moss growing on the rock face. "*Did you hear that?*" she whispered into her throat mic.

"*He is such an ass*," came a static reply. Veronica and Mikhail had established a private communication line before the team set out for the day. The line routed from *Hermes* through the Base Camp's comms equipment, then directly to Veronica's throat mic.

"He's just from another generation," said Veronica.

She could hear Mikhail sigh over her earpiece. "*You're too nice sometimes.*"

"Dr. Nizhny!" called Grey from further ahead. He had slowed his pace and was staring at something out of her sight.

"I'll talk to you later, sweetheart. Looks like he actually wants my opinion on something for once."

"*Call back soon. I'm getting bored up here!*" While Mikhail's tone was playful, Veronica detected a hint of anxiety.

She switched off her private line and quick-stepped toward Grey. As she passed beneath the large log which was obscuring her vision, she saw a small waterfall trickling between the boulders, feeding a tiny stream which ran through the center of the ravine.

"What's wrong?" It was then she noticed Grey was almost smiling.

He pointed to the little stream. "If this is a dead end, why isn't this place flooded?"

Veronica scowled under her breath.

"Hey? What's that?" asked Diamond as he approached Grey and Veronica.

Veronica turned, ready to explain it was a waterfall when she realized Diamond wasn't looking at the rivulet, he was listening intently. She paused and listened, too.

Low muffled moans were coming from the near distance, followed by a soft whinny, a whistle, and grunting.

"What is it?" repeated Diamond.

The group congregated by the small waterfall. They could all hear the strange sounds, originating from deeper in the ravine.

Amber's eyes lit up. "They're animal noises! And they sound close." Without waiting for the others, she took off, following the small stream deeper into the gorge.

"Wait! You don't know what's down there!" protested Diamond.

Amber ignored Diamond, moving quickly over boulders and under fallen trees. The flowing water grew in size, forming a shallow but wide stream further ahead. It increased in speed as the ravine suddenly opened up and dipped steeply downward, splashing dramatically over the rocks below. Amber approached the lip of the stream and her heart virtually leaped from her chest.

At the bottom of the depression, the narrow space opened into a huge gorge, surrounded by sheer walls, creating a hidden valley. In its center was a crystal clear lake, pooled water from the flowing stream. But it was the sight surrounding the lake that had taken Amber's breath away.

"Jesus Christ. It's a watering hole," she breathed in awe.

At the edge of the water all manner of lifeforms gathered in herds and family groups. Some snacked on nearby ferns while others lapped happily from the cool water. Amber counted at least four distinct animal species as well as several small pods of large beetles. Unlike the beetles, the other creatures were all vertebrates but she couldn't tell if they were reptiles, mammals, or something else entirely. The four species were completely different from one another, but with one key similarity; they were enormous.

Furthest from the base of the trickling water was an adult and child pair. While standing still, they stood on four legs, but when they moved to and from the water they reared up so they only used their back legs to walk. Their front legs had large elongated claws, perfect for digging in the mud.

Their bodies were covered in huge thick plates which overlapped like pine cone scales, from their noses all the way to the tip of their tails, which were decorated with bulbous and bony hammers. While they were as large as a domestic cow, the pair were dwarfed by the other creatures.

Near the armor-plated pair was an entire herd of elephant-sized organisms with hippo-like mouths and large bony crests on the backs of their heads, adorned with nasty-looking spikes. At the far side of the water a solitary long-necked creature was reaching for leaves from the overhanging trees which were dangling into the gorge from the ridge above. A single horn protruded from the middle of its forehead, while the end of its tail converged into a pointed blade. The final group of creatures were knee-deep in the water. There were two adults and three juveniles, a family group. Their mouths were long and flat, like a duck's bill, and they had large fleshy bulges on top of their snouts which engorged every so often, as the creatures trumpeted softly to one another.

"Oh, my God," said Joel, appearing by Amber's side with the rest of the crew.

Amber quickly engaged her GeniousWatch and began scanning the creatures to create digital renderings. Her heart raced with excitement as she watched them interact with each other and their surroundings. Their behaviors were reminiscent of herbivorous animals on Earth; congregating in groups and using relatively sheltered water sources.

The duck-billed sloth-like adults helped the juveniles reach kelp from the bottom of the lake. The crested herd formed a loose circle around their young while they played on the rocks. And the armor-plated pair kept their distance from the larger creatures.

Veronica turned to Grey angrily. "I thought you said this wasn't a dead end. You've led us into a cul-de-sac." The stream fed the lake below, which was surrounded by even taller and steeper walls than the ones in the ravine.

Grey grunted under his breath.

"It's okay," said Diamond, trying to defuse the tension. "I'm sure the Lieutenant will figure out a way for us to get around them. And don't forget, the other part of our mission is documenting life on the planet. I reckon we're super lucky to find so many different aliens in one spot!"

Veronica smiled at Diamond; she knew he was loyal to Grey and was only trying to play mediator.

Joel stepped away from the lip of the depression. While he shared the others' excitement, he was also unnerved by the presence of the animals. He took a sip of water, tilting his head back to get the last of the canteen's contents. He paused. At the top of the bluff, over their heads he saw a pair of large blue eyes hidden by the thick foliage. He held his breath. Whatever it was, it was staring directly at their little team. Joel elbowed Charles who was standing beside him.

Charles shoved Joel back, defensively. "Oi!"

Joel shook his head and placed a finger in front of his lips, signaling for Charles to be quiet. He pointed to the small grove where he'd seen the blue eyes, but they were gone.

Charles growled in annoyance. "What is it?"

Joel frowned. "Nothing. I thought I saw—" His thought was cut off as a series of boulders suddenly came tumbling down from the spot where he'd seen the blue eyes. The boulders rolled noisily down the steep slope, crashing into protruding rocks and starting a small rockslide.

The reaction at the watering hole was instant.

Every single animal snapped into flight-mode, rearing into the air, wailing and hollering. They began to charge in the only direction they could, up the slope of the stream, toward the humans.

"Go! Go! *Go!*" screamed Grey.

Everyone ran.

The ground vibrated beneath their feet as hundreds of tons of alien animals charged into the narrow pathway, tripping over one another as they ran. Large rocks which were easy to scale on the way there became obstacles for the fleeing crew. Grey, Joel, Veronica, and Diamond moved with agility, hurdling the boulders like athletes. Charles moved much slower than the others. He stumbled and slid, slipping in the muddy water as he struggled to keep up.

"I told you this would happen!" shouted Veronica over the thunderous vibrations.

"You can gloat later!" snapped Grey.

Despite their athleticism, the team were no match for the stampede. Members of the crested herd reached the team first, barreling through the thin pathway. Rocks and branches tumbled from the walls overhead. Suddenly the team were ducking and weaving between the huge legs of the barrage of animals. Diamond was clipped by one of the larger adults and almost fell flat on his face. He rolled into the fall and quickly regained his footing. Grey copped a kick to the shoulder from one of the smaller animals as it rumbled past. He shouted in pain, which only served to frighten the animals further.

"Over here!" called Veronica.

Everyone followed her voice, away from the center of the path, toward the waterfall which fed the small stream.

Joel looked around frantically; *where's Amber?*

"Amber!"

○ ○ ○ ● ○ ○ ○

Amber pressed herself against the large boulder in the center of the ravine, trying to flatten her body as much as possible. Water and debris assaulted her as the solitary long-necked creature ambled past. Unlike the rest of the crew, Amber hadn't run. As soon as she saw the stampede heading their way she found the largest boulder she could and crouched behind it.

She knew this wasn't threatening behavior, these creatures weren't trying to hurt the small humans. They were trying to get away from the falling rocks, which meant the humans had no reason to run; they just needed to get out of the way.

After several tense moments Amber opened her eyes. She moved slowly, peeking around the side of the rock; and came face to face with the armor-plated child. She froze. Up close it looked even stranger. Its eyes were small and positioned on the sides of its head but its nose was huge and black, like a dog. Tiny brown plates ran from just behind its rubbery nose along its head. Amber felt a faint sense of recognition. It reminded her of an oversized armadillo or a pangolin.

From behind, Amber felt a warm sensation on her neck and shoulders. She turned slowly, trying not to make any sudden movements. The armor-plated adult was standing behind her, breathing heavily. Amber kept still and avoided direct eye contact. The cow-sized creature moved awkwardly, waddling on its back legs and holding its front claws in front of itself. It hovered over her head and inhaled deeply. It was smelling her, trying to figure out what she was.

After several deep breaths the adult seemed to sigh, lowering its body slightly. Its body language relaxed as it continued to watch Amber curiously. Amber felt a strange and powerful sensation as she finally made eye contact with the enormous creature; something she had never felt before, something she couldn't put into words. Staring into the creature's eyes she didn't feel fear or threatened, she felt calm.

"*Amber!*" hollered Joel as he sprinted toward her, splashing through the shallow stream. He held his hand laser, pointing it directly at the adult.

Amber saw Joel and her heart stopped. "Joel! Don't!"

The adult reared backward in fright at Amber's sudden outburst. Its enormous claws splayed wide as it swung at Amber. It connected, scooping her into the air and throwing her back several feet. She landed heavily in the stream among the rocks.

Joel fired his laser repeatedly, striking the armored scales which ran along the adult's back. The blasts bounced off the plates, ricocheting into the ravine walls with a loud twang.

Amber moaned; she felt a dull ache on her forehead and was a little dizzy but was otherwise unscathed. "Don't!" she moaned as Joel continued to fire. "Joel! Stop it!"

With Amber out of the way, the adult stumbled to its child, keeping its back facing Joel to protect itself from the barrage of laser blasts. It shrieked in terror before scooping the smaller creature into its arms and scuttling back down the ravine, into the depths of the gorge once more.

Joel tried to help Amber to her feet. "Are you okay?"

She pushed him away. "What the hell were you thinking?" Beneath the mud and scratch marks, her face was red.

Joel shot back defensively. "Me? What were *you* thinking? That thing was about to tear you to pieces and this is the thanks I get!?"

Amber bristled. "It wasn't going to hurt me until you came in with your fucking cowboy act!" She pushed Joel aside and stumbled to her feet. The back of her head was throbbing now. She touched the area and pain shot through her scalp. She winced briefly.

"You're not invincible, Amber. You're lucky it's just a scrape. That thing could have gutted you if it wanted to," said Joel, irritated she was not grateful for his heroism.

Amber growled to herself and began walking back along the stream. She could feel the resentment burning in her chest but resisted the urge to fight back.

"You just can't admit you messed up and needed my help. Typical stubborn Amber."

She spun around, unable to resist this time. "*I'm* stubborn? You are so full of yourself! You think you're the smartest person alive, that you're better than everyone! Heaven forbid *you* make a mistake, couldn't possibly be something *you* did because that would mean you aren't the God you think you are." Amber turned away from Joel and lowered her voice again. "*You* put my life in danger just now, not me."

Joel didn't reply. He watched quietly as Amber backtracked up the ravine to catch up with the others. He felt equal parts anger and guilt. In a distant corner of his mind he considered if what she was saying could be true; had it been his actions that put her in danger? Or were his instincts on point, that she was already in trouble when he found her? They were on an alien planet with unknown lifeforms, unknown motivations, and unknown capabilities. Surely the best course of action was to go on the offensive? But it was also true he wasn't there. He hadn't seen why the creature approached Amber in the first place, and it didn't really look like it was threatening her.

Joel still felt he was in the right. Like Grey said, can't be too careful on an alien planet.

Joel and Amber caught up with the others who emerged further along the ravine. Their hair and clothes were soaked.

"What happened to you?" asked Amber.

Grey's eyes darted to Veronica. He pursed his lips. "Dr. Nizhny suggested we hide behind the waterfall while the herd moved through." He was clearly uncomfortable giving Veronica credit. "C'mon, it's getting late and it looks like the ravine is a dead end. Let's head back."

SECURITY

Base Camp, Arcadia—
18:00, 7 September, 2086

The weary group returned to camp after a long day of hiking. By the time they neared Base Camp the sun had already started to fall behind the nearby mountains, casting long grey shadows over the valley. Despite spending the entire day trekking through the jungle, the crew hadn't found a shred of evidence relating to the *Atlas* crew.

After their adventure in the gorge they had come across several more species of huge mutant insects, including an ant-like swarm of crawling creatures the size of rats and a fly/mosquito hybrid the size of a pigeon. They also found a bizarre group of small furry animals with pink skin and huge frog mouths, as well as several rodent-like creatures covered in fur which scurried around the underbrush.

As the crew approached the edge of the clearing Grey halted their movements, motioning to the security system in the distance. He extracted the small remote from his utility belt and switched off the perimeter.

"How do you know it's off?" asked Charles.

Grey didn't respond. He proceeded forward, safely crossing the invisible security line.

Charles waited for the others to cross, hanging back briefly to observe the small tripods up close.

"C'mon, Dr. Kendal," ordered Grey. "Get your ass inside so I can reset the perimeter before the sun goes down."

Charles took several steps away from the tripod so he was inside the perimeter.

As he did so, Grey pressed the remote again, arming the system.

Charles glanced once more at the small tripod. "Why does the system have to be on before the sun goes down?"

Grey glanced sideways at Charles, as though deciding whether to share his motives or not. "Because we don't know what's out there at night."

Charles frowned suspiciously as Grey walked away. "We don't know what's out there during the day either," he mused to himself.

At Base Camp, Veronica and Joel were already beginning to prepare their evening meal while Diamond lit the small campfire before the sun disappeared entirely.

While the others were busy, Amber discreetly slipped away from the camp, heading toward the edge of the clearing. She was still bothered by her fight with Joel and wanted some space from the others to cool down.

Amber sat on the slope of a partially toppled tree near a large gully of ferns and focused her attention on the forest. She could just make out Grey's security perimeter several feet away. Although the light was quickly fading she could still see the beautiful scenery around her. A soft mist had started to form among the small ferns, giving the whole area an other-worldly feeling.

Among the plants, Amber spotted a purple flower hidden by the growing shadows. It was beautiful and, like most things on this planet, huge; the size of both her hands put together. As she stepped away from the tree and crouched by the ferns, quietly examining the large purple flower, something moved in her peripheral vision. Amber spun quickly as something small and fast darted through the underbrush.

Amber held her breath. *Something had crossed the perimeter fence.*

She approached the ferns slowly, placing a hand on her laser, just in case.

"What're you doing?" asked Diamond, suddenly appearing behind her.

"Shh," she whispered. "I think I saw something."

Diamond followed her gaze as she continued to move into the ferns. Instinctively, he started to follow her.

The pair approached cautiously, trying not to make a sound. Amber gently placed her hand on a clump of ferns, clutching the laser tight in her other hand. In one swift motion she drew the leaves back and forced the gun into the gap.

"It's a rock," Diamond said, disappointed.

Amber squinted, lowering her laser. The rock was grey-brown in color, half buried in leaf litter and soil. Sitting flat against the rock were two pairs of large transparent wings, connected to a thin grey body at least the length of her forearm. Like the flower, the wings were each the size of Amber's hands. "No. It's another insect, but more like a dragonfly."

Amber crouched down so she could see the insectoid better. She quickly engaged the camera on her GeniousWatch to take holographs for their records. She lined up the rock and the "dragonfly" in her scope when she noticed something just beyond her focus; a pair of big blue eyes hiding in the underbrush a few feet away. Amber froze. The eyes were staring directly at her.

Diamond noticed Amber's sudden pause. "What's—?"

Without warning a creature sprang from the bushes, leaping at Amber with tremendous speed, knocking her to the ground. Her gun was thrown from her grasp, bouncing off a fallen log, out of reach. The creature pivoted quickly, taking Diamond by surprise. It kicked his legs out from under him, sending him to the ground. Everything happened so quickly, Amber couldn't even make out the size or shape of the figure assaulting them.

Amber rolled away, reaching under the log for her gun. The creature kicked her arm away. She rolled back and stared up at the figure, holding her hands up, ready to defend herself. This time she got a better look; it stood about four feet tall on two legs, covered in a heavy feathery coat. But it wasn't a bird. She looked closer and saw that instead of a beak it had a flat face covered in mottled feathers, with no visible features aside from a pair of striking blue eyes.

Suddenly the creature was thrown sideways, falling heavily to the ground and rolling away. Diamond stood behind the fallen figure, cradling Amber's laser.

Amber scrambled to her feet as Diamond aimed her laser. The small figure rolled onto its back. As it did so, Amber could see the feathers across its face had been pulled askew, partially masking its blue eyes. It sat up facing the barrel of the laser fearlessly.

Suddenly, the jungle vibrated as a menacing sound rumbled through the trees. The fallen creature sat upright, alert and agitated.

"What was that? Thunder?" asked Diamond.

Amber turned her attention to the darkening forest and her heart began to race. "Not thunder. Something big. Something alive. And I think it's coming this way."

Diamond took his eyes off the feathered creature for a moment and saw the look of terror on Amber's face. Slowly he lowered the laser as a huge dark shadow loomed just beyond the trees to their left. In a heartbeat, the feathery creature disappeared into the undergrowth.

Diamond grabbed Amber by the arm. "Back to camp. Now!"

○ ○ ○ ● ○ ○ ○

Joel lowered his laser briefly as Amber and Diamond emerged from the shadows. "Did you hear—" he started.

"We saw!" shouted Diamond as he scooped up his beloved explosives launcher.

"What is it?" asked Veronica nervously.

Amber shook her head. "I, I don't know. Something big. It sounded like an alligator, or a pissed-off elephant. I don't know."

Joel frowned. "Maybe one of the animals from the gorge followed us back here?" He shot an accusing look at Amber.

Amber shook her head. "This was different."

"What do we do?" asked Charles.

"We should hole-up in the ship," said Diamond.

"No need to hide." Grey exited a nearby tent. Unlike the others, his demeanor was calm. He pointed to one of the perimeter sensors in the distance. "We just need to stay alert and let the security system do its job. We're safe right where we are."

"You sure about that?" asked Charles. He was facing away from the rest of the group. His attention was focused on the shadowy perimeter fence; beads of sweat rolled down his face, which had turned a sickly pale white.

Everyone turned.

An enormous creature hovered at the edge of the clearing. It was at least ten meters tall, with legs as thick as a tree-trunk. Four long sharp claws on each foot dug into the earth creating a footprint the size of a small person. It stood upright, balancing with a huge tail which stretched behind its body.

Beneath one of its enormous human-sized feet were the smashed remains of a security tripod; it had never fired.

Nobody moved. Nobody breathed.

The huge beast parted its long crocodile-like snout, revealing a set of enormous teeth. Its skin was pebbled a dark reddish-brown and a huge sail ran down the center of its back. Its large eyes squinted as it examined the strange tiny beings in front of it.

Joel stared at the creature. "What the—"

The bipedal crocodilian behemoth let out a huge rippling roar. It was monstrous, resonating deep in the animal's throat. It was the same sound they'd heard moments earlier but amplified tenfold. Its open jaws revealed multiple rows of menacing serrated teeth.

Grey, still calm, quickly pulled out his automatic laser and fired several shots at the beast's face. Although it reeled from the blasts for a moment, it was relatively unscathed.

But now it was mad.

"*Run!*" screamed Veronica.

The creature lunged forward, shaking the earth violently as it charged into the clearing.

Everyone ran. In different directions.

Diamond headed directly for the lifeboat with Amber hot on his heels, while Charles, Joel, and Veronica ran straight into the trees.

For a moment, Grey didn't move. He continued to fire several shots at the huge creature, trying to force it into submission. When it continued to charge, Grey unshouldered his explosives launcher and aimed it at the crocodilian's enormous body. He clicked the firing mechanism and a small projectile blasted from the barrel; it missed. The earth trembled as the explosive charge hit the trunk of a nearby tree. A hot concentrated flash shattered the base of the trunk. The rest of the tree quickly toppled over, falling onto the front of the camouflaged lifeboat, momentarily blocking the path of the animal, and trapping Diamond and Amber inside.

Grey seized his chance and ran into the trees, following the others.

Together, the four humans scrambled through the dense jungle, keeping to the thickest parts of the undergrowth. Joel led the charge, keeping one eye on the creature behind, and the other on the surrounding forest. They could hear the pursuing beast reach the trees and smash through them like matchsticks.

Suddenly the jungle disappeared. The trees dropped away like a veil being lifted. Yawning before their eyes was a wide and fearsome-looking chasm, just like the one they had explored earlier that day. But this time, they were standing on the edge of the huge precipice. On the other side the jungle grew thick. The safety of the trees taunted them from across the gap.

Without missing a beat, Joel turned left, running along the lip of the chasm. The others followed closely, too terrified to stop.

"There!" called Grey, pointing ahead.

It was difficult to spot in the faded light but Joel could just see the outline of a huge fallen tree which bridged the gap. The group picked up their speed, heading for the makeshift overpass. The tree was enormous. When it was upright, it would have stood at least seventy meters tall. The top of the tree was missing; no leaves or ragged branches.

As soon as they reached the trunk, Joel ushered the others across. He could hear the crocodilian smash through the edge of the tree line, onto the open clifftop. It paused for a moment, before bellowing a deep horrendous sound as it spotted the fleeing humans only a short distance away.

As soon as Grey was across, Joel clambered onto the huge log. The moment he was on the tree he felt the fear begin to swell inside his chest. He knew he couldn't stop now; that thing would easily swallow him whole if it wanted to. Joel started to walk across, willing his legs to move faster.

"Carter, what are you doing? Get your ass over here!" demanded Grey.

Joel didn't look up. He focused on the log in front of him, watching each foot as he slowly made his way across. He could sense the vast empty space beneath his feet. He could feel his legs stiffening as fear began to consume him.

Joel felt bile rise in his throat as the crocodilian came charging toward the tree. For a moment, his leg muscles seized, slowing his pace even further; the fear was starting to paralyze him.

Grey was about to shout again but was cut off.

"You can do this!" Veronica stood on the far edge of the tree-bridge, waving Joel toward her. "Just focus on me, Joel. Only a few more steps! You are in control here!" called Veronica with enthusiasm.

Joel swallowed hard, fighting the urge to stop. He watched his feet move one after another across the surface of the bark, he listened to the soothing sound of Veronica's voice urging him on.

"That's it! Almost there!" called Veronica.

As soon as he was close enough, Veronica grabbed Joel's arm and dragged him to safety. Just as the crocodilian arrived at the far side of the chasm, Veronica and Joel leaped off the tree together. For a moment, everyone paused, watching as the crocodilian paced, eyeing the group hungrily.

Grey exhaled. "C'mon, let's keep mov—"

Before he could finish his thought, the crocodilian stepped onto the fallen tree-trunk. The wood of the tree squealed and snapped under its weight, but it held. The creature took another tentative step; the tree groaned again under the pressure.

"Shit," said Charles in disbelief.

As the animal took another step a sickening cracking sound echoed through the gully.

"It's not going to hold," said Joel with a hint of hope.

Another loud crack reverberated from the trunk. The crocodilian must have sensed it, too. Suddenly it began running across the now-weakened log, the cracking and splintering intensifying with each step.

"Go!" demanded Grey.

He didn't need to repeat himself.

The group took off into the jungle once more. Behind them, they could feel the earth shake as the gigantic predator landed heavily onto the south side of the chasm, followed promptly by the sound of shattered wood, tumbling down the cliff face.

"Move!" called Grey, urging the group forward.

"We're never going to outrun it!" snapped Charles.

They all knew he was right.

Suddenly Grey grabbed Joel by the arm. "Get them up there!" he shouted, pushing him toward an enormous tree which towered almost a hundred meters overhead. Its trunk was the size of a small car and its roots were huge and gnarled, forming a virtual stepladder which led to the higher branches. Behind them, the sound of the crocodilian's rolling snarls and growls rumbled through the trees.

Grey moved away from the others, trying to lure the creature south. "Hey! Over here!" he called.

The crocodilian turned its attention to Grey and followed him further into the thicket. Once it was far enough from the others, Grey aimed his explosives launcher at the behemoth again and pulled the trigger. Nothing happened; the barrel was jammed. Without missing a beat, he discarded the launcher and grabbed his laser, firing repeatedly at the creature's face. It ducked away allowing short bursts of laser fire to scorch the side of its torso.

While Grey distracted the creature, Joel waved Veronica and Charles toward the tree. Veronica grabbed at the roots and pulled herself up into the branches with amazing agility. Charles jumped into the tree and awkwardly clambered after her. Joel glanced back to Grey as he tried frantically to distract the animal. He crouched at the base, not willing to abandon the fight just yet.

Grey led the crocodilian further away, continuing to shout at the creature, drawing its attention. He walked backward with his laser at the ready, aimed at the beast's head. It walked slowly toward the noisy little man with a mixture of curiosity and anger. Grey looked down the barrel of the laser and prepared to fire when his foot slipped on some slick moss and he fell clumsily onto his back. Grey swore and rolled onto his side in time to see the creature lunging toward him. He fumbled for his gun and tried to aim.

The crocodilian was merely inches from Grey's face when a long thin projectile flew from an overhanging tree, lodging in the animal's eye. Blood exploded from its eye socket and it reeled, roaring in agony.

A small feathery creature, the size of a child, dropped from the overhanging branches. It crouched on the ground in front of the crocodilian and threw another long sharp object at its face. The beast turned away from the projectile, which skidded off to the side. The crocodilian lunged at the feathery creature which quickly scampered into the underbrush, crawling desperately into the relative safety of a rotting log.

Grey scrambled toward Joel at the base of the tree. "Get up there!" he ordered, hurling himself into the roots.

Joel looked around. He saw Veronica and Charles scaling the tree above his head, he saw Grey's discarded explosives launcher in the leaf litter, and he saw the small feathery creature who had just saved Grey's life, pinned down as the crocodilian clawed and snapped aggressively at it.

Joel made his decision.

He sprang from the base of the tree, grabbing Grey's explosives launcher. He ejected the old cartridge which was blocking the trigger and aimed the launcher at the monster.

"Hey! Crocodile face!" he hollered.

The crocodilian stopped clawing at the fallen log and turned slowly. Its left eye was dripping with blood, but it could still see Joel with its right eye. It hissed and snarled a deep guttural sound. Then it charged.

Joel lined up his shot.

The animal was running directly toward him, jaws open wide. Joel held his position, waiting for the perfect moment. His heart pounded; he could feel the sweat dripping down his brow.

Not yet.

The animal closed in quickly. Joel waited until it was only meters away, then he smiled and jammed his finger on the trigger. The launcher hissed and a small projectile shot from the barrel.

The crocodilian saw the projectile flying toward it and tried to pull away, but it was too late. The small explosive slammed into the beast's left arm and detonated on impact. The explosion blasted the creature's arm clear off in a grotesque spray of blood and flesh. The creature shrieked in agony, stumbling sideways from the shockwave. Its huge bulk swayed unsteadily as it moaned a pitiful and dejected sound.

For a moment, it stood its ground. Blood dribbled from its gaping eye-socket, jagged flesh hung loosely from the stump of its right shoulder. After several tense moments, the huge creature groaned softly before stumbling away, retreating into the darkness.

Without wasting time, Joel ran toward the feathery creature, but it had already scrambled up a nearby tree. Joel turned and raced toward Grey and the others, heaving himself onto the thick roots. He wheezed and panted as he pulled himself up, before finally leaning against the trunk of the tree to catch his breath.

"So, what the hell was that?" said Charles.

Joel shook his head. "I don't know. But with those jaws and that sail on its back it looked a hell of a lot like a . . ." he paused, unsure if he should say the word aloud, ". . . a dinosaur."

Charles scoffed. "A dinosaur? What're you on about? Are you trying to say *Hermes* took us back in time? That's insane!"

Joel shook his head. "Honestly, I don't know where we are. But that thing looked a hell of a lot like a member of the Spinosauridae family; the long jaws, the sail, and the whole fucking body shape. You don't have to be an expert to see the resemblance."

"Garkra," said a soft guttural voice overhead.

Sitting among the branches several feet above the group was the small feathery creature that had saved Grey's life. It mimicked the rolling hiss of the crocodilian, "*Grrrr-rrrr-rrr.*" It nodded to the animal's dismembered arm lying on the jungle floor and repeated, "Garkra."

"Did that thing just talk?" asked Charles.

As they stared in confusion, the small creature stood on the overhanging branch, clutched at the feathers around its face, and slowly removed its hooded mask.

"Holy shit! It's a woman?" exclaimed Charles.

Although she was the size of a child and her features were distorted, there was no mistaking her human-like appearance. Beneath her long blonde hair hid a pair of large blue eyes, which contrasted starkly against her brown skin. Joel felt a brief sense of recognition.

The woman clambered down the branches, moving slowly to show submission. As she descended, she removed her feathered cape and left it among the higher branches. She was virtually naked, lean and petite with narrow shoulders and large dexterous hands and feet like an ape.

She looked at the faces around her. "W-what you?" she stammered in English.

Charles cursed. "She speaks English! It's a karate fighting bird woman that speaks English!"

The small woman frowned at Charles's outburst, clearly confused by his comment. She crouched on the branch, staring at the humans surrounding her, examining their faces with a mixture of curiosity and caution.

Veronica shifted closer to the small woman, careful not to move too suddenly or make her feel threatened. "So that thing is called a *Garkra*?" she repeated, testing her comprehension and trying to start a dialogue.

The woman nodded. "Yes. Garkra," she said in clipped English.

Veronica pointed to her own chest, "I'm *Veronica.*" She pointed to Joel, "This is *Joel.*" Then she leaned closer to the small woman. "Do you have a name?"

The woman nodded, and pointed to her own chest, "This Faybin."

"Faybin, how do you know our language? Have you seen others like us before? Other humans?"

"Hu-man," said Faybin with a hint of recognition. "You hu-man? You *sky people*?"

"You've met others like us? Humans who came from the sky?"

Faybin nodded. "Yes."

"Where are they now?"

Faybin's eyes narrowed, she looked around at the strange faces and pulled away. "*Sky people* with Merna."

"Merna? What's a Merna?"

Faybin thought for a moment, searching for the right word. "Merna, Faybin people."

"Faybin people? Your people are called *Merna*?"

Faybin huffed, frustrated by the repetitive line of questioning.

Grey pulled himself to his feet on one of the lower branches, attempting to look Faybin in the eye. "Can you take us to the humans?"

Faybin bit her lower lip and glanced across the dark forest. "No. Dark. Wait. Light."

"Faybin," said Joel, noticing her hesitation. "What happens in the dark?"

Faybin stared Joel in the eye. "Garkra eat."

Breach

Base Camp, Arcadia—
09:00, 8 September, 2086

Amber stared at the outside world through the lifeboat's front window. She could see the morning sun shining through the tinted glass.

When they were attacked, Amber had followed Diamond's lead and ran straight into the lifeboat, expecting the others to be right behind them. The pair hid in the rear storage compartment, feeling the earth shake violently as something exploded outside. Soon after, the whole ship heaved as a huge mass crashed into it. For a brief moment, Amber thought the others had taken out the monster. That was until she heard its chilling roar as it made its way around the ship, fading into the distance. After several long and tense minutes, once they were certain the monster had passed, the pair emerged from the storage compartment and tried to open the airlock but it wouldn't budge.

Amber checked her watch; nine a.m. They'd been trapped inside the lifeboat for over twelve hours now. And there was still no sign of the others. She sat in the pilot's seat, staring absentmindedly through the window, deep in thought. Meanwhile, Diamond continued to pry and hammer at the lifeboat doors, as he had done almost all night.

Amber surveyed the damage outside. The attack had left the camp in shambles. Most of the tents were flattened and the communications equipment was crushed. From the edge of the curved window, Amber could just make out the tree-trunk jammed against the outer airlock door.

"It's never going to move," sighed Amber. "Not with that tree in the way."

Diamond ignored her comment and continued to work away at the door with a new implement. He kept his attention fixed on the door. "I should be out there. I shouldn't've gone to the ship. I should've stayed with the fight. The Lieutenant is gonna have my ass when they get back."

If they ever get back, thought Amber.

The last time they saw the others, they were being chased into the forest by a huge alien monster. Amber didn't expect them to return soon at all. For a moment, she thought about Joel. She pictured the resentment on his face when she accused him of almost getting her killed. In her heart, she knew Joel was at least partially right. She had acted carelessly and had put herself in an extremely dangerous situation. She was too stubborn to admit fault, especially to Joel. But with each passing hour, Amber began to realize she might never see him again.

The pit in her stomach deepened with guilt.

Amber tried to ignore Diamond's relentless hammering at the door. She tried to focus her thoughts on the creatures they had encountered on Arcadia so far; the monster that had attacked them, the herbivorous animals in the gorge, the giant insects throughout the jungle. There was something unsettling about the lifeforms they'd discovered, but Amber couldn't quite articulate her concerns. It was as though she was staring at a jigsaw puzzle, knowing the pieces should fit together somehow, yet unable to connect them in a meaningful way.

Diamond continued to hammer at the door.

"Diamond!" Amber finally snapped.

Diamond paused.

Amber immediately regretted her outburst. She knew he was just trying to help. She took a deep breath and looked around her. Unlike outside, the boat was relatively undisturbed, aside from the various tools beside the airlock. Diamond needed to keep his hands busy in order to keep his mind busy.

"Why don't you see if there's another way out of here? An emergency exit or something?" suggested Amber.

Diamond lowered the tool in his grasp. They both knew there was no other exit on the boat. They'd already scoured the entire ship searching for another way out. But he moved into the storage compartment regardless.

Diamond looked around the compartment curiously. It was much smaller than the equipment room aboard *Hermes*. It was the size of a butler's pantry and, like a pantry, its walls were lined with shelves bolted firmly in place. Sitting on the shelves was various gear that hadn't been unloaded; a spare tent, a couple of unlabeled crates, some medical supplies, and equipment for setting up the mobile laboratory.

Diamond moved around the length of the compartment, examining the walls behind the shelves. A small loose strap was sticking out of the mobile lab. Diamond tugged at it and the tab came away easily; several glass beakers tumbled out of the crate, shattering loudly.

"What the hell, Diamond?"

Diamond poked his head through the doorway which separated the two rooms. "I'm sorry, it's just . . ." He stopped mid-sentence.

"Just what?" asked Amber, looking back from the console.

Diamond's eyes were wide. "Aliens," he breathed.

Amber turned back to the window.

There they were.

A small group of alien creatures were standing at the edge of the field. They were unlike anything the team had seen so far. For a start, they were smaller than the behemoths from the gorge, about six feet tall. Their bodies and arms were covered in a fine layer of mottled brown and white feathers, but their legs and faces were bare, revealing grey-brown skin. Each creature's head, elbows, and tail were decorated with long and beautiful feathery crests of various colors.

The feathered creatures had stopped just beyond the perimeter fence.

Diamond approached Amber at the front of the ship slowly, his eyes fixed on the strange beings in the distance. "You think they're related to the feathery thing that attacked us yesterday?"

Amber shook her head. "No. These are something else."

Unlike the creature that had attacked them, these things had big and round heads, like a human, but with elongated lizard-like faces. Their eyes were huge compared to the rest of their body. Even from a distance, Amber could see their eyes were a sickly yellow color, not the brilliant blue they'd seen hiding in the ferns.

One of the creatures bent down and, using its three thin spindly fingers, picked an object from the ground. This one was slightly smaller than the others; its body was covered in a drab grey coloring and its head, elbow, and tail feathers were tinted with a soft purple. Judging from its smaller size and subtle coloring Amber guessed it was female. On Earth, male birds were usually larger than females and had more colorful and ornate plumage.

But these things sure as hell weren't birds.

The purple female gripped one of Grey's perimeter sensors. She sniffed the motion sensor cautiously and began bending the legs of the tripod, testing it. Amber's eyes widened; they could use tools. Another, larger member of the group pulled another sensor out of the ground and snapped it in half like a stick. Then the whole troop crossed the inactive perimeter fence, heading for the remains of the camp.

"I count at least eight," said Diamond. "They're moving this way but they don't seem to notice the ship. Guess the camouflage still works."

The creatures strode purposefully across the clearing, making directly for the camp. Amber's eyes were drawn to their feet; three elongated toes with sharp claws and an enormous curved inner claw on each creature's right foot. As they came closer she could hear soft chirping and purring sounds. One creature would nod to another and purr then the other would respond in kind.

Amber repositioned herself to get a better view. She spotted a small device strapped to the purple female's left forearm. "What the hell?"

"What is it?"

"The purple one, there's something on its arm?" said Amber.

The device was grey and white in color and looked almost mechanical. Yet it was wrapped around the creature's forearm like a fingerless metallic glove. The creature's claws protruded through the finger holes of the "glove" and three small flat discs sat on the back of the hand.

"They all have them?" whispered Amber, noticing the other creatures.

Each one wore the same grey-white device on its left hand and forearm. The "glove" ended at the elbow, so it didn't interfere with their larger elbow feathers. While their right arms were relaxed, swinging casually as they moved through the campsite, their left "gloved" arms were cocked at a ninety-degree angle.

Amber's eyes grew wide. "*They're coming toward us.*"

Directly outside the ship, the eight bird-lizard-aliens casually strolled through the camp, passing the boat without a second thought. The purple creature was the last to walk by, pausing as she reached the door obstructed by the fallen tree.

Purple visibly sniffed the air. She looked up sharply and extended her left arm, pointing to the hidden ship. Amber's mind raced. Somehow Purple knew the ship was there.

Slowly, Purple balled her fist so the small discs on the back of her knuckles were now aimed directly at the ship. From up close Amber could see the little discs begin to glow with a soft reddish pink. Suddenly, Purple squealed, letting out three echoing cries. Another, larger, creature quickly backtracked, joining Purple by the door while the rest of the troop continued on.

The two stragglers purred and growled to each other in soft tones.

Purple kept her arm fixed on the door while she inhaled deeply. Her nose reared up slightly and her nostrils flared. The other creature followed the same movement, sniffing the air. They stared at the fallen tree which was wedged against the ship's doorway.

A loud cry rang out, a call from one of the others who'd continued through the camp. Purple growled in reply but after a moment both creatures moved on, too, vanishing into the forest.

Once they were out of sight, Amber and Diamond collapsed onto the floor in relief.

Amber was breathing in heavy gasps. Her mind was racing. Everything about these creatures screamed intelligence. The way they coordinated their movements, the way they used tools and seemed to communicate with one another. But it was the device wrapped around each creature's arm which concerned Amber the most. The way Purple pointed it at the ship, the way she *aimed* the three discs. It wasn't just some strange alien technology.

"They have weapons," said Diamond with a mixture of intrigue and concern.

Amber rubbed her eyes, as though she were expecting to wake up from a bad dream.

"They're intelligent alien beings with weapons," repeated Diamond.

The pair sat in silence for a moment, trying to comprehend what they'd just seen.

Despite their unnatural, alien appearance there was something familiar about the two-legged creatures; another piece of the biological jigsaw puzzle Amber couldn't quite put together.

"Can you hear that?" Diamond turned his head abruptly.

"Hear what?"

He sat up. "It sounds like a radio." He looked around the floor. A soft static sound crackled nearby. The radio from the lifeboat was dangling from the console. Diamond grabbed the receiver. "I thought you said the comms equipment was busted up? Shouldn't the radio be dead?"

Amber cupped a hand on her forehead in realization. "The throat mics need the comms equipment to work. But the boat has a direct line to *Hermes!*" For the first time since they were attacked, Amber felt hope.

Diamond began punching at the control panel. "Dr. Ozero?"

There was no reply.

"C'mon, Ozero," he pleaded. "Pick up the damn thing!"

After several tense moments the receiver clicked and through the static they heard Mikhail's voice. "*Diamond, is that you? You're not going to believe this!*"

Jungle, Arcadia—
09:00, 8 September, 2086

The morning sun filtered through the canopy, creating small pools of light on the forest floor. Faybin, the miniature humanoid, led the way through the thick foliage.

The team had spent the night hiding in the large tree, taking turns on guard duty in case the crocodilian, "Garkra", showed up again. As soon as the sun began to peek over the horizon they had set off into the forest, following Faybin to find her people; the Merna.

Joel tried to insist they return to camp to make sure Amber and Diamond were okay, but he was out-voted. Faybin was also quick to point out that without the tree-bridge it would take forever to walk around the massive chasm. So, the team pressed ahead.

Faybin led the team south-west, diagonally toward the mountains in the distance. Aside from several small streams the forest was incredibly thick and difficult to traverse. Veronica and Joel stayed close to Grey who walked several paces behind Faybin, leaving Charles to bring up the rear alone. Since the attack, Charles had been unusually quiet; no snide remarks or inappropriate comments. He walked a short distance behind the others, deep in thought.

In truth, no one had been particularly chatty since the attack. Lack of sleep combined with a newfound fear and respect for Arcadia had left everyone a bit shaken.

Joel walked in silence beside Grey and Veronica. All he could think about was Amber. Every time he closed his eyes he saw the look on her face when she told him it was his fault for putting her life in danger. That look disturbed him. He had known Amber their whole lives and he had only seen that look once before.

Joel had always been very protective of Amber, but it became more of a burden as they grew older and she became more independent and adventurous. She was determined to prove herself to the world, but he couldn't help thinking of her as the insecure young woman he grew up with.

At the end of their first year as postgraduate students Amber announced she was going to spend the summer volunteering in war-torn South Africa to try and protect the largest nature reserve on the continent from industrial redevelopment. Joel had not reacted well. After days of arguing he eventually cracked.

"That's it! I'm putting my foot down! If you leave, we're finished. You have to choose." His face was flushed red with anger.

Amber narrowed her gaze. Her face was a somber combination of sadness and resentment. Her lips were pursed, her brow was furrowed, and her eyes were watery but she didn't shed a tear. "Then I guess this is goodbye." Without waiting for a response, Amber left their apartment and within twelve hours was on a plane to South Africa.

Joel had never expected her to call his bluff.

Over the years they'd rebuilt their friendship and their professional relationship. They had even secured a grant to work together on the Dinosaur Cove excavation. But their romantic relationship ended that day, and Joel was still plagued by that look.

After events with the Garkra the previous evening, Joel had tried to hail Amber on his throat mic, but couldn't get a signal. He wanted so desperately to return to camp in the morning, but he knew he had no choice.

After several hours of trekking through the thick forest, the trees thinned dramatically and the team stumbled onto a wide path which cut through the thicket. Towering overhead, the canopy arched inward creating a long and wide corridor. On either side the foliage was dense, but inside they moved freely, allowing everyone to pick up the pace.

Joel leaned toward Veronica and whispered, "Does it bother you there's a path in the middle of the jungle?"

Veronica looked around curiously. "The Mernas probably made it. If they can wear camouflaged clothing and learn English I wouldn't be surprised if they could build things, too."

Joel eyed Faybin further ahead, cautiously glancing behind every so often. The tunnel was as large as a double decker bus and the edges were clearly defined, as though any plants that tried to encroach were quickly stamped back. He shook his head. "I doubt it. It's way bigger than the Mernas would need. And it'd need some pretty big animals or heavy foot traffic to keep the forest from overgrowing. It almost looks like a—"

"What's that?" interrupted Grey.

"Oh, just commenting on the path in the jungle," said Veronica.

Grey looked around. "Oh."

"You don't seem very surprised," mused Charles from behind.

Grey didn't respond. He was impossible to read. He was a man of few words at the best of times, and when he did voice an opinion it usually lacked emotion or sentiment.

Charles tried again. "Don't suppose you can share any pearls of wisdom with us lesser folk now we're stuck in the big dangerous jungle?"

"If in doubt, shoot to kill," said Grey flatly.

Veronica and Joel exchanged a concerned look. "I hope he's talking about animals," she whispered.

HERMES

Hermes, Orbit—
09:00, 8 September, 2086

As Mikhail opened his eyes the blurry image of a beautiful turquoise ocean stared back at him. He blinked rapidly, allowing his vision to focus. Sitting before him was the floating translucent image of the holographic projector, sideways. Mikhail sat up slowly, slightly disorientated. The last thing he remembered was watching the team as they returned safely to Base Camp after a day of trekking through the wilderness. He felt relieved knowing that they, that *she,* were back in the safety of the camp.

Mikhail was still sitting at the observation table, but the hologram was now brightly lit by the sun; morning. He looked around the area and saw the near-empty bottle of vodka on the edge of the table. Guilt washed over him as his memory slowly returned.

After Veronica had shut off their personal comms line the previous afternoon he had tried to keep his mind busy by watching the security projections. But with the team gone, there was very little activity around Base Camp. Mikhail's mind began to wander.

His thoughts started to drift into dark territory; he was feeling isolated and alone. He began to play out "worst case scenarios;" like what he would do if something happened to the team, if they never returned to camp? What if they disappeared just like the *Atlas* crew? What if he lost Veronica?

Before long, Mikhail found himself back in the snow, surrounded by the bodies of his dead passengers; he was freezing to death, alone with his guilt.

He finally decided to have a drink to calm his mind and settle his nerves, just one.

He looked at the bottle in his hand, only a couple of mouthfuls were left. He sighed heavily and took a sip, trying to kill the disgusting taste in his mouth.

With a heavy yawn Mikhail stretched his muscles, feeling a tightness in his neck from sleeping at such an awkward angle. He glanced back at the hologram and frowned. When he fell asleep he must have messed up the settings on the control panel because the image was no longer focused on Base Camp. The entire projection had shifted to one of the furthermost cameras, which was pointed at the beach, ten kilometers from camp. For a moment he stared in awe at the crystal clear water, rising and breaking in white cascades along the golden sand. A few feet from the water, the beach merged seamlessly into the green and brown outskirts of the forest, creating a veritable smorgasbord of color. At the edge of the image he could see one of the smaller creeks running into the open water, slowly bubbling over rocks and twisting across the sand toward the ocean.

Mikhail sighed heavily and started to punch the controls to reset the image back to Base Camp. As he did so, the serenity of the image was disturbed as a small dark object emerged from the forest, moving quickly across the sand. Mikhail stopped what he was doing and sat up abruptly; pain shot through his head from a delayed hangover. He rubbed his throbbing temple with one hand and quickly adjusted the camera settings with the other, trying to sharpen the image. The blurry projectile continued to move as the hologram focused, darting left and right.

These weren't the movements of an inanimate object; this thing was alive.

As it darted across the open sand, Mikhail got a better look at the creature. It was running, upright, on two legs, but it had a long slender torso protruding from its front and back, creating a moving T shape. Mikhail adjusted the settings again, focusing the image further.

It was human.

Well, not quite human, but definitely humanoid; two legs, two arms, and dark tanned skin. The elongated torso wasn't part of the humanoid's body; it was carrying something long and slender, like a surfboard. The creature ran out of range of the camera, disappearing along the golden sand. Mikhail quickly took control of the monitor orb, detaching the small camera from its perch so he could follow the moving figure across the beach.

Now he had a better view, Mikhail could see the figure clearly. It was a young pygmy-sized man, with long dreadlocked blond hair. His upper body was exposed and muscular. Green tattoos of elaborate patterns decorated his arms and back. His lower half was covered in what could only be described as a feathery skirt.

Mikhail zoomed closer, trying to make out finer details. As the image rendered once more, he finally saw the expression on the small man's face; mouth ajar, eyes alert, muscles tense. He was terrified. He wasn't running toward the water, he was running *away* from the jungle.

As the small man reached the water's edge he threw his surfboard down and quickly climbed into a small hole in the center. The mini-man extracted a long thin object from inside the vessel. He pushed desperately away from the beach with his paddle and began rowing as though his life depended on it.

It was then Mikhail noticed movement at the opposite side of the image, near the forest. Trees rustled and shook violently before an enormous creature exploded onto the sand, snapping branches like toothpicks. It was huge, standing over two stories tall and at least fifteen meters long from head to tail. Its head was massive, with a huge round snout, but its arms were tiny compared to the rest of its body. Its skin was rough with brilliant gold and red markings.

Mikhail rubbed his eyes. It couldn't be? He grabbed one of Joel's cumbersome paper books sitting on the shelf beside him and flicked through the pages until he found it. He stared at the page for a moment, then glanced back to the projector. This creature was certainly bigger than the one in the book, but there was no mistaking the general body shape. It looked like a Tyrannosaurus Rex.

Something on the "Rex's" neck glinted in the sunlight. Mikhail refocused the image. Sitting just below its jaw, was a large unnatural brace of some sort. It was dark silver in color and it reflected light like frosted glass, sparkling like jewelry.

Before Mikhail had time to process what he was seeing, the Rex spotted the fleeing man and bared a set of huge stained teeth. It opened its jaws wide and moved straight for the ocean. The mini-man sat inside the small canoe, paddling like an Olympian. But the Rex was surprisingly fast, ploughing into the surf within seconds. Huge swells rose and fell beneath the tiny vessel, tossing the man around like a doll.

The Rex quickly caught up to the desperate canoer. The water barely reached its knees as it hovered over him. In one smooth motion the creature leaned forward, its mouth still open, and clamped down hard. Seawater erupted in a dramatic spray. The canoe shattered and splintered. The nose and tail fell with a splash back into the water below.

Mikhail closed his eyes and looked away from the projector. He felt his stomach lurch. The mini-man never stood a chance.

Slowly, Mikhail opened his eyes.

The man wasn't dead.

Inside the Rex's mouth he could see the mini-man wriggling desperately. The beast's teeth were locked together, forming a cage around the small man and the remnants of the canoe. Once the Rex had the man in its mouth it stood upright and turned back toward the jungle.

For a moment Mikhail sat in stunned silence, unsure of what he'd just witnessed. As the creature plodded out of sight Mikhail realized the Rex had no intention of eating the mini-man; it was taking him away. But where? Mikhail jumped onto the control panel again, moving the small monitor orb to follow the Rex down the beach and into the thick forest. He kept the camera at a safe distance, guiding it carefully through the trees.

The Rex headed north-west, back into the jungle, practically in a straight line. After several kilometers it came to a small river where it turned due west, following the bank of the river closely for a few hundred meters until the water was shallow enough to cross. Once over the water, the Rex swung northward where the jungle thinned abruptly.

It was a pathway; a pathway big enough for the enormous tyrannosaurus-like creature to walk with ease. The canopy grew around the edges of the path, creating a tunnel in the forest.

Mikhail felt ill as he thought about Veronica and the others somewhere down there. He glanced to the remains of the vodka bottle but shook his head, pushing the dark thoughts away. If something did happen down there, if the others needed his help, then he needed his wits about him.

As the Rex plodded through the jungle, Mikhail could occasionally see the man inside its mouth. Despite his situation the humanoid seemed unharmed; there was no blood and every so often he would squeeze an arm or leg between the Rex's teeth in a futile attempt to escape. The Rex moved stiffly and mechanically, its eyes lifeless and empty. Mikhail frowned as he stared at the image. Was the Rex saving his prize for later? Was it taking the mini-man back to its nest alive to teach its children how to hunt? Was it sick? Or confused? Whatever the reason, Mikhail couldn't shake the feeling it had something to do with the strange silver collar around its neck.

Eventually the Rex came to a depression in the jungle where the path led to a secluded valley. At the bottom a huge stone escarpment rose from the otherwise thick forest, towering over the enormous creature. The stone was smooth and black, but glistened like glass. It was not a natural formation; someone, or something, had built an enormous stone wall and erected it in the middle of the jungle.

"Holy shit," breathed Mikhail.

The path led directly to a section of the smooth stone wall where it receded inside itself, creating a large archway within the otherwise flawless surface. The Rex stopped outside the arch. For a moment it just stood there, motionless. After a minute or so the stone began to slide away within the wall itself, revealing a gaping hole. Mikhail pushed the orb forward, slowly, trying to angle the image so he could see inside.

"*Dr. Ozero!*" a voice burst in his ear, breaking his concentration. "*C'mon, Ozero! Pick up the damn thing!*" It was Diamond's voice resonating in his earpiece.

Mikhail glanced back at the projector but the creature was gone and the stone wall was sealed once more.

"Damn it!" he swore, quickly punching several keys, moving the solitary camera into a nearby tree so it faced the stone gate. He turned back to the control panel and reset the rest of the projector back to Base Camp.

Mikhail engaged the ship's microphone. "Diamond, is that you? You're not going to believe this!"

"*Finally! Dr. Ozero, where are the others?*"

"What do you mean?" Mikhail looked over to the projector table and his heart stopped. "Holy shit, what happened?"

"*Where've you been? We were attacked last night!*"

Mikhail's stomach tensed. "Attacked? By what? Is everyone okay?" Mikhail started punching at the control panel to bring up the recordings from the previous evening, when he was passed out.

Amber's voice interrupted the conversation. "*We don't know. It's just the two of us here. We're stuck in the boat. The others got away from camp when we were attacked, but we haven't seen them since. We can't do anything from here. Hoping you can use the cameras to find the others and make sure they're okay. There's some weird shit on this planet.*"

Mikhail thought about the small man in the canoe and the Rex wearing the shiny neck brace. "Yeah, I think I know what you mean. I'm pretty sure I saw a dinosaur capture a—"

Diamond's voice cut through the transmission, "*What's that? Shit . . . shit . . . they're coming back! Hurry! Find the oth—*" Static took over the radio.

Raid

Base Camp, Arcadia—
11:00, 8 September, 2086

Amber ducked beneath the control console of the lifeboat and peered through the window above her head. Outside, the aliens had re-emerged from the forest and were making their way toward the ship. This time there were only two. Amber recognized the smaller purple one from earlier. But the second one was completely different. It was larger than Purple with a long tail and clean white coloring on its body. The feathers on its head, elbows, and tail were long, sleek, and brilliant bright yellow. It reminded Amber of a sulphur-crested cockatoo. Based on its size and plumage, Amber figured this one was a male.

Purple walked in front of "Cockatoo," leading him to the door of the ship. The two creatures stopped a few meters away, observing the large tree which was wedged against the boat. They paused for a moment, inspecting the tree. Cockatoo turned toward the front of the ship, staring directly at the front window.

Diamond instinctively took up a defensive stance, ready to fight.

Amber held her position, confident they couldn't see her through the chameleonic tinting.

Cockatoo stepped around the tree, sniffing the air carefully and attentively. He approached the ship, stood directly beside the window, and stared inside. Amber held her breath; she could hear him sniffing and snorting less than a meter away from her, on the other side of the glass. He looked across the surface of the camouflage window and hissed.

He knew.

Slowly, Cockatoo moved down the length of the ship, returning to the airlock. As he did so, he extended his left arm, revealing the strange glove-like device which covered his hand and forearm. Cockatoo balled his claws into a fist and tilted his wrist downward. As he did so, the little discs on his knuckles began to glow with a soft pink light, gradually building in intensity to a vibrant red hue.

Cockatoo directed the red light at the fallen tree and turned his head away slightly.

Amber's eyes grew wide in realization.

Before she could react, Amber felt Diamond's strong arms pull her down, away from the window, just as a muffled lightning crack echoed outside, followed by the sound of something large crashing to the ground.

Amber raised her head; the ship was intact. She and Diamond lay face down on the small walkway just inside the inner airlock door. She looked up. Beyond the small porthole of the inner hatch she could see light inside the airlock, light that had previously been blocked by the fallen tree.

Amber's heart began to pound. Diamond grabbed her by the arm and pushed her across the walkway, into the storage compartment. Once inside, he hit the release button beside the hatch, sealing the room.

At that exact moment, the interior airlock door slid open.

Amber's mind was spinning. She tried to take deep breaths to keep a clear head but she was terrified. These creatures were not the lumbering herbivores they'd found in the gorge. They had forward-facing eyes for hunting, their feet were armed with huge sharp claws, and they clearly had an advanced sense of sight and smell. They were predators. They were *intelligent* predators. Amber's breathing quickened again.

The door separating the two compartments had a small opaque window around head height. From her vantage point, Amber could see the light on the other side of the window change as something large passed by. She froze, waiting for the shadow to move away. As the shadow receded, Amber crawled toward the rear of the compartment. She knew they couldn't just sit there waiting to be discovered; these things were smart enough to find the ship, remove the tree, and get inside. It wouldn't be long before they found the storage room.

Amber began gently and quietly sifting through the contents of the remaining crates and equipment on the shelving units, searching for a weapon of some sort. She moved items slowly and carefully, trying hard not to make a sound.

Nothing.

Amber recalled the gun in her holster and pulled it out quickly. She looked on the side of the laser and huffed. The power was almost empty. She'd forgotten to switch the laser off after the attack the previous night. There wasn't enough charge for a single shot. Amber placed it back in her holster and returned to the crates to find a power cartridge.

From behind, a clanging sound echoed through the storage room. Amber turned to scold Diamond for making so much noise when she realized what he was doing. He was dangling from the shelving unit against the starboard wall, climbing toward the ventilation grate in the roof.

Amber started to climb after him, scaling the shelves like a ladder. Together, they wrenched the cover from the vent. It fell heavily and unexpectedly, crashing loudly as it hit the metal floor.

Through the small window, Amber could see the shadows outside approach the compartment door. Cockatoo brought his face close to the window. Amber could see his yellow head feathers and enormous reptilian eye staring right at her. She turned back to Diamond, but he was already halfway into the vent. Once his long legs were inside, Amber grabbed the edge of the open grate and swung herself up into the narrow space.

Just as her feet disappeared into the darkness, she heard the internal door slide open.

The vent was barely big enough for a person to squeeze through. It ran around the length of the lifeboat in an elongated U shape, following the curve of the front windscreen and extending into the rear of the ship on the other side. Diamond led the way, commando crawling away from the hatch, taking them over the passenger compartment. He peered through one of the grates of the forward section and saw Purple below. No escape there.

"What's that?" whispered Amber from behind.

Through the darkness she could see a small square of fluorescent green and white near the front of the ship. Diamond crawled closer and saw the glowing green letters "EXIT," beside a square access panel. Next to the hatch was a large red release lever, and beneath the glowing sign, a small sticker read *Emergency exit: terrestrial use only.*

"What does that mean?" whispered Diamond.

"It means don't try to open the hatch when we're in space."

"Oh."

From below, Amber could hear loud shrill squeals as the creatures raided the storage compartment. She patted Diamond on the leg anxiously, urging him to open the hatch.

Diamond pulled the lever and with a soft hiss the hatch flew open and daylight flooded into the small shaft. He pulled his long body out of the hatch with Amber following close behind. As they stood on the roof, Amber realized that releasing the emergency hatch had deactivated the chameleonic shield. The white arrow-shaped ship was once again visible to the world.

Not that it mattered anymore.

Inside the boat, the squealing continued as the creatures became more frustrated. Amber felt her stomach tense with each consecutive outburst. They weren't the guttural roars of the monster that attacked them the previous evening; these were clicks, shrieks, and squawks; reminiscent of a dolphin or bird of prey. Amber moved slowly across the roof of the boat, holding the center fin for stability. She could see the airlock was still open below, and lying beside it were the remains of the fallen tree. She leaned over the roof's edge; the tree now lay in two large pieces. At one end the tree-trunk was broken and splintered, but the other end had been cut clean and precise, just like the tree stump in the middle of the field.

Amber felt a cold chill run down her spine. She took a deep breath, trying to collect her thoughts. They needed a plan. The ship sat at the edge of the open field, with its rear facing the forest, just a couple of feet away from a grove of tall trees with large sprawling branches. The external ladder was beside the airlock hatch; too close to the creatures inside. They could try sliding down the steep slope of the ship's sides and along the starboard-wing, but they'd risk being seen through the huge wraparound window.

Amber turned to Diamond. He was staring at the trees toward the rear of the ship. The branches looked strong but there was no way they'd make it across the gap. Plus, the roof was curved, which meant they'd likely slip if they even tried to run down its length.

Diamond nodded.

"We can't reach that from here!" protested Amber.

From below, they heard a high-pitched squeal which assaulted their ears like nails on a chalkboard. But the sound hadn't originated from inside the ship. Amber and Diamond turned in unison and saw the two alien creatures standing just outside the airlock door, staring at them through their huge yellow eyes.

They were exposed.

Amber made eye contact with Cockatoo. There was something about the look on his face that unnerved her. His eyes were cold and reptilian but also calculating and measured. Suddenly, with his eyes still fixed on Amber, Cockatoo sprang into the air in one swift move, leaping onto the roof of the lifeboat with amazing agility.

Amber's heart stopped.

Purple followed suit, leaping effortlessly onto the roof of the ship. The two creatures stood several feet away on the relatively flat surface above the cockpit.

"Holy shit! Those things can jump!" exclaimed Diamond.

His sudden outburst took the creatures by surprise. For a moment they paused.

Diamond used their hesitation to his advantage. He grabbed Amber by the arm and charged along the length of the central fin, toward the rear of the ship. They leaped off the roof in unison, reaching desperately for the branches.

Amber's fingertips wrapped around the curve of a thin branch. She dug her nails into the bark for grip. Above her head was a thicker branch, but it was too far to reach. Below her was a four-meter drop. Diamond had snagged a branch lower to the ground, to her left. He seemed stable enough, dangling from the branch. But Amber's grip was loosening fast. Her only hope was to swing to another branch and pray she could find a better foothold.

Wrapping her thumbs loosely around the bottom of the branch, Amber swung her body toward the trunk of the tree. She kicked her legs so she could wedge her foot into a small nook in the bark. Quickly, she pushed her body up, wrapping her arms around the branch. She kicked her leg up and looped it around the bough in her hand. Amber pulled herself onto the branch, clutching the trunk of the tree for stability.

Amber glanced back to the creatures on the roof of the boat. Cockatoo was still staring at her, calculating his next move. Before she had time to think, Cockatoo and Purple began running across the roof, their claws clanging loudly against the metal. As they hit the edge of the boat they lunged into the trees, catching branches just above Amber's head.

While the aliens were agile in their movements, they were not adept in climbing trees. Each one had managed to grab a branch but they couldn't get a good grip; their legs flailed wildly, rustling the branches and shaking leaves loose.

This was their chance.

Amber looked down, quickly assessing the distance.

Close enough.

Without hesitating, Amber jumped from the branches, rolling in the leaf litter as she hit the ground. She landed heavily, feeling the impact ricochet through her bones. She turned to check on Diamond but he was already rolling beside her.

In a heartbeat the pair shot off into the jungle, away from the campsite. They could hear the aliens still struggling in the tree, snapping at one another.

Amber felt a surge of adrenaline as they shot through the undergrowth. She could hear Diamond running behind her. They had no time to plan, no time to think about their next move. They were reacting on impulse. And they were running out of options.

Suddenly Amber heard Diamond shout out in pain. She turned just as a hot burning sensation struck her chest and rippled through her veins like a bolt of electricity. All the muscles in her body instantly went limp and she fell heavily to the ground, rolling several times on the damp earth. She came to a stop awkwardly on her stomach with her right ear flush against the ground. Her eyes were wide open, staring at the surrounding forest. Amber tried to move but her muscles didn't respond. She began to hyperventilate; she was paralyzed.

Amber, unable to speak, forced a moan in frustration.

Her moan was returned by another deeper sound: Diamond.

After a long and tense moment she heard the faint sound of footsteps approaching. Two large clawed feet walked into Amber's field of vision. She could just make out the shape of Cockatoo hovering over her like a hunter, ready to strike the final blow. Up close, Amber could see the skin on his foot was pebbly but soft. She saw his right foot with its enormous curved claw. Amber only knew of one creature on Earth with such a natural weapon.

Cockatoo crouched down so Amber could see his left hand and the small discs which were pointed directly at her face. Up close, she could see the glove in more detail. It was made from a strange material; a hybridized metal-fabric assembled in small overlapping segments like fish scales. This time the space inside the small discs glowed a soft blue. Cockatoo stood upright again and used his foot to roll Amber onto her back. Her body flipped over like a ragdoll.

Satisfied she wasn't going anywhere, Cockatoo lowered his weaponized arm and the light on the small discs faded once more. Purple approached Amber cautiously, crouching down so she could sift through her clothing. Purple stopped suddenly and withdrew Amber's laser from her holster; the small female began shrieking in excitement. Cockatoo looked at the laser, then glanced back to Amber. She could feel her heart beating hard in her chest as a tear rolled down her face.

Cockatoo took Amber by the arms and picked her off the ground, cradling her limp head.

Amber moaned again, trying desperately to scream.

Purple growled at Amber. She narrowed her gaze and aimed her gloved arm; the electric lights also glowed blue. Suddenly light blasted from the small discs like lightning and Amber's world went black.

TRUST

Merna Village, Arcadia—
12:00, 8 September, 2086

Joel paused as the group approached a huge wooden structure, marking the entrance to the Merna village. Several minutes earlier, Faybin had led them away from the huge path onto a smaller Merna-sized one. They were greeted by a large wooden archway, elaborately carved and decorated in flowers and greenery. White patterns were scrawled along the outer edge of the arch, like a warning or welcome sign. As soon as they spotted the arch Faybin visibly relaxed.

Joel stared at the archway, marveling at the signs of intelligence displayed by the Mernas. They used tools to cut down and carve the wooden frame, creatively decorated it, and they had the capacity not only to form their own language but to transfer that language into written form.

Faybin led the group through the arch along the smaller path. Within minutes, soft whispers began to drift through the trees. Joel slowed, trying to pinpoint the source of the sound. Beside him, Veronica touched his shoulder and pointed upward. At first all he saw were branches and leaves, swaying gently in the wind. It took a moment for him to realize that perched on those branches were small children. Their skin was covered in dried mud and their little bodies were wrapped in a layer of leaves and vines, camouflaged in the treetops.

One child, a girl, caught Joel's eye. She sat on the branch of a low-hanging tree. Her skin was painted with greens and browns. In her hand was a short pointed stick. She was young, no more than five or six years old, with short and matted yellow hair. She crouched on the branch with her feet apart, in a defensive position. From this angle, Joel could see the Merna's feet were larger and more dexterous than a human's; similar to an orangutan or chimpanzee.

Joel smiled and waved to the girl. She growled in response and stood upright, pointing her spear at the travelers. Joel frowned, wondering if waving was a sign of aggression here. The small girl and the other children suddenly scrambled away noisily, shrieking and hooting as they swung through the canopy.

After a short distance, the canopy receded, exposing the afternoon sky and the outskirts of a vibrant and bustling village. Joel paused as they entered the community proper; he could hardly believe his eyes. The village was set in a large clearing, at least three times the size of the one where they had set up Base Camp. It was covered in a soft layer of grass for the most part, with the exception of a large sparse area of exposed dirt which housed a huge central bonfire. Mernas of all shapes and sizes congregated around the central square. Women wove feathers and leaves together creating tunics and garments, men sat in small circles sharpening stone tools and butchering small animals. Many of the men and women had elaborately braided hair, decorated with colorful feathers and ornaments.

As the crew continued to follow Faybin into the village center, the surrounding Mernas stopped what they were doing and turned their attention to the humans.

Joel was fascinated by the Mernas' appearance. They were only about four feet high, with dark tanned skin and long blond hair. His analytic mind struggled to classify them. They had distinctive human traits, combining characteristics from the pygmies of Central Africa, who only grew to about five feet tall, and the Melanesian people of the Solomon Islands, who had blond hair and the darkest skin outside of Africa. But they also had distinctive ape-like features in their feet and faces. Their eyes and noses were proportionally larger than a human's, presumably giving them a better sense of sight and smell.

As they passed the central bonfire Faybin's mood changed again; this time she was animated and excited. "Come! Fast!"

Small huts were scattered around the outside of the center square. They were made from fallen tree ferns, vines, and branches, woven together like giant wicker baskets. They were teardrop in shape, with large rounded bases tapering to a pointed tip. At the base, under the lip of the rounded mid-section was a small circular opening, like a weaver bird's nest.

Mernas began to emerge from the huts watching nervously as the humans entered their village.

Veronica whispered to Joel, "If these people have met humans before, why do they seem so scared?"

Faybin brought the group to the far side of the village square where a small hill rose from the otherwise flat clearing. A group of older Mernas sat in a circle on the hill; they were different from the others. Besides their advanced age, they wore brightly colored feathery robes and headdresses, and elaborate tattoos and paint covered their faces and chests.

The elders glared at the humans with cold hard eyes.

Faybin brought the group before the older Mernas and began speaking quickly in her native tongue, addressing the elders. Joel watched the exchange closely. The elders were unimpressed. They looked over the humans with disdain, shaking their heads as Faybin continued to speak. In frustration, Faybin grabbed Veronica by the arm and pulled her closer to the council, forcing her to kneel before the elders.

For a long moment no one spoke. Villagers continued to congregate behind the group, waiting anxiously to hear the elders' response. The children had made their way down from the trees and were pushing toward the front of the crowd.

"Carter," whispered Grey. "I don't see any humans here."

Before Joel could respond, one of the elders stood up. It was the oldest and shortest woman in the group. Her hair was long and grey, braided in two long tendrils which almost touched the ground. With her thin frame and bony exterior she struggled to climb to her feet. Once standing though she was confident and poised, shuffling toward Veronica and eying her dismissively.

"Xylon," Faybin whispered to Veronica, nodding to the old woman.

"Human, come before," said Xylon. Her English was more advanced than Faybin's, but it was still clipped and stilted. Her gaze narrowed as she stepped closer to Veronica. Despite their height difference Veronica felt intimidated. "Human no friend. Human betray Merna."

Veronica gasped, but held her tongue.

"Human enemy. Human go." Without waiting for a reply, Xylon turned her back on Veronica and started to return to her seat with the other elders.

Joel stepped forward. "Wait!"

The crowd gasped at his outburst.

Xylon turned slowly, looking at Joel through thin stern eyes. Joel stepped forward and dropped to one knee as a sign of respect. He could see the anger in her eyes, but behind the anger, he saw fear.

Joel spoke slowly, with careful dictation. "We are not your enemy. We are not the humans you know. We have come to take them away. To take them home."

Faybin became anxious; she addressed Xylon. "Schmitt?"

Xylon grunted and looked to the other elders who nodded solemnly.

Faybin sprang to her feet and ran into one of the larger huts on the outskirts of the village. Within moments she returned, pushing a much taller man with pale dirty skin and unkempt greying hair. As the old man was directed toward the gathering Joel realized he wore clothes; they were ragged and filthy, but they were clothes nonetheless. The old man was almost two feet taller than Faybin but he walked in a submissive fashion, with his hands beside his body and his head bowed. As they neared the crowd the old man lifted his head slightly and, for the first time, noticed the group of humans standing before the elders.

"Oh, mein Gott!" he exclaimed in perfect German. He gazed at the faces, searching for something familiar. His mood softened slightly as he failed to recognize anyone. Faybin gently nudged him forward, until he was beside Joel and Veronica.

The old man frowned in confusion. "You are not my friends? But you are from Earth? Are you here to rescue me?" His German accent was heavy but his English was perfect.

Veronica's eyes lit up, she recognized his face from the mission briefing material; Professor Eckhart Schmitt, the German anthropologist. It was as though she'd been reunited with an old friend.

Before Veronica could speak, Xylon growled at Schmitt. He lowered himself to his knees, bowing before her. She spoke rapidly to him in her native language, pointing aggressively at Joel and Veronica.

"She says you call yourself *sky people,*" said Schmitt.

Joel stared in shock. "You speak Merna?"

Schmitt ignored Joel's remark. "She believes you are evil, that you are here to steal the *Light stone,* just like the others did."

"Tell her we are not here to steal anything. We don't even know what a light stone is," pleaded Veronica.

Schmitt turned to Xylon, speaking slowly in her language. She scoffed and waved a dismissive hand before crossing her arms defiantly. Faybin entered the conversation, clearly arguing on behalf of the humans. She pointed to Joel animatedly and mimicked the Garkra's roar.

After much back and forth, Xylon finally put up her hand and bowed her head. The conversation was over.

She addressed the team as Schmitt translated. "She says the last humans tricked the Mernas. They betrayed their trust and generosity. They brought great pain and fear to the village. But the other humans are gone now." Xylon looked at Faybin and sighed. "Faybin trusts you. She says you are not like the other humans, you are good people. You saved her from a Garkra."

Faybin looked at Joel as Xylon spoke, smiling appreciatively.

"You may stay. For one night. Then you must leave," translated Schmitt.

Xylon held up a hand to Schmitt and addressed the humans in English. "Xylon no trust human."

Hermes, Orbit—
14:00, 8 September, 2086

Mikhail stared at the projector in horror. He reset the recording again, dragging the time back to the moment he lost contact with Diamond and Amber. He felt so helpless aboard *Hermes*; alone and removed, with no way of contacting anyone on the ground. He replayed the recording and watched again as Amber and Diamond tried to escape the aliens only to be shot by their strange weapons.

At first, Mikhail couldn't tell if Amber and Diamond were still alive. But, considering the creatures were taking Amber away, he decided to follow them with the monitor orb; at least he tried to follow them. He stared at the images again, watching in slow motion as the creatures sprinted into the forest. Their speed was phenomenal. Even through the thick forest they moved as fast as cheetahs across the open savannah. They ran so fast Mikhail couldn't keep up. After a short while, he lost them; he lost Amber.

Mikhail adjusted the control panel again, shifting the image from Base Camp and the surrounding area to the lone camera he'd left by the enormous black stone wall.

When he lost the creatures in the jungle he realized, like the Rex with the small human, the aliens were heading north. So, he took a chance. He watched the gate for several minutes, fearful he'd misjudged the situation. But eventually two creatures appeared by the huge black wall, stood before the archway and waited for it to open. Mikhail watched the projector recording closely. The image began moving as the orb was removed from its perch, remotely operated by Mikhail. At the time, he was determined to see inside the gate. But he was too bold.

The projector showed the gate sliding open, growing in size as the orb drifted closer. Mikhail caught a glimpse of Amber in the large white alien's arms, cradling her like a sleeping child. He saw her eyes flutter, as she attempted to raise her head.

She was alive.

Mikhail sighed. Although he'd watched the image multiple times, he was still relieved to know Amber lived.

Suddenly the projector image shook violently. Half the image went black while the other half was blurred. Mikhail had tried to take control of the orb but a large yellow eye appeared, staring into the camera. After a moment, the eye receded and Mikhail saw the alien's face up-close. It was hideous. It had a large and bulging cranium with a long snout, big flaring nostrils, and huge yellow eyes.

Mikhail slowed the replay speed at this point. He watched carefully as the creature's long spindly finger entered the frame, growing incredibly large in size as it approached the camera, and then the projector image dissolved to nothing.

He shook his head in disbelief.

Mikhail turned to the control panel. One of the small nodules was no longer glowing red. The camera had been shut off; not destroyed or damaged; it had been turned off.

He moved the image back to Base Camp and shifted the time back to the present. Diamond still lay unmoving on the ground.

Mikhail sat back in the chair of the control panel in silence. He felt the familiar sense of dread and fear begin to encroach. But this time he felt another, stronger urge. He felt angry. These creatures had invaded their camp, knocked out his companions, and kidnapped his friend. As the anger grew in his chest, Mikhail felt a surge of adrenaline. The feelings of fear and isolation slowly subsided.

He didn't want to be numb this time.

Unbeknownst to Mikhail, while he was engrossed at the viewing platform in the science lab, a small red light was flashing on the control console in the cockpit, signaling a message had arrived from Earth. It had been flashing for hours now, but Mikhail hadn't even entered the cockpit since the previous day. So, the little red light continued to flash on and off, and Mikhail continued to watch the projector footage, praying Diamond would wake up soon.

AWAKE

Unknown, Arcadia—
14:00, 8 September, 2086

Amber's eyes felt heavy as she forced them open, blinking rapidly in the harsh light. Her memory was as fuzzy as her vision. The last thing she could remember was being trapped inside the lifeboat and calling Mikhail for help. She blinked again, trying to focus.

Amber tried to move her arms, but couldn't. The feeling jolted her memory slightly; being entirely conscious but unable to move. Her heart began to pound as she recalled running through the forest, and flashes of blue electricity. She started to take long control breaths, trying to calm her mind so she could remember what had happened. She focused on the flashing images and feelings; the electricity, it came from a weapon, she was shot by something; she remembered screaming, no, *trying* to scream, moaning, someone else was moaning, too?

Diamond!

Suddenly she saw Diamond in her mind's eye. She saw the look on his face as he lay paralyzed on the forest floor.

What had happened to Diamond?

Amber tried to move her head to gain her bearings. It was then she realized she was not paralyzed anymore. She could move her head to scan the surrounding area. But her stomach dropped as she realized the precariousness of her situation.

Her arms, legs, and body were imbedded within a large structure, made from some form of material she had never seen before. It was soft and gelatinous, molding to the shape of her body, but firmly holding her in place. The entire room was white and sterile, constructed from some sort of rough white metal and illuminated by a harsh glow emanating from the roof. Amber closed her eyes and continued to take slow controlled breaths.

To her right, she heard a soft rustling sound, like leaves blowing gently in the wind. After a brief silence, a shadow moved in her peripheral vision. She felt her chest tighten. The shadow moved again, this time on her left side. She caught a glimpse of something, it was soft and purple in color.

Purple.

More memories returned; the two aliens, Purple and Cockatoo. The invasion, the lifeboat, the trees; everything came flooding back. Amber felt her breathing increase again, all she could hear was her own long and heavy breaths.

Purple finally stepped into Amber's field of vision. She was truly a bizarre creature; part-human, part-bird, and part-something else. The greyish feathers which covered most of her body were small and thick, giving the impression of a fur coat. The coloring was darker near her shins, forearms, neck, and face. The longer purple feathers on her elbows, tail, and head were thicker and more stylish in comparison.

Despite their feathery coverings, these creatures were definitely not birds. They didn't have beaks or wings; instead they had elongated reptilian muzzles with two rows of sharp teeth and strong arms capable of picking up and manipulating objects.

As Purple moved around the edges of the white room she purred ominously to herself, sending chills down Amber's spine. She paid no attention to Amber as she began to touch seemingly invisible devices set into the rock wall. Amber contemplated trying to speak, to call for help, or demand to be released. But she knew it was pointless.

The white light illuminating the room changed abruptly to a soft yellow, bathing Amber in a beautiful golden glow. She could hear Purple still shuffling around the room, out of sight. She could also hear another foreign sound begin to build in intensity. Purple returned to Amber's field of vision and stopped at the front of the room. For the first time, Purple made eye contact with Amber, staring at her through cold emotionless eyes. Amber felt exposed and vulnerable.

The foreign sound began to whirr and build. Something was happening, something Amber couldn't see. She felt her blood run cold as Purple continued to stare at her. Her eyes were definitely reptilian; they were large and yellow with thin ovular pupils. Soulless.

The sound began to grow in volume and pitch. Amber felt the gelatinous table beneath her start to vibrate from the soundwaves. Her heart was pounding now. Sweat began to pour down her forehead. Her stomach twisted and turned. She was going to be sick.

Purple continued to stare at Amber.

The sound continued to increase.

The table vibrated more intensely.

Amber could feel every cell in her body shaking violently. She couldn't hold it in any longer.

"*Ahhhhhhhh!!!*" Amber screamed at the top of her lungs. It was as though the whirring sound in the room amplified her scream tenfold. Amber heard her own voice resonating in her ear as a deafening roar. She cut herself off quickly.

It was then she noticed Purple. This reptilian-bird woman was staring at her through cold yellow eyes, with jaws partially agape, and the corners of her mouth turned slightly upward.

She was smiling at Amber.

Purple touched the white wall and suddenly the intense sound and vibration began to subside, slowly drifting back into obscurity. Once the room was silent again, Purple approached Amber, still smiling. She placed her claws on the edge of the gelatinous table and the whole thing, with Amber still on it, began to slide away from the center of the room through a large opening in the rear.

Amber's face was assaulted by bright sunlight as they exited the white stone room. Over her head she saw the familiar sights of the jungle; leaves, branches, vines, and flowers. She could smell the earthiness of the leaf litter and for the briefest moment she felt calm.

But they weren't in the jungle anymore.

It took a moment for Amber to understand what she was seeing, to realize where she was. They were surrounded by trees, but they weren't normal trees. Every single plant they passed had been manipulated in such a way it formed a purposefully molded structure, ranging from only a few meters high, all the way to the canopy. The structures were huge and interwoven with their neighbors. Higher structures were connected to each other via long bridges woven together by thick living vines.

Alien creatures could be seen inside the structures, roaming up and down the alleys between the trees and along the vine-bridges. Each creature had the same general characteristics of the aliens Amber had already seen; fur-like feathers on their bodies, long crests on their heads, mouthfuls of sharp menacing teeth, and muscular legs with huge sickle-like claws. Some were slightly smaller with drabber coloring, females, while others were larger with beautiful ornamental head and tail feathers, males.

As Purple pushed Amber through the dense tree-buildings, still imbedded within the gelatinous table, she felt the other aliens' attention drawn to her. They stopped what they were doing and stared as she passed, like a scientific specimen being displayed on Main Street. Some creatures squawked and sneered, others snapped aggressively. Amber felt her heart rate increase again. She could practically feel the creatures salivating as she passed.

An intense buzzing sound whizzed past Amber's head; she could feel the wind from something moving quickly. After a moment she saw an enormous beetle. It flew through the tree-buildings with purpose. Within moments, several more beetles shot past, all heading in the same direction.

Purple rounded a huge hollowed tree with a trunk the size of a small house. An archway had been carved through the base of the trunk, creating a passageway deeper into the community. It was then Amber realized why the insects were making their way through the aliens' forest-home.

Beyond the huge hollowed tree-trunk, a flowing canal led to a beautiful garden filled with enormous and colorful flowers. Some flower buds were the size of cars, allowing the hefty beetles and other flying insects to land on the outstretched petals with ease. The bugs fed happily on the enormous plants. The canal pooled in the center of the garden where jets of water spurted into the sky every so often, showering the flowers and beetles in a soft mist.

One of the smaller, plain-looking aliens was wandering through a grove of flower stems as thick as tree-trunks. Sitting on top of the long stems were two large pink fleshy petals, connected in the middle by a seam. The edge of each petal was lined with a series of green spines, giving the plant a menacing appearance. The plain-looking alien was encouraging a group of large dragonfly-esque insects toward the menacing flowers. Three dragonflies landed on one flower and four landed on another. Without warning, the two petals of both flowers snapped shut like a mouse trap. The green spines interlocked perfectly, snaring the dragonflies inside. The plain-looking alien tapped the base of the stem, and moved toward the next large plant.

There was an entire field of enormous flytrap flowers. Some were closed tightly, others remained open and inviting for more insect prey.

The plain-looking alien turned its attention to one of the closed traps; leaping onto the outside of the petals it began gently massaging the space beneath the interlocking spines. The flytrap opened slowly, blooming at the command of the alien. Inside were two dead beetles. They were intact but entirely immobile. The alien lifted one from the trap and dropped it to the ground. It then leaped seamlessly back to the ground and the trap closed again. This time the trap-flower changed color, shifting to a pale grey-green.

Amber stared at the alien, holding its beetle prize, utterly puzzled by its behavior.

As if in response, the alien opened its jaws and clamped down on the dead insect. Even from a distance, Amber could hear the sickening crunch of the beetle's hard exoskeleton cracking as the alien feasted.

Amber turned her head away in disgust.

Purple continued to push Amber through the trees. Before long, Amber saw something large and black rising overhead. A huge shadow fell over her; the wall. It was a ten-meter-high black stone wall which ran as far as the eye could see. Several aliens hovered by a smaller section where a slab of rock was inset against the larger wall.

As Purple approached, the aliens nearby snapped to attention and suddenly the smaller slab began to recede inside the larger wall. From up-close, Amber could see the gate clearly. It was black stone, but polished like jewelry. She had seen this stone before. Obsidian; volcanic glass.

Purple began to push Amber through the new opening when one of the guards stopped them and examined Amber. The guard walked up to her cautiously. She followed it with her gaze, terrified of what it might do next.

Is this it?

Am I being served to the guards as their afternoon meal?

As Amber's head moved the guard shrieked in fright, squawking aggressively in her face. Purple snapped at the guard but it snarled at her in return. It came closer to Amber, bringing itself face to face with the small and fragile woman. Amber could feel its hot breath on her cheek, she could see its rough pebbly skin.

She wanted to scream again.

Purple pushed the guard away from Amber, defensively. It snarled again but Purple ignored it this time.

For a moment Amber felt grateful, as though Purple was protecting her.

Then Purple turned to Amber and raised her left arm. She balled her fist and aimed the small discs in Amber's direction. The light began to glow blue.

Shit.

Merna Village, Arcadia—
17:30, 8 September, 2086

As the sun started to drift toward the nearby mountains, long shadows fell across the Merna village. The air was still warm, but the fading sun brought with it a cool breeze and some reprieve from the humidity. After allowing the humans one night in the village to rest, Xylon had sent them with Schmitt to a relatively removed section of the settlement.

Schmitt had explained the Mernas were a superstitious people. They allowed him to stay with them because he could help them build tools, but he was forbidden from going to certain areas unescorted. He was not allowed to share the villagers' food or use the communal bonfire; he was generally segregated from the rest of the community.

Schmitt began to build a smaller fire in his little camp. Opposite him, Joel and Veronica sat on the soft grass quietly, staring into the growing flames as the German expertly built a fire using nothing more than two stones and some dried leaves. To Schmitt's left sat Charles, and to his right was Grey.

The growing light from the small fire danced and crackled across the old man's face as he stared vacantly into the flames. His eyes were weathered and sunken, but his gaze was alert. His clothes were ragged and filthy, his hair was grey and shaggy, and the bottom half of his face was covered with a wispy grey beard. His skin bore obvious marks of hardship; bruises, scars, and sores.

"So, are you here to rescue me?" asked Schmitt, doubtfully.

Joel and Veronica exchanged glances.

"Yes. Well, I mean, we did come to find your crew. But we also came to finish what you started. You know, to figure out if Arcadia can be colonized," said Joel.

The old man's eyes narrowed. He seemed to roll the words over in his mind, trying to make sense of them. "So, she *is* dead."

"What? Who's dead?" asked Joel.

The old man sighed heavily. "Our team included some of the greatest scientific minds of our time, but we were no match for this place. . . ." He trailed off as he poked at the campfire absentmindedly.

"Yeah, we know about you and your team. We've seen your files. You're Dr. Schmitt, the German exobiologist."

Schmitt looked sideways to Joel and shook his head sadly. "No. You are mistaking me for my wife."

"Oh," said Joel, feeling a little embarrassed.

Veronica leaned forward. "*Erika* Schmitt is the exobiologist. *Eckhart* Schmitt is an anthropologist."

Joel saw the concern on Veronica's face and recalled the last time she had identified Erika Schmitt, from the *Atlas* flight recorder.

Schmitt's eyes glistened as they held back tears. "But Erika was more than just a member of the crew. She was part of the original team that found Arcadia. She spearheaded the whole research project. It was only by her insistence they invited me. She convinced them if we did encounter civilized life we'd need an anthropologist, a cultural expert, to help communicate. I speak eighteen languages, well, nineteen if you include the local Merna dialect."

"Exobiologist," repeated Charles. "Interesting the first time around they send an expert on life outside of earth and this time they decide to send a *paleozoologist*. Now why would Irwin decide to send someone like Dr. Carter here, who specializes in *extinct* plants and animals?" Charles stared at Grey as he spoke.

Schmitt snapped up before Grey had a chance to respond. "You are Dr. Joel Carter? The Australian paleozoologist?"

"Yeah, sorry, we never actually introduced ourselves—"

Schmitt cut him off. "Then they must have received our message!" He jumped to his feet with excitement before sitting down again quickly, hunching over. "This is wonderful news. You see, Erika and I were separated almost two months after we arrived. She returned to the ship with one of the other crew members to send a message to the ISA, to update them on our progress so far, and tell them we found intelligent life."

"The Mernas," said Joel confidently.

Schmitt laughed. "The Mernas are an industrious people, yes. But they are simple hunter-gatherers." He paused, recognizing the look of confusion on the others' faces. "You have not seen them yet, have you?"

"Seen what?"

"On Earth, early humans once covered themselves in the skins of fearsome predators; tigers, wolves, bears. This was for warmth and camouflage, but it was also a sign of strength to their enemies. Now, have you noticed how the Mernas dress themselves?"

Joel thought back to the first time they saw Faybin, mistaking her for a beakless bird in her robe and mask. "They're covered in feathers."

"Precisely," said Schmitt, touching his nose.

Charles scoffed. "So, Mernas are afraid of birds?"

Schmitt shook his head. "I know you have not been here long, but have you seen any birds on this planet?"

Charles frowned. "No. Now that you mention it."

Schmitt nodded knowingly. He lowered his voice again. "There are no avian-like species on Arcadia; at least not the kind we are familiar with. But there is something else that has feathers. Something fearsome and cunning, something from your worst nightmares."

"What the hell is it?" asked Veronica with a hint of concern.

"The Mernas call them, *Adras.*" He whispered the word as though it were poison seeping from his lips.

Charles laughed. "Adra? That doesn't sound very scary?"

"Shh!" demanded Schmitt; he glanced over his shoulder, ensuring no Mernas were nearby. "You do not speak their name aloud inside the village. It is bad luck."

"You superstitious, Schmitt?" sneered Charles.

Schmitt narrowed his eyes. "You would be, too, if you had seen what I have seen."

Joel interrupted their exchange. "Okay, so there's some sort of intelligent feathery alien out there we haven't seen yet. And your wife sent a message to the ISA to warn them about these *Adras.* I still don't get it? Irwin told us no one on Earth ever heard from your team. So, what makes you think they did?"

"Erika's message must have arrived. Because they sent you." Schmitt stared intently at Joel.

"I still don't—"

"Your ship," said Grey, finally joining the conversation. "It was the *Atlas*, wasn't it?"

Schmitt shifted his attention to Grey. "Yes, I imagine you may have seen it in orbit? Did you find anything there? Any signs of my friends?"

Joel and Veronica looked at each other once more.

"We did," said Veronica, avoiding eye contact with the old German. "We didn't find much. But we did find bodies. A woman and a man."

"Bodies? On the ship?" he asked in disbelief.

Grey nodded. "It looked like someone fired a laser on board, shot a hole right through the ship's hull. The man died from exposure, but the woman took a laser blast to the chest."

The color drained from Schmitt's face. He leaned back on his haunches, his expression flat.

No one spoke for a moment.

After several minutes, Schmitt collected himself. His eyes were fixed on the fire. "As I'm sure you know, there were seven of us originally. In addition to my wife and I, there was Yoshi Kato, our medic; Zoe Martinez, our geologist, and Lachlan Armstrong, our chemist; we made up the research team. Then there was Guy Jackson and Tom Gilmore, our ex-SAS pilots. We were so excited when we arrived; the conditions for complex life were perfect, exactly as we had hoped. We spent weeks collecting samples and cataloguing plant and animal life. The similarities between Earthen and Arcadian life was phenomenal." Schmitt poked at the fire. His eyes glazed over slightly, but his tone remained flat and unemotional.

"We found the Mernas in the jungle, or I guess they found us. They were so curious and welcoming, inviting us into their home, treating us like royalty. They thought we were gods." He touched a scar on his cheek absentmindedly.

"But these *things* aren't afraid of the Mernas. They came right into the village, at night, in the middle of a huge storm. We didn't know we were under attack until it was too late. They didn't care about the Mernas, they came for us. By the time it was over Lachlan, Yoshi, and Zoe were gone. The following morning, Guy took Erika back to *Atlas*, to report to the ISA while Tom and I sought help from the Merna warriors to find the others. That was a long time ago."

"What happened after that?" asked Veronica. "What happened to make the Mernas hate humans so much?"

Schmitt's demeanor turned sour. "Arcadia is a very special place. It is truly unspoiled. There are rich deposits of precious stones and metals, fossil fuels, and other natural resources. The Mernas have a temple near the village which houses a precious stone; an enormous diamond, the size of a softball.

Charles raised an eyebrow. "A diamond?"

"Yes. The Mernas call it the *Light stone* and they worship it like a holy idol. They say it protects them from the Garkras, it brings them strength and power. The morning after the attack, after Erika and Guy had already left, the Mernas realized the stone was missing. They blamed us for their missing stone and imprisoned Tom and I."

The group fell silent for a moment.

"So, where is this Tom character now?" asked Charles.

Schmitt looked at Charles, narrowing his eyes. "I'll show you."

○ ○ ○ • ○ ○ ○

Schmitt led the group away from the central square of the village, through the various small teardrop huts, toward the darkness of the encroaching jungle. Once they reached the edge of the village proper, a few meters away from the tree line, Schmitt stopped suddenly. He brought the fiery torch in his hand close to the ground, illuminating the earth beneath his feet. Imbedded within the dirt was a large stone slab, half buried, with a symbol etched into it; an X enclosed in a square, overlaid with two vertical bars and two horizontal bars.

Schmitt moved the torch, lighting the space just beyond the stone. A wooden lattice structure had been laid across an enormous pit. The bars crisscrossed each other, forming a thick grid. At each corner were more flat stones, engraved with the same symbol as the one in front of them. The stones were huge and heavy.

"What is this place?" asked Joel.

Charles scowled. "It's a prison."

Schmitt leaned over the pit, holding the torch high so the light penetrated the darkness below. "Are you awake?" he called into the hole.

From the darkened pit they could hear a soft shuffling, followed by a loud sigh and a grunt. A deep hollow voice resonated from the pit, "What do you want?"

Schmitt knelt on the ground again, bringing the torch as close as he could to the grate. The orange light filtered weakly into the hole. Inside was a man; his face was gaunt and covered in filth and grime, and pockets of mud were crusted to his long hair and thick beard. A large scar could be seen on his forehead, its edges tinged pink and yellow.

"Allow me to introduce Tom Gilmore, diamond thief extraordinaire," said Schmitt dryly.

"My God," breathed Joel.

Inside the pit, Tom squinted in the firelight; his eyes were red and bloodshot. A long thick branch was stretched along his neck and shoulders and affixed to each of his outstretched wrists; he was virtually crucified.

"What happened to him?" asked Charles, keeping his eyes fixed on Tom.

Tom looked up at the sound of Charles's voice.

Schmitt left the torch on the ground and pushed to his feet, brushing dirt from his pants. "As it turns out, Tom and Guy decided to steal the *Light stone*. When the Mernas found out they imprisoned us, saying we had soiled their sacred territory. They accused us of being spies sent by the Adras."

Joel stared into the hole, to the face of the man inside. "That's why the Mernas don't trust humans."

"If they imprisoned both of you, why are you out here and he's in there?" asked Charles with a hint of skepticism.

Schmitt stared intently at Tom, his eyes filled with hate. "Because when I realized what they had done, I helped the Mernas get their stone back."

PRISON

Cave, Arcadia—17:30, 8 September, 2086

Amber's eyes stung. She blinked heavily, trying to clear her vision. She was somewhere dark. She could feel the cold hard ground beneath her head and arms, and there was a damp earthiness in the air; she was inside a cave.

Amber rolled slightly so she lay on her back; her muscles felt stiff and weak. She blinked again, her eyes finally starting to focus. She could just make out the dips and grooves of the limestone above her head. She followed the roof with her eyes, watching it curve downward in all directions.

Something grunted loudly in her ear.

Amber jumped at the unfamiliar sound. Dozens of faces were gazing wide-eyed at her. She jumped back again, scrambling along the cold ground. Small humanoid creatures stared back at her. She rubbed her eyes, letting her night vision adjust. Her confusion grew as the small humanoids took shape. They were indeed human-like, but shorter and with much larger mouths and eyes. Their skin was brown but their hair was long and blond.

Amber wiped cold sweat from her forehead. She squinted at the faces; each small humanoid wore some sort of brace around their necks, something smooth and reflective like jewelry, but soft and malleable. The humanoids seemed curious but unperturbed by her presence.

A few feet away, Amber could see a soft translucent glow coming from a ring of tall thin streaks of a blue-white light which stretched from the dirt floor ten feet into the air. The lights encircled Amber and the small humanoids, creating an enclosed space roughly the size of a two-car garage; it was a cage.

Suddenly the entire cave began to shake and the ground vibrated beneath their feet. The small humanoids shrieked like monkeys as they skittered to the back wall where a small portion of rock met the translucent streaks of light. Once the crowd had dispersed Amber could see past the light bars to the rest of the cave. More circles of light appeared in the distance. She counted a dozen structures with two lines of cages running parallel between the back wall and a wide archway at the front leading up a large stone ramp. From her vantage point she couldn't see much, but she could tell there was a soft natural light at the top of the ramp.

Amber moved closer to the bars to see the ramp better. As she approached she could feel warmth emanating from the blue-white light. A dark shadow cut through the natural light at the top of the ramp as something large made its way into the cavern. Above their heads came a heavy grinding sound and the whole area was bathed in natural light. A dozen square holes had been cut into the rocky slope of the roof, one over each enclosure. The light was soft but bright compared to the darkness of the cave; Amber guessed it must be dusk. With the area bathed in natural light, she could see more clearly. She was indeed inside a cave, but it was not a natural formation. It had been carved from the limestone with precision. Each cage held dozens of small humanoids who cried and howled as the roof holes opened.

Then she saw it.

At the bottom of the ramp standing over two stories tall was the muscular body of what she could only describe as a dinosaur. Like the creature that had attacked their camp, it was huge. But this one was different. Its jaws were shorter and rounded, its arms were tiny and useless, and it did not have a sail running down the length of its back.

Amber froze and closed her eyes, praying this was all some terrible dream. Opening her eyes again, she saw the red and gold creature standing tall on two legs; she could hear its deep breathing, and she felt the earth tremble as it moved.

This was no dream.

The creature was remarkable. It was an incredible size, with thick skin and enormous jaws designed for crushing bone and tearing flesh. Its head was large with small beady eyes, suggesting poor eyesight. However, its nostrils were wide and perfect for sniffing out prey. Its arms were small compared to the rest of its body, but its legs were enormous and muscular, suggesting it was fast. As the creature moved forward, the muscles on its legs rippled. Amber saw the long thick tail stretched behind the beast which acted as a counterbalance to its immense size.

Although it was absurd, Amber couldn't dispute the similarities between the creature standing in front of her and a long-extinct animal from Earth; a Tyrannosaurus Rex.

As the enormous beast neared her cage, Amber caught a glimpse of something large resting on its back. It moved again and Amber saw a smaller alien creature standing on the dinosaur's back in what she could only describe as a saddle.

Amber's mind spun as she tried to grasp the situation. The Rex edged closer. As she stared at the smaller alien sitting on the Rex's back she had a sudden feeling of familiarity. It was mostly white with a bright yellow crest; Cockatoo.

The Rex continued walking, heading straight for her cage. Amber realized she was sitting in the open, and it dawned on her why the small humanoids had scrambled to the back wall. She quickly crawled back, joining the others. The earth shook as the beast approached her enclosure. It stopped in front of her cage, moving its enormous body and head over the top of the streaks of blue-white light. Then, with incredible speed and agility, Cockatoo leapt from the Rex's back into the cage.

The Rex stood perfectly still, lifeless and mechanical.

Amber frowned; around its neck hung a thin glistening ring, a collar, made from the same material as the one worn by the small humanoids. Cockatoo stood for a moment and scanned over the faces in the crowd. His eyes fell on Amber and her heart jumped into her throat.

From within the crowd a female moved forward. Unlike the others, she was not afraid, walking toward Cockatoo with purpose. Amber watched carefully as Cockatoo turned his attention to the woman. She was much taller than the others, with soft tanned skin and dark brown hair.

The woman knelt before Cockatoo in a submissive position. She sat patiently closing her eyes, but listening intently. Cockatoo placed his clawed hand on her shoulder and closed his eyes.

After several minutes, the woman stood up, brushed herself off and returned to the group, casting a sideways glance to Amber. Cockatoo stood for another moment, staring directly at Amber before it sprang into the air and landed on the Rex's back with finesse. The Rex snapped to life and trudged back to the ramp into the fading daylight above. The light holes in the roof were closed again and the cave was returned to near-darkness.

Amber quickly moved to the taller woman. She stopped in her tracks; the woman was not like the others.

"Hablas español?" asked the woman curiously.

"You speak Spanish?" Amber searched her memory, trying to recall a Spanish crewmember from the first mission profile.

The woman half-smiled. "You speak English," she said with a heavy Latino accent.

Amber's mind clicked. She could see the woman's face in her mind, only her hair was shorter and styled, her face and clothes were clean, and she was smiling. "Zoe Martinez? The Argentinian geologist?"

The woman was unnervingly calm. "Correct."

Amber frowned. "What is this place? And what are those things?"

Zoe smiled. "That was an Adra. And we are inside an Adra holding cave. We have much to discuss, my friend."

○ ○ ○ ● ○ ○ ○

Amber and Zoe sat away from the small humanoids who had dispersed within the cage. They leaned against the back wall; Amber could feel the cold dampness of the limestone through her clothing.

"Adras?" repeated Amber.

"It is the name given to them by the Mernas." Zoe gestured to the small humanoids inside the cave.

"So, these *Adras* showed up to the *Mernas'* village, kidnapped you, and imprisoned you here? And you haven't seen anyone from your team since?" Amber shook her head in disbelief.

Zoe's gaze darted away, staring down the corridor toward one of the other cages. For a brief moment, Amber spotted a sadness in her eyes.

Zoe sighed heavily. "Not quite. Shortly after they brought me here, they brought another human to the cave; Yoshi, my crewmate. I thought he'd escaped the attack at the village, but I guess I was wrong. A Denkra carried him inside its mouth and put him in another cage on his own, down there near the entrance." She pointed to the giant ramp.

"Denkra?" repeated Amber.

"Sorry, I forget you are new here. There are two large carnivorous species on this continent; one looks like a giant upright crocodile, with long arms and a sail on its back."

"That's the creature that attacked our camp," interrupted Amber.

Zoe nodded. "They live in the forest and the Mernas call them Garkra which roughly means 'sharp claw.' Then there's the golden-red creatures with tiny arms and rounded jaws who walk around with Adras on their backs. The Mernas call them Denkras, which means 'sharp tooth.'"

"Like the thing that was in here before?"

"Precisely. When the Denkra brought Yoshi here I tried calling to him, but he couldn't hear me. He seemed disorientated, like he did not know where he was or what was happening. He did not even know I was here. Even from a distance I could see he was not well. He would not eat or drink. I started calling to the Adras when they came to feed us, I begged them to help him. Eventually he stopped moving altogether."

Zoe sat upright, her mood becoming serious. "Then the strangest thing happened. On the seventh day, when they came to feed him, they saw he was not moving at all. So, they came to my cage and I screamed at them to let me help him, but they just stared at me. I started crying, and I can't explain it, but I heard a voice in my head ask how to help him. I did not know what to make of it, so I replied with my thoughts. The Adras started chirping to each other very excited and then they took him away. I have not seen him since."

"I don't understand?"

"I do not really understand either. I could hear them speaking, but not with my ears; they were speaking in my mind. I know it sounds crazy. But I swear to you, I heard a voice in my head, in clear Spanish, ask me how to help him."

"Telepathy?" asked Amber, shaking her head in disbelief.

Zoe shrugged.

Amber glanced to the opposite side of the cage, to the spot where Zoe interacted with Cockatoo. "Was he speaking to you before? Communicating with you the same way?"

Zoe followed Amber's gaze. "Yes. They have spoken to me several times since then."

"So, what did he want?"

Zoe bit her lip, as though unsure if she should continue. "He was asking about you."

Light Stone

Merna Village, Arcadia—
05:00, 9 September, 2086

Tom slept awkwardly inside the damp pit, his arms still outstretched like a giant letter "T." He sat with his back against the earth, resting atop a pile of dried leaves and grasses. He leant his head against the wall, dozing lightly. Tom couldn't remember the last time he'd had a proper night's sleep, or the last time he felt truly rested. It was impossible to get comfortable in the hole with his arms restrained. But tonight, it was more than just discomfort that kept Tom awake. He couldn't stop thinking about the new humans and what it meant for him.

A sharp hiss interrupted his train of thought.

"*Psst.*"

Tom opened his eyes. It was dark; light from the waxing moon filtered through the lattice branches of his cage. He blinked several times, allowing his night vision to develop. Slowly, the light became more vibrant; he could see a shadow beyond the bars.

Tom made to speak.

"Shh!" whispered the figure.

Tom closed his mouth. The shadowy figure moved away from the grate. Outside, he could hear a shuffling sound, footsteps moving around the edge of the pit. He could hear scraping as one of the huge rocks which pinned the grate into place was rolled away.

Tom cleared his throat. "What are you doing?"

"*Shh!*" repeated the shadowy figure.

The shuffling sounds continued. Tom awkwardly pushed to his feet. He had to be careful not to fall over; it was hell trying to stand without the use of his arms. Once he was upright, he stepped closer to the front of the pit, trying to see the face of the mysterious visitor.

Suddenly the grate was lifted from its perch and thrown clear. Moonlight filled the hole as a thick tangle of dried knotted vines was thrown inside.

Tom raised an eyebrow. "I don't know how you expect me to—"

The shadowy figure quickly rappelled backward down the vine-rope. He extracted a serrated knife from his belt and stepped into the moonlight.

Tom froze at the sight of the knife.

○ ○ ○ ● ○ ○ ○

Joel awoke to the sounds of children's laughter. For a moment, in his semi-conscious state, he was reminded of his own childhood; laughing and playing with his best friend, Amber. It had been over thirty-six hours since he'd seen her. He tried to convince himself she was safe inside the lifeboat. She had plenty of food and water, the boat was extremely well camouflaged, and she had a Marine there to protect her. But something still nagged at the back of his mind. Something told him he had to get back there.

Joel stepped into the soft morning light and stretched his aching muscles. He saw Veronica and Schmitt by the small campfire, preparing breakfast. At least now they knew the whereabouts of some of the *Atlas* crew; two deceased, one incarcerated, and one alive. That still left three unknowns, but Joel didn't have time to think about the remaining crew. Right now he needed a plan to get back to Base Camp.

Joel stared at Schmitt as he crouched by the fire with Veronica. Schmitt knew the Mernas, he knew the language and their customs. But even with the German's help, Joel wasn't convinced they would be able to persuade Xylon and the elders to release Tom into their custody.

They needed more.

Joel approached the fire and noticed a small girl sitting beside Schmitt.

Joel eyed the little girl. "Morning. Who do we have here?"

"This little lady is Veyha." Schmitt gestured to the small girl who turned away shyly. For the first time since they had met him Schmitt was smiling.

"She speaks English," said Veronica, standing over the fire, clearly impressed.

"Is that so?" said Joel, turning to Schmitt.

The old anthropologist couldn't hide his pride. "Yes, I have been teaching the Merna English for some time now. The children have a little trouble speaking the words, and they use a fairly simple syntax, but they understand a lot after only a few months."

Joel saw the girl was staring at him through intense eyes. He recognized her. It was the same child who had been watching the group so closely when they first arrived. If the children knew English they might be able to help the humans argue their case, maybe gain sympathy with the elders?

"Hi, Veyha. My name's Joel," he said playfully.

The girl stood and eyed Joel up and down, warily. "You, sky people?"

Joel frowned. "Um, I don't think so?" He turned to Schmitt. "What are sky people?"

Schmitt shrugged. "For lack of a better translation, they are Gods, supreme beings who will come from the sky and bring salvation to the Mernas. They are remarkably similar to humans in that respect, believing in religious folklore and superstition."

Joel bowed his head modestly. "I'm sorry, kiddo. We aren't sky people."

The girl was cute but Joel doubted she'd be very useful in convincing the elders. He needed someone else, someone older, with more sway in the community. Joel looked across to the village square; it was barely daylight but most of the Mernas were already awake and going about their daily lives. As Joel made eye contact with various Mernas in the square, they promptly turned their noses up or glowered disapprovingly. He wasn't going to find many friends here.

"So, captain Vee," said Joel, addressing Veronica. "Have you given any thought to how we convince the Mernas to let us take that Tom guy with us when we leave?"

Veronica leaned over the glowing embers, watching a small parcel of root vegetables wrapped in a large broadleaf. "We were just discussing our options. From what Eckhart knows about the Mernas, they're not going to just let us walk away without a dispute. But if we can get Faybin on our side, convince her we are only here to take Tom away, we might have a chance."

Schmitt nodded in agreement. "As I said before, the Mernas are quite superstitious. We should be able to sell your arrival as a positive omen; the warrior humans have come to save the Mernas from the evil trickster.

Faybin already believes you were sent here by the sky people so it shouldn't be too difficult to extend the myth."

Joel nodded. "Sounds like a plan. Well, shouldn't we get moving then? Where is she? No point wasting time sitting around."

Veronica looked up from the fire; her eyes were soft and empathetic. "You know she's okay," she said in a soft nurturing tone. Despite the fact Veronica was almost ten years younger than Joel, she played the role of team-mother surprisingly well.

Joel laughed dryly, trying to brush off the idea he was hurting. "Who? Amber? Yeah, I know. I'm not worried. Do I look worried?" He forced his trademark cheesy grin. "C'mon, where are the others?"

While his face was all smiles, Veronica could see the worry behind his proud grey eyes. She shrugged. "Charles left to fetch firewood before dawn. And I don't know about Grey; was he still asleep when you left?"

Joel frowned. "When I left? I thought he was meant to be on watch? He wasn't here when you came out?"

Veronica frowned. "No, I've not seen him since last night."

In the distance an unfamiliar sound cut through the surrounding jungle. A loud twang followed by a muffled explosion. Veyha clutched Schmitt's arm tightly.

Veronica jumped to her feet and placed a hand on her holster. "Was that a laser blast? Maybe it was Amber? Or Diamond?"

Joel shook his head. "No."

There was a loud commotion in the bushes on the opposite side of the village square, shouts and screams from Merna men and women in the distance.

"What's happening?" asked Schmitt.

Suddenly a group of infuriated Mernas emerged from the trees, led by Faybin. They paused momentarily in the square, looking around the area angrily. When Faybin's gaze fell on Joel and the others her face hardened. Joel could feel her eyes burning through him. The angry mob charged toward the small group with purpose.

Faybin pointed her spear aggressively at Joel, shoving it in his face. "Faybin trust! You betray!" she cursed.

Joel felt the sharp point of the stone blade pressed firmly against his cheek. He held his hands up instinctively. "Woah! Wait! What did we do?"

"*Light stone,*" she breathed.

Two large Merna men took each of Joel's arms, pinning them behind his back; at the same time two large Merna women took Veronica's arms. The pair were pushed to the ground, forced to kneel before Faybin.

Schmitt stepped forward and began speaking Mernaese to Faybin, who still had a spear pointed at Joel's face. She responded quickly, pointing angrily at Joel and back toward the jungle path.

Schmitt shook his head in disbelief. "Oh, mein Gott. The *Light stone* has been stolen."

"Fucking Charles," snapped Joel. He tried to struggle against the Mernas who held his arms; they were strong for their size.

"We don't know it was him," protested Veronica.

Joel scoffed. "I knew he was a scumbag! Did you see the look on his face when Schmitt said it was a giant diamond? He was practically salivating."

Veronica shook her head. "I don't understand. How would he even know where it was?"

Schmitt sighed heavily. "Because he had help. It is my fault. I should never have shown you where Tom was being held."

Joel turned his attention to Faybin; her spear was still aimed aggressively in his direction. "Faybin, if Charles stole your stone then he betrayed us, too. We can help you find him."

Faybin shook her head angrily. "No! Lie!" She thrust her spear against the side of Joel's cheek, piercing the skin. Small droplets of blood trickled down his chin, staining his facial hair. But Joel didn't flinch.

"Please, let us help you," said Joel, keeping his voice even.

After a moment the harsh glare in Faybin's eyes softened. She relaxed the grip on her spear and paused, unsure how to proceed. After a moment she nodded to the four Mernas who were holding Joel and Veronica. "Xylon."

The two males holding Joel's arms hoisted him to his feet while the two women lifted Veronica. Schmitt followed, unguarded. Faybin led them through the network of huts until they came to one twice the size of any other. The entrance was decorated with beautiful flowers and feathers, woven together to form a circular wreath around the opening. Faybin halted before the flowery doorway and held up a hand to stop the others behind her. She signaled for the guards to release Joel and Veronica and motioned for them to enter.

Inside was dark. A tiny hearth sat in the center of the open space, giving the room a warm orange glow. Smoke from the hearth drifted up into the ceiling of the small hut, exiting via a little opening in the roof's tapered tip. Sitting on the opposite side of the fire-pit was the small and frail figure of Xylon. She prodded at the hearth, churning up the black coals, mixing them with the fiery embers.

Faybin whispered in Xylon's ear then took a seat beside her and motioned for the humans to sit. Schmitt, Veronica, and Joel obeyed. They sat in silence for a moment.

Xylon's face was hard. She stared at Joel and Veronica through angry eyes. She didn't say anything; she didn't need to say anything. Joel could tell she was filled with hate. The Mernas already distrusted humans. He could only imagine what they thought of them now.

Finally, Xylon spoke. She directed her comments to Joel and Veronica while Schmitt translated.

"She says she is very disappointed. The elders told her not to give humans another chance. Now they are being punished for her mistake."

Joel made to speak but Schmitt placed a hand on his shoulder, allowing Xylon to continue.

"She says you are to be sacrificed for your betrayal. Your presence in the village has clearly angered their gods and they require a blood sacrifice to seek forgiveness."

"What?" exclaimed Veronica. "They can't do that! You can't punish us for something they did! We only came here to take the other humans home; we were betrayed, too!"

Joel remained quiet, deep in thought, trying to measure their situation. The game had changed. They were never going to convince the Mernas they were sent by the gods to save them from the devil. They had brought the devil with them and, as far as the Mernas were concerned, they had lied their way into the village in order to steal their most sacred possession.

Xylon stared hard at Joel and Veronica. Her eyes locked with Joel's. For several moments she stared at him, judging him.

"She'll never trust us," said Joel flatly. "And why should she? We've done nothing to earn their trust. All we've done is proven humans are evil."

Xylon nodded her head quietly, understanding Joel's sentiment.

Joel addressed Xylon directly. "I'm sorry. I'm sorry for what our people have done to yours. We don't deserve your forgiveness, or your trust, but I *beg* you to give us a chance. We know the men who have betrayed you, we know where they are going and we can help you find them."

Xylon sat in silence. Unconvinced.

Veronica saw the firmness in Xylon's conviction. Joel was right, the Mernas had no reason to trust humans. They needed leverage.

Veronica's soft voice broke the silence. "Let Joel go. Send him to bring them back. Schmitt and I will stay here as insurance."

Xylon finally showed signs of wavering. She looked around the room, rolling the idea in her head. After a moment she snapped something at Veronica.

"She wants to know what happens to us if they fail; their God demands blood," said Schmitt.

Veronica bowed her head, still addressing Xylon. "If the others fail, then you have your sacrifice."

"What? Are you crazy?" exclaimed Joel.

Veronica turned to Joel; her face was stoic and calm. "We have nothing to offer the Mernas but our own lives."

Schmitt bowed his head. "She is right. Their laws require sacrifice. Otherwise they will never let you leave."

Joel turned back to Xylon. He rubbed his forehead, trying to think of an alternative option. Surely there was something else they could do? Something they could give the Mernas to prove themselves?

Veronica touched his arm gently. "It's okay."

Joel closed his eyes and nodded reluctantly, acknowledging the terms.

He opened his eyes and frowned at Xylon as another thought struck. "And if we capture them and return the stone? What do we get?"

From behind the group a deep gruff voice joined the conversation. "They help us find the remaining humans."

Everyone turned to see the shadowy figure of Lieutenant Grey standing in the doorway. Behind him stood a young and relatively tall male Merna.

Grey addressed Xylon. "If we succeed, if we return your stone and capture those bastards, then you send your best warriors to help us find the rest of our friends. And if we don't, then you have your sacrifice." He glanced down to Veronica and Schmitt.

Xylon stared at Grey for a moment. Hesitant.

Faybin whispered to Xylon and pointed to the Merna male behind Grey. The man was solid and wore many scars on his skin. After some hesitation, Xylon nodded.

Faybin addressed Grey. "You go." She pointed to her chest. "Faybin go." She pointed to the Merna standing by the entrance whose head was clean shaven and covered in dark green tattoos. "Faybin brother go." Finally, she looked to Veronica and Schmitt. "You stay."

Grey looked to Xylon and nodded. The deal was made.

AMBER

Cave, Arcadia—
05:30, 9 September, 2086

Amber lay quietly beside Zoe on the cold stone floor. The Mernas who shared their cage had been asleep for hours. Amber had given up on sleep. She sat staring intently at the darkened entrance ramp, unable to quiet the stream of thoughts in her head.

Zoe rolled over and opened her eyes; she saw Amber sitting up, cradling her knees. "You should try to sleep," she whispered.

Zoe's Spanish accent reminded Amber of the training ground in Buenos Aires. She remembered how excited she felt when they first found out about Arcadia and the mission. She remembered studying the topographical maps for hours, pawing through the atmospheric data, scanning the satellite images. She looked at Zoe lying on the ground; her face was dirty and her hair matted.

They had no idea.

"How long have you been here exactly?" whispered Amber.

Zoe opened an eye. She looked at Amber sitting against the wall and sighed. "I honestly couldn't tell you. Months?"

"How long were you here before they captured you?"

"We were here for a few weeks before we found the Mernas. Then we spent another couple of weeks living with them before the attack. That is when I was taken. But that was a long time ago, now."

Amber frowned. "I just can't make any sense of this place. These Adra things seem so savage and primitive, like something from a monster movie. But then they have these super advanced technologies like those arm-weapons. And they clearly control those big tyrannosaur-things. But how?" Amber spoke quickly, letting her thoughts tumble out. "And why would they capture us and keep us here? Why keep you for *months*? Why keep anyone? Are they storing the Merna people for food? They're clearly predators but they must have some huge source of food because I saw hundreds of them in their little community, so are they hunters or farmers?"

Zoe smiled.

"Did I say something funny?" asked Amber, slightly annoyed by Zoe's calm demeanor.

Zoe waved a hand in the air. "No, no. You just sound like me when I first came here. So many questions, so many logical questions. You clearly have the mind of a scientist. But you are asking the wrong questions."

Amber raised an eyebrow. "What are the right questions?"

Zoe smiled again. "You keep comparing the Adra society to things you know on Earth. Are they primitive or advanced? Do they hunt or farm? You even called the Denkra a "tyrannosaur." Did you ever think there might be something else in this universe? Another way of living? Another way of eating? Something that's neither primitive nor advanced, but a little bit of both. A balance between living in harmony with your surroundings and manipulating your environment for your own societal gains.

"Your instinct tells you to try and make sense of this world by putting unfamiliar things into boxes with familiar ideas and concepts. It's not your fault, that's how our brains are wired. But this place is nothing like our world. If you try to compare it to things you know then you will only create more questions. You will find answers, but only when you stop trying to understand everything through your own expectations."

Amber didn't like Zoe's tone. She spoke down to her, as though she were a child.

Zoe sighed, sensing Amber's annoyance. "Okay, I will tell you something you may not know about Arcadia. Something that might help you gain a little perspective. Did you know Arcadia is around four billion years old? The same age as Earth."

Amber shook her head. "No, I didn't know that."

"Do you know there's only one significant difference between Arcadia's sedimentary makeup and Earth's? *Iridium*. Or, more precisely, the *lack* of iridium." Zoe leaned forward as she spoke.

Amber relaxed her defensive position slightly. She knew iridium was a dense metallic element found in very rare quantities in Earth's crust. Natural deposits were far more common in extra-terrestrial bodies, like asteroids. Amber also knew about the sedimentary layer on Earth which contained concentrations of iridium hundreds of times greater than normal. Geologists concluded a giant asteroid struck the Earth around that time in the planet's history.

Zoe nodded solemnly, seeing the hint of recognition in Amber's eyes.

Suddenly the streaks of light surrounding the pair disappeared and the room was plunged into darkness. The cages were gone, but the Merna continued to sleep soundly.

"What's happening?" whispered Amber.

Zoe frowned. "I've only seen this once before; when they first brought me here the cage lights were inoperable, like someone had switched off the power."

Amber stood. "C'mon, if the cages are gone then this might be our best chance."

Zoe hesitated. "What? No, no, we shouldn't. The Adras will be here soon."

Amber ignored her and began to tip-toe down the central walkway between the now-invisible cages, trying not to wake the Mernas. Zoe huffed in frustration but followed Amber's lead regardless.

As they neared the entrance Amber could see a hint of daybreak outside. She heard the panicked squeals of several Adras in the distance. They crouched by the base of the ramp, quietly. Amber held her hand in the air, telling Zoe to wait.

"*We really shouldn't be doing this. The Adras will be here soon.*"

Amber ignored Zoe again.

After a moment, the panicked sounds outside began to settle. Silence quickly followed.

"Okay, now!" ordered Amber.

Before they had a chance to move a dozen Adras came bounding into the cavern, racing down the ramp in formation. One of them pointed its arm at Zoe and Amber and barked aggressively. Wrapped around its arm was the familiar glove-weapon with its glowing blue lights; they'd been caught. The rest of the Adras shrieked and hissed loudly as they entered the area, waking the sleeping Mernas.

More Adras flooded into the room, arms outstretched, aiming their weapons at the sleepy Mernas. They moved swiftly around the edge of the cavern, rounding up everyone inside. The Adras drove the Merna like sheep toward the ramp, moving them outside into the crisp morning air.

Zoe and Amber were herded with the rest of the group, towering over the shorter Mernas. As they reached the top of the ramp they were met by a low-hanging mist.

"Where are they taking us?" asked Amber.

Zoe was clearly annoyed. She shrugged. "I don't know."

The Adras circled the crowd, guiding them through the misty jungle. They walked on a large path which had clearly been etched through the jungle over time. The encroaching forest was littered with ferns, vines, and flowering plants. Attached to the trunk of many trees were beautiful bromeliads and philodendrons. Despite their situation, Amber couldn't help but appreciate the beautiful natural world around them.

As the group walked along the track a large stone structure emerged. It towered high above their heads and stretched for kilometers in a wide circular shape; the enormous stone wall. The group approached the familiar gate section of the wall. From the outside, the gate was dotted with decorative vertical lines, etched into the smooth black stone.

As they neared the gate, everyone stopped. The Adras stood before the wall and began squealing in sequential high-pitched screams. Amber still felt uneasy when she heard the Adras call. After a moment, the decorative gate began to slide away, receding into the external structure. From their vantage point, Amber could see a team of at least two dozen Adras inside, pushing the gate open, straining against its immense weight.

She frowned as the Adras struggled to move the stone slab. She thought back to the previous day, when the gate opened smoothly and mechanically.

Once the opening was wide enough the group was herded through and Amber was once again met with the massive tree-buildings. The Adras' community was much larger than it had first appeared. It was more than just a community. It was a city. A city *within* the rainforest. An alien city built from the living trees.

Zoe saw the look of awe on Amber's face. "It is impressive, isn't it?"

"It's incredible. How do they do it?"

Zoe smiled. "They create buildings by gently manipulating the trees as they grow to create livable spaces inside. This way the plants do not need to die for the Adras to create a shelter. But that is not the most impressive part. See those tall ones there?" She pointed toward the center of the city. A group of three tall spires sat deep in the forest city. They were hundreds of meters tall and incredibly thick, like a trio of skyscrapers. Two of the trees were fully formed, but their trunks weren't smooth like the smaller structures. They were ribbed and grooved, like interlocking fingers which created a tight seal. The third tree was different. It was just as tall as the others, but the trunk was full of huge Swiss cheese-like holes.

"They create those high-rise structures by taking the seeds of certain plants and placing them high in the canopy of an existing tree. The seed then grows roots which wrap around the interior tree and stretch down to the ground. The Adras manipulate the growth of the roots, creating space between the outer roots and the internal tree, forming a huge open space inside."

"Jesus Christ," said Amber, visibly impressed. "That must take years, or even decades."

"It can take a lifetime," said Zoe. She looked up at the tall skyscraper-tree and smiled. "But it sure beats the cities on Earth."

The group were herded into a series of smaller house-sized tree structures. As each Merna was ushered into a building its collar was checked.

Suddenly, Amber was seized by an Adra to her right. At the same moment Zoe was seized on her left. Amber called in fright as the leathery claw clutched her skin. When the Adra saw Amber was missing a collar it began barking to the others. Soon three large Adras dashed out from a nearby alleyway and took Amber away from the group. At the same moment, the Adras holding Zoe dashed away down the alleyway.

"Zoe! No! Let me go!" Amber kicked and struggled against her captors. The creature on her right extended its left arm and the small disc began to glow. It aimed the device at Amber who took the hint and stopped struggling.

Base Camp, Arcadia—
11:30, 9 September, 2086

By the time Joel and Grey reached Base Camp the sun was high in the sky. Dark clouds hung ominously in the distance, promising rain. The campsite was disheveled. Debris was everywhere, tents had been trampled, and the boat's camouflage mode had been deactivated, exposing it to the world. The huge tree which had been blocking the door to the lifeboat was now lying in pieces on the ground.

Joel felt his stomach sink at the sight of the camp.

He stared at the fallen tree. His mind flashed back to the attack. He'd seen Diamond and Amber run straight into the boat. He'd seen the explosive from Grey's launcher strike the tree, and had seen the tree lodge itself against the boat's hatch.

That same tree now lay in two separate pieces.

Joel knelt by one of the logs and ran his hand over the smooth cut. His blood ran cold. The tree hadn't broken apart on its own. It hadn't been smashed by the Garkra that attacked their camp. It had been cut with precision.

Joel followed Grey into the lifeboat. The interior was intact but there had clearly been something inside. Several of the passenger chairs had huge gashes down their center, like someone had taken a knife to the material. A light on the control console was blinking red, it was a warning signal: "*EMERGENCY ACCESS HULL BREACH. FLIGHT SYSTEM DISENGAGED.*"

Grey turned to Joel. "See if you can find the emergency access panel and seal it up. I want this boat operational in case things get dicey and we need a quick departure."

"Lieutenant?" Standing in the airlock, looking bruised and battered, was Diamond. "Oh, thank the Lord you're here!" he said, throwing his arms around Joel.

"Sergeant, report. What happened here? Where's Dr. Lytton?"

Diamond let go of Joel and stood to attention, keeping his eyes fixed on the ground. "They took her."

Joel felt lightheaded.

"Who did?" asked Grey.

Diamond hesitated, unsure if he should say the word aloud. "Aliens." Diamond quickly relayed the events of the previous day in detail. ". . . and then they took her and left me for dead."

Joel turned to Grey. "Sounds like the Adras Schmitt was talking about."

"What about Dr. Kendal?" said Grey, still addressing Diamond. "Did he come through the camp?"

Diamond shrugged. "I wouldn't know anything about that. When I was finally able to move again the first thing I did was try to track down Amber. Spent all damn night following alien footprints through the jungle. But I couldn't find her. I'm sorry, Lieutenant, I messed up," said Diamond, finally making eye contact with Grey.

Grey had been like a father to Diamond. They'd been in the same Marine unit since Diamond joined the corps almost fifteen years ago. Grey had not only trained Diamond to become a soldier, but he'd helped him become a man. The last thing Diamond wanted was to disappoint the Lieutenant.

"What happened before the aliens came. What were you doing?" asked Grey.

"We were talking to Dr. Ozero on the ship's radio."

Joel snapped his fingers. "Of course! He's got cameras set up all over this place."

"That's why I came back to camp, was hoping he might've seen where they took her," said Diamond.

"Good thinking. Dr. Carter, get Dr. Ozero on the comms," said Grey.

Joel slid into the pilot's chair and switched on the microphone.

"Mikhail, come in, this is Joel." He paused, waiting for a response. "Mikhail, again, this is Joel, come in."

Suddenly the speakers on the boat sprang to life, static whirred. There was relief in his voice. "*Carter? Joel? Is that you?*"

Joel clicked the receiver again. "Mikhail, yes, it's me. Listen—"

Mikhail cut him off, "*Thank Christ you're okay! Where have you been? Look, I don't know what the hell is happening down there but I have seen some pretty fucked-up shit.*"

"I know, mate. But right now I need your help. Have you seen Charles?"

"*Yes, he was at the camp. Turned up with some other guy. I'm guessing you found the missing team?*"

"They were here? What happened?" said Joel, ignoring Mikhail's question.

"*I tried to call the boat but he never picked up.*"

Joel exchanged a look with Grey. "What did he do next?"

"*After a while they came out and started looking over the outside of the boat, acting really weird. Anyway they mustn't have found whatever they were looking for because eventually they just left.*"

"They left? But where the hell would they go?"

"They're going after the other boat. The one at the *Atlas* team's camp," said Grey, putting the pieces together.

CITY

Adra City, Arcadia—
11:30, 9 September, 2086

Two Adra guards stayed close to the doorway of the tree-room where Amber had been taken. The room was small, about the size of a bedroom. The walls were made from branches which had been manipulated over time to grow at unnatural right angles.

Amber couldn't help but stare at the creatures by the doorway. They had characteristics from so many different animal classes. They had the posture of an emu or an ostrich but long muscular arms with three fingered hands capable of using tools, like a primate. Instead of beaks, they had lizard-like jaws full of sharp teeth, and each foot had a huge curved middle claw.

Suddenly the two creatures at the entrance parted, making space for another Adra to enter. Amber froze at the familiar figure standing in the doorway: Cockatoo. Unlike the ones guarding her, Cockatoo did not bear a weapon of any sort. He walked slightly more upright than the others, with an air of nobility. Amber guessed he was higher in the pecking order.

Cockatoo stepped inside the open space and reared high on his legs, ruffling the yellow feathers on his neck. He lowered his head, staring at Amber, then jerked his head toward the door, purring softly.

Amber looked to the doorway; the two Adras who had been guarding her were gone.

She hesitated.

Cockatoo snorted in frustration and repeated the gesture, motioning to Amber then outside.

Amber stood slowly. "You want me to follow you?"

Cockatoo turned and moved away from the small structure, allowing Amber to step through the doorway. She looked around the area cautiously. There were no other Adras in sight, no signs of her guards. For a moment,

Amber considered running. She looked to Cockatoo. He was unarmed, he was not threatening her, or forcing her to do anything. He was just asking her to follow him.

Letting curiosity get the better of her, Amber complied.

Cockatoo led Amber to another building, a few meters away. Inside was a long corridor, created by two large rows of bushes which curved inward, forming a passageway. Every few meters the bushes connected with other tree-structure rooms on the left hand side, while the right hand side and the roof had a series of small holes which had been molded into branch-walls. Fresh air and light filtered through the small holes.

As they approached the end of the corridor, a large space opened before them. In the center of the space was the thick trunk of an enormous tree which stretched high overhead. Amber looked upward and realized they were at the base of one of the large "skyscraper" trees. Wrapped around the outside of the trunk was a spiraling staircase of branches. Without breaking his stride, Cockatoo began ascending the staircase.

Amber followed.

Near the top of the structure was an open archway, leading to a vine-bridge which connected the large tree to its neighbor. As they passed through the arch, Amber could see intricate decorations and precious gemstones lining the inside of the arch. They were brilliant and perfectly cut stones of incredible size.

The pair emerged onto the large vine-bridge and, for the first time, Amber saw the city in its entirety. It had literally been crafted from the living forest. As far as she could tell it covered an area the size of a large town or small city. A clear waterway flowed uninhibited through the center of the trees, branching down the various roads and alleyways. The water pooled in several gardens, just like the one she had seen earlier, buzzing with insect life. Some buildings were made from semi-hollowed tree-trunks, others from carefully manipulating the growth of branches over time.

Amber counted hundreds of Adras moving busily through the city below. They progressed quickly along the alleyways. Entire troops of Adras, equipped with their weaponized arms, moved in sync, like an army platoon mobilizing for an attack.

The bridge connected to the second skyscraper-sized structure through another elaborately decorated archway. Amber and Cockatoo entered a huge chamber on the other side. The room was covered in greenery with a network of tangled vines.

Cockatoo stopped just inside the doorway, allowing Amber to pass. She slowed as she walked through, distracted by the series of beautiful gemstones which lined the doorframe. They were perfectly cut and aligned with precision. Amber edged toward the stones, reaching for one with her hand.

"Stop!"

Amber froze. A woman stood at the front of the room, a human woman with olive skin and brown hair.

"Zoe?"

Zoe watched Amber with soft eyes. She no longer wore tattered rags, but instead was draped in an elegant white silk gown. Zoe raised her arm and motioned for Amber to follow.

Amber hesitated. She turned to face Cockatoo, but he was already halfway across the vine-bridge, making his way back to the first spire. Amber took a deep breath and started to approach Zoe.

It was then she noticed two Adras sitting on elaborately decorated platforms at the front of the room. Amber couldn't explain it at first, but the pair had a sense of authority and poise about them, similar to Cockatoo. They were also unlike any of the Adras she'd seen so far. Their coloring was softer and their faces and feathers were weathered. The one on the right was covered in black and yellow stripes with bright yellow plumage along its head and tail. The one on the left was smaller with a white body and soft shades of blue across its head and tail, like a beautiful sapphire gemstone; Amber guessed it was another female.

Zoe approached the stripy male and the gemstone-colored female and bowed reverently. She took a seat between the two creatures. "Please, sit," she said to Amber, gesturing to some small flat white stones on the floor.

Amber frowned. The small female Adra, Gemstone, laid a hand on Zoe's shoulder and Zoe began to speak. Her voice was soft and tranquil, almost otherworldly.

"*We know why you are here,*" said Zoe.

Amber's jaw dropped.

Stripes laid a hand on Zoe's right shoulder. Her tone changed, this time it was rough and guttural. "*We know your world is dying.*"

Jesus Christ, thought Amber.

The Adras were using Zoe to speak to her.

Stripes removed his hand from Zoe's shoulder and stood. He was actually larger than the other Adras she'd seen, standing well over two meters tall. He edged away from his decorated throne, approaching Amber slowly. He cautiously stretched a single hand outward, offering it to her.

Amber stared at the claw, unsure how to respond. A strange sensation rippled through her mind. A male voice entered her consciousness and, as clear as her own inner monologue, whispered to her.

Let me show you.

Amber gasped, almost falling over in shock. She turned to Zoe, wide-eyed, for reassurance. Zoe's eyes were closed, her face expressionless. Amber turned back to Stripes. She saw his outstretched hand and tentatively reached for it.

As their fingers touched, Amber was struck by a blinding white light, a lightning bolt shooting through her mind, taking over her body. The world around her vanished; the sights, sounds, and sensations from the outside world evaporated and Amber was plunged into whiteness.

After a moment the light began to take shape, molding into a giant blue-green sphere surrounded by blackness; in the distance tiny white dots shimmered. The image grew in size and continents began to form and shift, floating across the surface of the planet like sailboats; crashing into each other and ripping apart again. The movement slowed down as the shape of the Americas took form. Suddenly a giant ball of rock hurtled through the atmosphere and smashed into the planet's crust, between the American continents. An enormous mushroom cloud stretched kilometers into the sky. Shockwaves rippled away from the fiery blast, followed by a dark cloud that extended around the entire globe, blanketing it in debris. The blue-green sphere quickly turned grey as the debris settled. For a moment, the little globe sat in silence.

Then the grey began to fade and the blue-green color returned. As it did, the image grew in size again, zooming in on the African continent, closer and closer until huge animals could be seen roaming the grasslands. Small bipedal creatures chased the enormous placid animals, killing the large beasts with their sticks and arrows. Humans.

The humans began massacring entire herds of animals. They butchered their way across the continent, moving north to an exposed land bridge between Africa and Europe. The image zoomed out again, following the humans as they spread into Europe and Asia, walking across more exposed land to the Americas and Australia. Behind them, the earth was scorched with fire. From the embers, giant sterile cities grew, mining pits scarred the land, and pollution stained the air and water. The green continents faded to a harsh yellow, stripped of their natural beauty. The image retracted again so the entire Earth was visible. The color of the oceans had turned a sickly brown and the atmosphere had become thick with smog. Amber recognized the image. It was the last thing she saw before they had engaged the *Phoenix* engine.

Amber felt sick and tried to shake the image from her mind.

Suddenly her vision was flooded white again. She found herself staring at another blue-green planet. She watched as the meteor soared toward the planet; but this time it flew harmlessly past, vanishing into the distance. The image grew again in size, zooming in on one of the large continents. A pack of two-legged dinosaurs were hunting a herd of sauropods. They moved swiftly, fierce and agile, racing beside the lumbering sauropods. Their huge muscular hind legs pushed them forward at lightning speed; their forearms were also muscled but sinuous, ending in four sharp claws. The dinosaurs were covered in a light coat of sleek thin feathers, with a feathery crest running along their heads and necks. Amber recognized the animals instantly; *Cerebraptors*. The raptors took down a single animal, while the rest of the herd escaped.

The image zoomed out again, this time following the raptors as they colonized the world. As they did so, the creatures began to change and distort in shape. Their postures straightened, their tails shrank, and their heads grew large and bulbous. Small groups split away geographically from the others, developing slightly different features to suit their environmental niche. One group settled among a vast scattered island chain, developing webbed feet and powerful dolphin-like tails. Another settled in the desert where they excavated enormous underground caverns, developing huge digging arms and large nocturnal eyes. And another settled in the snowy mountains near the northern magnetic pole, where their bodies and feathers thickened for warmth.

The image returned to the green forest near the equator. A solitary creature walked casually through a growing tree-city. An Adra.

At the center of the city were four enormous rainforest trees. The inner trees were fully grown but the roots from the parasitic outer trees were only half formed. Toward the edge of the city half-formed tree-buildings were gently being manipulated.

Suddenly a group of small humanoids appeared, draped in feathery tunics and riding on the backs of large animals. Amber recognized the animals from the gorge; as large as elephants with hippo-like mouths, lizard-like tails and large bony crests. The small humanoids attacked with ferocity, launching fiery arrows and spears. Their crested army stampeded through the city, trampling the half-finished buildings and the beautiful flower gardens.

The city and the surrounding forest burned to the ground.

The image shifted again, flying over the forest and the ocean to another landmass. An island surrounded by a huge glowing wall of light, just like the lights in the underground cages. The island grew in size as the image moved closer. Small Merna children emerged, playing and laughing happily. Several adult Mernas sat casually by a lagoon, while others danced around a bonfire. Large crested animals grazed on trees and grasses nearby.

Outside the glowing blue wall, Adras stood by a dock, guiding a group of skittish Mernas toward the entrance. The Adras outside the cage were sending in food and supplies, providing the Mernas with everything they needed. Outside the entrance was another large fire with the smoldering remains of Merna tools and weapons. The Adras were providing a safe haven for the Mernas, but not before stripping them of their independence.

Suddenly Amber's mind flashed white again and her senses returned. She fell to the ground, her knees weak. She clutched her head as a searing pain shot across her forehead. As she opened her eyes again, she saw the still-outstretched hand of Stripes. Tears began to fill her eyes.

"What is this place?" she asked, wiping a tear from her cheek.

Stripes gazed at Amber for a moment in silence.

Amber felt angry. "Why would you show me this?"

Stripes ruffled his feathers.

"They need your help," said Zoe. Her eyes were open again. She was still calm and relaxed, but she was in control. "They need *our* help."

Amber shook her head. "What are you talking about? Are you working for them?" Amber looked over Zoe's elegant robes, they were finely knitted feather strands which looked like silk. Amber gripped her stomach, still feeling weak after the strange out-of-body experience.

"They aren't the monsters you think they are," said Zoe.

Amber ignored her comment. She stared intently at Zoe, thinking about their earlier conversations. "Did they put you in the cave on purpose? Did they put you in there to manipulate me? To get me to trust you?"

Zoe didn't respond. She continued to stare at Amber through calm, cold eyes. After a moment, Zoe turned to Stripes and shook her head. "Take her away."

Base Camp, Arcadia—
12:00, 9 September, 2086

Diamond and Joel were crouched on the roof of the lifeboat. They'd closed the heavy emergency exit hatch and were in the process of resetting the system. Joel stayed on his hands and knees, all too aware of how high he was off the ground. He glanced at the exterior face of the access panel and saw a small round hole with the word "RESET" printed in large letters around its edges.

Joel tried to insert his finger inside the hole but it was too big. After a moment he tried again, this time using his pinkie finger. With a soft *clunk*, the door locked into place, hissing softly as the hatch created a perfect seal.

Diamond patted Joel on the back. "See, I knew your dainty scientist hands would come in handy! Now, just need a few more minutes to do some safety checks and reset the computer."

Joel stared at Diamond as he began running his hand over the newly sealed door. While he was acting like his happy-go-lucky self again, his eyes were bloodshot and red. "Diamond, what happened yesterday? Why did they take Amber?"

Diamond stopped running his hand over the door. His mood dampened instantly. "I don't know. I've been asking myself that same question. Why take her? Why her and not me? I don't have the answer, but I have a theory."

Joel frowned.

"I reckon it's because she had a gun. I'd left my launcher on the ship. But she kept her little laser in her belt. And they found it. It's like they knew what it was, that it was a weapon, and that made her a threat."

"Joel!" called Faybin. She was standing by the edge of the tree line, waving excitedly. "Come!"

Joel carefully made his way down the length of the ship's in-built ladder and followed Faybin into the forest. She was with her brother, Din, crouched over a disturbed patch of leaf litter, hovering cautiously. Faybin pointed to a small silver object on the ground.

Joel picked up the object. "It's Amber's watch." He felt his chest tighten.

The glass was cracked, and the features were inoperable. A still-image was frozen on the cracked screen, the last image she had captured before it broke. It was difficult to make out at first. The image was brown and curved, fat on one side, tapering to a thin point on the other; a piece of wood maybe? Or a bone?

Or a claw.

Faybin tapped Joel on the leg and pointed to a small section of damp earth. There was an impression in the soft mud. A footprint, with two elongated toes, tipped with claws, and one much shorter toe with a deep claw mark. "Adra," said Faybin, pointing to the print. She gestured to the mud nearby and Joel saw several more prints, similar to the one in front of them.

Joel felt a tear swelling in his eye. He gripped the watch tight then slipped it into his pocket.

"This is where they shot us."

Joel turned to see Diamond and Grey approaching. Faybin pointed to several places on the ground where leaf litter and dirt had been disturbed. "Adra," she said, following the trail with her fingers, pointing inland and to the north.

"I already tried following them," said Diamond, shaking his head. "The trail goes cold once it reaches the stream."

Din grunted, "Human." He was standing several feet away, deeper in the forest. Joel approached and saw a different set of tracks in the soft earth. These were oval shaped with ridges carved in the bottom: boots. Din pointed east, toward the nearby coast. "*Light stone.*"

Grey nodded to Diamond and Joel. "We go east. They've already got a head start on us and my guess is they know we're after them."

"Lieutenant? What about Amber?" protested Joel.

"We stick to the mission at hand. If these things are as intelligent as everyone says, then we're going to need the Mernas' help getting her back. For now, we focus on the stone."

"You can go find Charles. I'm going after Amber," said Joel defiantly.

Grey shrugged. "Fine. Go get yourself killed. A highly trained marine couldn't track her down but you should be perfectly capable of finding her, right?"

"Fuck you," retorted Joel. He could feel the resentment seething inside.

Grey remained reserved. "Argue all you want, Dr. Carter. My objective is to keep our people safe and to find the *Atlas* team. The best way to achieve both of those aims is not to go off half-cocked into the lion's den." Without waiting for a reply, Grey made his way back toward the lifeboat.

Joel swallowed hard. He wanted to punch Grey in the face. But he couldn't argue with the man's logic. As much as it pained him, Joel followed Grey to the lifeboat.

"Well, I hope you have a plan. Because we're never going to catch up to them on foot," said Joel bitterly.

Grey half-smiled and opened the large panel beneath the front window of the lifeboat. Inside were four compact MTVs: sleek two-seater crafts with two rotating fans on the underside, encased in a light alloy, and a huge engine at the rear. Grey heaved one of the bikes from the compartment; Din and Faybin jumped back as the large metal object landed heavily onto the ground.

The MTVs were reminiscent of early-century motorcycles, except instead of vertical wheels the MTV was propelled by a combination of horizontal vents and fans. The vents created an air cushion, allowing the vehicle to "hover" freely and practically fly across any terrain.

Grey turned to Joel. "That's why we're not going on foot."

Charles

**Hermes*, Orbit—12:30,*
9 September, 2086

Once again, Mikhail watched the monitor orbs around Base Camp as Grey, Diamond, and Joel left with the MTVs and the small humanoids. He felt so useless. All he could do was watch as his crew explored the surface of a strange planet with no guidance and no way to communicate.

Mikhail's mind flashed back to the woman and man they found on the *Atlas*. He wondered if the man with the pilot's badge had also been left alone aboard the ship. Had he gone mad? Is that why he shot the older woman? He recalled the holograph from the woman's last entry, she said he'd cut the comms when she tried to send a message to Earth.

Earth!

Mikhail cursed himself for not considering it sooner. He had been so engrossed with the projection table he had completely forgotten about his responsibilities as sentry, one of which was to send regular reports back to the ISA. Quickly, Mikhail entered the cockpit. As soon as he crossed the bulkhead doors he saw the small red light on the control console; a message had arrived from Earth.

"Shit," he said to himself.

He sat in the pilot's chair and played the message. Irwin's face took over *Hermes*' front window and he was clearly agitated.

Irwin was alone in the communications room. He shook his head as he spoke. "*Hermes, this is Irwin. I don't want to alarm you but, but we found Montello's body. We don't know what happened exactly, but the coroner says it was blunt force trauma that killed him. His face was covered in bruises and blood. It looks like he was murdered,*" he said, almost choking on his own words.

Mikhail's stomach twisted into knots.

Irwin swallowed hard. "*His body was found near the perimeter wall. The investigators believe it happened the day of the launch. There aren't any clear suspects yet, but they're not ruling anyone out. That includes the crew. I'll let you know when we hear more.*"

The image faded and the window was clear once more, providing a beautiful view of Arcadia from space.

Mikhail's heart was racing. A bombshell had just been dropped on him but he had no way of contacting the others, no way of getting the word out.

He looked down at the console and saw the red light was still flashing; another message? He pressed play and Irwin's face reappeared. This time he was covered in sweat; his button-down shirt was half-open, revealing a stained white tank top. He was sitting at the console with an open bottle of whisky. "*It was him,*" he said, almost sobbing. "*I should have known it was him. I sent him with you. I put all your lives in danger. That slimy English bastard!*" Irwin cursed and rubbed his face dejectedly.

Charles.

Irwin took a swig of whisky. "*That's not even the worst part. How's that for ridiculous? The murder isn't the worst part of this whole thing. They identified the body of the real Charles Kendal a few days ago. The body they pulled from the Oxford fire wasn't the janitor. It seemed like such an open and shut case at the time, no one thought to check the dental records of the deceased; after all, illegals don't usually have dental records. But when they found the deceased man's skull had been fractured, they decided to check anyway. And this body did have a record. It was the body of Dr. Charles Kendal.*"

Irwin looked away from the camera for a moment, then he stared right down the lens. Mikhail felt a twinge of dread. It was as though he were looking directly into Irwin's eyes. "*I have no idea who I sent with you.*"

Jungle, Arcadia—
12:30, 9 September, 2086

Tom rubbed the wounds on his wrists. The vines that kept him crucified to the wooden stake had left his skin raw and bloodied. But at least he was free. He eyed the man walking in front of him curiously. His dark hair had shades of grey peppered through, as did his facial hair which was starting to grow into a thin beard. His face was weathered and hard, it wasn't the face of a scientist who'd spent his life in a laboratory.

"So, *Dr. Charles Kendal*, Irwin actually sent you to save us?" asked Tom.

Up ahead, Charles was climbing over a huge fallen tree. He paused and turned to face Tom. "Is that so hard to believe? After everything you'd worked so hard for, as if anyone would just throw that away."

Tom shook his head. "You have to admit, it's a bit suspicious. You said Erika sent a message to Earth telling them not to come here? It's almost like they never saw her message?"

Charles shrugged. "I wouldn't know anything about that. It was hard to tell exactly what happened from the recorder. All I know is when your buddy, Guy, killed that old German lady he also Kamikazed himself by shooting a hole in the goddamn ship."

Tom didn't react.

"Guess it's sort of ironic she jabbed him with a sedative before she died."

Tom still didn't react.

"What I want to know is why your buddy shot that poor woman in the first place? Seems like a bit of a reckless act if you ask me."

Tom's face hardened. "He did what had to be done."

Up ahead the forest thinned dramatically as the trees gave way to open space and beautiful white sand. The pair emerged from the forest to a brilliant sight. Dark ominous clouds hung over the open ocean in front of them; a wave of clouds was rolling toward the land. Beneath these, the water was a deep dark blue, fading to a beautiful luminescent green as it met the shore.

Tom said, "Pretty, isn't it? You know, if you're into that kind of thing."

Charles patted his knapsack. "Not as pretty as this baby." Charles froze, squinting and looking around the area cautiously. "*Can you hear that?*"

For a few seconds all Tom could hear was the rolling waves crashing gently on the sand. "I don't—" Then he heard it, a faint humming in the distance. Tom frowned. "Thunder?"

Charles shook his head and grabbed Tom by the arm, pulling him back into the jungle and shoving him into a small gully.

"What is it?" asked Tom, rubbing his sore arms.

"Shh!" demanded Charles. "It's an MTV."

The pair lay close to the ground, concealed by the low-lying foliage. The soft humming grew in volume until three silver MTVs burst from the jungle a few hundred meters to their right, straight into the middle of the delta where one of the creeks met the ocean.

"Son of a bitch," whispered Charles. "I thought you said the little people would kill the rest of the humans once they realized their stone was gone?"

Tom shook his head. "After what happened to me I was sure they would."

There were three bikes; Grey and a male Merna on one, Joel and a female Merna on another, and Diamond on the third.

"We can't stay here," whispered Tom. He looked at Charles's bag. "Our old camp is on the beach, about two kilometers south from here. Take the stone and get to that lifeboat."

"What about you?" whispered Charles.

Tom grabbed the laser from Charles's holster. "I'll meet up with you later." Without another word, Tom sprang to his feet and ran north, along the beach. He kept low but stayed close enough to the forest to attract attention.

Charles pressed his body further into the ground, trying to conceal his presence. After a few seconds he lifted his head slightly. The male Merna was searching through the nearby foliage. After a moment he started pointing animatedly toward the beach, in the direction Tom had run. The small male ran up to Grey and jumped on the back of his bike. Grey and Diamond gunned their throttles in pursuit.

Charles held his breath; Tom's plan was working.

"Joel!" a female voice screamed to Charles's left. He turned and saw the small female staring directly at him, only a meter away. "Joel! Joel!"

Charles sprang to his feet and ran as fast as his legs would carry him.

Joel heard Faybin's screams from just beyond the tree line. In the corner of his eye he saw a figure moving beyond the trees. Joel gunned the throttle of the bike and brought it back toward the forest to get a better look; it was Charles. He was moving fast. Joel accelerated, moving parallel to Charles along the beach.

Joel shouted over the hum of the bike. "Charles! Charles! Stop!"

Charles saw the bike approaching and quickened his pace, changing course to move deeper into the thick overgrowth. Joel guided the bike back into the forest. Charles moved swiftly through the trees, darting back and forth, making it impossible for Joel to catch up. Thunder rolled in the distance and large fat drops of rain began to fall from the dark clouds above.

Joel carefully brought the bike as close as he could toward Charles, edging himself into position. As soon as he was close enough, Joel launched himself from the bike, swallowing Charles in his arms.

The pair landed heavily, rolling on the damp ground as rain began to pelt down. As they connected with the earth Charles's knapsack flew from his shoulder. Within seconds he was back on his feet, scrambling through the foliage, looking for his bag.

Joel wheezed, winded from the impact. But he was soon on his feet, too. He launched forward, crash-tackling Charles from behind, throwing him to the ground and sliding in the dirt. Joel scrambled onto Charles's back, pulling his arms behind his body, pinning him down. Charles lay flat on his stomach with his arms pulled back and his shoulder blades inches apart; he screamed out in pain.

"What the hell were you thinking?" bellowed Joel, unable to control his anger.

"Get off me!" yelled Charles as rain began to hammer down around them.

Joel relaxed his grip and pulled Charles's wrists to the base of his back. With one hand he unhitched his utility belt, removed its small compartments, and wrapped it around Charles's wrists.

"Where's the stone?" demanded Joel as he hauled Charles to his feet.

Charles intentionally spat as he spoke. "I dropped it. When you tackled me."

Joel began fishing through the thick ferns with Charles in his custody. "How could you be so stupid, Charles? How could you *steal* their stone? Are you trying to get us all killed? What the fuck were you thinking?" Joel poked behind a clump of damp leaves but found nothing.

Charles was silent; his eyes followed Joel like a predator stalking its prey. He kept his body rigid and tense. Joel didn't notice.

Joel pulled back a wide flat leaf and, to his relief, he saw the bag. He picked it up and opened the flap, revealing the stone. It was enormous, the size of a softball, perfectly cut, and amazingly clear with a soft green coloring. Joel examined it closely, it was not the raw unprocessed mineral he had expected. The cut was flawless, as though it had been carved by a laser. It was far too advanced to be Merna work.

"Jesus Christ," he breathed.

Thump.

Joel fell to the ground hard as the shockwave rippled through his nervous system. He rolled in pain and watched through double vision as Charles leaped over his head, with Joel's belt still dangling from his left wrist. With his right hand, Charles snatched the pack. Joel grabbed his ankles and ripped his feet out from beneath him. Charles slipped, landing heavily on the wet earth, winding him momentarily.

Joel took his chance and sprang on top of Charles, ignoring the throbbing pain in his head.

Charles kicked and squirmed. "Get off of me!" he shouted, elbowing Joel in the face.

Joel lost his grip and Charles scrambled to his feet. Joel was hot on his heels, swinging wide with a right hook. Charles turned just in time and ducked out of the way. As Joel recoiled, Charles spun around with lightning speed and grabbed him by the collar, thrusting him against a nearby tree, pressing his elbow into Joel's throat, cutting off his air supply.

"Not so tough now, are you? Where's your military friends to come and save you?" Charles pushed his elbow harder into Joel's throat, pinning him against the tree.

He was surprisingly strong.

Joel struggled as his oxygen supply was restricted. "Charles, listen to me. That stone isn't what you think it is," he wheezed.

"Stop callin' me Charles!" he snarled. For a moment, his proper Queen's English accent slipped, revealing a subtle cockney twang.

Joel stopped resisting. The rain continued to fall in heavy droplets all around.

Charles laughed to himself; his grip on Joel's neck loosened. Charles shook his head, still laughing, "You think *I* don't know what the stone is?"

Joel was silent.

"You don't know nothin' 'bout this place." His accent was thicker now.

Joel stared into Charles's eyes. His gaze was hard and cold. Joel had never been this close to Charles's face before. He'd never looked into his eyes. Around the edge of his blue irises Joel could see traces of an olive-brown hue. He frowned; the only time he'd heard of this type of iris coloring was from surgical re-coloration; an elective cosmetic procedure to permanently change a person's eye color.

Joel's gaze narrowed as it finally clicked. "You're not Charles Kendal."

The man holding Joel smirked; he stepped back slightly, further relaxing his grip on Joel's throat. "Congratulations, Dr. Carter. That's the first intelligent thing you've said since we met. Guessin' it was the eyes that gave me away, eh? They can do amazing things with plastic surgery these days. Did you know you can have elective facial surgery in less than an hour? As long as you can pay for it."

Joel frowned. "Who are you?"

"Edward Gilmore, happy to make your acquaintance," he sneered.

In a distant corner of his mind Joel recalled the name Gilmore. His face must have betrayed his thoughts.

"You recognize the name, don't ya?"

"T-Tom," stammered Joel. "Tom Gilmore? You two are related?"

"Well done, Carter. Keep it up and you might actually figure out why we *really* came to this planet." He pulled the belt from his wrist using his teeth and lashed the strap around Joel's wrists. "Tom's my brother."

"Your brother? That's not possible, the population laws?"

Edward looped the belt again and secured the strap. "Laws don't stop everything. There are laws against rape; but that didn't stop my daddy from conceiving me. There are laws against murder; but that didn't stop the state from executing him for his crime. There are laws about aborting rape pregnancies; but that didn't stop my mother from keeping me. And what did she get for her troubles? For saving the life of an innocent infant? Stripped of her rights as a citizen, exiled from the community, and left to raise two boys alone in the slums of Liverpool."

"I don't understand. What happened to the real Dr. Kendal?" asked Joel.

Edward pulled Joel away from the tree and started guiding him through the forest, back toward the beach. He clicked his tongue. "Tut, tut, Dr. Carter. You were doin' so well on your own."

Joel swallowed hard. "You killed him."

Edward pulled Joel around a tree; they could almost see the beach again. "Ooh, so close! Charles was a pretentious prick anyway. Thought he was the smartest man in the room, but he was clueless, really. I mean, who doesn't question a janitor hanging around a university lab in the middle of the night?"

Joel's mind was spinning as he tried to absorb this new information. "You killed Charles Kendal."

Edward retorted, "I'm not a monster. The fire killed him. I just had the courtesy to make sure he wasn't conscious when it started."

Joel thought back to the moment he met "Dr. Kendal" at the briefing. He wasn't surprised by the news, in fact he seemed to know Irwin wasn't telling the full story.

"You knew about the first mission?"

Edward smiled involuntarily. "Tom had been keeping me up to date for a while. We'd already pooled all our resources getting him onto the first mission, but when things went pear-shaped I had to be on the next one, by whatever means necessary." As he spoke they exited the thick forest, returning to the open air of the beach.

The pair moved south, along the sandy shore. In the distance, several small dunes rose from the flat surface. Four mounds were arrayed around a single larger mound. As the pair came closer, the mounds began to flap and sway in the ocean breeze; chameleonic tents.

Edward visibly relaxed at the sight of the *Atlas* camp.

As they made their way into the camp Joel could just make out the camouflaged outline of the lifeboat. The domed tents were discretely dotted around the boat. Even the communication equipment was still standing erect and untouched.

Edward pressed the release lever on the lifeboat's outer airlock doors. Nothing happened. He stepped back and looked over the ship gritting his teeth. "Fucking ship has no power!"

"What's that?" whispered Joel, standing behind Edward, near the edge of the forest.

"I'm not falling for that," said Edward, raising an eyebrow.

In a heartbeat, Joel turned and ran into the nearby forest.

Edward frowned. He turned slowly and, to his horror, saw a troop of aliens making their way down the beach. Eight creatures walked upright; they were lizard-like in appearance and yet their heads and tails were decorated with long delicate feathers: Adras.

Edward sprinted into the forest after Joel. Together they scrambled beneath a mound of fallen branches and leaves, trying to hide from the approaching creatures. The pair held their breath as the alien-beings approached the camp. They were sniffing the area, searching for something.

Joel could feel his heart throbbing in his chest. From their vantage point, they could see the feet of the Adras as they passed. Their legs were covered in a thin layer of soft feathers, fading to a hard pebbly skin near their huge and menacing clawed feet. Each foot had an enormous curved inner claw. Joel recalled the image from Amber's watch and the strange footprint they'd seen in the mud near Base Camp.

The Adras continued moving through the camp, searching each tent and structure. After several long minutes the creatures moved on, entering the jungle further down the beach. Joel frowned; they were heading in the same direction as Grey.

The pair lay in silence for several more minutes, until they were satisfied the Adras were gone. Joel turned to Edward and made to speak but froze. Edward was already on his feet, aiming Joel's own laser in his face.

"What're you doing?" said Joel, frozen in place.

His cold eyes stared at Joel. "I'm sorry, Doc, but you know too much now. I can't let you walk away from this one. Honestly, I am sorry." He switched off the safety.

"*Argh!*" Edward stumbled forward gripping his leg. To his horror a spear had impaled his right thigh. Edward dropped the gun and fell to his knees as pain rippled through his body.

He began to stand again but froze as the cold pointed tip of a blade pressed at the back of his neck.

"Light stone," a harsh female voice whispered in Edward's ear. Faybin stood behind the fallen man, with a sharp stone blade. She nodded at Joel lying in the mud.

Joel nodded back. "I guess we're even now," he said, smiling in relief.

Tom

Beach, Arcadia—
13:00, 9 September, 2086

Grey's bike shot along the sand like a bullet with Diamond following close behind. Rain started to pelt down on the beach. Din squeezed Grey's waist to keep from falling off. To their left, Tom moved swiftly, zigzagging through the palm trees which lined the edge of the forest. Grey and Diamond increased their speed, bringing their bikes parallel with the fleeing man. Tom instantly changed course, turning sharply left and heading deeper into the undergrowth.

"Fuck!" cursed Grey. He pulled the bike handles, following Tom into the forest. As soon as they left the beach, Grey and Diamond were forced to slow their approach. Wet branches and leaves assaulted them as they pushed further into the thickening forest.

Tom continued to run. Without slowing down, or even looking back, he aimed the laser over his right shoulder and discharged several shots that flew wild. One of the shots grazed the side of Diamond's bike, causing him to veer off course. Diamond engaged the bike's brakes but it was too late; he careened down a steep gully, plunging into a thicket of tangled vines.

After the volley of laser fire Grey slowed the bike further. Din patted Grey's side, encouraging him to pick up speed. Grey hesitated. He kept moving forward, but no faster than running speed. They glided between the trees, over low-growing ferns, under fallen logs. The rain started to hammer down, killing their visibility. Tom was nothing more than a shadow fading in the distance.

Din smacked Grey on his shoulder. "Go! Go!" he demanded.

Grey brought the bike closer, edging his way toward Tom. As they approached, Tom turned and fired. Grey swerved the bike dramatically to the right and three laser blasts missed the bike by centimeters, striking a nearby tree instead. The bark on the tree exploded in small bursts of fire. Grey pulled the bike around again but reduced their speed once more.

Din grew more frustrated. "Go!"

Grey growled under his breath. He eased the bike forward, trying to get closer to Tom, but not close enough he would fire his laser again. Suddenly Tom burst into a field of small ferns which grew to about ankle height. He was assaulted with the pounding rain, but the unobstructed space gave him the freedom he needed to pick up his pace.

The MTV entered the clearing but Grey continued to keep his distance. He felt pressure on his shoulder from Din and was about to snap at the small humanoid when suddenly Tom dropped mid-step, disappearing beneath the layer of ferns. Grey quickly engaged the MTV's brakes and the bike came to a slow stop, hovering several inches off the ground.

The pressure on his shoulder eased and Grey turned to see Din holding a crudely constructed weapon. It was a projectile launcher, a simple device, like a cross between a bow and a slingshot. Din placed a hand into a small pouch on his waist and extracted a pointed object. It was a flat star-shaped stone with pointed tips. Din held it carefully in the middle of the sharp points.

Despite himself, Grey was impressed with the small humanoid. He nodded, wiping the heavy raindrops from his eyes and smiled. "Good work."

The pair stepped off the bike and slowly pulled out their respective weapons. Grey aimed his laser forward, in the direction Tom had fallen. Din placed one of the starred projectiles into his sling-bow and mirrored Grey's movements. They saw Tom's foot sticking out of the ferns and slowed their approach. Tom's leg was in spasm, his boot twitched awkwardly.

Grey quickly pulled back the leaves concealing Tom's body. He was lying on his back, his whole body convulsed while his hands clutched at his neck. Within seconds he began frothing from the mouth like a rabid dog.

"Jesus Christ!" said Grey, quickly holstering his weapon. He knelt by Tom's shaking body and peeled his hands away from his neck; the small star protruded from his throat and small droplets of blood dribbled down his neck. Grey frowned in confusion. "I don't get it?" He pulled the small star from Tom's neck and placed his hand against the open wound to apply pressure.

Grey addressed Din. "What's happening? He's hardly bleeding at all?"

Din stood over Tom's fallen body; his face was stoic, his eyes cold. He held up one of the small stars. "Sacrifice."

Grey looked at the star he had removed from Tom's neck and realized each tip of the small projectile was covered in a sticky sap. He sniffed the star and a pungent odor wafted into his nostrils: poison.

Tom's body began to shake violently. The white foam oozing from his mouth turned a sickly red as blood entered his esophagus.

"Shit!" cursed Grey, rolling the stricken man over onto his side. "Shit! Shit!"

Tom's body seized violently again. His arms and legs stiffened as his muscles contracted, his head arched back at an unnatural angle. After several seconds his body suddenly went limp, flopping flat and silent on the ground.

Grey placed his fingers on Tom's throat; there was no pulse.

He cursed again. Grey turned to Din angrily. "You killed him! We didn't need to kill him!"

Din's face remained unchanged. "*Light stone*. Sacrifice."

Grey sat back on his haunches and wiped the rainwater from his brow. He sat in silence for a moment, staring at Tom's body. It wasn't meant to be like this. Grey didn't care much for Arcadia or the Mernas, he cared about his mission; to keep the humans safe, *all* the humans. Now a man was dead because of a stupid stone.

Grey began sifting through the dead man's clothes, searching for the stone.

"He doesn't have it," he growled.

Din shook his head angrily. "*Light stone,*" he demanded. Din approached Tom's body and started patting down his clothes.

"He doesn't have it," repeated Grey tersely.

Din ignored him and continued to sift through the dead man's clothes.

"C'mon, it must be with Dr. Kendal."

As they made their way to the bike Grey paused, turning back to Tom's lifeless body. Whatever the man had done, he didn't deserve to die like that; he didn't deserve to die at all. For a moment Grey felt sorry for Tom. He watched Din walk casually back to the bike and felt his insides turn cold. He would not underestimate the Mernas again.

Tom's body lay quietly among the ferns. Rain fell heavily through the canopy, drenching everything in sight. Foam still dripped slowly from the corner of his mouth, gradually washed away by the rain. Water rolled down his neck, wiping away traces of blood from his throat. A crack of lightning flashed in the distance, beyond the trees. Thunder quickly followed, rolling across the forest like a tidal wave. The jungle fell silent again.

Suddenly there was movement.

Eight large Adras moved cautiously through the quiet jungle. They paused simultaneously at the sight of Tom's lifeless body on the forest floor. The largest creature signaled to the others to stay back while he approached.

The large Adra crouched by the body and felt his neck for a pulse; nothing.

He hung his head while the others stood in silence. After a moment he began gently patting down the body. After several minutes the large Adra shook his head, stood, and signaled to the others to follow.

Adra City, Arcadia—
16:30, 9 September, 2086

Amber sat alone in her secluded tree-room. After her encounter with Stripes and Gemstone, she was returned to the small room with only a bowl of water and a plate of fruits and root vegetables. Small droplets of water trickled through tiny cracks between the manipulated branches. Outside, the thunder and rain had finally stopped. Amber sat beside the food platter, picking at small oddly-shaped items.

Zoe's words echoed in Amber's mind like a song stuck in her head: *If you try to compare it to things you know then you will only create more questions. You will find answers, but only when you stop trying to understand everything through your own expectations.*

Maybe Zoe hadn't been brainwashed. Maybe her time with the Adras had given her a new perspective. Maybe she was seeing this place for what it really was.

Since the moment Amber first came across the Adras she had viewed them as monstrous aliens. Their appearance, their behavior, even the sounds they made were like something from a horror movie. But this wasn't a movie. These weren't imaginary monsters or fictional aliens, they were real lifeforms on a real planet. Lifeforms with their own set of unique behaviors and abilities.

Amber thought back to her ecological training. She had been taught that all of life was fueled by three basic motivations; to find sustenance, to reproduce, and to avoid death. The Adras were clearly excelling at all three, but they didn't stop at their own survival. The tree-city was evidence of their desire to preserve other forms of life. Their chosen food source was insects; a genus which reproduces in huge numbers and if left unchecked can devastate entire ecosystems. Even their weapons were designed to paralyze, not to kill. Everything about their behavior supported the idea they were motivated by more than their own existence.

"Holá, Amber."

Amber was startled at the sudden voice, interrupting her train of thought.

"Zoe?" She squinted at the shadowy figure by the doorway. Amber shuffled to the back of the tree-room, slightly guarded.

"There is no need for that. I would like you to come with me." Zoe offered Amber her hand.

She ignored Zoe's outstretched hand but stood slowly at her request. Zoe nodded to the two Adras outside the door and without saying a word, they left their post, allowing Amber and Zoe to move freely. Amber hesitated for a moment. Zoe's behavior continued to confuse and intrigue her. With nothing to lose, Amber followed Zoe into the tree-city.

"I know you must be angry with me, you feel I lied to you before," said Zoe.

Amber didn't respond.

Zoe led Amber away from her secluded room, into the depths of the Adra city. The trees grew in tight groves all around them. At a glance, each structure looked like a normal tree. But on close inspection they were anything but normal. Their branches were twisted and contorted at unnatural angles, creating useful spaces for the Adra community.

"You have every right to be angry," said Zoe. "But I promise you, nothing I said in the cave was untrue. I was captured by the Adras several weeks after we arrived and I was kept in the cave cages where I saw Yoshi for the last time."

Amber eyed Zoe as they walked deeper into the city, moving toward the large skyscraper-sized trees. Zoe was still dressed in a long flowing gown. She was a far cry from the dirty and frightened prisoner Amber had met inside the cave. She was a stranger, just another alien thing in this alien world.

"What I did not tell you, is what I have learned since that day."

Zoe led Amber to a small grove surrounded by a thick hedge which grew to the height of Amber's waist. Inside the hedge, the earth was carpeted in thick lush grass. And playing happily on the grass were a dozen small Adras. Most were tiny fledglings, hardly bigger than a chicken. They were grey in color and covered in a soft downy layer of feathers. The smallest creatures were entirely grey. As they increased in size, their soft down thinned, giving way to sleek and colorful feathers.

A solitary adult Adra moved among the brood, snapping occasionally when their play became too rough. Amber recognized the Adra she referred to as Purple.

Zoe continued, "The pack leaders, the ones you met earlier, they showed me the same things they showed you. They did this because they want our help. They know the Mernas will never trust them. But they might trust humans. The Adras have been relocating Mernas for generations, trying to protect them from themselves. They want to send all the Mernas to a protected island where they can live peacefully."

Amber still didn't respond. She gazed at their surroundings and realized the nursery hedge was situated beside the large skyscraper-trees. From the outside, Amber could see the two fully formed buildings were slightly blackened. She could also see inside the third, half-formed building. Dozens of Adras were hovering inside the structure at various levels, setting up and adjusting braces between the inner and outer plants. It reminded Amber of building scaffolding.

"It just doesn't feel right," said Amber, finally engaging in the conversation. "The Adras don't just want to protect Mernas, they want to domesticate them."

Zoe sighed. "That was my thought, too, at first. But I have come to see things differently. Like the Adras, I have seen the similarities between Mernas and humans. They are aggressive and stubborn. They kill each other in sporting battles; sacrifice innocents in the name of their Gods. They *need* to be domesticated."

Amber looked at the position of the nursery again in relation to the two tall skyscrapers and the third half-formed one. The hedge which encircled the nursery was the same size as the base of the other three trees. Something clicked in Amber's mind.

"This used to be a tree-building," she said, eyeing the hedge.

Zoe smiled at Amber's perceptiveness. "You finally recognized it."

Amber stared at the two blackened trees. "The Mernas burnt down the tree-buildings."

Zoe nodded. "Yes. The Mernas have attacked the Adra city many times over the generations. Some of their attacks have been devastating for the Adras, burning down hundred-year-old tree-buildings. But they are a resilient species. They replant most of the trees they lose." She nodded to the half-formed structure. "And where they cannot replant, they repurpose the space." She nodded to the nursery. "Both serve as a reminder of the tenacious nature of the Adra community."

Zoe and Amber stood in silence for a moment, watching the children playing inside the nursery.

Amber thought back to the images she had seen in the visions; the fiery trail of destruction left behind as humans colonized Earth, the visible desolation of the atmosphere and the water, cities and industry scarring the land. From a distance it certainly seemed like humans were a plague on the Earth. Amber thought back to another image, to the second blue-green planet and the asteroid which flew harmlessly past.

"When you commented on the lack of iridium in Arcadia's sedimentary makeup, you weren't suggesting . . . I mean, it's ridiculous, isn't it?" asked Amber.

Zoe nodded. "Yes. I believe Arcadia and Earth are one and the same."

Amber was stunned for a moment. "How is that possible?"

"I do not know for sure but I think it has something to do with the *Phoenix* engine. It was new technology and it was never properly tested. Looking back, we should have been more skeptical. The coincidence was just too great. Almost immediately after they started using the *Phoenix* they found exactly what they were looking for. I guess it never occurred to anyone they might be looking in a mirror."

Amber frowned. "The *Phoenix*? But that was designed to teleport a spacecraft to the furthest reaches of the universe?"

"In principle, yes. The basic premise of the *Phoenix* is it opens and stabilizes a singularity, a hole in space-time. On the other side of the hole is another part of the universe, billions of light years away." Zoe paused, trying to find the words to explain her thoughts. "But what if instead of opening a hole to another point in our universe, the drive created a wormhole to *another* universe? How would we know the difference?"

Amber raised an eyebrow. "A parallel universe? That's a bit science fictioney, isn't it?" Amber looked at the Adra children playing among the soft grass. "Then again, I guess we are on another planet with tiny humanoids, alien overlords, and T-Rex wandering around. Maybe we are in a science fiction movie after all," she laughed dryly.

As the pair spoke, another Adra arrived at the nursery. This one was larger than Purple and tucked carefully in its arms was a large ovular shape; an egg. It was bigger than an ostrich egg, creamy in color and speckled pink. The Adra held it very carefully, a parent cradling a newborn. As it entered the hedge it nuzzled one of the larger children before leaving together.

"I'm not exactly a theoretical physicist," continued Zoe. "But if the multiverse theory is correct, if there are an infinite number of universes, then it is possible there is a version of Earth where the dinosaurs were never wiped out by that asteroid. And in that universe, it would be equally possible dinosaurs would have continued to evolve and flourish naturally. The rise of mammals would not have taken place, and the most intelligent species of the dinosaur era could have evolved into complex beings beyond anything ever seen on Earth."

Amber smiled at the irony; clearly Zoe was not familiar with her work back home. It seemed like a lifetime ago she and Joel were presenting their findings on the *Cerebraptor* and their theory that raptors would have evolved to a point well beyond humankind.

"We were right," she whispered to herself.

As the light of the day started to fade, more Adras arrived at the nursery. Each one left with more of the children until eventually only Purple remained. Amber and Zoe watched Purple as she studiously collected any small trinkets left behind and stored them in a neat pile in the center of the grass.

"We should be getting back," said Zoe.

As the pair left the now-empty nursery, Amber turned to Zoe. "Say you're right, say we're in another universe where the Chicxulub asteroid never struck the Earth. How do you explain everything else? How did the dinosaurs survive other extinction-level events like global warming, or the ice ages, or geological anomalies like super volcanic eruptions? And if mammals never had a chance to thrive, how do you explain the Mernas? They're clearly mammalian in appearance. But according to evolutionary theory they shouldn't exist here. Also, what happened to avian birds? They started to surface in the Cretaceous era, so where did they all go?"

Zoe shook her head. "I do not have all the answers. I do not know how the Mernas came into existence, what happened to avian birds, or why the raptors changed so drastically but the Denkras look so similar to their ancestors."

Amber scratched her head. "Well, the Tyrannosaur resemblance actually makes sense, biologically speaking." As she spoke Amber could see her now-familiar tree-room sitting at the base of a wide kapok tree. "Apex predators with virtually unchanged body structures are common. Just look at crocodilians; they've stuck with pretty much the same general design for about two hundred million years. Or sharks, where the earliest fossils date back to over 400 million years. Aside from slight modifications here and there, if the formula works why change it?"

Zoe escorted Amber to her room. "I don't know much about that sort of thing. What I *do* know is the Adras are smart, smarter than anything we've *ever* seen on Earth."

As they entered the room the large Adras which had been on guard also returned.

Amber looked sideways at Zoe, still unsure of her behavior. "So, what happens now? What happens if I don't agree to help the Adras domesticate the Mernas?"

Zoe patted Amber's shoulder. "I don't really know. But for now, you should get some sleep."

Base Camp, Arcadia—
18:00, 9 September, 2086

The unfamiliar sound of shouting cut through Diamond's subconscious. He shifted uncomfortably on one of the lifeboat seats, trying to sleep. The shouting increased in volume and changed in pitch, deeper this time. Slowly the muffled sounds turned into stilted words as Diamond's mind drifted back into the conscious world. He blinked, clearing his vision.

Diamond grimaced as he stretched his stiff muscles and looked out the forward wraparound window of the lifeboat. The sky was dark, with a soft tinge of orange in the distance. He quietly exited the boat to find Din and Grey arguing animatedly.

Diamond walked slowly around the nose of the ship, catching snippets of their conversation.

"I don't care if it's getting dark. We need to get back to your village as soon as possible," growled Grey.

"No. No dark. Garkra eat," protested Din.

The pair were hovering around the firepit which was stoked with fresh kindling. From the looks of it, Din was preparing to hunker down for the night, but Grey wanted to return to the village.

Diamond knew the only thing Grey hated more than being told what to do was being told what to do by a civilian. He could only imagine the Lieutenant's frustration at being bossed around by a primitive miniature humanoid.

"What's all the shouting about?" asked Diamond.

Grey rubbed the space between his eyes, massaging a stress headache. "This pipsqueak thinks it's too dangerous to travel after sunset and is *insisting* we camp here for the night."

Din was calmer than Grey. He crouched by the firewood in the middle of a small pit. "You go. You Garkra eat," said Din nonchalantly.

Diamond scratched his head. "Sir, where are Dr. Carter and the lady Merna? Isn't this conversation pointless until they get back?"

Grey's expression relaxed. "I don't know." He shot a sideways glance to Din who was still building the small fire. Grey nodded subtly, leading Diamond several steps away. "I think we may have a problem with our little friends," he whispered.

"What do you mean?"

Grey continued to move Diamond away, into the forest. "I don't trust them. They're not the pathetic primitives I thought they were."

"Why? What happened?"

Grey kept Din within his sights but led Diamond far enough into the trees that they could converse in private. "Din shot Tom with a poisoned dart. I'm not saying the guy didn't deserve to be punished after everything he's put us through, but the look on that little guy's face was . . ." he paused, searching for the right word, "…ruthless. He died in front of us, seizing and gagging. Fucking brutal way to go."

"Jesus Christ," breathed Diamond.

Grey glanced back toward Din. "I don't trust these people. They're holding our team as insurance. So, what happens if we don't return tonight?"

"While I can't argue that, if we return without the stone won't they just kill all of us anyway?"

Before Grey could answer a soft humming interrupted their conversation. Grey and Diamond instinctively placed a hand on their lasers, peering into the greying forest. The humming grew in volume.

Suddenly Joel's MTV shot through the trees like a race car, skidding to a stop. Joel saw Grey and Diamond holding their lasers and laughed. "Is that the thanks we get for bringing the stone back?"

Faybin sat on Joel's lap cradling a knapsack reverently.

"You found it!" Diamond couldn't hide the excitement from his voice.

"Yup. We also found *him.*" Joel leaned to the side so Diamond and Grey could see the man sitting on the back of the MTV.

Grey was actually relieved to see Charles alive. He was bloodied and bruised, his wrists were bound together, and his left leg was bandaged, but he was alive.

"What happened to his leg?" asked Diamond.

Joel gestured to Faybin. "She put a spear through it. Little lady saved my life."

Grey watched Faybin climb off the MTV and quickly run toward Din by the campfire. For a moment he wondered if he had judged the Mernas too quickly.

Joel looked around the camp. "Where's Tom?"

Grey's expression soured. "Tom didn't make it back."

"He what?" a deep gravelly voice interrupted their conversation.

Everyone turned to the man on the back of the bike. His face was hard and his eyes cold. He glared at Grey with animosity.

Joel touched Grey's shoulder. "Lieutenant, may I introduce the man formerly known as Charles Kendal; Tom's brother, Edward Gilmore."

Grey's eyes narrowed. "Brother?"

Edward continued to stare at Grey through hate-filled eyes. "What happened?"

The image of Tom's convulsing body vomiting blood and foam entered Grey's mind. He shook his head, pushing the images aside. He returned Edward's cold gaze. "He didn't make it."

"So, what now?" asked Diamond, trying to defuse the tension.

Grey turned back to Joel. "Din is insisting we stay here for the night because he's afraid of the Garkra."

Joel nodded. "Faybin said the same thing. And considering the Mernas know this place a hell of a lot better than we do, we'd be stupid not to listen."

"While I agree with the sentiment, I'm not comfortable leaving our people with the Mernas one minute longer than we need to," pressed Grey.

Joel shook his head. "If we want the Mernas to trust us then we need to start trusting them, too."

Grey growled. "Fine. But to be safe everyone is staying in the ship where it's secure. And I want a sentry on duty 'round the clock' just in case."

Return

Jungle, Arcadia—
06:00, 10 September, 2086

Joel and the team got moving at the crack of dawn. It was so early a thick fog still clung ominously to the forest. The sun had barely peeked over the horizon, but the sky was light enough they could move with ease. They took three MTVs again; Grey and Edward on one, Diamond and Din on another, and Joel and Faybin on the third.

The journey to the Merna village took a fraction of the time with the MTVs, turning a half-day walk into a mere half-hour ride. As they raced through the dimly lit forest Joel finally felt a brief moment of relief. From the outside, it seemed like everything on this planet was against them. A Garkra had tried to eat them, the Mernas had tried to sacrifice them, and they had even been betrayed by their own people. But their luck was about to change. With the *Light stone* in hand they'd be able to regain the Mernas' trust and could focus their attention on the only thing Joel really cared about, finding Amber.

As they approached the village the rising sun was casting long streaks of light through the trees. The fog had thinned but still hung in the air like a gentle veil. Grey, Diamond, and Joel slowed their bikes as they passed through the entrance archway.

Joel's stomach dropped.

The area was deserted. Not a single sound could be heard from the village or the surrounding forest.

Something wasn't right.

The three bikes came to a halt near the central bonfire, which was reduced to cold ashes.

To their right came a loud cry. "Joel!" Veronica came running from one of the nearby huts; she sprinted toward Joel and threw her arms around him.

Joel felt her trembling slightly. "I'm glad to see you, too," he said, slightly confused.

"You found Diamond," said Veronica in relief. She looked around the area, glancing between the faces of the returning crew, and frowned curiously; she was looking for Amber.

Joel shook his head, fighting back the pain.

Behind Veronica, Schmitt exited a hut with Veyha by his side. At the sound of Veronica's cries, Merna faces began poking out of the nearby teardrop huts, clearly agitated and yet relieved at the sight of the returning party. Veyha ran to greet them, throwing her arms around Faybin and burying her head in the latter's shoulder. The smile on Faybin's face melted as she exchanged words with Veyha. She shot a discerning look to Joel as she stroked Veyha's long golden hair.

"What happened here?" asked Joel tentatively.

Schmitt sighed heavily. "There's something you need to know." His voice was tranquil and calm but Joel could sense pain in his eyes.

Veyha suddenly appeared by Joel's side. "*Light stone*?"

"Hang on a second, Schmitt." Joel smiled at the small girl. He reached into his knapsack and pulled out the *Light stone*, holding it high so everyone could see. It was so large it filled his hand easily. The morning sunlight glinted off the stone, producing a stunning emerald green shine. The quiet village suddenly erupted with enthusiastic cheering. Several Mernas approached, patting the group on their arms as a sign of appreciation.

"What happened to Charles?" asked Veronica, suddenly noticing the man sitting on the back of Grey's bike. He sat with his hands still bound. His leg had been bandaged using medical supplies from the lifeboat.

Joel nodded to Diamond. "Fill them in on the details." He turned to Faybin. "Let's get this stone back to the temple so we can put this whole mess behind us." He started to follow Faybin into the forest before pausing and addressing Schmitt. "Sorry, what were you saying?"

Schmitt bowed his head. "Come, it will be easier to explain as we return the stone."

The pair quickly took off after Faybin who led them through the maze of huts, to the very edge of the village. They came to a small path cut into the edge of the forest.

"So, what do I need to know?" asked Joel.

"It's about the *Light stone.* The Mernas may worship it like a holy idol but it is by no means *theirs.*"

Joel thought back to the first time he saw the stone. The perfect laser-like cut, the flawless color and shape. He knew it was too advanced for the Mernas. "So, whose is it?"

Schmitt lowered his voice slightly. "The Adras. The Mernas believe the stone has magical properties. That it brings light where there is darkness, that it keeps Garkras and Adras away from their village, that it protects and guides them."

As they spoke, the path ended abruptly less than one hundred meters from the edge of the village. Faybin paused for a moment in the middle of a small clearing, next to a dead hollow tree. The tree-hollow was large, larger than a natural hollow should be, large enough for a human to enter with ease. Faybin stepped inside and was swallowed by the darkness.

Schmitt continued, "The truth is, the Mernas aren't entirely wrong. They just don't understand *how* the stone does all these things."

Schmitt and Joel followed Faybin into the darkness. Inside the tree was a huge space, far larger than it appeared from the outside. It was dark, but Joel's night vision quickly adapted to the small amount of light offered by the large opening. Faybin was standing beside a strange inorganic contraption. It was a big smooth glass-like cylinder which stretched from the floor up through the hollow tree above their heads. At about chest height, an ovular hole was cut in the center of the cylinder. Inside the hole sat a platform with four small grappling prongs.

Faybin reached a hand to Joel. "*Light stone.*"

Joel handed Faybin the stone. She took it with reverence and gently placed it atop the small grappling prongs. Almost instantly, the entire room lit up with a bright white light. Joel was blinded momentarily from the brightness. After a few seconds his eyes adjusted again. The walls of the hollow were covered in small crystals which shone like lightbulbs. He looked back to the stone and frowned. It had lost its green coloring, replaced by a fiery red hue which seemed to radiate in a wide halo around the stone.

Joel turned to Schmitt, awaiting an explanation.

Schmitt half-smiled. "As far as I can tell the stone harnesses both solar and geothermal energy, like a giant conductor." As he spoke, the old

German pointed to the strange-looking cylinder which ran all the way to the top of the canopy and down into the earth beneath them.

Joel saw Faybin smile momentarily. But her smile quickly faded.

Schmitt sighed. "When active, the stone emits a powerful magnetic field which the Garkras can't stand, keeping the Mernas safe as long as they stay within the vicinity of the village. The stone also keeps the Adras away, in a manner of speaking. It provides energy to their community. And because the Mernas treat this station like a temple, the Adras have no need to maintain the space themselves. So, they don't come near the station or the village, provided the power is on. But, when the power goes out—"

"They come looking for answers," said Joel, finally understanding. He saw the saddened look on Faybin's face and recalled the empty and eerily quiet village. "They *came* looking for answers."

Schmitt nodded. "Yes. They came yesterday afternoon, searching for the stone. When they did not find it, they took the Merna elders instead."

Joel finally understood. The one Merna he had not seen on their return. "Xylon."

Veronica was silent for a moment. She stood several meters away from the MTVs with Diamond and Grey. Edward sat on the back of Grey's bike, brooding quietly.

Veronica shook her head. "I knew it. I knew he was a lying scumbag. That crap about the fire; I bet he started it. I just don't get why, though? Why go to all this trouble?"

Diamond shrugged. "You'd have to ask him that."

Veronica eyed Edward with suspicion. "What's your game? Why go to all this effort? Killing the real Charles? Undergoing plastic surgery? Taking on his identity? For what? A piece of jewelry on an alien planet?"

Edward scoffed. "You expect me to just tell you everything? I'm not a bloody Bond villain."

As they spoke, Veyha clambered over the MTVs, poking at the various instruments. She opened the lid to one of the storage compartments which hung on either side of the bike and started to climb inside the small box.

"Get away from that," snapped Grey.

Veyha dropped the lid and jumped back in fright, scuttling to the other side of the bike.

"The Adras have taken the Merna elders," interrupted Joel.

Everyone turned to see Joel and Schmitt returning with Faybin.

Joel shook his head. "I don't know why, insurance maybe? Punishment? I don't know. But now the Mernas have as much reason to help us get our people back as we do to help them get theirs."

Grey nodded. "We heard. And I agree, our priority needs to be finding our people. But first, we need to secure him," he gestured to Edward.

"We could keep him in the prison pit," said Schmitt.

Grey shook his head, thinking back to Tom's convulsing body. "No. There's no telling what the Mernas will do if we leave him here. I want him supervised by a crewmember."

Veronica thought for a moment. "The most secure place right now is *Hermes*. There's nowhere for him to run in space."

Grey rolled the idea over. "Sounds good. Sergeant—"

Veronica cut him off. "With all due respect, Lieutenant, this sounds like something you need a pilot for, not a Marine. You and Diamond should stay here and get the Merna warriors ready." Veronica was annoyed at the familiar patronizing tone from Grey, but this time she was determined to assert her position.

Grey eyed her sideways. "I don't like it."

"I'm not asking for your permission. If I take one of the bikes back to the lifeboat we can dock with *Hermes* in a couple of hours. It's about time Mikhail and I switched shifts anyway."

Grey growled slightly under his breath. "Fine."

Veronica concealed a smile. She climbed onto the front seat of Grey's bike and revved the engines.

Joel gave Veronica a quick hug. "Watch him closely," he whispered.

Veronica nodded. "I'll be fine. Go get Amber back."

Adra City, Arcadia—
06:00, 10 September, 2086

Amber lay on her back on the floor of her small tree-room. She had managed to secure a couple of hours' sleep during the night, but her mind refused to switch off. It was too busy trying to make sense of everything she had seen and heard. Trying to assemble the jigsaw pieces and make meaning of this place.

Suddenly the two Adras standing guard by the door stepped aside and Cockatoo entered the small room. He stared at Amber lying on the floor and snorted. Amber didn't react; she eyed Cockatoo with a sense of intrigue. For the first time, she didn't feel any fear. Something in her gut told her they had no intention of harming her.

After a moment Cockatoo motioned for Amber to follow him.

Amber stood. "Where are we going this time?" she asked casually.

Cockatoo stepped closer to Amber, staring intently into her eyes. She heard a voice in her head; it was deep and smooth, like a jazz singer.

There's something you need to see.

Amber felt butterflies in her stomach at the strange sensation, as though someone was whispering directly into her auditory cortex. She picked herself off the ground and followed Cockatoo through the city.

It was still relatively dark outside, but there were already signs of daylight by the time the pair reached the city gate, which was partially ajar.

Cockatoo led Amber deep into the jungle. They walked for hours through the undergrowth. Slowly the pre-morning chill was replaced by the warmth of daybreak. Streams of light danced sideways through the trees as the sun peeked over the horizon in the distance. Amber couldn't help but feel a sense of relief being immersed in the forest once more. The familiarity of the natural world reignited her sense of hope and wonder.

With the rising sun, all manner of animal life began to emerge. Tiny carnivorous creatures with the face of a crocodile and the body of a mouse skittered across the forest floor, feasting on the rotting carcass of what Amber could only describe as a toad the size of a cow. Enormous and spectacularly colored insects scaled the equally enormous trees. An entire family of four-legged herbivores grazed in an open field. Their backs were covered in sharp spines like a porcupine, and long tentacles extended from the sides of their faces, searching for food.

The pair hiked for the better part of the morning until the forest finally began to thin and Amber spotted the ocean. Without thinking, she dashed ahead, through the palms and mangroves onto soft white sand. The water was a beautiful deep blue, and crashed in elegant white crests on the sand.

For the first time since they'd landed on Arcadia, Amber felt at peace.

Her tranquility was interrupted by the soft purring of Cockatoo from behind. She heard the smooth jazz voice in her mind again.

Over here.

Amber followed Cockatoo back into the trees. The analytical part of her mind wondered if the tone of the telepathic voices in her head was a reflection of her own expectations or if the creatures actually projected unique vocal tones.

She was led to a large patch of ferns which appeared to carpet the forest floor in greenery. Cockatoo stopped and turned back to Amber expectantly.

Amber paused. "What is it?"

Cockatoo nodded to something hidden beneath the foliage. Amber followed his motions and, to her horror, she saw a man's boot sticking out from the ferns.

"Oh, God!" she exclaimed, diving to the ground. She pulled the leaves back and saw a body lying on the damp ground. She saw the man's face; it was gaunt, sickly blue and pale. But it wasn't a member of her team. Amber shook her head in confusion. "What happened here? Who is this?" But she already knew the answer. Beneath his thick beard and filthy hair she saw the familiar ISA pilot's badge. "He's from the *Atlas*." She stared at the body, it couldn't have been more than a day old.

Cockatoo held up a small object in his clawed hand. It was a star-shaped stone with pointed edges. It wasn't human, and it was too primitive to belong to the Adras. Amber thought back to the small humanoids who occupied the cave. She recalled images of the Adras cultivating their precious tree-city and the small humanoids who viciously attacked, burning it to the ground. It was a Merna weapon.

A Merna had killed a human.

Amber turned to Cockatoo with anger in her voice. "Why did you bring me here? Why are you showing me this?"

Cockatoo stared at Amber, unblinking. His face was stoic. As her eyes connected with his, Amber felt a pang of guilt.

You know why.

Arrival

Hermes, Orbit—
09:30, 10 September, 2086

"*Mikhail!*" Veronica's voice echoed through *Hermes* like a ghost. "*Mikhail, pick up! I'm in the lifeboat on my way to you.*"

Mikhail sat up abruptly, startled by the unexpected sounds.

After speaking with Grey and Joel the previous day, he had kept a close eye on Base Camp, observing as the team took the MTVs into the jungle and as they returned again later that day. Knowing they were secured in the boat and there was nothing further he could do, Mikhail had finally allowed himself to leave the viewing platform and attempted a proper night's sleep in the living quarters.

The last thing he expected was to be woken by Veronica's voice.

"*Mikhail? Where are you?*" repeated Veronica over the ship's speakers.

Mikhail leaped out of bed and stumbled across the living quarters to the ladder which led to the upper deck. He engaged the small communication panel in the wall. "Veronica? It's so good to hear your voice! Are you okay? Is anyone else with you?"

Her voice was tense. "*I'll explain later. I'm only a few minutes out. Prep the loading dock.*"

Veronica angled the lifeboat effortlessly toward the hovering mass of *Hermes* as it orbited Arcadia. She glanced over her shoulder. Behind her sat Edward, strapped to his seat. His hands were still bound together, his eyes were closed, and his face was stoic and placid. He had been eerily quiet since they left the Merna village. Veronica disliked being alone with him.

As they approached *Hermes,* the lights surrounding the lifeboat-shaped hole switched on, guiding Veronica into docking position. Once she was within range, the auto-guidance system kicked in and brought the two vessels into perfect alignment. The boat slipped into place with a comforting whoosh of air pressurizing. For a brief moment Veronica relaxed.

Mikhail waited eagerly just inside the airlock. The hatch hissed as the airlock released. The doors slid open smoothly and, to Mikhail's surprise, a man fell from the open hatch.

Before Mikhail could react, Veronica leaned out. "Wait here," she said before disappearing back inside the boat.

The man on the floor stirred and pushed up onto his hands and knees. Mikhail finally saw his face. It was bruised and filthy, but he recognized the man's cold blue eyes, sharp features, and salt-and-pepper hair.

"Charles," he breathed. He shook his head, recalling Irwin's last message. "No, not Charles."

As Edward tried to stand, Veronica appeared again and kicked him hard; he fell back to the floor. "His name is Edward Gilmore," she said bitterly. Veronica opened a nearby cupboard marked "security" and pulled out a pair of handcuffs. "We need to secure him until we're ready to leave."

Mikhail didn't need to be told twice. "Where do you want him?"

Veronica eyed the bulkhead doors at the back of the science lab. "In the storage compartment. It's one of the few places that can be locked from the outside."

"Veronica," squeaked a tiny voice from inside the airlock.

Mikhail and Veronica spun around in surprise. A tiny child stood in the airlock. She was very small, with brown skin and golden blonde hair.

"Veyha! What are you doing here?"

Veyha bowed her head sheepishly. "Sky people."

Veronica's surprise quickly turned to sympathy. "You wanted to see where the sky people came from? Oh, Veyha."

Mikhail tapped Veronica on the shoulder. "You can explain her later."

Together they dragged Edward into the storage compartment and sat his limp body by the huge steel doors which led to the engine room. He didn't resist, closing his eyes lazily and allowing himself to be dragged. Mikhail attached one set of the cuffs to Edward's wrist and the other to the steel door. Edward still didn't resist. He sat quietly while he was restrained and opened his eyes in time to see the pair leave the room and lock the door behind them.

Veronica threw her arms around Mikhail and hugged him tight; her body was trembling as she finally released the stress and anxiety that had built up over the past few days. Despite her height and cool demeanor, she felt so small and fragile in his arms. The warmth of her breath against his neck was strangely calming. He held her in silence, waiting for her quivering body to settle. He never wanted to let go.

After a few minutes Veronica looked up. "I guess you have a few questions."

○ ○ ○ ● ○ ○ ○

Veronica and Mikhail sat at the dining table of the kitchen. Veyha sat quietly, marveling at the strangeness all around her. Mikhail had prepared some hot chocolate for her. At first she was wary of the warm liquid, but once it had cooled she lapped at it hungrily. Veronica sat at the opposite end of the table nursing a mug of coffee. The huge floating body of Arcadia was just visible through the enormous window which wrapped around the front section of *Hermes*. It seemed so small and unassuming from this distance.

"Did you see where they took Amber?" asked Veronica, sipping her coffee slowly.

"Sort of. They took her to the same place they took the small man from the beach. I wanted to get a better look inside the gate but one of the aliens saw the orb and switched it off."

"You mean it broke?" asked Veronica.

"No, turned it off. It actually used the 'off' switch."

Veronica sat back in her seat, taking in the new information.

Mikhail touched her hand gently. "Vee, I'm glad you are okay."

As Veronica stared into Mikhail's eyes she could sense something was wrong. She could hear the angst in his voice and could see the relief on his face. Her gaze shifted focus, landing on the bench behind Mikhail, to the empty vodka bottle.

"You started drinking again," she said flatly.

Mikhail's face dropped.

Veronica could see the guilt in his eyes. She took his hand in hers and kissed it. "Mikhail, I'm so sorry. I can't believe I left you up here on your own. You must have felt so helpless and alone. I should have known better."

Mikhail was taken aback. "*You're* sorry?"

Veronica stroked Mikhail's hand gently. "Did you really think I didn't know about the crash? Your mother told me everything a few years ago. She thanked me for bringing you back to her."

Mikhail was stunned. "You've known for years? You've known all this time and you stayed with me anyway?"

Veronica stifled a laugh. "Of course I did. I know everything about you. I know you are smart and strong, you are a hopeless romantic but you are stubborn and strong-willed. I know you have your demons and I know you have the strength to overcome them."

Mikhail felt recharged by her words.

"But you still need to be careful down there," she continued.

"*I* need to be careful?"

Veronica nodded. "Yes. Because you are going down this time. Someone needs to keep an eye on Edward but the crew still needs help down there. You know more about this planet than me or anyone else, and you know where the Adras took Amber."

"I don't want to leave you again. I was a mess without you." He took her hand in his and kissed it gently.

Veronica smiled weakly. "You are stronger than you think, my love. You have been up here for days battling your demons alone. Imagine what you could achieve down there. I don't want you to leave either, but the others need you, now more than ever."

"What about her?" he asked, pointing to Veyha.

"Veyha stay! Veyha stay Veronica!" shouted the little girl.

Her outburst took Veronica by surprise. Veyha must have understood English better than she realized. Veronica shrugged. "It's probably safer for her to stay here for now. Her people are about to go to war."

Veronica and Mikhail quickly loaded the pre-packed supplies into the lifeboat. Veronica showed no emotion as she moved busily around the cabin, but Mikhail could sense her anxiety.

"You can use the MTV to get to the Merna village. I pre-programmed the location so the bike can take you straight there. The Garkras only seem to hunt at night so you should be fine for now. I don't know much about the Adras, but they have the Mernas scared shitless, so stay on your toes."

Mikhail laughed. "Bet you never thought you'd say that."

She offered him a weak smile; he was always trying to make her smile.

Veronica handed Mikhail a case of shortwave radio transceivers. "These should be useful on the ground with the comms equipment down."

As he took the case from her, their eyes locked. Without saying another word Mikhail kissed Veronica tenderly. Veronica felt a passionate longing mixed with a fearful dread. She didn't know if she wanted to scream or cry.

After a moment, they pulled back and Mikhail placed a hand on the side of Veronica's face as tears began to roll down her cheek.

"Don't do anything stupid down there," she whispered, trying to control her emotions.

Mikhail stared into her brown eyes and whispered, "I love you."

Adra City, Arcadia—
12:00, 10 September, 2086

Amber followed Cockatoo through the now-familiar gate which surrounded the Adra city. Her mind was still buzzing after seeing the *Atlas* man's dead body. Although she had no way of knowing what had happened, something about the look on his face sent shivers down her spine.

With her thoughts distracted, Amber didn't notice she was not being taken back to her solitary tree-room. She was being led deeper into the city, toward the large skyscraper-trees.

As they ascended the various levels inside one of the large structures, Amber realized something was different this time. The rooms which hung between the inner and outer trees were no longer empty. Each room had two or three small humanoids inside, although they weren't the same Mernas Amber had seen inside the cave. They were much older and they lacked the familiar brace around their necks.

But it wasn't the Mernas that captured Amber's attention. A soft blue light glinted from the entrance to each tree-room. The doorways were covered in a thin translucent sheet of blue-white light.

As they neared the top of the staircase, Cockatoo stopped and placed his hand beside the door of the nearest tree-room. The panel of light disappeared and Amber was ushered inside. By the time she turned around the light had returned and Cockatoo was out of sight. Amber frowned as she stared at the panel of light, reaching to touch the strange surface.

"I wouldn't do that if I were you," came a voice from behind.

Amber spun in surprise.

Zoe sat casually on the other side of the room. She was seated on a series of vines which had been woven together to create a hammock-like structure. Amber glanced around the room curiously. It was constructed from the roots of the parasitic tree which formed the outer layer of the huge skyscraper. Various branches and vines were draped across the room. The floor was carpeted in a soft and luscious layer of mosses. It was like walking on a sponge bed. The walls had been molded to form several large openings, allowing natural light to fill the open space.

"What is this place?"

Zoe spoke with an eerie calmness. "This is my chamber. Be careful of the light-shield. It's non-lethal, but it'll give you quite a jolt if you touch it."

Amber eyed the panel of blue-white light closely, careful to keep her distance. The small gemstones which lined the edges of the doorframe were glowing white and humming softly, like a refrigerator.

"Jesus. They have electricity?"

"It's not quite electricity, at least not as we know it. As I said before, I'm no physicist, but I believe it has something to do with electromagnetism and a huge gem called a *Light stone*."

"*Light stone*?" said Amber, glancing sideways at Zoe.

Zoe half-laughed. "The name might sound silly, but the stone is a remarkable example of the Adras' intelligence. It is used to harness geothermal and solar energy which it relays to the city. They use it for everything."

Amber approached one of the large "windows" built into the wall of the room. The same blue light shimmered across the open space, protecting the room from the elements. Outside Amber could see more light-shields lining the ground-level doorways and the higher windows of the taller trees. "If they're so reliant on this power, why is this the first time I've seen it?"

Zoe raised an eyebrow. "What do you think formed the 'bars' inside the cave? Or powered the medi-lab you were taken to for health screening? When the power went out in the cave I knew the stone must have been removed. Which means someone from your team must have stolen it."

Amber turned back to Zoe and frowned suspiciously. "How can you be so sure it was a human? It could have been one of those small humanoids?"

"The Mernas would never remove the stone. When they realized the magnetic field it generated also kept away large predators they built their village right next door. For the most part, it was beneficial for everyone. The Mernas treated the station like a temple. And the Adras and Garkras stayed away from the village, providing a safe environment for the villagers. The Mernas know better than to touch the stone. Humans, on the other hand, go stomping around like they own the universe. They come here pretending to be on a scientific mission, but really are looking for a new host planet to consume. We are like the cosmic equivalent of a virus." For the first time since they had met, Zoe's calm demeanor faltered, replaced by a subtle but deep-seeded resentment.

Amber half-laughed, "You sound like Joel."

In all honesty, Amber sympathized with Zoe's sentiment. The more time she spent on Arcadia, the more she began to question the ethics of their mission.

Amber turned back to the window and gazed across the beautiful tree-city. "It's a wonder the Adras don't just kill us all and be done with it. Seriously, why don't the Adras take us out? They know we're here and *why* we're here. They're clearly intelligent, so why let an invasive alien species continue to run around wreaking havoc?"

Zoe finally stood from her hammock and joined Amber by the window. "Because the Adras aren't just clever animals who figured out how to use tools. They are perceptive and discerning. They recognize humanity's potential for love and compassion, as well as for greed and destruction. Despite our flaws, the Adras would never kill a human or a Merna if they could help it. It's just not in their nature."

Amber thought back to the body of the ISA pilot. "The Adras took me into the jungle today. They brought me to the body of a human man, one of the *Atlas* pilots. At first I thought they were trying to threaten me; to show me what would happen if we didn't comply. But they didn't kill him. He was killed by a Merna. I think they showed me his body so I'd finally understand who the real threat was. And to help me realize what you've been trying to say all along; the Adras want to help the Mernas, to protect them from themselves." Amber turned back to the window. "To stop them becoming like us."

Merna Village, Arcadia—
12:00, 10 September, 2086

"Mikhail!" said Joel as an MTV cruised into the Merna village.

Mikhail brought the bike to a halt in the village square. Dozens of Mernas stood nearby in full battle camouflage. Their bodies were decorated with elaborate green and brown markings, while their chests and groins were covered in the thick hide of some sort of animal. Most of the warriors carried spears and slingshots as they practiced a ceremonial war dance.

Mikhail frowned as some of the taller, stronger Mernas walked past, carrying lasers.

"About time you joined the party," said Joel playfully.

Mikhail turned his attention back to Joel. "I know where they've taken Amber." At that moment, he saw Grey and Diamond standing off to the side with a handful of armed Mernas, showing them how to use the lasers. "What's going on here?"

Joel's heart leapt into his throat. "You know where they took Amber? Where is she?"

"There's a compound north of here, a huge stone-walled fortress. I followed the aliens with a monitor orb after they invaded the camp. It's the same place the dinosaur-thing took the tiny man."

"The dinosaur-thing is called a Garkra, and the tiny man was a Merna," said Joel.

Faybin's ears pricked up. "Garkra? Merna?" Her voice was concerned. She turned to Schmitt and spoke rapidly in her native language.

"She wants to know what the Garkra and Merna looked like," said Schmitt.

Mikhail thought for a moment. "Honestly, the dinosaur-thing looked like a T-Rex; big head, tiny arms, and it was red and gold. The man had dark skin and long hair and green tattoos all over his body. Oh, and he was carrying a canoe, a boat of some sort. He turned up at the beach, like he was planning to paddle over the ocean."

Faybin's eyes welled as Schmitt translated. She whispered, "Naru. Denkra."

Schmitt sighed heavily with recognition. "That creature wasn't a Garkra. It was another type of large carnivore called a Denkra. They are like servants of the Adras. And the small man you saw was her husband. Naru had been sent on a scouting mission to find Katchu, the promised land. The elders of the tribe often send their strongest, bravest warriors to search for Katchu. Many warriors have been lost at sea, others have been captured by Adras. Naru is one of the strongest and smartest Merna warriors. He's been chosen for this mission many times before but he had always returned safely; until now."

Joel saw the pain on Faybin's face. "We'll find Naru. If they took him to the same place they took Amber then that's probably where we'll find the elders, too. We're all going to the same place."

Mikhail frowned as a pair of Mernas walked past carrying guns. "What's going on here?" he repeated.

Joel ignored Mikhail's question. "Lieutenant!"

Grey looked over and noticed Mikhail had arrived with the bike. He left Diamond and the Mernas to their training. "Welcome to Arcadia, Dr. Ozero. I see you've met Dr. Schmitt."

"Mikhail knows where they took Amber. We should go ahead and scout out the place, don't you think?" Joel could hardly contain his enthusiasm.

Grey nodded. "It would be helpful to have a scout."

Joel turned back to Mikhail. "Which way is it from here?"

Mikhail stared at Joel for a moment, frowning. "What is going on here?" he asked, for the third time.

Joel paused. He saw the Mernas training with Diamond and shrugged. "Didn't she tell you? The Mernas are helping us find Amber and the others. They've volunteered every able-bodied person they have."

Mikhail frowned. "I know I just got here but is that really the best option? I mean, you're giving them lasers. Who's to say they won't shoot each other, or you, by accident?"

Grey shook his head. "If we're going to war, we need to be armed. Who knows what sort of alien technology these Adras have? Besides, I've seen what the Mernas' weapons can do to a man. If they're going to shoot me by accident, at least with our weapons I'll die quickly."

Mikhail shook his head. "I'm not going to argue with you. But I still think this is a bad idea." He reached into his backpack and pulled out two small transceivers. It was a small black device with an antenna sticking out of the top. He handed one to Grey. "Vee figured these would come in handy."

Grey took the device and half-smiled. He looked over it fondly. "A walkie-talkie? I haven't seen one of these since I was a kid."

Joel climbed onto the back of Mikhail's MTV. "Yes, yes, it's amazing how old technology can still come in handy," he said dismissively. "Mikhail, let's move."

The bike raced through the trees, heading north. They moved slowly at first, carefully navigating through the thick undergrowth. The mountain towered over the bike in the near distance, dwarfing the pair of humans beneath its sheer green rock face. A cascade of misting waterfalls toppled over the cliff, sending beautiful sprays of water into the valley below. At the base of the mountain, the falling water pooled, creating a small stream.

Mikhail pulled the handles hard to the left, veering toward the stream. The bike crashed through the branches of some low-lying bushes, careening over the lip of the stream bank. As the MTV hit the surface, the nose briefly dipped under the water, splashing over the handlebars. As soon as they hit the water additional pressure jets kicked in and the bike rose several inches over the surface. Without any obstacles in its way, the MTV accelerated quickly, flying over the small body of water like it was an open highway.

To their left was the sheer rock face of the cliff, covered in moss and lichen. To their right was a thin riverbank covered in grasses; beyond that was the thick jungle. They were sandwiched between greenery.

The forest thinned as the stream expanded into a flowing river. After another few kilometers Mikhail slowed the bike. Ahead, the waterway turned into a torrential current as the landscape dipped into a valley. Mikhail brought the bike away from the water, back into the jungle. They paused at the crest of the hill to get their bearings.

From the hillside, they could see the bottom of the steep decline where a huge stone wall rose from the ground. Slick leafy debris lined the sloping descent, but the foliage thinned dramatically at the bottom, leaving an exposed grassy plain about five meters wide around the edge of the wall. The river to their left raced down the valley and ran directly beneath the wall.

"This is it. This is where they took Amber," said Mikhail.

From their vantage point they could just make out the location of the gate to their right. Mikhail slid the MTV forward slowly, gently gliding it down the slope. When the bike reached the bottom of the incline, faint sounds of life could be heard inside the compound. Mikhail kept the bike away from the tree line, cautious to remain hidden.

They moved parallel to the wall, following it east, making their way to the great gate. As they approached, Joel finally saw its immense size. The gate towered several stories high. It was a ten-meter-high and ten-meter-wide decoratively carved stone slab, inlaid against the even larger stone wall which stretched several meters higher and beyond their line of sight in both directions. Joel felt dwarfed against the structure.

"Please tell me there's another way in?" said Joel, staring at the impenetrable entrance.

"Not that I've seen."

Once they were positioned outside the gate, Mikhail brought the bike to a stop and the pair dismounted. They pushed the MTV deeper into the forest, covering it with fallen branches in an effort to conceal their presence.

"C'mon, we need to get a better view," whispered Joel as he crept toward the tree line.

At the edge of the forest a huge fallen log provided some cover. They could see several Adras patrolling around the decorated entrance, moving with purpose along its length. Mikhail and Joel froze at the sight of them. It was the first time they'd seen the Adras in full.

Every Adra by the gate was either red and black or mottled grey in color, but they all had missing head and tail feathers and their left arms and hands were covered in a strange glove-like device.

They crouched lower.

"What do we do now?" whispered Mikhail.

Joel shrugged. "We find a way inside."

DISTRACTION

***Hermes*, Orbit—**
14:00, 10 September, 2086

Veronica stared wide-eyed at the 3D projections as they danced animatedly over the table. She paused the recording and moved the timeframe back again. She was watching the events which led to Amber's capture, for the fourth time. Veronica wanted to watch the recording from every possible angle. Something didn't feel right about the whole thing. Like why the Adras targeted their camp in the first place? And why they took Amber but left Diamond behind? As the scene ended again, Veronica sat back in her chair and stared at the table, deep in thought.

Veyha pulled at her sleeve. "Veronica," she whispered, pointing to the hologram. "Naru?" she asked, with a hint of hope in her voice.

Veronica frowned, searching her mind for the meaning of the word. "Naru? What's Naru?"

Veyha thought for a moment, trying to find the words. She pointed the index finger on her left hand in the air. "Faybin." She then held her right index finger in the air. "Naru." She rubbed the tip of her two fingers together; a child's view of adults kissing.

"Naru and Faybin? He's her husband?"

Veyha rolled the word over in her mind. "Hus-band, yes, yes. Hus-band." She thought for another moment and held up her fingers again then rubbed them against her own cheeks, smiling. "Veyha, Faybin, Naru."

Veronica frowned. "I don't—Oh? Oh! They're your parents? Faybin and Naru are your parents?"

"Yes! Pa-rents." Veyha smiled, proud of herself. She pointed to the observation table again. "Naru?"

Veronica looked back to the table; she could see the campsite and the surrounding forest. "I'm sorry, sweetheart. The cameras can't see *everything*, they only show us what we want them to see."

"Veyha want Naru. Want see, yes?" She squinted at the image.

"I'm sorry, I can't show you Naru. I don't even know—"

Veyha huffed, and ran to the opposite side of the viewing table; she began to push buttons at random. "Naru! Veyha want Naru!" The image above the table jumped and scrambled as Veyha mashed the controls.

Veronica walked around the table and pulled the small girl into her arms.

"Veyha want Naru!" Tears welled in her eyes.

"I'm sorry, but I can't help you. I don't know where Naru is." She stroked Veyha's hair and rocked back and forth gently.

Suddenly there was a loud crash from inside the storage room. Veyha clutched Veronica's arm in fright. Another loud thump followed by a metallic clang echoed through *Hermes* like a shockwave.

"Stay here," whispered Veronica, placing a hand on her laser.

Veyha shifted nervously as Veronica moved slowly through the science lab, toward the bulkhead doors. There was another thump; Veronica jumped slightly. She stood flat against the wall beside the door and inched closer to the small porthole. She couldn't see anything; Edward was gone. A sick feeling swelled in her stomach. She reached for the latch and slowly undid the lock. She slipped her fingers around the handle and in one swift motion threw the door open and aimed her laser into the room.

It was empty.

She kept her laser in front of her, walking forward several steps. Suddenly Veronica was grabbed from behind and a sharp serrated knife was pushed against her throat. She made to scream but she felt a hot sweaty hand clamp down over her mouth.

"That wasn't very smart now, was it?" whispered Edward.

Veronica could feel his hot breath on her neck. Her breathing increased as Edward released her mouth and pried the laser from her hand. He dug her own gun into her back, all the while keeping the knife pressed to her throat. Together they exited the storage room and moved back into the science lab.

Veyha was gone.

"Where's the little one?" he asked gruffly.

Veronica swallowed hard, trying to keep her neck still. "She went back down with Mikhail. I'm the only one here."

Edward took the gun away from her back and relaxed his grasp on the knife. He pushed Veronica through the science lab and into the cockpit.

"Sit down," he ordered as they came to the main control panel.

Veronica sat in the pilot's seat but kept her eyes fixed on Edward. Suddenly she felt a gentle tickling on her calf. She cast her eyes downward but kept her head still. A tiny face was staring back at her.

Edward looked around the room cautiously.

"I told you I'm the only one here," repeated Veronica.

Edward looked at Veronica through narrow, intense eyes. "You aren't very good at frisking, are ya'? Not even a pat-down? Did it honestly never occur to you I might 'ave a weapon?"

"What do you want from me?" Veronica fought the urge to look down again.

"Nothin' you can give me, love. But somethin' you can help me get." He walked slowly around to her left and sat in the co-pilot's seat. In the blink of an eye he reached under the panel and seized Veyha by the hair, pulling her up and pointing the laser at her head.

Veyha screamed.

Edward pulled her onto his lap and held her tight.

"Leave her alone!" Veronica screamed, lunging forward.

He pulled away quickly and held the laser firmly against Veyha's small head. "Tut, tut, tut. Wouldn't want me to panic and accidentally pull the trigger."

Veronica froze. Her eyes moved between the laser and Veyha's panic-stricken face. She slowly moved back into her seat. "What do you want?"

"I'm goin' back down. You're gonna remote control the second boat and guide me to this location." He tapped the screen of the control panel.

Veronica frowned. "Fine, just let the girl go and I'll send you back down."

Edward laughed. "Really? You think I'd leave me leverage behind? Afraid I need the little one as, let's call it, insurance."

Veronica saw the look of terror on Veyha's face, but she had no choice.

Slowly, Veronica stood with her hands in the air, showing submission. She moved with Edward and Veyha to the airlock where the second lifeboat sat, unused. Veronica opened the outer hatch and watched, helplessly, as Edward disappeared inside. She sealed the exterior door with a sharp metallic clang, clenching her fists in frustration.

Veronica returned to the control panel. "Please, don't hurt her," she whispered.

Merna Village, Arcadia—
14:00, 10 September, 2086

Grey stared at Schmitt, his eyes hard and judgmental. Schmitt was in his late sixties, at least a decade older than Grey. His body bore the unmistakable signs of hardship. He was thin and gangly with a greying beard, a small scar on his right cheek, and a slight limp. The man was in no condition to fight.

Schmitt was angry. "I must protest. You will need me to communicate with the Mernas, to coordinate your attack. I am no spring chicken, but you need me out there."

Grey's gaze narrowed, but he didn't respond.

Schmitt threw his arms in the air in frustration. "Give me one good reason why I should stay behind!"

Grey continued to stare for a moment longer, collecting his thoughts. "I don't think you should stay behind at all," said Grey, a plan forming in his mind.

Schmitt paused, waiting for Grey to continue.

"I want you to lead the children, the elderly, and anyone else who is unable to fight far away from the village."

"How dare you!" spat Schmitt.

Grey kept his eyes fixed and his voice level. "With the warriors gone, the village won't be safe from the Adras. These people need protection. But I can't lead the charge and protect the villagers at the same time. I need someone I trust, someone who knows the area, but someone who can still look after them." He paused and leaned close to Schmitt's face. "Can I count on you?"

Schmitt hesitated, it was not the explanation he had expected. "I, I can do that, yes," he stammered. A thought struck Schmitt. "Actually, I know the perfect place. The beach, where we first set up camp; the camouflaging on the boat is solar powered so it should still be operational even if the ship is not. That will at least give us somewhere to hide."

Grey concealed a smile. "Very well, Dr. Schmitt. The villagers are your responsibility. I want them mobilized within the hour. Make sure you hit the beach before nightfall."

Schmitt, somewhat pleased with his newfound responsibility, trotted off to begin rounding up the remaining villagers.

Grey smirked, another problem solved. He addressed Diamond and cleared his throat. "Sergeant, alert the warriors, we're moving out in ten minutes."

Grey turned his attention back to the Merna warriors. From his best estimates, he counted around two hundred villagers in total. For their part, the Mernas were a resilient people. Every member of the village was trained from a young age. Children were taught to scale trees for safety, how to use small weapons, and how to build a fire. If he excluded those unable to fight, the youngest children, the elderly, and the infirmed, he was left with close to one hundred and thirty able-bodied fighters, armed with spears, a handful of lasers, and two US Marines.

It would never be enough.

The warrior-army made their way north-west toward the base of the mountain. Unlike Joel and Mikhail who reached the stream in a matter of minutes on the MTV, it took the better part of the afternoon for the warrior-army to arrive at the waterfall. Water cascaded gracefully over the cliff, spraying down in a showery mist. At its base, the falls pooled into a rather tempting swimming hole, giving birth to three long and winding streams which diverged north, north-east, and east from the cliffs.

Once the small army reached the pool, they followed the northward stream, staying parallel to the cliffs overhead. After several kilometers the stream quickly expanded into a flowing river. The larger the river grew, the thinner the forest became.

Before long, the sun began to move behind the cliffs, plunging the valley into an eerie grey-blue. With visibility dropping and just over one hundred warriors, Grey knew they would be no match for an armed force of super-intelligent alien beings.

He needed a plan.

On the far side of the river was sheer rock from the overhanging cliffs. Vines, mosses, and lichen covered the exposed rock, forming a thick layer of green. On the near side of the river, the bank sloped gently away from the water creating a flat clearing which was covered in nothing more than a thin layer of silt and resilient grasses and shrubs, evidence of seasonal flooding. A few meters back from the waterline the thin grasses exploded into a grove of small trees and bushes, increasing in size as they moved further from the water.

Grey stopped. It was perfect.

"What's going on, Lieutenant? I thought the compound was still a few clicks away?" asked Diamond.

"It is. But we're not going to storm the compound. We need to draw the Adras away to give Dr. Carter and Dr. Ozero a chance to get *inside*."

Diamond looked around the dimly lit riverbank and frowned. "And how exactly are you planning to do that from here?"

Grey smiled again.

Through a combination of English, sign language, and swearing, Grey coordinated the construction of a giant pile of wood, sticks, and grass. The Mernas heaved enormous dead trees onto the pile, cutting them down to size with lasers. Long thin branches were piled into a tee-pee shape, and mounds of dried grasses and leaves were inserted into the tee-pee's center. The final structure towered over the small Mernas, stretching almost as tall as Diamond. It was wide, too, designed to last for hours.

Diamond stood back from the completed structure. "Great plan, Lieutenant. Make it seem like the threat is out here, nowhere near the compound. That way no one gets hurt."

Grey raised an eyebrow. He'd always had a soft spot for Diamond. He was a good soldier, always followed orders and tried his hardest. But he lacked the ruthlessness of a true warrior. Grey, on the other hand, was a seasoned vet. He knew sometimes sacrifices had to be made for the greater good.

"C'mon, it's getting dark. Let's light her up." Grey patted Diamond on the shoulder.

The fire grew rapidly, consuming the sticks and grasses hungrily. Within seconds the entire pile was alight, sending flames several meters into the air. Grey smiled.

He turned to Diamond. "Okay, time for the smokers."

Diamond and several Merna men and women carried sizable leafy branches toward the flaming pile. Now the kindling had caught and established a large and hot fire, it was time to add something moist, something to send up plumes of billowing smoke. Diamond and the Mernas heaved their leafy branches onto the pile and immediately thick white smoke began to stretch high into the sky, filling the air with the unmistakable smell of burning wood.

Diamond quickly backed away from the fire as the heat grew in intensity.

Grey's smiled broadened. The light from the fire cast long shadows which danced across his face, giving him a somewhat sinister appearance. "That should get their attention."

EDWARD

**Merna Village, Arcadia—
17:30, 10 September, 2086**

The lifeboat touched down in the center of the Merna village. The wide clearing was the perfect place to land now the Mernas were off fighting the humans' war. Edward stepped out of the boat with Veyha in his custody. He opened a large side panel and extracted an MTV from the storage compartment.

Edward returned to the control panel inside and engaged the microphone. "Much obliged, Dr. Nizhny."

There was a pause on the intercom. "*You got what you wanted. Now let the girl go.*"

Edward smiled to himself momentarily before firing multiple laser rounds into the control panel, breaking off communication with *Hermes* and disabling both the remote and manual flight controls.

"Now there's only one way off this rock," he said to himself.

He stepped outside and sealed the hatch behind him. Veyha sat on the back of the bike, her hands and feet bound by a rope Edward had found aboard the lifeboat. Her eyes, red from crying, were fixed on Edward.

He made his way through the huts and the thick vegetation, to the temple Tom had shown him only days earlier. As much as it pained him to know his brother would not be joining him on the return trip, he took solace in the fact he was finishing what the two of them had started. Tom would be proud to know his baby brother was going to succeed. That he would no longer be at the bottom of the pecking order. That he was finally going to have the life they had always dreamed of.

He made his way toward the tree-hollow, hidden among the tangle of vines and creepers. As he reached the entrance, Edward slowly pushed back the encroaching plants and moved into the darkened room. Without warning, the room lit up with a blinding incandescent light. Edward turned away, closing his eyes for a moment, allowing them to adjust to the glare. As he reopened his eyes he could see the treated bark which lined the inside of the tree-hollow. Small gemstones glowed softly like fireflies, illuminating the base of the tree. And sitting in the middle of the near-empty space was the *Light stone,* balancing on its four-pronged perch inside the glass-like cylinder.

Edward smiled as a wave of excitement washed over him. He approached the stone, which glowed red like a ruby, and placed a hand on the base of the pedestal. As his sweaty hand came into contact with the stone he felt a small electrical shock and pulled away quickly.

"What the?" he said aloud. Tom had extracted the stone last time, while Edward stood guard.

Edward pulled off his jacket and threw it over the stone, scooping it away from its perch, avoiding a shock. The gemstones in the hollow immediately stopped glowing, plunging the area into darkness. Edward quickly made his way outside again.

As he returned to the village, he unwrapped the stone from his jacket and was excited to see the red hue had disappeared, replaced by a beautiful clear emerald green. While Edward was not actually a geologist, he had spent enough time in Dr. Kendal's lab to know, in addition to being very rare on Earth, Alexandrite had an amazing ability to change color from green in natural light to red in incandescent light. Even if the stone didn't hold the key to limitless clean energy, it would be worth a mint back home because of its unique geological qualities.

But it did hold the key. Which meant it was priceless.

As Edward returned to the village square he paused. The girl was gone.

For a moment he hesitated, contemplating his next move. The girl was useful as leverage, but now he had the stone there was no point wasting time trying to find her. Right now, he needed to get to Base Camp, take the remaining lifeboat back to *Hermes,* and get the hell off this planet.

Looking down to the stone cradled in his arms, Edward smiled.

He quickly mounted the bike and gunned the throttle, taking off like a gunshot. The bike raced along the cleared path in the trees. As night approached the heat of the day subsided. A small sense of giddiness came over Edward as he rode. He was on the home stretch now. It would take the others hours before they found Amber; plenty of time to get to the boat.

He would obviously need to take care of Veronica once she brought him back to *Hermes*. It would have been easier to coerce her if he still had the little girl. That darn little girl. He thought he had tied her up so well. It was only by sheer luck he found rope in the first—

Edward was struck in the chest as he rode directly into that very same rope which was pulled taut across his path. The impact threw him violently backward, allowing the bike to speed forward without a rider, crashing into a nearby tree. The jacket he cradled so delicately was thrown clear.

He hit the earth with tremendous force. Edward could feel his bones crack from the impact. A surge of pain swelled through his chest as he struggled for breath, wheezing desperately. He rolled as he hit the ground, coughing up a small pool of blood. His vision was blurred but he could just make out a small and agile figure as it scampered past and scooped up his jacket.

"Oi! You little shit!" he cursed, but the figure was undeterred.

He tried to pull himself to his feet but a searing pain shot through his body like fire. He lay on the soft dirt, wheezing heavily. It felt as though shards of glass were dancing inside his lungs. He looked up again, blinking to clear his vision. Slowly the image of the little girl came into focus as she extracted the stone from his jacket.

"Girl! Drop it!" he shouted, desperately.

Veyha paused, looking back to the battered and fallen figure of Edward. She stuck out her tongue and blew a raspberry at him before scaling the nearest tree and disappearing into the dark canopy.

Edward gritted his teeth and, with all his strength, clambered onto the crashed bike with its motor still running. Pain shot through his body with each step. Veyha was nowhere to be seen; she'd vanished into the forest like a phantom. Edward sat on the bike to compose himself. The pain in his chest was getting worse, his breathing was labored and shallow. He didn't have much time.

To his surprise the bike was still functional, although it was trailing a small cloud of pungent electrical smoke. He brought the battered vehicle back to the open path, steering it in the direction the little girl had fled. The bike hovered above the ground, sliding along at walking speed.

Edward groaned heavily as the reality of his situation hit. He had lost the girl and the stone, his ribs were most likely broken, and he was definitely bleeding internally. He glanced down to his leg and saw blood saturating his pants. Without medical assistance, he wasn't going to survive.

With no other option, Edward pulled the throttle on the bike gently, increasing his speed. The surrounding jungle was getting darker. Stars shone brightly in the clear sky. As the strength drained from his body, Edward could no longer control the bike. He watched, helplessly, as it drifted off the path, colliding with the roots of a huge buttress tree. Edward tumbled unceremoniously to the ground, struggling for breath.

He had done everything in his power to come on this trip. He had killed two men, undergone facial reconstructive surgery, bribed, blackmailed, and bullied whoever he needed. But it wasn't enough. He had lost his identity, his brother, and the stone. And now, he was going to lose his life.

A sickly smell of decaying flesh wafted into his nostrils. Edward opened his eyes and, to his surprise, several feet away, behind the huge buttress tree, lay the half-eaten and decayed body of a dead Garkra. Despite its deteriorated form, he could tell from the small bite marks that scavengers had been feasting on this trophy kill for months. He frowned at the sight; what on this planet could possibly kill a Garkra?

As if in response to his query, a monstrous roar rippled through the forest.

Edward's eyes widened. He could hear something large walking toward him. He could feel the earth shake as an enormous body approached. Although Edward knew he'd be dead from his injuries in a matter of hours, his fight to survive was still strong. He mustered every ounce of strength he had left and dragged his broken body into the relative safety of a small cleft between the twisting buttress roots. He leaned against the roots, sitting upright and staring outward at the path.

As he stared at the trees, Edward suddenly remembered the conversation between Joel and Veronica when they first discovered the giant pathway. They'd said it was too large to belong to the Mernas and such a structure would require big animals and heavy foot traffic. He also recalled the Mernas' warnings about travelling at night, because that's when—

His train of thought was interrupted as a large shadow fell over his hiding place.

Adra City, Arcadia—
17:30, 10 September, 2086

Joel and Mikhail had been watching the gate for hours. They hid behind the large log, observing the various comings and goings of the Adras. Joel stared at the wall, his frustrations mounting. Amber was in there, somewhere, but the place was a fortress. The wall was slick and offered no purchase for climbing. The gate was under constant guard by at least three large and armed Adras. And, as far as they could tell, the wall ran around the entire length of the community.

For a moment Joel wondered *why* the city was so well defended. What could these intelligent beings possibly be guarding themselves against? At first, he assumed the size and material were chosen to defend against the huge Garkras which roamed the forest. But why seal the gate? And why make the wall slick?

In the time Joel and Mikhail had been watching the wall, the gate had only been opened a handful of times, either upon return of an Adra from the outside, or someone departing. Each time it opened, the pair were offered a brief glance at the inner workings of the compound. The gate was never opened for long, and it never seemed to completely retract. Beyond the wall there were more trees growing in tightly packed groves. They also caught a glimpse of the river which indeed ran beneath the huge wall.

There was no way of knowing how many Adras were on the other side. From the outside, they could hear the strange otherworldly sounds of shrieks and chirps, muffled by the large black stone. Occasionally swarms of huge insects flew over the wall, into the heart of the city.

As the heat of the day subsided, a chilly wind blew through the trees. With the sun hidden behind the mountain, a grey shadow fell over the jungle.

Mikhail squinted at the river. "What about the waterway? We know the river runs beneath the wall over there."

Joel kept his eyes fixed on the gate. "Too many unknowns. We don't know what happens to the water under the wall. Or if they have sentries on the other side. Our best bet is to wait until Grey arrives with the Mernas. If they can draw the Adras' attention, we might have the cover we need to sneak inside."

Mikhail contemplated the idea for a moment and frowned. "When Grey attacks, won't they seal the gate? If they're under siege surely they wouldn't just open the doors for anyone to wander in? We need another plan," he demanded.

Joel didn't reply.

"What if we move further down the wall, away from the sentries, and construct a ladder out of branches or a grappling hook from vines?"

Joel kept his eyes fixed on the gate, watching the Adra patrol, deep in thought.

Mikhail became frustrated. "We need another plan. I thought you wanted to get Amber back?"

Joel finally took his eyes off the gate. He glared at Mikhail with a mixture of pain and anger. He spoke through clenched teeth. "Everything I have done over the past few days has been in an effort to get her back."

Mikhail's frustration was quashed instantly. He saw the anguish on Joel's face; his eyes were red and glazed, his muscles tense. Mikhail shook his head and frowned. "I'm sorry. I thought you two were just professional associates, I had no idea you were, well, you know."

Joel shook his head, embarrassed he'd let his emotions get the better of him. "What are you talking about?" he said dismissively.

"*You know,*" Mikhail nodded suggestively.

Joel turned his attention back to the gate. "It's not like that."

Mikhail eyed Joel thoughtfully. He recognized his pain. He had experienced the same torment, the same anxiety and fear aboard *Hermes* over the past few days. Joel didn't have to say it aloud; his actions spoke louder than words ever could.

"What's that?" asked Joel; his attention was back on the gate. "What's it doing?"

Mikhail turned to the gate. One of the smaller Adras, a thin gangly creature, had stopped its patrol and was sniffing the air, inhaling and exhaling sharply. Its head moved in circles, its nostrils flaring. It leaned toward the ground and back up into the air.

"It can smell something," said Joel, lowering his voice.

Suddenly, the creature turned sharply, staring in their direction.

Both men held their breath. The creature started to move away from the gate, directly toward their hiding spot. Several shrill calls rang out from the other guards. They jumped and pointed in agitation toward the river. In response to the behavior of the other sentries, the lone creature changed its path, veering toward the river.

"Can you smell that?"

Mikhail sniffed the air; smoke.

Slowly, the gate began to slide open with ease. And, for the first time, retracted entirely within the enormous black structure. An army of Adras quickly emerged from the city; Joel counted dozens of the creatures. Each one was equipped with the same glove-weapon. The troop quickly fanned out, away from the wall, onto the grassy plain.

"Joel," whispered a voice from the trees.

Joel and Mikhail looked up and saw the faint outline of a body sitting in the leaves. "Faybin?"

"*Shh!*" She held a hand over her mouth. "*Come.*"

The pair scaled the trunk and clambered into the branches where Faybin sat with Din. Faybin handed them a handful of damp leaves and flowers and quickly began rubbing them on her own skin.

"What? Why?" asked Mikhail.

Faybin sniffed the air with exaggerated movements as she rubbed the leaves on her body and hands. Mikhail sniffed Faybin's hand; it reeked of sweet eucalyptus.

"Oh!" he said, understanding. Mikhail quickly mirrored her behavior, rubbing the foliage against his skin, masking his scent.

Din sat away from the others, on a higher branch with a better view of the wall.

"What's going on?" whispered Joel.

"Danger," said Din.

The little group sat silently in the trees, watching wide-eyed as more Adras marched through the fully retracted gate. They were organized and coordinated, like a military unit mobilizing in perfect formation. They moved in sync toward the river and up the ravine, disappearing into the forest beyond.

With the gate open, Joel and Mikhail could finally see the city in its entirety. It was incredible. Every living plant had been purposefully shaped and cultivated to create beautiful structures, covered with layers of vines and mosses. Soft blue plates of light lay across the open holes of the tree-buildings, bathing the city in an otherworldly glow.

They sat in silence for several minutes, waiting for the Adras to move out of sight, until they were certain the coast was clear.

Joel turned to Faybin. "Where are Grey and the others?"

Faybin thought for a moment, searching for the right word. "Fire. Faybin help Joel. Adra fire."

Joel smiled briefly. "Clever man. Keep the fight out there." He turned back to the gate and, to his surprise, saw it was still open. He smiled. "Now's our chance."

One by one, Joel, Mikhail, and the Mernas slipped from the tree. They moved swiftly and quietly across the grassy plain under the cover of dusk. As they approached the gate, keeping flat against the outer wall, Joel paused, signaling for the others to stop, too. He peered around the lip of the wall; the streets were deserted. The blue lights that had bathed the area only minutes earlier were gone, too, leaving the place in near-darkness.

Inside, the city of strange-looking tree-buildings spread before them. In the distance, three giant skyscraper-sized trees marked the center of the city.

"I bet that's where they took her," said Joel, pointing to the tower-trees. Without waiting for a response he slipped around the gate, stepping into an open courtyard.

"Wait! We don't know anything about this place!" called Mikhail.

But Joel was already halfway across the courtyard, heading for the relative cover of a nearby network of bushes. He quickly disappeared into the shadows. After a moment, Joel leaned out and motioned for the others to follow.

Mikhail scowled under his breath. A moment ago Joel had seemed so calm and calculated. Now he was running off half-cocked into an alien city. Mikhail nodded to Faybin before darting across the open courtyard. Faybin followed closely behind.

As the team regrouped among the shadowy roots, Mikhail heard a soft scuffling sound coming from the other side of the huge kapok tree. Joel waved for Din to join them.

"Wait—" started Mikhail.

Din followed Joel's instructions and began to scamper across the open courtyard. A harsh high-pitched shriek cut through the silence. Din turned toward the sound, still running hard, and crashed heavily into a small and rather startled purple Adra. The collision sent the pair skidding across the ground. They rolled together, terrified.

The small purple Adra began squawking frantically, flailing its limbs wildly. Din was trapped beneath the panic-stricken creature; his spear had been thrown clear during the collision. Like a true warrior, Din extracted his stone blade and began stabbing blindly beneath the Adra's heavy body. Purple screamed, becoming louder and more desperate.

Within moments, a dozen Adras had rushed out of the nearby buildings, drawn by the commotion.

"Jesus Christ!" cursed Joel. He grabbed a laser from his belt, switched off the safety and aimed.

"They're not armed?" said Mikhail.

Joel ignored his comment. "Follow my lead." In a heartbeat, Joel loosed two shots at the Adras exiting the buildings. The creatures shrieked in surprise and quickly retreated as the laser blasts cut through the wooden branch-walls.

"Wait! Goddammit!" cursed Mikhail as Joel fired wildly into the crowd.

Several Adras were struck by loose laser shots; they screamed in pain, a shrieking, ear-piercing sound. More Adras came running into the courtyard; this time they were armed.

Din and Purple lay in the middle of the firefight. Din continued to stab at Purple's underbelly. She was panicking now. She flailed her arms and legs at Din, trying to defend herself. Din shouted in pain as the huge sickle-like claws shredded his soft skin. Din's wails became frantic as the wounds multiplied and deepened. Suddenly, both beings stopped screaming and Din's body fell flat against the ground. Purple continued to thrash for a moment until she was able to scramble to her feet.

Purple crouched down, clutching several deep lacerations along her stomach. Blood oozed from the open wounds. She let out a mournful cry before hobbling into the nearest building.

"Din!" screamed Faybin over the sound of the lasers; the pain in her voice was palpable.

Mikhail turned at Faybin's scream; he saw Din's body lying motionless on the ground and cursed under his breath. "Faybin! Get out of here! Find the others!"

Faybin gazed at her brother; tears welled in her eyes. She shook her head, clearing her mind before taking off toward the tower-trees.

Retreat

Bonfire, Arcadia—
18:30, 10 September, 2086

Diamond crouched by the tree line, well away from the heat of the bonfire. Beside him lay Grey, staring intently into the black forest beyond. They'd been in position for over an hour now, waiting patiently for the Adras to arrive from the compound.

"C'mon, you bastards. Schmitt said these things are attracted to fire. They should come in droves to put it out. It'll be like shooting fish in a barrel," said Grey.

Diamond shook his head. "Wait? I thought the whole point of the fire was nobody needed to get hurt?"

Grey kept his eyes fixed forward. "The point of the fire is to keep the fight out here so Carter and the others can get inside. We're still going to take down as many of the fuckers as we can when they get here."

"Sir? Do we really need to take them out? Can't we just keep hiding? Or draw their attention further away?"

Grey cast a sideways look at Diamond. He had never questioned an order like this before. "Aren't you mad? Don't you want to get even with them for what they did to you? They infiltrated your camp, kidnapped your crewmate, and left you for dead in the jungle. They made you look weak. I'd be mad as hell," he said, turning back to the fire.

Diamond hesitated. "I guess, but, I mean, they had their reasons for doing what they did. Think how we'd react if we found a foreign spaceship with two aliens on board? And then if we found out one of 'em had a weapon? I reckon we'd have gone on the defensive, too."

Grey shook his head, clearly disappointed. "You're a good kid, Sergeant. But you have a lot to learn. These things aren't like us. They don't use reason or logic. They're animals, big scary animals that think they're top dog around here. We're going to show them who's in charge now."

Grey motioned for silence, pointing into the darkness. Diamond peered through the leaves of the low-hanging ferns; he couldn't see anything in the shadows. A twig snapped in the distance. Diamond froze.

A large shadow crept along the edge of the river. It was bigger than a Merna, greater than a human, and it moved slowly, rigidly. While its details were hidden among the shadows, Diamond could tell it was walking upright on two legs and it had a large head and a tail. For a brief moment, he had a faint feeling of recognition, of something he had seen shortly after they had arrived. The creature's movements were stiff, like an overgrown turkey searching for food, stepping lightly and bobbing down every so often. It was alone, a scout.

"Adra?" whispered Grey.

A nearby Merna pointed to the creature and whispered back, "Adra."

The lone scout made straight for the bonfire. It broke through the trees beside the river and was suddenly bathed in the fire's light. It was larger than Diamond first thought, at least six and a half feet tall. It was so alien, with its swollen head and feathery coat. Its body was mostly a drab grey-black but it had a brilliant crimson-red hue along its head, neck, and tail. Its body was covered in scars, its long feathers were broken; it had seen battle before.

As the scout approached the fire it sniffed the air. Curiously, it seemed to relax when it saw the bonfire. Sniffing and looking around, it suddenly became rigid again, tensing at some unseen scent.

"Do you think it can smell us?" whispered Diamond.

Grey didn't respond.

Diamond turned to Grey, about to repeat his question when he realized the Lieutenant was no longer beside him. He had moved to the edge of the tree line and was crouching in the shadows, leaning on one knee. In his hands was a Marine-issued explosives launcher; the barrel was pressed against his shoulder. But the launcher wasn't pointed at the Adra. It was aimed directly into the bonfire.

Diamond's eyes grew wide as he realized what Grey was doing. Before he could react he heard his beloved weapon click and instinctively buried his head in the dirt.

The fire exploded with tremendous force, sending flaming debris in all directions. Diamond felt an intense burning sensation on his leg. He quickly rolled over smacking the flames on his pants.

At the same moment, an ungodly scream assaulted his ears. Diamond looked up. Past the smoldering remains of the bonfire lay the writhing body of the Adra scout, its feathers burned like paper. It rolled, desperately trying to extinguish the flames. It screamed in pain as the fire engulfed its body. Diamond felt sick.

He sprang to his feet and pulled a hand laser from his belt. He aimed carefully and shot the scout in the head. The screaming stopped instantly and the burning Adra's body fell limply to the ground.

"Sergeant! What are you doing?" Grey's tense voice cut across the grassy plain.

A nearby tree cracked as the flames began to spread through the forest. The vegetation had been engulfed by the fire, spreading through the grass and leaf litter. Mernas ran to the water to extinguish their burning garments.

Diamond ignored the outrage in Grey's voice. "I had to put that poor thing out of its misery, it wasn't gonna survive. It was suffering."

Grey's face was hard. "It was meant to suffer. It was meant to scream. We need to draw the rest of its troop here."

Diamond didn't respond. He stared at Grey with ambivalence. This was the man who had trained him to be a soldier, the man who had helped turn him into a man, and the closest thing he had to a father figure. But now, Diamond hardly recognized the person standing in front of him.

Another tree cracked nearby; this time the sound was followed by a loud snap as a huge dead branch toppled from the intense heat. Diamond grabbed Grey by the shirt, pulling him away from the path of the falling limb. They dived into the sand together, narrowly escaping the falling body of wood.

Grey pulled Diamond to his feet. "C'mon, the rest of its troop won't be far behind now. Things are about to get messy."

As if on cue, a shrill cry rang out in the distance. It was an otherworldly sound.

Grey turned his attention to the Mernas, who were swatting at burning piles of leaves and embers. The fire was spreading quickly, consuming everything in sight. He barked orders at the Mernas, urging them to get back into formation to prepare for what was coming.

Without warning, a hundred shadowy creatures stormed onto the riverbank, approaching the site of their fallen companion. Despite the intense fire raging all around, the Adras remained calm. One creature carried a small cube-shaped device. It set the cube beside the scout's body and pressed a trigger. Suddenly the entire cube lit up with an incredible yellow light. The radiance seemed to grow from within the device, forming a golden sphere which expanded rapidly. As the illumination reached the scout's dead body, the fire consuming its corpse was smothered. The light continued to grow, engulfing the bonfire and the nearby trees. As it grew, it extinguished any flame it came into contact with.

When the spherical light reached its apex it contracted again, slowly shrinking back into the small black box. It had extinguished a twenty-meter periphery. Outside that boundary, flames still ravaged the forest. But the area inside the sphere had been completely neutralized. All that remained were the smoldering embers of the bonfire and the scout's lifeless body.

The Adra who had placed the device quickly scooped it up again, and ran toward another area of the forest which was still burning out of control. He repeated the action and more forest was extinguished.

With the Adras distracted by the fire, Grey seized his opportunity. He pulled out his explosives launcher once more and aimed into the crowd of Adras.

"Now!" he shouted to the Mernas as his finger pressed down on the trigger. The small bullet-size wad of explosives shot into the crowd and exploded on impact. Billows of dirt and silt erupted into the air. Several Adras were thrown clear of the impact zone. One unfortunate creature, the one closest to the initial blast, was torn to pieces. Limbs were ripped from its body in a grotesque spray of blood.

At the same moment, the nearby Merna warriors pulled out the human weapons Grey had given them and began firing wildly into the crowd. Half a dozen Adras were struck by laser blasts, screaming in pain. Two more dropped where they stood, killed instantly from blasts to the head and chest.

As lasers blasted across the riverside, the Adras turned their attention to the tree line and began firing their gloved weapons. Electricity sizzled from the strange devices, lighting up the jungle like a strobe light. In reply, the remaining Merna warriors burst from the trees, wielding stone-tipped spears and poisoned slingshots.

The riverbank had become a battlefield.

Diamond lay hidden in the tree line. He fired his laser in the direction of the oncoming Adras, but made sure his shots were too high or too wide. None of this sat well with him. He couldn't quite put his finger on it, but for the first time in his life he couldn't follow Grey's orders.

Several Mernas were struck by the electrical blasts of the Adras' weapons. They fell instantly, lying wide-eyed on the ground. One of the taller Merna men wielding a gun fell directly beside Diamond as he lay flat in the tree line. Diamond made eye contact with the fallen man and saw the terror frozen on his face. He frowned; the man was not dead. He was still breathing but he was unable to move. Diamond holstered his weapon.

Within minutes, any Merna carrying a gun had been shot. The Adras were targeting the human weapons first. From his vantage point, Diamond could just see Grey lying several feet away. He had also stopped firing, allowing the Merna warriors to continue the fight alone.

Diamond could see the uncertainty in Grey's eyes. Despite the smaller Adra force than they had expected, Diamond knew Grey was out of his league. The army of small humanoids had spears and a handful of guns. The Adras had weapons and technology beyond their imagination.

Grey looked around the still-burning forest. Mernas were dropping like flies as they were struck by the Adras' electric pulses. They had no choice.

"*Retreat!*"

Adra City, Arcadia—
18:30, 10 September, 2086

Amber stared at the blue panel of light which covered the window on the outer wall of the tree-room. She sat inside one of the vine-hammocks inside Zoe's chambers, gently swinging back and forth. The sky outside was growing dark, accentuating the glowing blue light.

Amber was fascinated by the room which held her and Zoe; it was so raw and primitive and yet so technologically advanced. It was a lot like the Adras themselves: ancient beings who evolved slowly, at one with nature, and yet, more advanced than humans could ever hope to be. For a brief moment, Amber considered what life would be like—

Suddenly the blue light disappeared, plunging the room into near-darkness.

"What happened?" asked Zoe, startled.

"I, I don't know?" stammered Amber. "The light's gone. Doesn't that mean the power's out?"

"That doesn't make any sense? The power just came back on this morning."

Amber turned her attention to the large window. She could feel the crisp evening air which was now free to flow inside the room. The city was shrouded in darkness. There were no signs of the blue-white light anywhere.

"What's happening?" asked Zoe nervously.

"Nothing? The city is deserted? What does that mean?"

Zoe shook her head. "I have no idea. This has never happened before."

"So, what do we—"

Amber's thought was interrupted by several shrill cries which pierced the relative silence outside. It was an Adra screaming. The sound was followed immediately by the thud of laser blasts, and louder screams and cries; human screams.

Amber gasped, "Holy shit. Did you hear that? That was a human!"

Zoe shook her head. "It might not be human. Mernas sound very similar."

Amber leaned out the open window, trying to see the commotion. "Human, Merna, whatever; we have to do something." Through the darkness, the flashing lights of the firefight stood out like a beacon. Not far from the city gate Amber could just make out the bodies of an Adra and a humanoid rolling on the ground in what appeared to be hand-to-hand combat.

"An Adra is killing someone!" Amber felt sick as both sets of screams grew wild and panicked.

"What? That can't be right," said Zoe in disbelief.

Suddenly the humanoid screams ceased, leaving only the soft shrieking of the Adra as it picked itself off the ground and disappeared into the shadows.

Amber's face dropped. "Oh, my God. They killed someone, the Adras just killed someone. I thought you said the Adras would never kill anyone?" Amber was clearly agitated.

Zoe shook her head, equally bewildered.

Amber grabbed Zoe by the arm and pulled her to the exposed doorway. "We need to get out of here."

The inner tree stood before them, with its winding staircase branches. There were no signs of movement anywhere.

"Wait, we don't know what happened out there," protested Zoe.

"That's why we need to go," retorted Amber.

She slipped around the edge of the door, making her way down the steps below. Outside they could still hear the sound of laser blasts. In reply to the lasers, they could also hear the buzzing of electricity, like tiny cracks of lightning.

As they approached the next room along the descending stairway, Amber paused. She leaned against the doorframe again and peered inside. The room contained three older Mernas; two shorter females and a slightly taller male. Each one had elaborately decorated headdresses and their skin was covered in colorful tattoos. They were huddled at the back of the room, clearly terrified by the commotion.

Zoe looked inside the room. "Xylon?"

The older of the two women turned around in fright. She saw Zoe standing by the door and her expression changed immediately; she was mad.

"You know these people?" asked Amber.

Zoe moved inside slowly. "These are the village elders, the leaders of the Mernas."

"Why is she staring at you like you're the devil?"

Zoe shrugged. "I guess because the last time we saw each other was the night I was taken by the Adras. As far as the Mernas are concerned, anyone taken by the Adras are never seen again. What are you doing here?" said Zoe, addressing Xylon.

Xylon was silent for a moment. She eyed Zoe suspiciously before grunting, "*Light stone stolen. Sky people.*" Xylon nodded toward Amber.

Amber saw Xylon's gesture. "Me? What do I have to do with anything?"

"She doesn't mean you, personally. She just means 'you' as one of the new humans." Zoe turned back to Xylon. "But if the *Sky people* stole the stone, why did the Adras bring *you* here?"

Xylon grunted, "*Sacrifice.*"

Zoe shook her head. "No. The Adras aren't like that. They don't want to hurt anyone."

Amber scoffed. "Did you see what just happened out there? They just killed someone!"

Zoe was disoriented and confused. "No, no, that's not them."

Outside the entrance to the room, they heard a soft shuffling. Zoe and Amber stepped away from the door as a shadow fell across the staircase. Everyone held their breath.

"Zoe?" came a voice from the steps.

Amber and Zoe froze as the shadowy figure entered the tree-room.

"Faybin?" said Zoe in surprise.

A young Merna woman entered the doorway.

"Zoe!" she exclaimed. Faybin noticed the elders huddled at the back of the room. "Xylon? Evoah? Omath?" She hugged the elders lovingly. After a moment Faybin's delight was replaced by a sense of urgency. "Move. Now."

As they exited the room, Amber and Zoe were greeted by five more Mernas; the elders Amber had seen in lower tree-rooms. Faybin led the way down the winding staircase which wrapped around the center of the enormous rainforest tree. The small group exited the base of the tree-building into a network of bushes and walkways. They headed through the shadows of the city, toward the sounds of the fight.

Suddenly the laser blasts ceased and silence fell on the city. Amber and Zoe exchanged a concerned look.

The group burst into the open courtyard, colliding with two terrified creatures. Faybin quickly drew her spear, pointing it aggressively at their assailants.

"Joel? Joel!" exclaimed Amber, unable to control herself.

"Amber!"

The pair ran into each other's arms, embracing tightly. Amber felt tears welling in her eyes but fought them back. Her voice cracked involuntarily. "You came for me?"

Joel brushed Amber's long red hair behind her ear and stifled a laugh. He pulled something small from his pocket, Amber's GeniousWatch. "Of course I did. Thought you might want this back."

Amber took the small watch. Without thinking, she threw her arms around Joel again, kissing him passionately. Joel didn't resist. He pulled her body closer as they embraced.

"It's 'not like that,' huh?" sniggered Mikhail.

A soft static sound crackled from Mikhail's belt. He had almost forgotten about the small transceiver.

"This is Mikhail, come again?" he said into the small black box.

After a few moments the radio clicked to life. It was Grey. "*Repeat, things are getting hot here. We're pulling out. Hope we gave you enough time.*"

Mikhail engaged the transceiver. "Got in fine, Lieutenant. Just need to get out now. Thanks for the diversion."

"*Good luck; we'll meet you at the rendezvous point as planned.*"

"Copy that. We'll see you soon." Mikhail looked at the small black device in his hand and for a moment he thought about Veronica alone aboard *Hermes*. He switched channels and pressed the receiver again. "Veronica, do you copy?"

There was no response.

"Vee, are you there?"

After another tense moment a female voice came over the speaker; it was flat and soft. "*Mikhail? Mikhail, I've been trying to get in touch with you. He, he got out. Edward is back on the surface, and, and he took Veyha,*" she sobbed softly.

"Veyha?" Faybin heard the name.

"Where is he now?" asked Mikhail.

"*I sent him back down, to the Merna village. I think he's going after the stone again. I'm so sorry, I had to. He was going to hurt her.*"

"It's okay, it's not your fault. How long ago was that? Is the other boat still at the village?"

Veronica sniffed, collecting herself. "*I don't know, a couple of hours ago? The boat is still at the village but he disabled the control panel after they landed.*"

"Don't worry, Vee. We'll find him. You just sit tight and make sure *Hermes* is ready to leave as soon as we get back." Mikhail tried to sound positive but he knew Veronica would hear the uncertainty in his voice.

He switched off the transceiver. "Okay, lovebirds, I hate to break up this beautiful reunion but things just got more complicated. Edward is back and he's after the stone again."

The beaming smiles melted from Joel and Amber's faces instantly.

"Who's Edward?" asked Amber.

Joel scratched his bristly chin. "I'll explain later. For now, we need to get the hell out of here."

Zoe protested, "Wait. You don't understand." Before she could continue a bolt of electricity struck her left shoulder. She collapsed into Amber's arms. Her entire left side was limp but her right side was unaffected.

"Zoe!" cried Amber.

"Move!" shouted Joel.

Everyone scattered impulsively, diving for cover where they could. A small team of Adras had appeared in the surrounding treetops and vine-bridges which encircled the courtyard.

"Amber! Get the Mernas out of here!" hollered Joel as he lay awkwardly, pinned behind an unfinished tree-building. "Mikhail! Take out the one on the right; I'll get the one on the left!"

Mikhail nodded and fired several shots toward the right vine-bridge. He hit his target in the head with incredible precision. The Adra fell lifelessly off the bridge, slapping into the earth below like a sack of rice. An electrical shot grazed the knotted roots directly above Mikhail's head. He ducked instinctively, concealed behind the larger groves at the base of the tree. He could feel the residual electric charge ripple down the trunk. Mikhail looked up and saw a black smudge in the space where his head had been a second ago. He frowned; the black mark looked like someone had rubbed charcoal against the side of the tree, but the bark was completely intact. He rubbed a finger over the mark and it came off cleanly.

"Mikhail! Get your head back in the game!" snapped Joel.

Joel had taken down the second Adra. It was sprawled awkwardly over the left bridge. He was focusing his attention on the closer attackers now, directly opposite their position.

Joel turned to Amber, who was cradling Zoe's semi-limp body. He hollered over the noise of the laser blasts, "Get ready to run! Mikhail, lay down cover fire on my mark." They halted their shots for a moment. "Now!"

Together, Joel and Mikhail started firing aggressively at the attacking Adras. At the same moment, Amber and Faybin scooped up Zoe and started running with the Merna elders across the courtyard toward the still-open gate. The moonlight illuminated the bloodstained ground. It was like something from a horror movie.

As they passed Din's mutilated body, Amber slowed her pace momentarily. The wounds on his torso, arms, and legs were random and erratic. A bloody stone blade still sat loosely in his fingers.

"Come!" ordered Faybin, urging Amber to pick up the pace.

The group ran through the gate, continuing deep into the forest outside the wall. After a moment, Joel and Mikhail came sprinting through, following the others into the forest, desperate to hide among the thick foliage.

After a few hundred meters Joel and Mikhail stopped running.

"What are you doing?" asked Amber.

Joel caught his breath. "You need to take the Mernas back to Base Camp."

"Me? What about you? Where are you going?" queried Amber, shifting Zoe's weight across her shoulder.

Joel could see the confusion in her eyes. "I'm sorry. There's so much to explain but we don't have time right now." He addressed Faybin, who was also assisting Zoe through the forest. "Faybin, do you know how to get to our camp from here?"

Faybin looked at the wall behind them which was just visible through the thick undergrowth. She looked upward, noting the position of the moon over their heads. "Yes. Camp," she said, pointing south-east.

"Take the elders back to Base Camp. Grey and the warriors will meet you there." Joel turned back to Mikhail. "We have no chance of catching him on foot but the MTV should still be hidden in the trees over there."

Amber paused. She felt defensive, as though Joel was being overprotective again. But she wasn't in a place to argue, not this time. Even if he was trying to protect her, she'd spent the last few days imprisoned inside the Adra city; she knew nothing about the world outside the walls or what had happened while she was gone.

Amber touched Joel's arm. "Be careful out there."

Joel offered her a weak smile before taking off into the darkness.

Rendezvous

Base Camp, Arcadia—
23:00, 10 September, 2086

Amber poked at the newly created fire. It crackled and stirred as she prodded at the burning wood. It was late, the moon was high and the forest was still.

On the other side of the fire, Faybin and the Merna elders dozed on the soft grass while they waited for Grey and the others to return. Amber was on watch. With the security system down, they couldn't be too careful. Inside a nearby tent, the only one which was still standing, Zoe was sleeping off the partial-paralysis. Aside from a loss of feeling and muscle control, she was completely unharmed.

After the altercation in the city, Amber wasn't sure what to make of the Adras anymore. Zoe seemed so confused when the fighting broke out. She truly believed the Adras were incapable of killing a human or a Merna. But Amber saw it with her own eyes. The Adra didn't paralyze the small man. It killed him.

She turned back to the fire and poked at it again.

But why?

Amber recalled her earlier speculations about the Adras' behavior, that they seemed motivated by more than their own survival, that they wanted to preserve life in all its forms. She thought about her interactions with Stripes and Gemstone in the tower-tree. They showed her visions of the Mernas ruthlessly attacking the Adra city, but the Adras did not retaliate. They didn't kill the small creatures even to defend themselves. Instead, they built a safe haven for the Mernas, somewhere far away where they could live in peace. The Mernas had no real reason to fear these creatures. No reason beyond their own superstitions.

Amber pictured the wounds on the small man's body and the bloody knife by his side. His wounds were erratic. They didn't look like deliberate injuries, they pointed to a struggle, an accident.

Maybe Zoe was right. Maybe the Adras were the altruistic creatures she thought them to be. Stephen Hawking, one of the greatest minds in scientific history, once said if humans did not colonize space then they would face their own extinction. He was right. After all, that's why they were on Arcadia in the first place. Instead of cleaning up the mistakes of humanity, they were just going to jump ship.

Amber pictured the solitary Merna's body among the dead Adras which littered the courtyard. Dozens of hyper-intelligent creatures were gunned down just to retrieve her and the others. Murdered in their own backyard. Even if an Adra had killed a Merna, it was nothing compared to the trail of destruction left by the humans.

She found her thoughts turning darker.

Maybe humans were not meant to colonize space. Maybe they were meant to lie in the bed they made for themselves, to face their own extinction.

Amber thought back to their first days on Arcadia, to their first hike into the forest and the amazing creatures they'd seen in the gorge. Thinking back, it was almost laughable she hadn't put two and two together. The armored pair, the crested herd, the duck-billed family; these were all distinctive dinosaur characteristics. Although the species had changed over the millennia, there was no arguing the similarities between the creatures in the gorge and dinosaur genera like Ankylosaurs, Torosaurus, and Hadrosaurus.

It certainly seemed like this version of Earth was better off than the one they had left behind. The biggest threat on this planet was not the dominant intelligent species but the small primate-like creatures who ran around wreaking havoc. Amber's gaze shifted to the Mernas as they slept by the fire. She couldn't help but wonder how these hominids came into existence in the first place. If the Cretaceous mass extinction never took place, then primate-like mammals should never have had the chance to develop into complex beings.

Zoe's words began to echo in Amber's mind again. She was still trying to understand Arcadia through her own experiences. Maybe the evolutionary rules of Earth didn't apply here? Maybe the evolution of primates was not dependent on the extinction of the dinosaurs after all? Maybe she didn't know as much about evolution as she thought?

A nearby rustling interrupted Amber's thoughts. Her mind flashed again to their early days on the planet, to the Garkra that attacked their camp. Her stomach tensed. The bushes rustled again, louder this time. The noise was enough to wake Faybin and the elders from their light sleep.

The rustling continued until, to their surprise, Lieutenant Grey and Diamond emerged. They strode into the camp with the Merna warriors close behind; soot and ash covered everyone's skin.

"Jesus. What happened to you guys?" asked Amber.

Grey cleared his throat. "Welcome back, Dr. Lytton. I see you found the elders, too. Very good. What about the *Atlas* crew?"

Amber nodded to the tent. "I found Dr. Martinez. She's sleeping off some paralysis after taking a shot from one of the Adras."

Grey looked around the immediate area. "Where's Dr. Carter and Dr. Ozero?"

"Apparently Edward escaped, so they've taken an MTV to go find him. Can you tell me who the fuck 'Edward' is?"

Grey grimaced. "He's a lying son of a bitch. I knew I shouldn't have left him with Dr. Nizhny. He needed a proper guard not a babysitter." Grey saw the confusion on Amber's face and quickly explained Charles's true identity.

Amber's eyes grew wide. "Gilmore?" she repeated with a hint of recognition.

"Exactly," said Grey.

Amber flashed back to the man's body she had seen in the jungle, wearing an ISA uniform and a pilot's badge. It was the beard and filthy hair that threw her off at the time. Tom Gilmore's photo in the mission profile always showed a clean-shaven and full-cheeked man. But the body she saw was haggard and gaunt.

Zoe's smooth Argentinian accent interrupted Amber and Grey's exchange. "We cannot stay here. If the stone is missing again, this is the first place the Adras are going to come to find it. Before humans arrived on this planet, the Adras never had a reason to worry about the Merna village being so close to the stone." Zoe addressed Grey directly.

He nodded. "Which means they'll come straight to us to find it. All right, let's move."

The group walked in single file through the forest. The Mernas were on edge; they knew the dangers of roaming the forest at night, but they also knew they weren't safe at the humans' camp while the *Light stone* was missing. Amber and Zoe kept back from the rest of the group while Grey and Diamond led the way.

They walked in near silence, careful not to draw attention to themselves. Without the luxury of the MTVs, it took hours to reach the beach. As they approached, the dense vegetation eventually thinned, giving way to a wide open space filled with sand and water. The night sky was brilliant, lit up with millions of tiny stars, and an enormous white moon. The stars reflected off the calm water, giving the whole scene a peaceful and tranquil feeling.

After another hour of walking, small twinkles of light could be seen in the distance; the unmistakable light of campfires on the beach. The *Atlas* camp. Everyone quickened their pace. The Merna warriors were eager to reunite with their families.

"Dr. Schmitt! Dr. Schmitt, are you here?" called Grey as they approached.

Within minutes heads began poking out of the various camouflaged tents; excited faces leapt from their hiding places and ran into the arms of their loved ones. Schmitt's weary face emerged from the lifeboat. When he saw Zoe among the Mernas his eyes lit up.

"Zoe? You're okay!" he said as they embraced warmly.

"It's so good to see you, Eckhart. Where are the others?" she said, looking around expectantly.

The giddy expression on Schmitt's face melted. "We have much to discuss, my friend."

Jungle, Arcadia—
01:00, 11 September, 2086

Joel and Mikhail moved slowly through the jungle, gliding the MTV along the uneven ground. Joel steered the bike carefully through the trees, keeping it at walking pace to minimize noise. It was hard to see anything in the dark beyond the MTV's small headlight.

Since leaving the city, the pair had taken the bike straight to Base Camp, arriving well ahead of Amber and the others. Joel figured if Edward had destroyed the controls of the second lifeboat, then he must be planning to take the first boat, stranding the rest of them on Arcadia. It had taken hardly any time to reach camp with the bikes, but the lifeboat was exactly where Mikhail had left it. Joel knew Edward wouldn't be going for the *Atlas* boat this time, now he knew it had no power. That meant he must still be on his way to Base Camp from the Merna village.

Mikhail sat behind Joel, loosely holding his waist to keep steady. "Did you notice their guns are non-lethal?"

Joel was caught off-guard. "What? What guns?"

Mikhail stared at the laser holstered in Joel's belt, thinking about the altercation in the city. "The Adras' weapons, the glove-things on their arms, they aren't designed to kill, just to incapacitate. When we were escaping I saw one of their shots hit the tree behind me, but it was completely fine. In fact, when I touched the black mark it just wiped away."

Joel shrugged, keeping his eyes on the dark forest ahead. "We don't know what they're capable of. Maybe the electrical impulse is only fatal to animal organisms but not plants?"

Mikhail shrugged. "How do you explain Zoe? She was hit when we were escaping but she was only paralyzed down her left side; *paralyzed.*" He repeated the word for emphasis.

Joel rolled the idea in his mind; he couldn't argue the point. He found himself nodding involuntarily.

Mikhail continued, "It's like their weapons interrupt the somatic nervous system, so the victim can't move, but it leaves the autonomic nervous system untouched. Removing possible threats but keeping them alive. Like a fast-acting tranquilizer dart. Makes our lasers feel pretty aggressive." Mikhail kept his eyes fixed on Joel's gun.

"*Dr. Carter, come in,*" came a static voice over the small black transceiver.

Mikhail pulled the box from his utility belt. "This is Mikhail, what's going on, Lieutenant?"

"*Dr. Ozero, there's been a change of plans. We've relocated to the back-up meeting point. Base Camp isn't safe with the stone missing.*"

"Copy that. We'll let you know if we find anything." As Mikhail spoke he realized Joel had slowed the bike to a near-crawl.

"What're you doing?"

Joel sniffed the air. "Can't you smell that?"

Mikhail could smell an acrid burning; it was faint, but it was definitely there. He looked around the area for the source of the smell. "Residue from the bonfire?"

Joel shook his head and continued to inhale deeply. "No, it smells electrical."

Joel turned the handles of the bike, veering toward the source of the smell. After several minutes the bike reached a huge open space. Joel recognized the formation from their first trek into the jungle with Faybin. It was a pathway. But they were further north this time, new ground.

The bike glided over the relatively flat surface of the path with ease, but Joel continued to keep their speed low. The ground was largely dirt with remnants of bark and leaf litter scattered from the nearby forest. Rocks protruded from the earth every so often. The area was eerily quiet; even the familiar croaks and chirps of hidden animals were virtually inaudible.

"I don't like this," remarked Joel.

"Hey, what's that?" Mikhail tapped Joel's shoulder and pointed to something up ahead. A soft glow penetrated the surrounding blackness.

Joel brought the bike off-course again, steering it into the forest, toward the shadowy shape. The still-smoldering wreckage of an MTV lay crumpled among the foliage; its engine was sputtering quietly; smoke poured from the sparking wreck.

"I guess we found the source of the smell," said Joel.

Joel brought the bike to a halt to examine the wreckage. The MTV was totaled; it had clearly collided with something at high speed; the nose of the vehicle was crumpled, the fans beneath the craft were poking out like a gruesome compound fracture. Joel examined the huge buttress roots which stood defiantly beside the bike. While it was obvious the roots had stopped the craft in its tracks, there were no signs of a high-speed collision.

Joel scratched his head. "The bike didn't crash here. At least, not initially. It doesn't make any sense."

Mikhail crouched over the wreckage. He leaned closer to the bike and saw small droplets of red spatter across the left side. The droplets led to a large pool of blood nearby, partially concealed by the shadows. Lying beside the bloody pool was a small object; an e-cigarette. Mikhail picked up the small silver cylinder and held it up for Joel to see.

"At least we know he was here. Now where did he go?" said Joel.

Mikhail looked up and frowned. At the same moment, the stench of rotting flesh assaulted his nostrils. Mikhail quickly held his breath to avoid vomiting. Joel smelled it, too.

Laying on the other side of one of the huge buttress roots was the mangled body of a dead Garkra. Mikhail could still make out its long crocodilian snout and the remains of a thin sail which ran down the length of its back.

"Fucking hell," breathed Mikhail.

Joel crouched down to examine the area. Two distinct sets of enormous footprints were imbedded in the mud. One had four elongated toes, matching the toes of the Garkra carcass in front of them. The second were different, three fat clawed toes. Joel looked up and noticed something hanging from a nearby tree. It was a small black fabric container, about the size of a pocketbook.

He stood and approached the buttress tree. The roots were huge and knotted together, creating large hollow spaces, large enough for a person to squeeze inside. And wedged at the edge of one of the intersecting roots was the small black pouch. As Joel approached he could see the letters "ISA" printed clearly in the bottom left corner.

"What is it?" asked Mikhail.

Joel shook his head, "It's an ISA medical field kit." The kit was hanging from a bright red carabiner which was snagged between two roots. Joel tugged at the kit but the carabiner didn't move. Mikhail approached and together they pried it away from the tree. Inside were basic field medical supplies; gauze, saline, antibiotics. Joel shrugged and attached the carabiner to the belt loop of his pants.

As he looked up again, Joel saw a pair of soft black eyes staring back at him from deeper in the crevice. Something was alive inside.

"What's that?" asked Mikhail, placing a hand on his laser.

Joel stared at the eyes for a moment. "Edward?"

His question was met with a soft wet cough. The cough of someone who was in a very bad way. "Well done," came a hoarse reply from the shadows.

As Joel's eyes adjusted to the darkness, he could just make out the figure of Edward slumped inside the roots. He was hunched sideways, clutching his abdomen, clearly struggling to hold himself upright.

"Where's the girl?" asked Joel, narrowing his gaze.

"And the stone?" continued Mikhail.

Edward chuckled, a rattling, damaged laugh. "Can you believe it? I was outwitted by a midget child."

Joel looked down at Edward in his sorry state and shrugged. "Honestly? Yeah, I can."

Edward shrugged. "Doesn't matter now. They're both long gone."

Joel shook his head. "All of this for a stupid diamond?"

Edward sighed heavily, as though there were a lead block sitting on his chest. "Alexandrite."

"Alexandrite?"

"Yeah. The stone ain't a diamond, champ. It's Alexandrite, one of the rarest gems on Earth. And even more expensive since the mines went dry a few years ago. That baby would be worth a small fortune."

Mikhail shook his head. "But it's still just a stone."

A thin smile crept across Edward's lips. "You still have no idea, eh? You think it's just a pretty rock that might net a few million back home."

Joel recalled his earlier conversation with Schmitt. "It's a power source. More than that, it's technology. *Valuable* technology. It would make all our existing ways of generating power obsolete."

"You'd have an all-out bidding war between energy companies to get their hands on it," continued Mikhail, picking up Joel's train of thought.

Both men stared at Edward expectantly.

He shook his head. "Sure, energy companies would pay through the nose to get their hands on this puppy. But it's the ones who would want to keep it hidden from the world that'd offer the most."

Joel grabbed Edward by the arm and dragged him from his hiding place. He howled in agony but was otherwise incapable of resisting. "You self-centered scum," spat Joel as he dragged Edward into the open.

Edward rolled on the soft earth, wincing in agony. "Eat me."

Before Joel could respond, a soft whistling sound cut through the relative silence of the forest. Everyone froze. The sound was high-pitched and came in long fluctuating hoots. It sounded like a bird.

Joel listened carefully. He licked his lips and whistled, returning the call; long high-pitched fluctuations.

"What are you—" Mikhail was cut off by another whistle, quicker this time, excited.

Joel stifled a laugh. "It's Veyha! Veyha!" he cried, his voice carrying through the trees. "*Veyha!*"

Mikhail smacked Joel hard on the arm. "What are you doing? Are you trying to get us killed?" Mikhail eyed the nearby Garkra carcass.

Joel pushed Mikhail away defensively. "Calm down, I know predators. If whatever killed that was still hungry, it would've come back to finish the job by now."

"Just because it doesn't want to eat rotten meat doesn't mean it won't attack," Mikhail shot back.

Joel laughed derisively. "I'm a paleozoologist. I think I know a thing or two about animal behavior."

"Pfft, you study fossils on Earth. These are living creatures on an alien planet," scoffed Edward, who still lay in the middle of the open path.

Before Joel could respond, a tiny blonde head appeared on the branches above them.

"Joel?" said Veyha, visibly excited.

"Veyha!" called Joel in reply.

The small girl quickly scrambled down the tree and ran into the open arms of Joel. "Are you okay? Did he hurt you? Where's the stone?"

Veyha wrinkled her nose and pointed at Edward. "Bad. Dumb."

Mikhail smiled. "Can't argue with that."

Joel rubbed the tiny Merna's arm. "Where's the stone, kiddo?"

Veyha smiled broadly, pleased with herself. From beneath her feathery garments she extracted the enormous Alexandrite diamond. Joel smiled and ruffled Veyha's hair. "I'm so proud of you!"

Veyha beamed.

Joel felt a soft spot for the little girl. She reminded him of another strong-willed and brave little girl he'd known back home. It was Amber who had stood up to bullies when they were kids. She was never afraid to speak up for what she believed in. For a moment, Joel remembered embracing Amber only hours earlier, remembered the intense feeling of relief and adoration. He wished he was with her now.

In the corner of his eye, Joel saw a large shadow fall over the enormous path, blocking the moonlight overhead. The shadow was accompanied by a soft hissing, followed by a rolling and menacing growl.

Joel and Mikhail froze. Veyha buried her face into Joel's leg, moaning softly.

The earth trembled as the huge shadow began to move along the path. It approached the broken and bleeding body of Edward Gilmore who still lay on the path several feet behind Joel and Mikhail. As it neared, Joel felt a pit forming in his stomach; the long crocodilian snout, the huge sail along its back, the bloody stump where its left arm should have been. The creature stared at Joel through its one good eye and for a moment Joel could have sworn it recognized him. As though it somehow knew who he was, that he was the one who had blown its arm off.

The huge beast looked down at Edward, lying on his back. It growled softly as it sniffed the small human.

Curiously, Edward didn't panic.

He opened his eyes and saw the enormous jaws hovering over his head. The two beings stared at each other for a moment before Edward took a deep breath and shouted, "Go on! Just fucking eat me already!"

The one-armed Garkra roared aggressively at the small man's outburst before opening its jaws and scooping Edward's upper body into its mouth, biting down hard.

Edward was gone.

"Son of a bitch," Mikhail breathed, too afraid to move.

Joel placed his hand over Veyha's eyes. He saw the terror on Mikhail's face. Mikhail hadn't seen a Garkra before. It was then Joel realized the Garkra was standing between them and the MTV, their only form of escape.

Once it was finished with Edward, the huge creature turned its attention to the remaining humanoids. It stared at them for a second, growling softly like an alligator with deep and throaty rumbles, as though it were deciding what to do next.

"Mikhail, take Veyha to the bike," whispered Joel.

"What? What're you—"

The Garkra let out a bellowing cry which rolled through the jungle like thunder.

"Now!" demanded Joel, pushing Mikhail and Veyha into the cover of the buttress roots. As he did so he pulled his laser from its holster and began firing wildly at the Garkra's face. The creature ducked and the laser blasts flew past its head unscathed. Joel felt his stomach clench at this behavior. The Garkra remembered the lasers. Joel continued firing as he ran in the opposite direction of the buttress tree. The one-armed crocodilian continued to duck, but was struck by a loose shot. It howled in pain and took off after Joel.

Joel sprinted across the open path and dove into the thick underbrush of the surrounding forest. The Garkra was hot on his heels, lunging and snapping aggressively as it chased him into the forest. Its enormous bulk snapped branches like toothpicks, shaking entire trees as it forced its way into the thicket. The creature lunged again, snarling loudly. Joel rolled along the wet earth, barely avoiding a mouthful of teeth. It snapped down on the leaf litter, spitting and spluttering to expel the dirt and grit from its jaws. Joel continued to roll onto his feet but the Garkra was right behind him.

It snapped at him again. Joel felt his heart sink as he was jerked backward from his hips. It had caught his utility belt in its front teeth. The force caught Joel by surprise and he lost the laser in his grasp. He was hauled from the ground and swung through the air like a ragdoll. He turned awkwardly and saw the gruesome gaping hole where the beast's left eye should have been. It was still bloodied and red, oozing yellow and white pus. The Garkra shook its head violently again, and Joel's belt snapped.

Joel was thrown across the forest, landing heavily with a loud smack. His body seared with pain as the wind was knocked out of him. But he couldn't stop now. He rolled again and saw the Garkra was still several meters away; its jaws were wide open revealing his belt still dangling between its teeth. Joel scrambled to his feet; pain shot through his chest but he couldn't stop. In the corner of his eye, he spotted a huge rotten log to his right; it was the size of a small car and had been mostly hollowed out in its center.

Joel sprinted toward the log. As he did so, the Garkra finally dislodged the belt from its teeth and charged toward him. Just as Joel dove inside, snapping jaws plunged into the opening. Joel crawled quickly down the length of the log as the Garkra's huge bulk crumpled the weak opening like a soda can. Several feet of the log disintegrated as pieces of rotten wood shattered and fell away.

Joel continued to crawl through the darkness as the beast snapped at the opening behind him. Suddenly Joel touched something soft and gelatinous inside the dead wood. He couldn't see anything but he could hear a sickening ticking and twitching sound. He scrambled backward several paces but the one-armed Garkra was still snapping desperately at the opening. Joel paused as he felt a tickling sensation running across his arms. He scrambled back further, toward the opening, but the tickling sensation followed him, dancing across his legs.

Without warning the section of bark above Joel's head collapsed as the Garkra's snout ploughed through the rotting wood. Joel instinctively pulled away, again avoiding snapping jaws by centimeters. As the Garkra pulled its snout out of the hole momentarily, Joel caught a glimpse of something else hiding inside the dead tree. Sitting to his left was a gigantic insect larva with a fat white body the size of a pig, and two long tentacles which twitched in the air, searching for food. It had no eyes or ears, but it did have a huge circular mouth with rows upon rows of terrifying teeth.

Joel recoiled in horror and quickly scrambled toward the original opening, which was no longer under attack from the Garkra. Suddenly, one of the larva's tickling tentacles wrapped around Joel's ankle, squeezing like a boa constrictor. It was surprisingly strong. The larva began to drag Joel along the length of the log, beneath the gaping hole the Garkra had punched into the wood overhead.

Joel braced himself, then grabbed the tentacle around his ankle and started to pull back. After several heaving strains, it was now the larva who was being dragged toward him. The larva hissed aggressively and splayed its menacing mouth opening, ready to take a bite out of Joel's calf.

Before the larva could sink its teeth in, the Garkra's face reappeared through the gaping hole. Its jaws snapped down on the huge larva and the tentacle around Joel's ankle went limp.

Without wasting any time, Joel crawled desperately out of the log while the one-armed Garkra was distracted by the juicy insect.

Mikhail sat on the bike, with Veyha tucked away in one of the storage compartments. They saw Joel burst from the jungle, waving at them to start the motor.

"Go! Go! Go!" he shouted as he jumped onto the back of the bike. "Let's get the hell off this planet!"

ATTACK

Atlas Camp, Arcadia—
03:00, 11 September, 2086

"Lieutenant!" called Joel. The MTV sprang from the trees like a metal panther, skidding to a halt just outside the *Atlas* campsite.

Amber rolled over, groggy from dozing by the fire. Beside her, Diamond and Grey also stirred at the sound of Joel and Mikhail arriving.

"We need to get out of here!" demanded Joel, walking briskly through the camp.

The Mernas had built several small fires along the beach. Most of the villagers were now resting quietly. Zoe and Faybin had taken the elders to the relative comfort and safety of the abandoned *Atlas* lifeboat.

Amber climbed to her feet quickly at the sound of Joel's voice.

Grey frowned. "What is it? Did you find Edward?"

Joel pulled Edward's e-cigarette from his pocket and threw it to Grey. "We found him. But we don't need to worry about him anymore." Joel glanced to Veyha sitting patiently on the back of the MTV.

"Veyha!" exclaimed Faybin as she ran across the sand.

Veyha was startled by the sound of her own name. "Faybin?" Xylon followed close behind. "Xylon! Faybin!" Veyha squeaked with delight. She leaped from the bike and raced into the open arms of her mother and grandmother. The Mernas on the beach began to stir at the sound of Veyha reuniting with her family.

"You found the girl, too? Well done. What about the stone?" asked Grey.

"Lieutenant, we don't have time for this. We only got ahead of it because we had the bike, but it'll be here soon," pressed Mikhail.

Suddenly, the nearby trees began to rustle as though assaulted by a gust of wind. Soft purring drifted through the misty air. The Mernas froze. The guttural purring continued as the trees rustled in quick succession around the edge of the beach camp, accompanied by a ghostly twittering.

Slowly, three dozen Adras emerged from the trees, fanning out along the beach surrounding the camp. Grey, Diamond, Joel, and Mikhail instinctively pulled out their lasers and aimed.

The Adras didn't attack.

Amber frowned. This wasn't aggressive behavior. They stood calmly with their arms pointed upward. Their weaponized gloves were dormant. They had cut off all exits, pinning the humans and the Mernas between them and the ocean. But they weren't attacking. They were just standing still with their arms in the air.

They were displaying submission.

Amber's eyes grew wide as she saw the faces within the crowd of Adras. Leading the troop was the familiar form of Cockatoo. But it wasn't his presence that had caught Amber's attention. Behind Cockatoo stood the weathered faces of Stripes and Gemstone, the Adra leaders. Seeing all three Adras standing together, something clicked in Amber's mind; the yellow along Stripes' decorative feathers, Gemstone's white body. They were Cockatoo's parents.

For a brief moment, Amber made eye contact with Cockatoo.

Light stone, the smooth jazz voice whispered in her mind.

"Attack!" Grey's booming voice rang out across the beach as he fired his laser into the semi-circle of Adras. Mikhail and Joel followed suit and fired several rounds into the fray.

"Wait!" called Amber, but it was too late.

The Mernas responded immediately, launching their poisonous projectiles and stone spears at the Adras. Mernas scrambled across the sand, lunging at the Adras with their primitive weapons. In that moment it was as though their fear of the feathered creatures had evaporated, giving way to a terrifying tenacity. They attacked aggressively and without mercy.

With no other option, the Adras engaged their gloved weapons. The small discs began to glow with a brilliant electric blue as the creatures started firing at the attacking Mernas. Cockatoo ushered Gemstone and Stripes into the forest before turning his attention to the Mernas. The Adras' shots were precise and effective. Every Merna who was hit collapsed on the spot, eyes wide open, paralyzed. Xylon was struck in the chest, collapsing like a ragdoll where she stood.

"Xylon!" screamed Veyha.

Faybin turned at the sound of Veyha's scream. She saw Xylon's body in the sand and her face hardened. Faybin scooped Veyha into her arms and ran for the lifeboat.

Schmitt fumbled, trying to extract the laser from his belt. He finally pulled it out, aimed it at a nearby Adra, and pulled the trigger, only to hear the dead click of the safety. The Adra in his sights swiftly fired an electrical blast into Schmitt's stomach. The old German fell to the sand heavily; his laser flew from his grasp.

From the airlock of the lifeboat Zoe watched in horror as the carnage unfolded outside. "Stop! Everyone, stop! They don't want to hurt you!"

Grey ignored Zoe's pleas. "Someone give me some cover! I'm going for the big white one." Grey sprang into action, running lengthways down the beach, drawing the fire of the oncoming attackers.

Mikhail and Joel responded quickly, firing into the Adras at the tree line. The group immediately ducked behind the shadows. Grey ran directly toward the leader of the pack, Cockatoo. He extracted a six-inch bowie knife from a sheath on his belt and, before Cockatoo knew what was happening, Grey crash-tackled him, trying to stab his soft stomach. Cockatoo rolled with amazing agility at the last second, missing the knife but taking the full force of Grey's tackle. Together they tumbled backward onto the sand. The Lieutenant's explosives launcher flew from his shoulder, landing several feet away.

Grey quickly regained his bearings and in a flash was on top of Cockatoo. He thrust the knife toward the alien's throat, but Cockatoo parried the attack with his weaponized arm. Grey slashed at the exposed skin of Cockatoo's upper limb. A burst of blood exploded from the Adra's shoulder and his attack arm went limp. Cockatoo elbowed his assailant in the nose with his good arm. Grey could hear his own nose crack under the force. While he was disorientated, Cockatoo took his chance, grabbing Grey with his good arm and rolling him onto the ground, trying to pin him down.

Grey quickly thrust his knife upward. Cockatoo reeled to avoid the blade. Grey followed with a lightning fast jab with his left hand. He connected with Cockatoo's ribcage, knocking the wind out of the huge creature. Cockatoo rolled off of Grey and continued rolling into the outskirts of the forest's edge.

"Not so fast!" Grey sprang to his feet and charged toward Cockatoo, leaping onto his back and plunging his knife into Cockatoo's right shoulder. Cockatoo shrieked in agony. He quickly reached both arms over his head, grabbed Grey by the shirt, and rolled him over his shoulder, throwing him into the dirt.

Grey rolled on the ground, surprised at the strength of his adversary. He still gripped the large knife in his hand, poised and ready to strike again. For a moment, Grey made eye contact with the huge creature standing several feet away. Its eyes were cold and emotionless.

Suddenly, the Lieutenant heard a smooth voice in his mind.

You don't have to do this.

Grey froze. He glanced around but couldn't see the source of the sound. Just the large wounded shape of Cockatoo standing before him. His left arm was damaged, his right shoulder was wounded. He wasn't going to put up much of a fight anymore.

Stop—

Grey pounced, ignoring the strange voice in his head.

Cockatoo had not expected Grey to strike so fast. The knife connected again, this time driving deep into Cockatoo's chest. Cockatoo howled. It was a harrowing, gut-wrenching sound. Slowly the huge white and yellow Adra collapsed onto the sand. Grey quickly scrambled to his feet, nursing his broken and bleeding nose. He looked down on Cockatoo and made eye contact once more.

You don't have to do this, the voice whispered in his mind again.

Grey frowned. For a brief moment, he wondered if the voice he'd heard had somehow come from the dying creature.

As Cockatoo took his last breath, Grey heard a rustling sound to his right, in the shadows of the forest's edge. He picked up his explosives launcher and smiled. "And where do you think you're going?" he said to himself.

When the fighting broke out on the beach, Diamond had not followed Grey's order. He'd seen the way the Adras were behaving when they arrived. He'd seen Grey's ruthless treatment of them at the bonfire. It wasn't right.

Amber lay beside Diamond in the sand dunes as the fighting raged all around them. "We have to stop this. Talk to Grey, he'll listen to you."

Diamond shook his head. "He won't listen to me. He's got it in his head the Adras are the enemy. He's going to do everything in his power to take them down."

"We have to try. Where is he now?"

"There!" called Diamond. He was pointing to the tree line a few hundred meters away as a human-shaped figure slipped into the shadows of the forest.

"C'mon." Amber grabbed Diamond's arm and they raced across the beach and into the forest.

The huge rainforest trees muffled the sounds of gunfire from the beach. Amber and Diamond moved carefully, trying to keep their distance from Grey. They stayed several paces back, watching as he carried his explosives launcher at the ready. After a few hundred meters, he stopped and raised the launcher to his shoulder.

Beyond his shadow, Amber could just make out the figures of Stripes and Gemstone hiding among the thick foliage. They were alone and unarmed. They didn't even know Grey had them in his sights.

"Lieutenant! Stop!" called Amber impulsively.

Grey was startled at the sound of her voice. He shrugged her off. "Stay back, Dr. Lytton. This doesn't concern you."

Amber ignored his order and continued to approach.

"Sir, with all due respect, we were wrong about these guys," said Diamond. "They aren't the bad guys. They didn't come here looking for a fight. I don't think they want anyone to get hurt."

Grey bristled. "You don't know what you're talking about, boy. These things don't have feelings. They don't care if anyone gets hurt. They're just monsters."

"You're the monster here! You're the alien being that's invaded their home and is literally holding a gun to their head!" Diamond swallowed hard. He'd never spoken like that to Grey before.

Grey's face remained cold and indifferent. "You're too soft."

At the sound of their exchange, the pair of Adras turned abruptly. They saw the launcher in Grey's hands and Amber and Diamond standing nearby. Amber made eye contact with Gemstone. A tranquil voice entered her consciousness.

Help us.

Amber could see the panic and desperation in her eyes.

"Grey! Stop!" she screamed. Without thinking, Amber sprinted through the trees and stepped in front of Grey and the launcher, putting herself between him and the Adras. She stared down the barrel of the launcher as it hovered less than a meter from her face. "Put it down. You don't have to do this."

"Get out of the way. Don't make me shoot you, too." He spoke through gritted teeth, clearly losing patience. Grey pulled the scope up to his eye, staring at Amber.

Amber watched in horror as Grey placed his finger on the trigger. He wasn't backing down.

A loud ear-splitting shot echoed through the forest.

Amber's heart stopped. After a long moment she finally opened her eyes. She felt her body; it was unscathed. She looked around frantically. Stripes and Gemstone were unharmed, too.

Grey hadn't fired.

He still stood several feet from her. He still held the launcher, aimed directly at her. But now his eyes were wide and his breathing was quick and shallow. He dropped the launcher and fell to his knees, his head hung loosely on his neck. Finally, Amber saw the jagged hole at the back of his head. Grey inhaled one last time as his whole body flopped clumsily to the ground.

Amber exhaled, unaware she had been holding her breath. She clutched her heart in a futile attempt to slow its racing speed. Her hands were clammy and damp patches of sweat stained her clothing. Amber felt her knees weaken as she lowered herself to the ground.

It was only then she saw Diamond, standing behind Grey's lifeless body. His arm was still outstretched, gripping the hand-laser tight. Slowly his arm relaxed and the laser tumbled from his grasp. His eyes filled with tears. "I'm . . . I'm sorry," he sobbed.

Stripes placed a hand on Amber's shoulder and a guttural voice entered her mind.

Thank you.

Amber turned to face Stripes, unable to hold back her emotions. "Thank you?"

For saving our lives.

Amber stared at Stripes; his face was pained but he seemed genuinely grateful; there was no anger, no desire for revenge. Amber felt a pit in her stomach, an intense feeling of guilt and grief she had never felt before.

She wiped a tear from her cheek. "Diamond, we have to stop this. They aren't monsters. They're just trying to put an end to all this bloodshed. We're the real enemy here. I get it now," she said, directing her last comment to Stripes.

Cavalry

Atlas Camp, Arcadia—
05:00, 11 September, 2086

On the beach, Mikhail and Joel watched Grey take out Cockatoo and then disappear into the forest. Before they could react, two smaller Adras burst from the trees, moving fast and low. And they were heading straight for Joel and Mikhail. Both were small, mostly grey in color, with softer and fluffier feathers than the others; juveniles. The young Adras were fast and ferocious but they lacked the familiar glove-weapon of the adults.

The larger of the two approached Mikhail with phenomenal speed. With its arms outstretched, it tackled him hard. Mikhail's gun was knocked from his grasp as the pair rolled across the sand, into the water together.

"Mikhail!" called Joel, as they disappeared under the crashing waves.

Mikhail scrambled to his feet in the knee-deep water, waiting for the Adra to gain its bearings, ready for a fist fight. Just as the juvenile was about to stand, Mikhail swung wide with a left hook, connecting hard with the juvenile's face. The small Adra reeled, reaching out to grab something for stability. Its claws seized Mikhail's shirt and pulled both of them under the water again. This time, the pair were caught by the riptide, rolling upside-down in the churning waves.

After a tense moment, they resurfaced several meters along the beach, bringing them in line with the lifeboat. They both coughed and spluttered. Neither was trying to fight the other anymore, they were desperately trying to make their way out of the water, away from the tide. After several moments, Mikhail found his footing and steadied himself in the waves. He grabbed the small juvenile's claw as it flailed and helped it scramble to shore. They flopped onto the sand together and for a moment, they lay quietly on the beach.

The smaller of the two juveniles was slower and more calculating in its approach. It stood before Joel, snarling and shrieking, and kicking its right leg in a show of aggression. It held its claws in front of its body defensively and crouched low. Joel could see its enormous curved toe, perfect for gutting a small mammal like himself.

Joel aimed his gun at the juvenile's head.

"Joel, stop!" Zoe's voice was shrill and frantic.

Joel hesitated just as the juvenile sprang into the air like a frog, its enormous clawed toe poised in front of its body. It was quick and agile, but it was still young. It had misjudged its aim. Instead of hitting Joel's chest or abdomen its huge toe caught his left leg and sliced a four-inch gash down the side of his thigh. Joel howled in pain. He caught the juvenile as it struck him and, to his surprise, it was incredibly light. Without missing a beat, Joel pivoted his whole body and threw the juvenile into the sand behind him. It rolled once but was quickly back on its feet.

Joel snatched his laser from the sand and aimed at the juvenile's head again.

"Joel! Stop it!" demanded Zoe.

Suddenly a tremendous roar reverberated through the air. It rolled across the beach like a tsunami. Everyone stopped dead in their tracks. The humans, the Mernas, and the Adras all froze instantly.

"It's here," whispered Joel under his breath.

The earth shook as the enormous body of the one-armed Garkra crashed through the trees, onto the beach. It paused for a moment, surveying the area. It seemed even bigger out in the open, towering over the comparatively tiny creatures on the beach. Its huge shadow, cast by the full moon, was splayed across the sand like a demon.

"Run!" screamed Joel.

The Garkra lunged toward the camp. A nearby Adra turned quickly and fired at the beast, but the shot went wide. The Garkra watched the flash of blue electricity fly past its head as it dove toward the guilty Adra, jaws agape. The latter shrieked in terror as the crocodilian scooped it into its mouth and bit down hard. The Adra's shrieks stopped dead, replaced by the sounds of bones shattering as blood exploded from the giant creature's jaws. Its limbs flopped instantly, dangling lifelessly between the Garkra's teeth.

Joel hobbled toward the boat, clutching desperately at the wound on his leg, trying to stifle the flow of blood.

At the sound of the Garkra's arrival, Mikhail and the juvenile had also scrambled to their feet and sprinted from the waterline to the lifeboat. Zoe pulled Joel, Mikhail, and the juvenile inside, closing the airlock behind them. Mikhail leaned against the door for a moment, panting for breath.

Inside the boat, a dozen Merna children and the seven remaining elders were crouched in fear among the lifeboat's passenger seats. Faybin squeezed Veyha tight in her arms, staring at the small grey juvenile with a mixture of fear and confusion. The juvenile looked so small standing beside Zoe and Mikhail. The ferocity it had displayed only moments earlier was gone. Its eyes were wide as they darted between the Garkra on the beach outside, and the Mernas huddled at the back of the boat. It was scared.

It was dark inside the boat. The only light came from the bright moon as it filtered through the large wraparound window.

Joel crouched by the glass. "The Adras are gone," he said to no one in particular.

"The others are still out there, we have to do something," said Mikhail.

"We can't—"

The whole boat suddenly lifted off the ground, crashing down violently. Metal squeaked and scraped, making a horrible sound. The juvenile and the Merna children screamed in panic. Suddenly the large menacing face of the Garkra appeared by the front window, baring its bloodstained jaws. It still had the Adra's weaponized glove-arm lodged between its teeth.

The one-armed Garkra reared backward then slammed its enormous head into the side of the boat. This time the glass on the huge front window splintered into spider webs. The Garkra spun around and rammed its muscular tail into the window. The cracks spread further.

"It's going to break!" screamed Zoe.

"Everyone to the back of the boat!" called Joel.

While the others retreated to the rear compartment, Mikhail paused. He saw the Mernas huddled at the back of the ship, they were terrified. For a moment, his world slowed down. He recalled the fearful screams of his passengers when his plane had crashed. He heard Veronica's voice in his mind; *you're stronger than you think*. In that moment, Mikhail felt his fears dissolve away, as though some unseen force was washing his conscience clean, giving him a second chance.

He knew what he had to do.

Mikhail turned to face the front window with determination. The Garkra's head appeared again. It paused and gazed through the splintered glass with its huge reptilian eye. Mikhail snatched a laser from a nearby weapons crate and jumped into the pilot's seat.

"What're you doing? Get back here! That thing will demolish you!" called Joel.

"For once, just trust me."

Mikhail held his breath as the huge creature spun around once more, pivoting on its enormous feet and slamming its muscular tail into the window. The weakened glass shattered into a million pieces, showering Mikhail in broken shards. The children and the juvenile screamed again as the beast roared aggressively, opening its jaws wide.

Mikhail fired several laser blasts directly into the creature's mouth. It reeled from the shots, hacking and coughing. In that moment, Mikhail leaped through the now-open space. He slid down the nose of the boat and ran as fast as his legs would carry him. As he ran across the beach, he fired randomly into the creature's torso and legs, drawing its attention away from the lifeboat.

"Mikhail!" called Joel from the rear of the boat.

"Hey! You! Come and get me!" taunted Mikhail as he ran toward the water.

The Garkra was disorientated, shaking its head, trying to dislodge the taste of the laser blasts. It growled a deep throaty sound and turned to follow Mikhail toward the ocean. Mikhail ran straight into the water and dove beneath the surface, hoping to hide himself in the darkened depths.

Joel watched helplessly as the creature left the front of the ship and followed Mikhail into the water. "C'mon, everyone! Out the window!"

Zoe and Joel began hauling the others through the open hole that used to be the window.

"Where do we go when we're out?" asked Zoe.

Joel lifted one of the Merna children through the open space. "Take them into the forest. Find the tallest, thickest trees you can and climb."

After the Mernas were out Zoe helped the small Adra across the broken glass. She smiled as it shot off down the beach to join its family. Joel and Zoe clambered over the broken glass into the darkness beyond. Zoe ran into the forest after Faybin and the others. Joel hobbled slowly to the tree line. The pain in his leg made it impossible to move quickly. Once he was in the relative safety of the trees, he stopped to catch his breath and to keep an eye on Mikhail.

In the water, Mikhail was paddling desperately, ducking beneath the surface and swimming several lengths before coming up again. He was trying to confuse the creature, trying to throw off its sense of direction. The Garkra snapped and growled at the waves in frustration. A massive wave crashed down on Mikhail just as he was about to dive again. He was plunged underwater, turned upside-down and rolled over. He couldn't tell which way was up. After several panicked moments Mikhail broke the surface; he was facing the horizon, which was starting to show signs of daylight.

Without warning, an enormous foot smashed down on top of him, plunging him underwater and pushing him into the sand below. His lungs burned, he didn't have enough oxygen. There was no time to take a breath. Just as he was about to black out, the foot released its grip and Mikhail desperately made his way to the surface, gasping for air.

As soon as he breached, Mikhail's heart stopped.

He saw the insides of the Garkra's mouth, lined with razor-sharp teeth. He could smell the foul stench of rotting flesh. Mikhail cast his eyes back to the shore and saw Joel and the others had made it to safety.

He closed his eyes and Mikhail's world went black.

Hermes, Orbit—
05:30, 11 September, 2086

Veronica sat in near-darkness aboard *Hermes*. The only light came from the viewing platform as she watched the battle raging on below, helplessly. She had held her breath as Mikhail and the small Adra tumbled through the water. She'd bit her knuckles when the Garkra attacked the lifeboat. She'd cursed Mikhail as he lured the beast back to the water.

As the Garkra's jaws clamped down over Mikhail's small figure, Veronica froze. Her limbs went cold as adrenaline flooded her veins. Her stomach lurched. Her hearing and vision blurred as though she had been punched in the head. For half a heartbeat the world stopped.

Emotions came flooding out of Veronica all at once. She screamed as loud as her lungs would allow. Tears streamed down her cheeks. She rocked back and forth muttering, "No, no, no."

It took all her strength not to collapse to the floor. She could still hear his voice whispering in her ear, still smell his musk, and feel the warmth of his hand on her cheek as they said their final goodbye. He was safe aboard *Hermes*. It should have been her that went back down.

It's my fault.

Suddenly the viewing platform sprang to life again as a second enormous creature barreled through the trees at the edge of the jungle. The animal charged across the beach. Unlike the Garkra, this creature had a huge head and massive rounded jaws. Its legs were thick and muscular, but it only had three claws on each foot. A Denkra. The silver brace around the creature's neck glinted in the moonlight like jewelry. The Denkra lunged, thrusting itself across the beach and into the water. As it entered the surf, the Garkra quickly swung left, narrowly avoiding a face full of teeth. Pivoting with speed which defied its size, the Garkra used its tail like a gigantic whip and knocked the Denkra into the ocean. The water exploded beneath the beast as it crashed into the waves.

With the Denkra underwater, the Garkra lunged, jaws bared. Its teeth locked onto the Denkra's neck and clamped down. Blood sprayed everywhere and the animal howled in pain, a harrowing and unholy sound. Using its huge back legs, the Denkra kicked its captor, slicing a huge gash in the side of the Garkra's right thigh, causing the animal to release its grip. The Denkra quickly found its footing and charged, like a battering ram, slamming the Garkra with its thick skull, shattering its ribcage.

The Garkra stumbled to regain its footing and swung its tail trying to knock the Denkra off balance, but the larger beast ducked quickly and lunged again at the Garkra's neck. This time the Denkra hit its target, biting its neck hard and shaking violently.

Veronica shifted the image around, trying to find the rest of her team. At the edge of the forest was a human-sized body, Joel. She held her breath. He was alive. She could see him shuffling around, trying to get a better view of the two titans battling in the water. To his left, there was a disturbance in the undergrowth. A shadowy figure darted toward him. Joel aimed his gun. It was another human, Amber. After a brief exchange Veronica saw Joel pull something large and green from his bag. Amber snatched it and disappeared into the forest again.

Before Veronica had time to comprehend what was happening, a horde of Adras burst from the trees onto the beach. They moved in perfect formation, heading straight for the monsters battling in the water. The Denkra continued to hold the Garkra's neck in its grasp, shaking its head like a dog with a chew toy. The crocodilian flailed its right arm, desperately trying to connect with the Denkra. But it was too strong. The more the Garkra thrashed, the harder its attacker bit down.

The one-armed Garkra howled and groaned in desperation as the Adras formed a defensive semi-circle around the battle, providing a gap for one of their troop to pass through. The yellow and black leader strode through the pack, carrying the *Light stone*. He held the stone high in the air while the remaining Adras aimed their arm-mounted weapons. The three discs on the knuckles of the Adras' weapons were no longer glowing blue; this time they glowed a brilliant bright red.

The Adras simultaneously fired their weapons. Bolts of red lightning struck the stone, illuminating it like a lightbulb. It glowed against the dim light of impending dawn, lighting up the entire beach in an eerie crimson glow. At the same moment, the Denkra released its grip on the Garkra's neck.

The Garkra bellowed an ungodly sound which reverberated across the sand, penetrating into the jungle. The huge creature was being assaulted by some unseen force. It swayed left and right in agony, as though something were pressing on its brain. It roared again before turning and running down the beach, disappearing into the darkness.

Once the Garkra was gone the Adras lowered their weapons. The bright red light dissipated and the stone reverted to a soft emerald green.

Veronica stared at the viewing table, unsure of what she had just witnessed.

Atlas Camp, Arcadia—
06:00, 11 September, 2086

Soft morning light slowly spread across the beach. White sand stretched for miles in both directions. The only obscurity was the dark and desolate area inhabited by the remaining survivors. Aside from the crashing of the waves the beach was silent.

Stripes and Gemstone stood on the shore, letting the water wash over their feet. They were looking over the beach, watching Amber and Diamond as they checked the bodies of Mernas and Adras for signs of life. Every time it was the same outcome; the Mernas were paralyzed but unharmed; the Adras, on the other hand, had been fatally struck by the humans' lasers, severely wounded by the Mernas' spears, or gruesomely poisoned by the Mernas' darts.

Amber turned to Stripes, feeling weighed down by guilt. "They're dead. Not a single Merna casualty, but almost every Adra is dead."

Stripes closed his eyes and nodded, placing a hand on Gemstone's shoulder. She nuzzled into him, sighing heavily.

Joel emerged from the battered lifeboat with a fresh bandage on his leg. The medical kit he'd found in the forest had a field staple which he used on his thigh. Blood still seeped through to the bandage, soaking it red. Joel's eyes darted between Amber and Stripes suspiciously. He hobbled forward, trying to keep the weight off his injured leg.

"We have to help them," said Amber, as Joel stumbled across the sand.

Joel raised an eyebrow. "We have to what?"

"We have to help them. It's the least we can do."

"You want us to help the Adras? The same creatures who kidnapped you? Who attacked us and killed half the Merna tribe?"

Amber shook her head. "The Mernas aren't dead, they're just paralyzed. And did *they* attack *us*?"

Joel thought back; the Adras had arrived with their weapons subdued and their hands in the air. It wasn't until Grey called for attack that they started to fire.

"No, now that you mention it. But what about you? Why did they kidnap you?"

"It's not like that. It's a long story but, for once, just trust me." She touched his arm gently.

Joel felt his chest tighten. They were the last words Mikhail had said before diving through the window to his death. Joel saw the sincerity on Amber's face. He couldn't deny she probably knew more about the Adras than he did. And he did trust her.

Suddenly a deep guttural voice entered Joel's consciousness.

Help us.

Joel stepped backward, startled. "What was that?" He looked around for the source of the sound, his eyes falling on Stripes in disbelief.

Gemstone stepped forward, making eye contact with Joel. A different voice entered his mind; this time it was soft and feminine.

Please, help us, help them.

Joel turned to Amber, his eyes wide. "What's happening right now? Am I dying?"

Amber laughed. She leaned forward and whispered, "Joel, we were right. The Adras are more advanced than anything on Earth, *sixty-five million years more advanced.*" She couldn't hide the lilt of excitement in her voice.

Joel's eyes grew wide at the implication.

Amber glanced to the bodies on the beach. "The Adras saw the Mernas' ancestors getting smarter. They saw they were aggressive and unpredictable, but they were also intelligent and compassionate. I don't know how, but they know about us, too. They've seen what humans did to Earth, they've seen our capacity for destruction and they've seen the Mernas' potential for becoming just like us. So, they've done everything in their power to keep them in check. To stop them from turning *into* us." Amber shifted her attention to the Adra corpses. "They were right to be so concerned."

Faybin and Zoe sat patiently in the treetops with Veyha and the Merna elders. The commotion on the beach had fallen silent a little while ago and the sun was now rising over the horizon.

"C'mon, I think it's over," said Zoe.

Faybin saw the streams of sunlight filter through the canopy and visibly relaxed. She motioned to the elders, who nodded, and the group made their way down the tree, heading back to the beach. As they approached, they saw the familiar shape of the *Atlas* camp; the domed camouflaged tents and the now-battered lifeboat. They could hear voices.

Faybin and Zoe crawled closer to the edge of the forest, hiding in the shadows. They could see the beach and the remaining humans. Amber and Joel were standing near the Adra leaders by the camp while Diamond continued to examine the bodies on the beach.

Faybin's eyes were focused on the beach, but not on the Adras. Zoe followed her gaze. Merna bodies were scattered along the sand, dotting the beach like sunbathers. Faybin's eyes narrowed, fixing on the body of Xylon. She pursed her lips and clenched her fists.

"Adra," said Faybin through gritted teeth. She reached beneath her feathery tunic and extracted one of the humans' lasers. She had paid close attention to the humans and their weapons. "Adra kill Din. Adra kill Xylon. Faybin kill Adra."

Without another word, Faybin started marching toward the camp.

Zoe sprang to her feet. "Faybin! Wait! Stop!"

At the sound of Zoe's shouts everybody turned to see Faybin several meters down the beach. She was aiming the laser directly at Stripes, her face hard and angry.

"Faybin? What're you doing?" called Joel.

Faybin scowled as she continued to approach. "Adra kill Merna."

Joel saw Faybin glancing from the Adras back to the beach. It took him a moment to realize she was looking at a body on the beach. The paralyzed body of Xylon.

"She thinks they're dead," he said aloud. Joel quickly broke from the group, hobbling to the fallen figure of Xylon on the sand. It had been several hours since the attack started. Joel prayed that was enough time. He crouched over Xylon's frail body and took out his canteen, dripping water on her face. No response. He lifted her shoulders and shook her gently. Still no response.

"C'mon," he whispered to himself.

"Joel!" screamed Faybin in outrage.

"Xylon?" came a soft voice from the tree line. Veyha emerged from her hiding place. "Xylon!" she repeated as she sprinted to the body of her grandmother. She pushed Joel aside and threw her arms around Xylon, laying across her chest. She wept uncontrollably, repeating her name.

Faybin stood before Stripes and Gemstone with the laser still fixed at Stripes. She watched Veyha sobbing over Xylon's lifeless body. Her anger intensified. "Adra kill Xylon! Faybin kill Adra!" she screamed, placing her finger on the trigger.

"Ah!" screamed Veyha. Her ear was pressed against Xylon's chest, but she was no longer crying. Veyha moved her head across Xylon's chest, over her heart. "Thump, thump!" she screamed.

Faybin kept the gun fixed on Stripes as she cautiously walked over to Xylon's body. She moved Veyha aside, gently, and pressed her ear against Xylon's chest.

"Faybin?" said Xylon weakly.

Faybin jumped back, startled. She dropped the laser as Xylon's eyes fluttered open, adjusting to the brightness of the rising sun. Her eyes moved between Faybin and Veyha and she smiled. Faybin stroked Xylon's hand as tears began to stream down her cheeks. All her anger and hatred melted into relief. Veyha threw her arms around Xylon's neck and squeezed her tight. "Xylon!"

"Can someone please explain to me what the hell is going on?"

Everyone turned. Standing by the shore was the weathered and battered figure of Schmitt. All along the beach the fallen Mernas were slowly regaining movement.

Faybin froze in shock as one after another the Mernas seemingly rose from the dead.

Joel placed a hand on Faybin's shoulder. "Faybin, we need to talk."

Amber approached, crouching beside Joel. "Xylon, Faybin, the Adras don't want to be your enemy. They know you are good people and you just want what's best for the Mernas. That's what they want, too."

Faybin shook her head. "Adra steal Merna."

Amber nodded. "I know. I know they've taken Mernas in the past. But they only took them so they could send them somewhere safe, somewhere where there are no Adras and no Garkras. They just want to help."

Faybin frowned, taking in Amber's words. "Katchu?"

Zoe joined the conversation. "Yes. The Adras have been taking Mernas to Katchu for a long time now. I have seen many Mernas brought to the city and taken away again. Your friends and family are alive."

Zoe gestured for Stripes and Gemstone to approach.

Faybin and Xylon recoiled as the two Adras came closer. Stripes still held the green-tinted *Light stone*. He crouched before Xylon and Faybin and held the stone so they could see it clearly. The small sphere changed dramatically. Deep inside the stone an image developed. An island grew in size within the small diamond, an island surrounded by tall streaks of blue-white light. Dozens of Mernas roamed the island freely and happily. They laughed and played without a care.

But one Merna in particular caught Faybin's eye. A small and muscular Merna man, with long dreadlocked blond hair. His arms and back were decorated with elaborate green tattoos. She recognized him instantly.

"Naru?" she said, clutching at the stone in disbelief.

"Naru is alive. He found Katchu and he's waiting for you to join him," said Zoe.

Veyha snatched the stone from Faybin. "Naru! Naru Katchu!" She turned to Faybin with excitement.

Faybin turned to Xylon for guidance. All their fallen comrades were awake now and had started to congregate around Faybin and her little family. Faybin felt a small hand tugging at her arm.

"Sky people," said Veyha, pointing to Amber and the remaining humans. "Sky people take Merna to Katchu," she said in surprisingly eloquent English.

Faybin smiled. She nodded to Amber and Zoe. "Yes. Sky people take Merna to Katchu."

KATCHU

Adra City, Arcadia—
09:00, 12 September, 2086

Joel opened his eyes slowly. He was inside a white room. The walls were made from some sort of rendered stone, giving the room a rugged but sterile feeling. A light shone directly down on him from the roof, assaulting his delicate eyes. Joel tried to move but his body was held firmly in place. He lifted his head. He was lying inside a small tank, about the size of a bathtub. But this bathtub was not filled with water. His body was immersed in a thick yellow gelatinous substance which had molded to the shape of his body.

Amber's face suddenly appeared in Joel's field of vision, hovering over him like an apparition. "Morning, how're you feeling?"

Joel was relieved to hear her voice. He felt disoriented and confused. "Where am I? How long was I out?" His voice was hoarse.

Amber smiled, brushing her hair behind her ear. She looked refreshed and rested. "You're inside the Adra city. Stripes gave you some medication for your leg. It knocked you out pretty hard, so they took you to the medical unit to rest and recover. You've been asleep for about a day."

Joel raised an eyebrow. "Stripes?"

Amber laughed. "Oh, that's just what I call the male leader, the yellow and black one."

Joel smiled involuntarily. "And did you say they have medicine?"

Amber shrugged. "I guess on Earth we'd call it medicine. But this is way more advanced than anything we have back home. The stuff Stripes gave you is like a cocktail of painkillers, antibiotics, and an enzyme that stimulates tissue regeneration. It's pretty amazing, take a look for yourself."

Amber touched something outside Joel's field of vision and suddenly the stiff jelly-like substance encasing his body began to warm, quickly melting into a liquid state. Joel was able to move. He sat up, thankful for the ability to control himself again. Joel could finally see his injured leg. Beneath the surface of the liquid, his thigh was covered in a thin translucent wrap, like saranwrap. He could see the remnants of his wound. The medical staples had been removed and fresh pink skin had already grown beneath the wrap. The skin was tender and bruised around the edges, but the scar looked like it was weeks old, not hours.

"Well, I'll be damned."

As Joel looked up he saw an Adra in the room with them. His eyes grew wide as he recognized the small purple creature that had collided with Din in the courtyard. The one who Din had stabbed repeatedly with his small stone knife. She wore the same translucent saranwrap around her abdomen. Beneath the wrap, new skin was already growing, repairing the damage.

"C'mon, the Mernas are almost ready," said Amber, offering her hand.

Joel took her hand and awkwardly pulled himself out of the sticky yellow liquid. "Ready for what?"

Amber smiled.

She hooked Joel's arm over her neck, helping take some of his weight. With her assistance, Joel hobbled out of the room. He was surprised by how little his leg hurt; he hardly needed Amber's help, although for the moment he was happy to have her so close.

The pair emerged into the elaborate tree-city. They walked for several minutes before coming to the main courtyard. Joel recognized it from the night they rescued Amber and the others, although it was certainly something else in daylight.

Amber saw Joel staring at the tree-city. "They use the same growth enzyme with their construction. Instead of chopping down a hundred-year-old tree and using the wood to build a frame, they grow and cultivate a mature tree-building in less than ten years."

Joel saw the look of adoration on Amber's face as she talked about the tree-buildings. There was something different about her, something that had always been there but which Joel had never seen this clearly before. It was as though her passion and excitement were radiating outward, making her appear even more beautiful on the outside. This place really was paradise to her.

A procession of Adras carried various Merna artifacts from the great gate across the courtyard, disappearing into the network of alleyways. The earth shook beneath their feet as an enormous Denkra plodded casually past. It looked just like the one from the beach, with the now-familiar collar around its neck, glinting in the morning light. Strapped to its back was a saddle containing a single Adra and all sorts of material from the Merna village; huts, tools, garments.

Joel looked to Amber expectantly. He knew she had already gone into lecture mode.

Amber laughed. "I'm sure you've figured out the Denkra are descendants of the Tyrannosaurus. They were domesticated over time by the Adras with the help of the Electro-Transmitters."

"Electro what?"

"Electro-Transmitters. See the collar? It's a quartz-encrusted transmitter which targets the Alpha brain waves of the wearer by picking up neurological signals from the Adras. Primitive species, like the Denkra, don't even know they're being controlled. The Mernas, on the other hand, are too advanced to be manipulated in the same way. But the Adras give them similar collars for tagging and surveillance."

The Denkra continued to walk through the courtyard, following the length of the winding canal which cut through the city. Joel and Amber followed the huge beast along the length of the canal. They passed several gardens which were bursting with plant and insect life. Adras congregated in social groups inside the gardens, munching happily on insects. Amber explained the symbiotic relationship the Adras had developed with the enormous flytrap flowers. The flytraps caught a hundred times more insects than they needed to survive, so they shared their catch with the Adras. In return the Adras provided water and protection for the flytraps inside the city walls.

The canal flowed right through the city, ending at another enormous stone gate several kilometers away. The gate was retracted now so the Denkra and Adras could move freely. As Amber and Joel left the confines of the city they were assaulted with a salty gust of wind and the strong scent of the ocean.

The canal flowed beneath the great wall, draining into a large inlet which connected to the ocean a short distance away. The back gate led to a long dirt ramp which flattened to a stone "dock" at the water's edge. Diamond, Zoe, and Schmitt congregated on the dock waving Amber and Joel over.

"It's about time you got here!" called Diamond.

As they approached, Joel caught a glimpse of something huge floating in the water. Sitting just below the waterline, like an enormous inflatable toy, was another remarkably dinosaur-like creature. Its body was at least twenty meters long and largely hidden beneath the surface. Its head was long and flat with a tapered snout and serrated teeth. Its flippers alone were the size of a human and its tail stretched behind its body like a sea-serpent.

"What is *that*?"

Diamond was visibly excited. "It's a Denkravon, a water-dinosaur! That's how the Adras move things over water. Isn't it cool?"

Despite its ferocious appearance, the creature was calm and docile at the edge of the dock. Around its neck was the familiar quartz-encrusted Electro-Transmitter, and floating behind the dinosaur was a large open container filled with Merna possessions. The large Denkra Joel and Amber had been following stopped beside the Denkravon, allowing Adras to leap onto its back and transfer its cargo to the open container.

Mernas had already started to gather on the dock, staring at the Denkravon with a mixed sense of awe and trepidation. Among the crowd of Mernas, Xylon, Faybin, and Veyha emerged. Veyha let go of Faybin's hand and ran into Joel's arms, hugging him tight.

"Joel come Katchu," she pleaded.

"I can't, kiddo. The island is only for Mernas."

Zoe interrupted the exchange. "That's not entirely accurate."

"You must be Joel!" called a deep Scottish voice from inside the cargo container.

Two humans stood at the edge of the vessel. One was a small Japanese man with grey wisps in his jet-black hair, the other was a big burly man with wild red hair and a thick red beard. Beside them was a muscular Merna man with long blond dreadlocks, covered in green tattoos.

Zoe smiled. "Joel, Amber, meet Yoshi Kato and Lachlan Armstrong. They've been living on Katchu for several months now." Yoshi and Lachlan clambered over the edge of the container, joining the others on the dock.

The Merna man followed Lachlan and Yoshi onto the dock. As he did so, he scooped Veyha into his arms. She squealed with delight and hugged him tight. Faybin touched the male on his arm and pressed her forehead against his in a sign of affection.

Zoe continued, "And this is Naru. Faybin's husband and Veyha's father."

Joel watched Naru nuzzle with Veyha. Joel felt a soft spot for the little girl and her family. At that moment, he felt a hand take his. He looked down to see Amber casually wrapping her fingers around his. He gripped her hand and squeezed.

Yoshi saw the small black pouch on Joel's pants. "Hey! You found my medi-kit!"

Joel looked down. "You can have it back if you want?"

Yoshi smiled, a big toothy grin. "Nah, you keep it. The Adras have much better medication anyway."

Diamond patted Yoshi on the shoulder. "Maybe the Adras can give us some of their meds to take back with us? I guess even if we didn't find another home for humanity at least we rescued the *Atlas* crew and found some cool stuff!"

The *Atlas* team looked at one another sheepishly.

"Not quite," said Lachlan in his thick Scottish accent. "We've been talking and, as far as the ISA is concerned, you never found us. Or better yet, you did find us, but we were already dead. Killed on a hostile alien world!" He waved his arms in the air dramatically.

Yoshi, Zoe, and Schmitt smiled.

Diamond shook his head. "What are you talking about? We came here to rescue you."

Yoshi patted Diamond's shoulder. "The thing is, we don't really need rescuing. You're right, this place isn't meant to be a new home for humans. It's doing pretty damn well on its own. And, let's face it, if more humans came here they'd just screw it up. But, for those of us who are here, it feels like a waste not to take advantage of the hand we've been dealt."

Joel looked around the area. The beautiful crystal clear water, the salty smell of the ocean, the huge obsidian wall of the Adra city. He couldn't argue with their logic. Arcadia wasn't exactly an untouched wilderness, but it was a cultivated and protected version of Earth.

"So, you're going to stay with the Adras?" asked Diamond.

Schmitt shook his head. "No, no. We're going with the Mernas to Katchu. We can help them assimilate to their new home and act as mediators between them and the Adras. That's exactly what Lachlan and Yoshi have been doing for the past few months."

Amber watched the Mernas begin to climb aboard the huge container floating behind the Denkravon. She thought about the beautiful island she'd seen in her visions, the Mernas laughing happily, surrounded by herbivorous animals, without a care in the world.

Amber turned to Zoe. "I get it. I think I *finally* get it."

Zoe smiled and embraced Amber tightly.

Diamond shrugged. "I guess technically we still completed our mission because we found the missing team. I don't quite get it myself, but if you want to stay here, well, good luck with everything." He shook hands with the *Atlas* team.

Schmitt shook Joel's hand. "Just tell Irwin we were long dead before you arrived. Killed by the savage and hyper intelligent aliens." He winked playfully. It was the first time Joel had seen Schmitt so happy.

Everyone said their goodbyes, and Faybin and her family boarded the cargo container with the remaining *Atlas* team. Naru held Veyha in his arms so she could see over the side.

Once the last Merna had boarded, a team of Adras stepped in to detach the container from the dock. They stepped back and the Denkravon snapped to life, dipping its head below the water. The container eased away, moving down the inlet, toward the open ocean.

Hermes, Orbit—
12:00, 12 September, 2086

The lifeboat door opened with a hiss as the pressure equalized. Amber stepped onto the science deck of *Hermes* while Diamond helped Joel. Standing just inside the airlock hatch was Veronica.

As their eyes met, Amber felt an overwhelming sense of guilt. She couldn't imagine what it would have been like for Veronica these past few days; forced to send Edward back to the surface with Veyha as his prisoner. Able to watch as events below unfolded, but unable to communicate. Watching in horror as her partner was killed by a monster below.

Veronica clearly hadn't slept; her eyes were red from crying.

"Oh, Veronica," sighed Amber.

Veronica took a deep breath, trying to hold herself together. "It's too much. It's just too much, too fast." Tears began to stream down her cheeks.

Amber embraced Veronica, hugging her tight. Despite their height difference, Veronica felt so fragile in Amber's arms. Joel and Diamond stood behind the women as they embraced. Everyone was silent for a moment, as if paying an unspoken reverence to their fallen comrades.

"I want him back. It's my fault he's gone," whispered Veronica.

Amber stroked Veronica's back gently. "Don't say that."

She continued to weep softly into Amber's shoulder. "I never should have sent him down there. I should have gone back down. It should have been me."

Joel touched Veronica's shoulder. "It was nobody's fault." Joel recalled the look on Mikhail's face as he sat in the pilot seat of the *Atlas* lifeboat. He knew he was risking his life. "Mikhail saved our lives. If it wasn't for his actions on the beach, that thing would have killed everyone inside the boat. He's a hero."

The weary group made their way to the lower level of *Hermes*, into the kitchen. The bright blue marble of Arcadia hovered in the large window like an enormous sentinel watching over them. They were all too aware of the empty seats around the table. Diamond made some coffee while Amber and Veronica took a seat. Joel stood in the doorway, leaning against the wall, deep in thought.

It seemed like a lifetime since they'd first arrived. And yet, only days earlier Grey and Mikhail were alive and well, Edward Gilmore was still Charles Kendal, and they had no idea if the *Atlas* team were even alive. They were blissfully unaware of Mernas and Adras, Garkras and Denkras.

Joel was first to break the silence. "Not a single human or Merna was actually killed by an Adra, at least not on purpose. But how many Adras did we kill?"

Diamond handed a coffee mug to Joel. "I've seen a few fights in my day. I've been on the frontline of wars and on recon missions. I've seen what humans do to each other over stupid things like politics and religion." He placed two more cups on the table and took a seat, nursing a coffee of his own. "Adras don't fight like humans. They don't fight over bullshit. They only came to the beach because we had their power source. They came to our bonfire to put out the mess we made. They came to our camp because, let's face it, we were alien invaders planning to take over the world. But what did we do in only a few days? Stole their magic stone, twice, burnt down half a forest, tried to kill their leaders, and killed I don't know how many of their friends and family."

No one responded. They had all been thinking the same thing. They had all noticed the stream of death and destruction that started with their arrival.

"So, what now?" asked Veronica.

Joel scratched his chin which was now covered in a generous fuzz. "I don't know. Do we tell the ISA about the Adras and the Mernas? What do we say happened to the rest of the crew? What do we say happened to all their expensive equipment?"

Diamond shook his head. "Uncle Hugh put a lot of money into this project. If we go back and say 'the place is livable but we can't go because someone else is already there,' I'm pretty sure all he's going to hear is 'the place is livable.'"

Amber looked at the empty chairs around the table and the cold and sterile kitchen. She thought back to the last thing she had seen before they engaged the *Phoenix* drive; the view of Earth as nothing more than a dirty and polluted wasteland. She glanced out the window once more and saw the pristine body of Arcadia staring back at her.

"What if we don't tell the ISA anything?" A thought began to crystallize in her mind.

"How does that make any sense? 'Hi, Mr. Irwin, thanks for the interstellar trip, nothing to report.' I don't think he'll accept that," said Joel.

Amber turned to address Joel directly. "We tell them nothing, as in, we never make it back to Earth."

Joel shook his head. "What? You mean stay here?"

Amber shrugged. "Why not? The *Atlas* crew are staying. Why can't we?"

"That's crazy. What about our lives back home? We can't just abandon everything?"

"Can you honestly tell me you wouldn't prefer to stay? What is there on Earth that's worth going back to?" asked Amber.

Diamond and Veronica nodded absentmindedly.

Joel saw them nodding. "You can't be serious? What about our work? Our families? Our livelihoods?"

Veronica looked to Diamond and shrugged. "We just lost the only people that matter to us in this world."

"What about the ISA? Surely they'll send reinforcements if we just disappear."

Diamond frowned. "Will they? Uncle Hugh already said this mission was his last chance. He had to fight pretty hard just to get us here. If they lose *another* team the project will be dead in the water."

Joel shook his head. "I don't know."

Amber took his hand and smiled warmly. "Trust me."

Joel stared into Amber's brilliant blue eyes. He felt butterflies fill his chest. Once upon a time he had let Amber slip away because he was afraid. Afraid of losing her. Afraid of loving her. But he wasn't afraid anymore. The only thing that mattered to him in this world was staring him in the face.

He took a deep breath. "Okay. Let's do it."

Epilogue

Irwin Institute, Buenos Aires—
19:30, 24 September, 2086

Hugh Irwin sat at the long mahogany dining table of his elaborately decorated banquet hall. He was alone in the oversized room, with a solitary butler standing quietly by the door. Despite the silence, Irwin's mind was alert and active. All he could think about was *Hermes*, Arcadia, and his crew. It was all he had thought about for weeks, ever since they had left Earth.

Irwin stared at his tender eye fillet steak and took a sip of his Macallan Seventy-Year-Old scotch whisky. He let the liquid swill in his mouth to savor the oaky flavor.

Irwin lived alone in his mansion with a large staff who served only him. While he knew the house was full of people, he still felt alone as he ate his dinner. It wasn't the crew he worried about as much as the progress they were making. If they could just bring back some proof; living specimens, data readouts, even just an image of the planet's biodiversity. If he could show the world there was another planet capable of supporting complex life, able to be colonized, the government would have no choice but to listen to him. And he'd go down in history as the man who saved the human race from extinction.

Irwin smiled at the thought and pushed the last piece of steak into his mouth.

Things had become complicated since the *Hermes* left. The image of Montello's bruised and bloodied corpse flashed in Irwin's mind. He'd tried for many weeks to forget the horrible sight, and he'd tried even harder to not think about the implications for his mission. For all he knew the crew still had no idea Charles was not who he said he was, that he was a murderer who'd conned his way onto the mission for god-only-knew what reason.

"Will there be anything else, sir?" asked Sebastian, from the doorway. Sebastian was tall and thin; he looked positively skeletal next to Irwin's ample frame.

"No, thank you, Sebastian." Irwin wiped his mouth and leaned backward in his chair, taking another sip of his expensive drink. "Take a seat, old boy."

Sebastian looked at Irwin for a second, unsure if he'd heard right. "Yes, sir. Thank you, sir." He stepped away from the door and took a seat.

"Tell me, Sebastian, do you have any children?" asked Irwin, resting his elbows on the table and pouring a second glass of whisky.

Sebastian frowned. "No, sir, I am not married and I have no children."

Irwin nodded, handing Sebastian a drink. "Me neither. All I have is my sister's son. She passed away quite a few years back, you see, left me as the child's guardian. But I'm a busy man, as you know, and I didn't have time to raise a child. So, I sent him to a military academy in the States. I feel bad for not spending more time with the boy. Now I don't know if I'll ever see him again."

"That's terrible, sir," said Sebastian, who stared awkwardly at the expensive drink in front of him, unsure if he should take a sip.

Irwin shook his head. "Call me Hugh."

"Yes, sir, I mean, Hugh."

Suddenly the door to the dining room flew open and a young man ran inside. "Mr. Irwin! They want you at the ISA! It's about *Hermes*!"

Irwin jumped to his feet and ran out of the room as fast as his legs would carry him, leaving Sebastian to finish the rest of his whisky in peace.

○ ○ ○ ● ○ ○ ○

Irwin and the young man burst through the doors of the main control room. Irwin was wheezing and puffing. He bent over and leaned on the desk for support.

"Where . . . is . . . it?" he puffed.

The lead controller, Martín, looked up. "Señor Hugh! Gracias a Dios, you are here."

"Where is *Hermes*?" repeated Irwin as he caught his breath and moved to the main console. "What happened to my ship, Marty?"

Martín punched several buttons on the control panel. "We do not know. As far as we can tell, *Hermes* is still in orbit around Arcadia."

"But they're okay? They're there?"

Martín punched more controls. "They have been there for a couple of weeks now. But that is not why I called for you. Sir, we finally received footage from the security cameras we installed on *Hermes*. We will not be left in the dark this time."

The lights in the control room dimmed and an image formed in the center of the control table. A large 3D image of the inside of *Hermes* was displayed on the table. The image took a few minutes to render, slowly forming a blurred video.

"The image quality is not great, but considering how far the data has travelled it is a miracle we are getting anything at all," said Martín, pleased with himself.

The image focused further but remained soft and pixelated. They could see the various compartments inside the ship, the sleeping quarters, the kitchen, the cockpit. And they could see the *Hermes* crew. The timestamp was 11:00 a.m., September 6, 2086, the day they arrived at Arcadia. Each member of the crew was boarding the lifeboat with the exception of Mikhail, who simply hugged Veronica and returned to the control panel.

"Well done, Marty! Well done!" Irwin beamed.

"The bad news is there is only about a week's worth of footage. The cameras are motion operated. So, if there is no one on board to trigger the sensors, they switch off. And after September 12, the footage ends."

Irwin frowned. "A week? Show me the last thirty minutes."

Martín punched the controls again and the image shifted in time, jumping ahead seven days, until the timestamp read 12:30 p.m., September 12, 2086.

The image was focused on the kitchen of *Hermes*. Only four crew members were visible: Amber, Joel, Veronica, and Diamond. Irwin relaxed slightly at the sight of his nephew. The crew sat at the table drinking coffee.

The four crew members were discussing something; their faces were blurry but he could see them looking between one another and gesturing with their hands. Within minutes the crew's mood seemed to elevate. Amber was animated and excited about something, Diamond and Veronica had raised their heads and were nodding, but Joel was still shaking his head. Then Joel's mood seemed to change, too.

The crew stood up from the table and hugged each other. Then they disbanded from the kitchen, collecting various equipment and belongings from the living quarters and storage compartment, piling them onto the lifeboat.

"What are they doing?" said Irwin to no one in particular.

The crew boarded the lifeboat. Diamond was the last to board. He paused in the airlock and looked over *Hermes* for a moment. He saluted the ship before engaging the airlock. After a few minutes the footage cut out and the image dissolved into obscurity.

Irwin was speechless. He looked around the room and saw everyone had the same look of confusion and uncertainty. No one knew what to say or how to react.

"Is that it? That doesn't tell me anything? Marty, when are we getting more footage?"

Martín grimaced. "Sir, like I said, there is no more footage. I am pretty sure we just witnessed the crew abandoning *Hermes*."

Irwin's face reddened. "Rubbish! Your cameras must be broken. I knew I shouldn't have trusted you with such an important job."

Martín growled under his breath.

"What about the footage from the monitor orbs? Have we received that yet?"

Martín prodded at the control panel again. "Yes. But the file is much larger than the security footage. It will take another week or so to fully load."

Irwin groaned. "Show me what we have so far, just the start. That might be enough."

Martín shifted his position to another place along the large square-shaped control panel. He pressed several controls, engaging the partially downloaded images.

Brilliant colors lit up the table, a vibrant green forest materialized in front of their eyes. Trees were interspersed with beautiful flowers and vines. In the center of the image was the *Hermes* camp, although with such poor resolution it was nothing more than a handful of indiscernible blobs.

Irwin's face lit up. It was beautiful, picturesque, exactly what he'd hoped for.

"Yes! Look at that! That's all the proof I need." He turned to another member of the operations team. "Get the PR team down here. I want that image cleaned up and sent to every media station in every major city around the world."

"Sir?" asked Martín, slightly confused. "But we still do not know what happened to the crew. It might not be safe. Surely we should wait until we can see the rest of the footage."

"We'll have plenty of time to watch the rest of it while we're preparing for Phase Two. If the crew are alive and voluntarily went back to the surface that means the planet is livable. Which means right now we need to get the world behind us to start pressuring the government for more resources."

Martín raised an eyebrow. "Phase Two?"

Irwin smiled as he stared at the image. "Colonization."

Acknowledgements

First, I would like to acknowledge the ongoing love and support of my parents, Ann and David Borg, who not only read multiple manuscript drafts over the years, but even helped me attempt to publish the original version of *Edge of Extinction* when I was sixteen. I would also like to acknowledge Chantelle Staggard for putting up with me and for reading multiple drafts during the years that we lived together. To Katie Travers for proofreading a very early draft, and to Eliza Renouf, for proof-reading one of the final ones. Most of all, I would like to acknowledge my husband, Adrian Bucca, who has been my biggest fan, my biggest critic, and a significant source of inspiration for different character personality traits.

Special mention must also be made for the team at WiDo and E. L. Marker. In particular I would like to thank my editor, Stephanie Procopio, for her incredibly useful feedback and WiDo's Managing Editor, Karen Gowen, for giving me the opportunity to share *Edge of Extinction* with the world.

About the Author

Kim Borg is an academic, writer, and self-proclaimed nerd. She is a Social and Behavioural Researcher at Monash University in Australia and is one of few people to actually enjoy undertaking a PhD. Kim spends most of her free time watching action-adventure movies and science and nature documentaries. These interests, combined with her expertise in human behaviour, give Kim's writing the unique flavour of an adventurous science-fiction film put to paper. Through her research and her novels, Kim's ambition is to educate as well as entertain.